KING'S CRISIS

KING'S CRISIS

THE PAWN STRATAGEM BOOK III

DARIN KENNEDY

Charlotte, NC

FALSTAFF
BOOKS

WWW.FALSTAFFBOOKS.COM

*To Neil Peart and Neil Gaiman,
the first of whom will never read this
and the second of whom I hope someday might.*

Play the opening like a book,
the middle game like a magician,
and the endgame like a machine.
- Rudolf Spielman

1

TRITABULA

R ed sky in morning, sailor's warning.

Steven Bauer stared up at the cloudless heavens from the roof of their Manhattan hotel. They'd considered moving on yet again after Zed tracked them to New York after their return from their shared banishment across both continent and century, but Grey had wisely convinced him and the rest of the White to stay. The half-month since their homecoming, other than for the momentary invasion by their sworn enemy, had passed uneventfully for the most part. That is until three days before, when the usual pinks and blues of early morning had gone absent in favor of a more menacing hue to mark the sun's inevitable reappearance.

Somehow, Steven mused, *I don't think this is what the mariners of the past were talking about.*

Deep crimson stretched from horizon to horizon as it had for days. Newscasters and meteorologists across the globe pontificated about various weather phenomena, astronomic events, or even global warming as possible causes, while others in the public eye openly questioned whether the end times were finally upon us.

For once, the doomsayers and apocalypse believers were closer to the truth.

With the universe out of balance, a great correction was eminent, and a shift down the spectrum for the heavens above represented the least of the world's problems.

"The time of the Game swiftly approaches." Archie's voice, from across Steven's shoulder, raised the hairs on his neck. "We must all be ready."

"Looks that way." Steven turned, his inexplicable discomfort at being alone in the White Bishop's presence as pervasive as ever. "How much time do you think we have?"

"Based on what I've seen in visions from the past iterations of the Game, a day or two." Archie joined him at the roof's edge. "Three at most."

"So," Steven gripped the rail at the roof's edge with both hands, his knuckles white, "this is it."

"It would appear so."

"And no further sign of the Black?"

Archie shook his head. "None."

Two weeks had passed since Zed tracked the lot of them down to an otherwise unremarkable coffee shop mere blocks from their perch and delivered a not-so-veiled threat of his intention to win this latest iteration of the Game by any means necessary. The intervening disappearance of the Black from their lives as well as the relative cessation of the natural disasters brought on by the coming correction had left Steven and the others in a strange limbo.

Their lives, albeit uprooted from their usual day-to-day from before the Game, had resumed at least a semblance of normalcy. Still, not one of them had slept a full night since their return to their proper century. Despite the strange calm before the coming storm, each remained all too aware that a fight to the death awaited them at a time and place decided at the dawn of the universe.

Their hotel sat atop the strongest metaphysical crossing in the Midtown area. Though the amenities were anything but opulent, there was one thing Steven had learned from the Zed of 1890: real estate truly is all about location, location, location. The ability to travel anywhere by way of the *Hvitr Kyll* without risk of fatigue had priority, for, as Archie repeated incessantly, the Game was nigh. The blood red sky above their heads, growing darker with each successive sunrise, only stoked their anxieties.

Steven released the rail and began to pace. "How will we know when it's time?"

"Oh, we'll know." Archie sighed. "From what Grey has told us and from what I've seen in visions over the years, the Game will deliver us all to this continent's dominant locus of disruption at some preordained time. God help us all if we're not ready." His head tilted to one side. "I trust you remember what we witnessed in Antarctica."

"Remember?" A chill stole up Steven's spine at the intertwined memories of the inescapable cold of the seventh continent and the horrific ending of the third iteration of Grey's Game. "How can I forget?" He ran his fingers through brown curls that hadn't seen scissors in weeks. "So, at some point over the next seventy-two hours, we're going to get plucked from wherever we are on the planet and placed on a giant chessboard to fight Zed for the fate of the world?"

"From what I can put together based on the countless visions I've had over the years, there will likely be a bit more preamble than that, but yes." Archie lowered his head. "That's exactly what's going to happen."

"And then, ready or not, here they come." Fragments of their various battles with the Black cascaded through Steven's memory, the chill already creeping up his back manifesting as a full-on shiver. "No more archaic rules protecting us. No more interventions from unseen referees in the sky. Just force on force, violence against violence." He let out a resigned sigh. "We've been lucky so far, but if there's one thing I know about chess, it's that no game ends with all the pieces on the board."

"Unfortunately, Steven, your insight is closer to the truth than even you know." Grey's voice, absent for days, came from the dim beyond the door leading down into the hotel. "For the thousandth time, I must again apologize that it has come to this."

Steven's ancient mentor strode across the roof clad in his usual checkered tunic and dark pants, his long grey duster draped from his shoulders despite the muggy New York October. Though Grey rarely shed what was in effect a modern version of wizard's robes, Steven also recognized that the man had only days prior been rescued from a time loop that left him exposed and starving atop an Antarctic glacier for God knows how long.

Months? Years? Even longer?

Would the man's bones ever feel warm again?

"No need for any more apologies." Steven cracked his neck in an attempt to release the tension in his shoulders. "This Game of yours is finally upon us, and, like it or not, it's almost time to play."

"How long, Grey?" Archie asked. "The skies have been red for days, though it seems the natural disasters along the continent have abated since the earthquake that destroyed the Brooklyn Bridge." The priest sat on the ledge at the building's edge. "Will we be called today? Tomorrow?"

"Sadly, I have no idea." Grey shook his head. "The Game, for all the rules we set in place, is nothing but the vain attempt of two desperate men to bridle a wild horse whose hooves can shake the universe. One does not ask when such a mighty creature will rear but simply prepares to be thrown."

"Cryptic as ever." Steven crossed his arms. "Is that really your best answer?"

"We could all be drawn to the Board a moment from now or days hence." With a frustrated huff, Grey shoved his hands into the pockets of his grey duster. "That is why each of you must rest, prepare, and steel yourselves for the ordeal to come."

"Not much else we can do." Steven's eyes flicked in the direction of the door leading down to their friends. "By the way, Grey, it's good to see you. Curious, you planning on sticking around long enough to say hello to the others? As far as I know, Archie and I are the only ones awake but..." He paused, smiling as the rising sun finally cleared the treetops to the east. "Lena in particular has been asking after you."

"Miss Cervantes." Grey's face too broke into a smile. "If there is a more delightful person on this planet..."

"You've chosen quite the early arrival time." Archie squinted into the bright rays of the strangely scarlet sun. "I trust there's a reason."

"When one reaches my age, sleep becomes more an option than a necessity." Grey inhaled sharply through his nose. "I had hoped to find someone awake at this hour but was more than ready to enjoy alone the last breeze of evening and the glory of what may be one of my final sunrises."

"I've been up before the sun every day since our return." Archie crossed his arms. "I may not share your centuries on this planet, but sleep has proven elusive for me as well."

"For all of us." Steven grunted. "Even Emilio has bags under his eyes."

Grey let out a long breath, his shoulders slumping. "I would expect nothing less."

"So, Grey, enough beating about the bush." Archie's lips drew down to a thin line. "To what do we owe the pleasure of today's visit?"

"Yeah." Steven's eyes narrowed. "It's been days since your last drive-by. What's going on?"

Grey cleared his throat. "With the advent of the crimson sky, certain priorities demanded my attention."

"Priorities best faced alone, I'm guessing?" Steven did little to keep the frustration from his tone. "Seeing as how you didn't invite any of us along or even let us know where you were going." His voice grew quiet. "Again."

"I did what needed to be done," Grey whispered, "and, you might recall, I did take time to say goodbye to everyone before I left." He raised an open hand. "My apologies if my sudden departure left you disconcerted."

"Disconcerted?" Steven trembled with anger. "Try pissed off. Scared senseless. Terrified." His hands balled into fists before his chest. "The sky turns blood red and you disappear with barely an explanation, knowing full well at any minute we could be called upon to fight for our lives, and the person supposed to lead us into battle is God knows where." His hands dropped to his sides. "How'd you think we were going to respond?"

Grey lowered his head in a rare show of shame. "Again, my apologies, but everything I did was necessary."

Steven let out a frustrated sigh. "As always."

"To be fair, Grey, you did leave us in good hands." Archie grinned in a futile attempt to break the tension. "Steven has been keeping us all fed and watered. Even managed to put together a bit of strategic training."

"'How to Survive a Massacre 101' with Professor Bauer." Steven scoffed. "Everyone was riveted."

"I would expect no less." Grey smiled, ignoring the sarcasm in Steven's tone. "The others have always looked to you for—"

"But that's just it." Steven's cheeks grew hot. "Whether or not the others look up to me, believe in me, or whatever, I don't know how to lead them through this. I'm *not* qualified." He turned to face the still rising sun. "This is your stupid Game, Grey. You should be the one here leading everyone. Come hell or high water, I'll follow you to the end, and you know it." His voice cracked. "But I can't be responsible for everyone's lives. Don't ask that of me." He pulled the pawn icon from his pocket and held it before his face. "Never forget, the Game proclaimed me a mere foot soldier in all of this."

"What does that matter, Steven Bauer?" Grey looked on him with a fatherly smile. "No matter your position on the Board, when the chips are down, the others all look to you. I may wear the crown in this Game, but among our number, you are the one they all respect, the one on whom they all depend, the one who *must* lead."

"Lead from the front," Archie said with an oddly gleeful snicker. "Isn't that what the advice books always say?"

Steven ignored the crawling sensation at the back of his scalp at the White Bishop's odd proclamation. "Look, Grey. I get it. I'm the one that gathered them all together. Saved them from a bunch of super-powered assassins hell bent on wiping them out. Led them against every natural disaster the world could throw at us. Even managed to get everybody back to the right decade in one piece. And for what?" He raised a hand to the crimson sky above their heads. "So they can all fight to the death in a Game none of us ever asked to play?"

"You *have* performed admirably throughout this ordeal." Grey smiled. "And surpassed even my wildest expectations."

Steven bristled despite the compliment. "But I led only because there was no one else who could. If you're here now bearing the crown, why does the burden still fall to me?"

"Listen to your own words." Grey stepped forward and clasped his shoulder. "You led out of necessity. As the Bard wrote centuries ago, 'Some are born great, some achieve greatness, and some have greatness thrust upon them.' Do not ignore that which you have already proven beyond a shadow of a doubt. You *are* a leader, Steven, and, more importantly, you are *their* leader. All I ask is that you strive to be what you already are."

Still since their time in Antarctica, the metallic dragonfly that had warned Steven of countless dangers since he first accepted Ruth Pedone's gift fluttered in his pocket.

"Amaryllis?" Before he could retrieve the metallic dragonfly from his pocket, another familiar voice sounded from the roof's opposite corner.

"*Dios mío!* Grey!" Lena stepped from the doorway leading down into the hotel wearing a baggy sweatshirt and plaid pajama pants. "You're back."

"Indeed, I am, Miss Cervantes." Grey inclined his head in her direction, his brow furrowing when he saw the concern etched in the girl's features. "Is everything all right, my dear?"

"Whatever you're talking about is going to have to wait." Lena trembled, though the morning air was anything but chilly. "You all need to come inside. Now."

"What is it?" Steven asked.

"It's on every station. Everybody's up and watching." Lena bit her lip. "You're not going to believe it."

And with that, the girl disappeared back into the darkness of the stairwell.

"Well," Steven muttered as he strode toward the doorway, "that can't be good."

"Have faith." Archie gave his back a gentle slap. "Perhaps this once, it's not bad news."

He shot the priest a side-eyed glare. "You can't possibly be serious."

"Confession?" The priest let out a lone bitter laugh. "Even *I* didn't believe me this time."

Steven, Archie, and Grey followed Lena down the flight of stairs to their floor.

"Hurry." Lena waited at the entrance to the big double suite they'd shared for weeks. "It's happening now."

Steven stepped through the door to find Audrey, Emilio, and Niklaus, all still in their night clothes, huddled before the flat screen TV that rested on a table in the suite's common room. Lena joined Emilio on the couch, the two interlacing fingers as if it were the most natural thing in the world. Steven's gaze rested briefly on Audrey's trembling arm. He fought the desire to follow Emilio's example as he brought his attention to the matter at hand.

What he found on the screen more than explained the tears rolling down her freckled cheeks.

The scene, most likely shot from a news helicopter, depicted three figures battling the winds atop the Gateway Arch in St. Louis, a trio Steven knew all too well.

On their knees, Audrey's mother and grandfather visibly shook from fear and cold and wind. To their rear, Wahnahtah, the Black Pawn, stood impassive in his dark Plains warrior garb. With one of his quiver of barbed arrows trained on Deborah Richards' back, he kept a close eye on both her and the elderly Woody Buchanan.

"Mom?" Audrey buried her face in her hands as the newscaster vacillated between theories ranging from terrorist attacks to publicity stunts for upcoming movies. "Grandpa?"

Steven knelt by her side and pulled her tight to him. "We'll save them, Audrey. I swear."

"It's another trap." Audrey met his gaze, her eyes red with angry tears. "You know it. I know it."

He sighed in frustration. "Doesn't change the fact that we have to do something."

"Oh my God." Niklaus' eyes grew wide. "Look."

The newscaster shifted to another breaking story, the feed from St. Louis moving to a small box in the lower right corner as a new image filled the screen: another helicopter view, this time of Hoover Dam engulfed end-to-end by an inferno of black flame with only the center spared from the dark conflagration. There, a second pair of figures, one familiar to Steven and one unknown, huddled together beneath the smug gaze of one who filled his core with equal parts anger, hate, and dread.

Scant feet from the dam's edge, his father rested on his knees next to a stunning woman with platinum blonde hair dressed in a torn formal gown. Behind them, the Black Queen grinned malevolently, her serpentine scepter held aloft, as per her standard, like a conductor's baton. The flames danced atop the dam at her pleasure, at times drawing close enough to nip at her two hostages like a pack of hungry dogs.

"Dad." Steven murmured even as Niklaus whispered another name.

"Victoria?" The Rook's cheeks went white. "But how?"

"Victoria?" Steven asked, fighting to keep his breathing even. "Wait. Your ex?"

"I haven't seen her since the day you found me on top of that skyscraper in Atlanta. Losing her sent me into a spiral that almost killed me." Niklaus lowered his head. "In more ways than one." He allowed his gaze to return to the screen. "Still, she doesn't deserve this."

"Why would they have gone after her, though?" Steven stared unblinking at the image of his father on the screen. "Or even known who she was to you in the first place?"

"Face it, Steven." Emilio seethed with anger. "We still don't know how they knew to come for *us*." His gaze dropped to the pouch at Steven's waist. "Last I checked, your little bag of tricks was the only thing that could pick us needles out of the haystack." His eyes shifted in Grey's direction. "And 'old and grizzled' there still hasn't given us so much as a *cryptic* answer for that one."

Grey's already morose expression darkened in frustration. "Would that I could, Emilio." He returned his attention to the screen where Donald Bauer glared with unbridle defiance at the woman they knew as Magdalene Byrne. "Still, regardless of how they know what they know, a more important question remains: What do we do about it?"

"We go to them." Audrey stood, hands balled into fists at her sides. "We save the ones we love." She pointed to the screen. "We fight back."

"And what if the Black does the unthinkable?" Steven's eyes blazed. "What if they wait for us to arrive and then…"

"Don't say it." She took his hand. "We're all already thinking it."

"Let's not forget they each stand upon a national monument with who knows how many tourists around." Archie lowered his head as if in prayer. "And Hoover Dam. If the Black Queen were to bring the full force of her power to bear at such a place…"

"Catastrophe." Grey's voice grew quiet. "Death." He looked to Steven. "Everything the Game was designed to avoid."

"Forget what I said before, Grey." A potent mix of compassion and resignation filled Steven. "There'll be time later for beating ourselves up over past mistakes we've made."

"Still, your loved ones are in danger because of a decision I made centuries before any of you were born." Grey lowered his head in a humble bow. "To all of you, my deepest regrets."

"I'm pretty sure you weren't counting on your best friend threatening to kill innocent hostages to win this Game you two came up with to save the world." Emilio crammed a fist into an open palm. "But here we are, yet again." He pulled Lena tight to him. "Apologies later. Time to go kick some ass." His brow furrowed as the young woman who held his heart pulled away from him and rose from their spot on the floor. "Right, Lena? Like Audrey said, we fight back, don't we?"

"Yes, but…" Her face drew up in a pensive mien. "What if—"

"What if *what*?" Emilio shot up from the floor and rested a gentle hand on each of Lena's shoulders. "They've got our people. What else do we need to know?"

"Look." Lena pulled away a second time and strode to the room's lone window. "I pushed hard for us to go to New York and save all those people on the Brooklyn Bridge. We all know how that turned out."

"Saving those people wasn't just the right decision, Lena." Steven joined her by the rectangle of glass. "It was the only decision."

"Still," she continued, "that doesn't change the fact the whole thing was an ambush, albeit one we didn't know about. Audrey said it. This has mousetrap written all over it."

"With cheese for each and every one of us." Archie stared at the screen, any hint of mischief or contempt absent from his concerned expression. "Look."

Both the Gateway Arch and Hoover Dam had disappeared from the screen, replaced by live images from the National Mall in Washington D.C. Between the columns that housed Abraham Lincoln's marble visage, a trio of figures waited, none of them familiar. On one side of the screen, a middle-aged woman with dark hair and tawny skin dressed in a pullover and jeans knelt trembling on the hard stone; on the other, a young girl with dark brown complexion and intricate braids wearing a dirty school uniform lay curled in a ball crying. A towering figure clad in a jet-black version of Emilio's conquistador armor stood over them, a basket-hilted rapier at his waist, a spiked flail held loosely in one hand, and a round metallic shield hung on his opposite forearm.

As the newscaster again launched into wild speculation as to what it all meant and who the people involved in this trio of bizarre hostage situations might be, Lena swooned.

"*Tía* Renata," she said as Emilio caught her mid-fall.

"Wait," Steven asked. "That woman is your aunt?"

"*Sí.*" Lena dropped briefly into Spanish. "*Mi tía amada.*" She trembled as Emilio lowered her onto the couch. "Wait. This is happening now, right? That means she's alive." She broke into tears. "But…"

Though his heart went out to Lena, Steven's attention was drawn even more to Archie as the old man stared silently at the terrified little girl on the screen.

"Clarissa." The old priest's voice shook with a potent mixture of fear and anger. "Those bastards."

"Archie," Steven asked, "who's the girl?"

"That's Clarissa." He reached toward the screen, a fine tremor overtaking his outstretched fingers. "My great-granddaughter."

"Great-granddaughter?" Niklaus asked. "But…"

Archie shot him a cross look. "I haven't always been a priest, Mr. Zamek."

"That's not what I meant." Niklaus stepped back, hands raised before him, a faint smile on his lips. "Other than Grey, you may be the oldest of us, but sometimes you forget you don't exactly look the part of doting granddad these days."

Archie's trembling hand balled into a fist before dropping to his side. "My apologies. It's just...I wasn't prepared to see that." His eyes narrowed. "I had no idea they had *my* family as well."

Before Steven could ask the next logical question, Emilio drew close to the screen.

"And who is *this* supposed to be?" He pointed to the dark conquistador, his face obscured in the shadows beneath his curved helmet. "I thought the Black Knight was a samurai."

"A *dead* samurai." Audrey's eyes narrowed. "Trust me on that one."

"A new player in our Game, then, though how such a thing is possible lies beyond my understanding." Grey paced the room. "For the moment, at least, it seems that Black is back to a full complement."

"With their Rook and King currently unaccounted for," Niklaus added.

"And a Piece we still have yet to meet." Archie steepled his fingers before his lips. "My opposite."

"Their Bishop." Steven narrowed his eyes at Grey. "Any idea why Zed might be holding back one of his Pieces?"

"To be honest, I have not the first clue. No one knows Zed better than me, yet even I cannot fathom the intricacies of his current machinations. Not to mention, as I have told all of you many times, not one of the previous iterations of the Game has played out even remotely like this one."

"Zed has already proven himself a cheat." Niklaus crossed his arms. "No doubt the Black Bishop is one of several aces he's keeping up his sleeve."

"In the end, it doesn't matter." Steven motioned for everyone to gather round. "Those bastards have our people, and even though we're walking into yet another trap, the time for action is now." His gaze meandered around the circle, catching the eye of each of the White, and took the measure of what he found in each of their gazes.

Audrey, sad but resolute.

Emilio, angry and ready to fight.

Lena, distraught but focused.

Niklaus, as unflappable as ever.

Archie, trembling with rage, the ever-present twinkle in his eye notably absent.

And Grey, beaming with pride and admiration.

Time to lead from the front, Steven thought. *God help us all.*

2

ZWISCHENZUG

"Greetings, Bauer." Atop Hoover Dam, Magdalene studied Steven and his two Pawn doppelgangers in their anachronistic uniforms with clear amusement, her two hostages huddled at her feet. Dark flames threatened from either end of the dam, leaving only fifty feet or so of open concrete on which to stand. A pair of news helicopters circled, the wash from their rotors making their already precarious perch even more dangerous. "We thought this little display might get your attention."

Steven locked eyes with his dad, the terror in Donald's face more than matched by the resilience he'd always found in the man's steady gaze. "Step away from my father, Magdalene. He has no part in this."

"To the contrary, little Pawn," she answered, running a tongue across her even teeth. "He has a very large part in this."

In a blinding flash, Niklaus appeared beside the three Pawns and stretched out a hand toward the other hostage. "Don't be afraid, Victoria. We're going to get you out of this."

The platinum blonde in the shredded blue velvet gown looked up into his face as if she'd seen a ghost. "Nik?"

"Yeah." Niklaus rolled his shoulders as if he carried the weight of the world. "It's me."

"But how?" Her voice quavered as she teetered on the edge of panic at the Black Queen's feet. "Why?"

"Quiet," Magdalene whispered, silencing the woman. "You'll have plenty of time to chitchat once this little negotiation is over."

"Negotiation?" Steven grumbled. "And what exactly might you be here to negotiate?"

"The terms of your surrender." The Black Queen waved her scepter over her two captives with a magician's flourish. "The lives of all your loved ones spared at the low cost of the icons that grant you your power." Her gaze fell to Steven's hip. "As well as that pouch you wear on your belt, Pawn."

His cheeks hot with anger, Steven forced a laugh at Magdalene's demand. "Like you wouldn't kill us all the very next second."

Her eyes went half-closed with derision. "You speak as if that were not already the outcome barreling toward you like an out-of-control train."

"You talk big." Niklaus gripped the rook icon so tightly, his fist shook. "But as I understand it, you haven't won a fight with us yet."

It was Magdalene's turn to laugh. "I hold the lives of your lover and Bauer's very flesh and blood in my hands, and you deign to think your situation is anything less than abject defeat? Now, who's delusional, Mr. Zamek?"

"My *lover*?" Niklaus stepped forward, head hung low. "This woman means nothing to me."

Victoria's eyes grew wide even as the Black Queen's narrowed. "I'm no fool, Rook. You can say what you want, but a blind man could see the unrequited passion in your eyes." Her taloned hand went to the woman's slender neck. "As for this pretty cut of meat, I snatched her from a lovely charity event last evening. I must say, the handsome man at her side seemed quite concerned." Her grip intensified, leaving the woman gasping for air. "Mere weeks, Zamek, and she's already moved on." Magdalene's smile grew wide. "Your pitiful attempt to feign indifference only makes this all the sweeter."

"I won't warn you again." Niklaus' skin shifted from flesh and blood to cool white marble, his voice dropping into the crushed granite tones of the White Rook. "Victoria has no part in this. Let. Her. Go."

Magdalene held tight for another second and then flung Victoria to the unforgiving concrete. "As you wish, though don't mistake my momentary mercy as anything but that." Her gaze flicked down at her beautiful hostage. "The only reason she remains breathing is the simple fact that you still care for her, a fact that grows plainer by the second."

Niklaus tensed, and Steven worried he might lunge for the Black Queen's throat.

"Back down." He rested a hand on the Rook's marbled shoulder. "Don't let her get under your skin."

"She's way deeper than that," he growled. "One more word and I'm going to rip off her fucking head."

"Nik, relax." Steven swallowed back his own fear, never forgetting that his own father's life rested in the balance as well. "Let me handle this."

"All right." His massive form slackened an iota. "But if she touches Victoria again..."

Steven returned his attention to Magdalene. "I take it the others are being given similar terms?"

"But of course," she sneered, her head tilting to one side as if listening to someone. "As we designed, you've divided your forces, and each group will have to come to their own decision regarding our offer." She let out a self-satisfied sigh. "Even if you and your Rook stand strong in the face of adversity, the coming Game will be impossible to win if, say, your Queen, Bishop, or Knight decide to capitulate."

Steven cast his mind wide, stretching the ever-present link between him and his seven Pawn brethren east from the Nevada-Arizona border. Atop the Gateway Arch in St. Louis where he'd sent a third of the White, the kaleidoscope vision of a second trio Pawns revealed their Queen facing off against his opposite, the dark Plains warrior, Wahnahtah. The Black Pawn, as smug as his dark Queen, kept his bow drawn, the barbed tip of his nocked arrow wavering between Audrey's mother and grandfather as the wind whipped around them, threatening to hurl either or both of his captives to the earth far below.

An internal blink and the scene shifted to the National Mall in Washington D.C. where Steven had sent the remainder of their team. Lena and Emilio atop Rocinante charged up the stairs leading to the Lincoln Memorial with Archie and the two remaining White Pawns close behind. At the top of the stairs stood a Piece none of them had yet to meet, a new and very different Black Knight. His armor a dark mirror of Emilio's bright conquistador trappings, the enigmatic steel-clad figure stood guard over Lena's aunt and Archie's great-grand-daughter, his dark steed armored with barding of dull metal. The pair of hostages knelt together, terrified and confused, but for the moment, alive.

"Never." Steven brought his attention back to the matter at hand as the dark flames surrounding them all inched ever closer. "Regardless of your treachery and deception," he said, the words coming from somewhere deep inside, "the White will stand against you and your dark King, no matter the cost."

The Black Queen's smile diminished a shade. "You would sacrifice the lives of your loved ones to earn the right to die by my hand on a checkered battlefield in a war that no one will ever remember?"

"We were chosen specifically from a continent of millions to oppose you." Steven took a step forward. "You attempted to kill us all before the Game could claim us and failed. You scattered us across decades and left us powerless in an effort to keep us from the Game, and in doing so, only solidified our resolve. And now, you—"

"Hold your tongue, Steven Bauer." Magdalene leveled her scepter at him, its serpent eyes glowing a deep violet. "Let's not leave that middle part quite so quickly." Black flame smoldered in her green eyes. "In deference to the wishes of my King, I've held my tongue for weeks since our 'initial' encounter. Do not think for a moment, however, that I have forgotten events that for you likely occurred days ago, but for me led to seventy-five years of suffering."

Steven braced for an attack, but Magdalene, surprisingly, kept her composure. Flashes of the woman before them, thrashing and screaming as her hair and dress caught fire during their encounter in

1936, filtered through his mind. Neither the mental images of her blistered skin nor the memories of her high-pitched wailing approached the horror of the sickening aroma of her charred flesh, a strangely sweet stench he would never forget.

Three quarters of a century of smoldering hatred stood before him, the embers of a decision made a lifetime ago returned to even the score.

"Your little firebomb almost killed me." Her voice remained strangely quiet. "And for years, I wished it had. The pain, the scars, the ridicule." Her face twisted into a thundercloud of anger. "I was once the toast of the town, the girl every man wanted and every woman wanted to be. But after our little skirmish at Franco's place, no man would even look at me." Black fire crackled at the tip of her scepter. "Scarred, hairless, my beautiful voice left but a harsh whisper, what man would?" Dark sparks engulfed the implement of her power and enveloped her fist in a sphere of ebon flame. "How ironic that the self-same inferno that once ruined my life now obeys my every command?"

Steven halted his slow advance on the Black Queen, he and his two doppelgangers keeping an eye on the surrounding dark conflagration that blocked their every avenue of escape. "Your argument is with us, Magdalene. The Game involves only those of us who were chosen. Let our family members and loved ones go. Enough innocents have lost their lives already as a result of Grey and Zed's Game—"

"And several more near and dear to you will die as well if you don't do exactly as I say." Magdalene held out her free hand, her fingers curled like talons. "Your icons and the *Hvitr Kyll*. Now."

"Don't do it, Steven," Donald whispered, the first words his father had spoken since he and Niklaus had appeared atop Hoover Dam. "I don't understand everything that's going on here, but I know it's a hell of a lot more important than the few years I've got left on this world."

"Silence!" The Black Queen swung her scepter, the crack of metal on bone as its bejeweled tip impacted the side of his father's head leaving Steven nauseated. "You'll speak when I tell you to speak, old man."

"Big talk coming from a woman who's pushing a hundred."

Niklaus pounded a rocky fist into his marble hand, the sound like a thunderclap. "The Game certainly did *you* some favors."

"And if we win, it's a favor I don't have to pay back." Her gaze shot from Niklaus to Steven. "A second chance, Bauer," her eyes narrowed in loathing. "at the life *you* took from *me*."

"Is that what Zed told you? That you get to keep all this?" He studied Magdalene like a snake charmer matching gazes with a swaying cobra. "Because Grey told *me* the exact opposite."

Surprise, doubt, and suspicion warred across Magdalene's features. "And what exactly is it your mysterious mentor claims to be the truth?"

"That any benefit gained from the Game lasts only until that iteration reaches completion."

"And when it's over," Niklaus added, "everybody goes back to the way they were."

"Assuming, of course, they survive the experience." Flashes from Egypt, Stonehenge, and Antarctica flitted across Steven's subconscious followed by a flash of Audrey's smiling gaze, the White Queen's visage, as was often the case these days, accompanied by a twinge of sadness. "Either way, as I understand it, your time is running out."

"Lies." Magdalene's green eyes darkened even as the flames encroaching from either side drew closer. "Zed has assured me the energies he will assume after our inevitable victory will leave him with more than enough power to make this body with all its youth and vitality my permanent state."

"Zed promised you immortality?" Niklaus asked, his voice like rocky thunder. "And you believed him?"

"Niklaus," Victoria gasped. "Please..."

"Too late, my dear." Magdalene stepped directly behind the woman and raised the dark scepter above her head. "While Steven's dear father seems more than ready to accept whatever fate befalls him, it would seem that you are not yet ready to die. Perhaps watching you burn will shut this imbecile's marble mouth."

"No," Niklaus cried out, the word hitting Steven's ears like a jackhammer punching through concrete. "Don't."

"Beg." She brought the flaming scepter so close to Victoria's face that the woman's hair smoldered. "Beg me for her life."

"Enough." Steven stepped in front of Niklaus, his two Pawn brethren maintaining watch on the surrounding flames. "Let's end this."

"I couldn't agree more, Bauer." Magdalene pulled her scepter to her shoulder. "No more stalling. Make your choice and pray I like your answer."

Steven looked to his father. "Dad?"

"Can't tell you if a snake is going to strike or not." Donald smiled at his son, a river of blood and sweat coursing down the side of his face. "Do whatever you have to do, and I'll do the same." His gaze shot to Victoria, who sat sobbing and listing to one side as if she were about to keel over. "Understand?"

A memory two decades old came rushing back as if it were moments ago. Steven and his father had gone on a camping trip to the mountains of Virginia and taken one of his friends from elementary school, a boy named Cody Hendricks who had grown up to become one of the top cardiothoracic surgeons on the east coast. In fifth grade, however, he'd been just another shrimpy kid who knew far too much about Jedi Knights and Spider-Man for his own good.

The three of them had hiked almost a mile to a fishing hole Donald had been visiting since he was a kid. On their way back with a cooler full of largemouth bass and catfish, Steven drew back at a sound he would never forget: the telltale buzz of a timber rattlesnake.

He and his father both froze in place, knowing all too well what waited on the other side of the tree that had fallen across the trail. Cody, on the other hand, was too busy pontificating about his favorite comic book and stepped across without a second thought. His scream as the coiled snake struck his boot cut short the captivating debate of who'd win in a fight to the death between Batman and Wolverine. The sound of the rattler's wide head ricocheting off the leather, like a boxer striking the heavy bag with a quick jab, echoed in Steven's mind, as did the dread that gathered in the pit of his stomach as the snake coiled for another strike.

"Hold still, Cody," Donald whispered. "If you move, it'll strike again, and it might aim higher this time."

"But," Cody began to cry, "I'm scared."

"Don't move." Steven remained still as his father had taught him. "Dad will get you out of this. I promise."

"I'm going to die." The boy shook from head to toe, and Steven worried the snake would smell his fear and strike. "I don't want to die."

"Steven." Donald focused, ignoring the boy's whimper. "I need you to distract the snake while I get Cody out of harm's way."

"Distract the snake?" He barely got out the words as fear took his breath. "How?"

"I don't know," his dad whispered, never taking his eyes off Cody. "Grab a stick or something."

"But, Dad, what if the snake bites me instead?" He took a hesitant step back.

"Hold still, Steven. I need your help and so does Cody. Time to step up." Donald fixed Steven with a look he reserved for only their most serious talks. *Do whatever you have to do, and I'll do the same. Understand?*

Steven's mind snapped back to the present where he awaited his father's signal as he had two decades before.

"Now!" Donald leaped from his low crouch and tackled a surprised Victoria, forcing her to the dam's concrete surface. "Steven, go!"

"Shield," shouted a trio of identical voices as Steven and his pair of Pawn doppelgangers dove to defend the helpless hostages from the Black Queen's flames, three circles of metal materializing on their arms and interlocking into what appeared a three-petaled flower of platinum half a second before the dark fireball struck.

"Nik," Steven shouted as ebon sparks ran off the trio of shields like a torrential downpour from hell itself. "Now's your chance. Take her down."

Niklaus rushed the Black Queen, but if he expected Magdalene Byrne to be caught unawares twice in a row, he was sorely mistaken. Without a word, she swept her scepter in his direction and sent the dark flames from both sides of the dam charging at him, a two-pronged fiery stampede of darkness.

"Steven..." he groaned as the twin jets of black flame hit him head-long in the chest, driving his rocky form back toward the edge of the dam. "Help."

"I'm coming." With the Queen's attention now focused on Niklaus, Steven disengaged from the other two Pawns, leaving them to defend his father and Victoria, and rushed to Niklaus' side. Contrary to the battle plan they'd discussed back in Manhattan, the White Rook remained his native height, a far cry from his full mass and power.

His attention is split over this woman, and it's going to get him killed.

"Snap out of it, Nik." Steven stepped in front of Niklaus and held his shield before him, the glowing circle of metal a boulder amid a river of black fire. "Don't you dare let her win this."

"You have only so many shields, Bauer. One little opening..." The Queen, a vindictive smile upon her face, sent another ball of ebon fire flying at the pair of Pawns defending her hostages. "And I'll kill you all."

"No..." Niklaus winced, his stony gaze following the path of the dark fireball. "Victoria."

"Dammit, Nik. Focus." Steven brought his shield high and leaned into the jet of black flame. "Get big and finish this."

"You got it." With a crackling roar like a splitting glacier, Niklaus began to grow, drawing substance from the enormous mass of concrete at his feet. In seconds, he towered over Steven at three times his height, his shoulders as broad as a locomotive and his arms and legs like tree trunks. "Round two, Your Highness?"

"Actually, I have a better idea." The Black Queen held aloft her serpentine scepter of dark platinum. "You two once left me to burn. Perhaps I should show you the same courtesy." Her gaze shot to the dam's edge. "Unless, of course, you all choose to jump."

Before Steven could take a breath, a platform of shimmering darkness appeared beneath the Black Queen's feet. With a sardonic flourish and a hate-filled glare, she vanished from sight, the swirl of ebon energy that marked her departure gone in an instant. With the sudden absence of their dark mistress, the flames surrounding them grew only higher. Black fire swept at them from either side along the top of the dam until only a scant few feet of concrete remained. The pair of Pawns jerked Donald and Victoria up from the ground and pulled them to the free edge of the dam as the dark conflagration drew closer and closer.

Niklaus stared across the flames at the placid surface of Lake Mead. "Millions of gallons of water just a few steps away, and we're all going to die in a fire."

"Can you get bigger and carry us through the flames?" Steven asked.

"I could, but if I pull any more mass from the dam—"

"The whole thing could split wide open." His eyes narrowed. "It's up to me, then." With a single glance over the edge, he tore the pouch from his belt and held it before him. "All right. Everyone lay a hand on the pouch, and I'll get us out of here."

The two Pawn doppelgangers dissolved into Steven's form, leaving only four figures atop Hoover Dam. Niklaus dropped to one knee behind Magdalene's erstwhile hostages in an effort to shield them from the flames and brought his giant hand into the circle to touch the *Hvitr Kyll*. With but a moment's hesitation, Donald reached in as well, his only hope of survival held in his son's grip.

"Do it, Son," his father whispered through gritted teeth as his pants leg began to smolder. "We're out of time."

"Not yet." Steven's gaze shot to the edge of the dam where Victoria lay curled up in a fetal position, the hem of her tattered dress smoking as the blue velvet threatened to burst into flame. "Not without her."

"Come on, Victoria," came Niklaus' granite-voiced plea. "Get up. Grab the pouch. Steven can save us all, if you'll let him."

"We're all going to burn," she whimpered as if she hadn't heard a word he'd said. "God, please save me. I don't want to die."

"Steven?" Niklaus' marble brow furrowed. "What do we do?"

"Sorry, Nik." His fingers tightened around the mouth of the pouch. "She has to come willingly."

"The flames are almost on us." His father held tight to the pouch. "It has to be now."

Steven scoured his memory for anything he could say to get the woman's attention and then, abandoning the Austrian accent that usually accompanied the famous words, knelt by the woman and held out his hand.

"Victoria Van Doren," he grunted, "come with me if you want to live."

The woman snapped out of her panic and looked Steven square in the eye. "But—"

"No buts," he shouted. "We have to go. Now!"

She hesitated a second longer before reaching out and grasping his steady hand. No sooner did their fingers touch than Steven whispered them all away in a flash of silver, a grateful thought bringing an exhausted smile to his face.

Thank you, Arnold Schwarzenegger.

3

MINEFIELD

local news helicopter hovered a safe distance from St. Louis' gleaming Gateway Arch, the monument's apex more crowded than at any time in recent memory. Where three figures had been before, now six huddled atop the highest point in the city as if daring gravity to come knocking.

Another standoff, a second trio of White Pawns watched with trepidation as their lone remaining opposite repeated a not-so-innocent children's rhyme, the aim of the Black Pawn's barbed arrow vacillating between Audrey's mother and grandfather beneath the foreboding crimson sky.

"Eeny." He leveled the missile's cruel tip at Woody's back even as the whipping wind threatened to tear the elderly man from the stainless-steel surface and hurl him into oblivion.

"Meeny." The bow shifted subtly in his hand, redirecting the barbed point at Deborah's head.

"Miney." He again trained the arrow on the trembling old man who decades before had fought in the most horrible war the world had ever seen.

"Moe." Drawing the string back another inch, the dark archer's fingers brushed the corner of his cruel smile.

"No..." Audrey appeared in a flash, her plaintive cry sending Steven's heart racing as the Black Pawn brought his bow to rest, its dark missile aimed squarely between Deborah's shoulder blades. "Please."

"Audrey?" Her mother got out before her captor pressed the point of the drawn arrow into the back of her neck. "You're okay?"

For a moment, Steven chalked up Deborah's wide eyes to her daughter's impossible arrival, but the relief in her mother's gaze far outweighed either the surprise or even the despair. Then it dawned on him: The last time she'd seen Audrey, her only child had been eaten alive by the yoked demons of cancer and chemotherapy. To see her hale and hearty after all this time must have been quite a shock.

"Quiet." The Black Pawn stepped back from Deborah and offered her daughter the subtlest of bows. "Thank you for coming, Richards. I'd hoped you'd attend to your current familial crisis personally." Then, with a snide flick of his eyes, he added, "Greetings, *Bauer*."

"Looking pretty lonely up here, Wahnahtah." The first Pawn leveled his pike at the Plains warrior in their midst.

"Though you appear to be faring pretty well." The second Pawn followed suit, directing the gleaming tip of his spear-axe at the Black Pawn's midsection.

"To rise above such a *crushing* defeat." The third Pawn, positioned between his two brothers, brought his shield up before his chest and offered a conciliatory smile. "And still show your face at work the next day."

The Black Pawn's fingers twitched, sending the drawn bowstring rolling toward his fingertips.

"Stop it, Steven." Audrey shot a sidelong glance at the trio of Pawns. "Don't antagonize him."

The center Pawn took a breath, his eyes narrowing at his opponent. "I'm just answering our friend here in the only language he seems to understand."

Her voice dropped to a low whisper. "And when it's your family whose lives are on the line, feel free to lead with all the bravado you like."

A dual flash from the remainder of his Pawn brethren hit Steven simultaneously, taking his breath.

One vision revealed another trio of Pawns flanking a troubled Niklaus as they faced off against a grinning Black Queen atop Hoover Dam, its concrete surface alight end-to-end with darkest flame.

The other conveyed a twofold view from the final pair of Pawns in Washington D.C. Archie, his staff held aloft in a defensive posture, stood his ground by one of the Lincoln Memorial's columns as Lena and Emilio, both astride an armored Rocinante, rushed the menacing new Black Knight, all of them mere feet from the seated marble figure of the nation's sixteenth president. Atop his own fully barded mount, their enemy whirled a shimmering black flail as if daring the pair of hostages kneeling before him to so much as breathe. As the ebon horse reared, Lena's aunt listed to one side while Archie's great-granddaughter curled her knees back into her chest and covered her head with her hands like she'd no doubt been taught in school.

All of their loved ones sat firmly under Zed's thumb, and only a trio of miracles would get the lot of them through the next moments alive.

"Not as much fun when it's your people on the line, is it, Bauer?" Wahnahtah stepped close behind Deborah and pulled the bowstring another inch past his chin. "I've been looking forward to this day."

Before Steven could respond, a new sound hit his ears: the rhythmic whopping of a second helicopter. A glance across his shoulder revealed a black-and-white chopper headed directly for them.

"This is the St. Louis Police," came a voice over loudspeaker as the helicopter pulled into a hover above the Arch. "Put down your weapons and surrender. We have you surrounded. Repeat, we have you all surrounded."

"Pardon me, if you will." Wahnahtah's voice went quiet as he raised his bow. "The reporters were a necessary evil to bring you here, but I believe Zed would agree the local authorities have no jurisdiction over our little chat." A wicked grin spread across his face. "Here, let me show you a new trick I've learned."

"No!" Steven shouted.

"Fear not, Bauer. I have plenty of barbs remaining in my quiver for you."

The Black Pawn drew his bowstring and fired but a single arrow, the resulting impact beyond anything a lone shaft of wood and stone should have wrought. The sound of metal on metal and shattering glass filled the air, the force of the Pawn's missile sending the chopper spinning out of control.

Steven's eyes traced the flailing helicopter's descent. "Audrey, can you—"

"Already on it." A tendril of silver mist flew from Audrey's hand and encircled the wounded helicopter's landing skids. At first, the intervention made matters worse, sending the chopper lurching to one side and nearly forcing it from the sky, but by then, the matter was simply a battle of her will and the laws of physics.

A battle Audrey won handily.

"Bravo," Wahnahtah intoned as the police helicopter limped away with smoke pouring from its engine. "Grey chose his Queen well." He returned his attention to Steven. "Don't think I haven't noticed the way you look at her, by the way." He released a mocking sigh. "Though I wonder how she'll look back in the future if I slay her mother right here in front of you and you're too impotent to stop me?"

"Don't even think about it, you bastard." The frantic fear left Audrey's gaze, replaced by steely resolve. A low white mist billowed from around her feet as an octet of shimmering orbs of silver energy materialized around her, all eight revolving about her shoulders in a slow orbit. "You, little man, are all that remains of Black's front line. Harm one hair on either of their heads, and I swear it will be the last thing you ever do."

"And in that exchange, the Black King will have sacrificed a single Pawn to compromise the enemy Queen for the remainder of the Game." Wahnahtah raised one shoulder in a dismissive shrug. "You may have the numerical advantage for now, Audrey Richards, but I fear the sight of your mother and grandfather being put down like dogs as you stand by helpless might be difficult to scrub from your mind."

"In that case, we have again reached an impasse." The White Pawn to the far right lowered his pike all of an inch. "We can't attack you without risking the lives of your captives, and you know all too well your life is forfeit the moment you harm either of them. You may be quick, Wahnahtah, but if you think you can fire more than once before Audrey crushes you like an aluminum can, you're deluding yourself." In an instant, the three Pawn doppelgangers fused together into a single unarmed form, the remaining avatar of the White's front line taking Audrey's hand. "You and your compatriots clearly wished to draw us out and divide us. The only question remaining, then, is what you hoped to accomplish." Steven's eyes narrowed. "Tell me, what does Zed want?"

"What he wants, Bauer, are your icons, and with them, your power." Wahnahtah's gaze shifted to Audrey. "For the lives of your loved ones, the King demands only your unequivocal surrender." The tip of his nocked arrow remained fixed on her mother's back. "Stand down, Richards, and deliver your icon to me, and you and your family may live to see another day." His eyes shot to Steven. "As for you, fellow Pawn, behave, and I might even agree to allow your safe passage as well."

"Don't do it, Audrey." Woody, her grandfather, had remained silent since their arrival. Still, Steven had kept a close eye on the man throughout the interchange. Anything but a coward, the elderly man had merely been biding his time, waiting for the right moment to speak. "No matter what he threatens, don't give in to this madman."

The Black Pawn's foot shot out in a quick kick, sending Woody face first into the cold steel of the Arch.

"Silence, old man," Wahnahtah hissed.

"I stormed the beach at Normandy on D-Day, you piece of dog excrement." Woody pushed himself back onto his knees, his already cold gaze made all the more vicious by the blood trickling from his nose. "Do you think I'm afraid of your little bow and arrow?"

The Black Pawn growled through bared teeth. "If you don't value your own life, perhaps a different motivation." He drew even closer to Deborah and rested the tip of his nocked arrow at her temple.

Audrey's mother whimpered but didn't budge an inch. "Don't worry about me, honey. Listen to your grandfather, no matter what."

"She's right, Audrey." Steven squeezed her hand in his. "You have the power here, and he knows it."

Wahnahtah drew the arrow's razor point across Deborah's cheek-bone, leaving a thin line of crimson in its wake. "Queen she may be, but I think we all know who holds the cards here."

Steven's thoughts raced. Though his consciousness now resided in three different states across the North American continent, there remained but one pouch, and it hung at another Pawn's waist hundreds of miles away. The Black Pawn stood guard over the hatch-like doorway leading down into the stainless-steel monument, taking away that option as well. That left only one other way down from this, the tallest man-made arch in the world. Only a miracle and more luck than he deserved had saved him when he dove from atop a skyscraper to save Niklaus weeks before, and he knew better than to count on such providence twice.

"Tell me this, Wahnahtah." Steven worked a different tack. "You are the last remaining of eight Black Pawns, the dispatched seven each borne from your very flesh and soul. With the others gone and, as I understand it, never to return, this is it for you. If you fall today, there's no reset button. No 'Get Out of Jail Free' card." He tilted his head to one side. "What could Zed have possibly promised you that was so compelling you'd risk your life alone against the two of us?"

"More than your narrow mind can possibly imagine, Bauer." At Wahnahtah's laugh, Amaryllis pinched Steven below the collarbone for the second time that day. "And whoever said that I was alone?"

No sooner had the Black Pawn finished his question than the arch beneath them shook as if an earthquake had struck. The tremor tore Audrey from Steven and sent the White Queen stumbling toward the edge of the monument's newly pitched surface.

"Audrey!" He rushed after her, his feet performing a drunken dance as he tried to maintain his balance atop the shuddering monu-ment. "Grab my hand." He dove to his knees and shot out an arm for the woman who'd become his every morning's first thought, but it was too little, too late.

"Steven!" Her fingers brushed his as she slid over the edge. "Look out!" Her wide-eyed gape focused on something across his shoulder just before she vanished from sight, the terror in her eyes forcing a single word to his lips.

"Shield," he whispered, his arm shooting up reflexively in defense. No sooner had the metallic disc reappeared on Steven's forearm than it clanged like a church bell, struck by one of Wahnahtah's lethal arrows. The force of the impact nearly sent him off the edge after Audrey, but somehow, he held his position. The Black Pawn's barbed shaft fell and rolled toward the edge as the already precarious perch shifted from stainless steel to dark granite.

"Dammit." Steven clambered to his feet. "They brought their Rook."

"That's all right, Steven." Audrey rose back into view atop a bank of silver mist the size of a small yacht. "You brought your Queen."

Steven leaped from the top of the steel-made-stone arch and landed beside her, the novelty and wonder of being able to walk atop a cloud a distant memory. "Thanks for the save."

"I am so done with this stupid Game," she muttered as she pulled close to Wahnahtah, the Black Pawn standing over her mother and grandfather with a salacious smile. "Kid gloves are officially off, Pawn," she proclaimed between gritted teeth. "Give me one good reason why I shouldn't snap your neck for threatening my family."

Wahnahtah, another arrow already nocked and at the ready, raised his shoulder in a mocking shrug. "Because you value their continued existence more than you do your mission." He tilted his head to one side, amused. "Or even your own already doomed life."

Audrey's eyes drew down to slits. "Touch either of them, and I'll kill you without a thought."

"And yet, here I am, still breathing." He stamped his foot on the dark granite at his feet. "Anytime now, dear."

In answer, the black stone surface beneath Deborah and Woody flowed up and over the kneeling captives like fingers of ink, forming rocky bonds up to each of their waists. A breath later, the 630-foot structure that had become synonymous with St. Louis over the preceding half-century began to warp as if collapsing under its own weight. With the roar of a dozen avalanches, the Gateway Arch ripped itself in half at its apex, leaving Wahnahtah and his two captives on one side of the breach and the remaining leg coiling like a six-hundred-foot-long serpent preparing to strike.

Audrey's mother and grandfather screamed in unison as the rocky shackles enveloped their bodies and encircled their necks. Still, Steven suspected their lives were safe for the moment, as the pair were all the leverage the Black Pawn held against a furious White Queen. The same, however, couldn't be said for him and Audrey, a fact made crystal clear as the Arch's opposite leg hurtled at them, an impossibly huge tentacle of black stone.

"Not today," the White Queen whispered as she inclined her head to the right, sending the bulwark of mist holding them aloft flying to one side. "Watch my flank, Steven. I can't dodge architecture and arrows at the same time."

"Got it." As Audrey continued to evade swing after swing of what was effectively a mountain-sized flail, Steven kept his shield held high. Shaft after shaft of Wahnahtah's relentless assault from the apex of what had become a curved tower of dark granite ricocheted off the circle of platinum, the memory of Audrey's nearly fatal wound weeks before by one of the Black Pawn's arrows as fresh in his mind as yesterday.

"How many arrows can he possibly be carrying?" he shouted.

"Seriously?" Audrey's sarcasm cut through the din. "We're currently avoiding getting crushed by a sixty-story hunk of animated rock while riding atop a magic cloud of silver." She tilted her head to one side and the bank of mist evaded yet another pass of the flogging mass of granite. "And you're impressed by a bottomless quiver of arrows?"

"Point taken." He dove to block a missile meant for her knee. "Literally."

"So, how the hell do we get out of this and get my family away from that maniac?"

"I'm working on it." A sudden brush against Steven's thoughts brought new hope. "Wait."

"What is it?" Audrey asked as they barely evaded the dark stone's latest flailing strike.

"The cavalry." Steven peered over the edge of the cloudy bulwark, a wide smile spreading across his face. "Okay, this may sound crazy, but take us straight down and fast."

With a nod, she sent the dais of mist plummeting downward, the enormous mass of stone hurtling after them like a giant hand attempting to swat an escaping fly. "It's gaining on us." Panic rose in her voice. "What now?"

"Straight down." He glanced up for but half a second, his attention focused earthward. "Keep going."

"But, Steven—"

"You're going to have to trust me," he glanced up again, the fist of dark stone mere feet above them and gaining. "Straight down, fast as you can, and don't stop."

"But I can't see where we're going," she grunted through gritted teeth.

"Then let me be your eyes." Steven's voice took on that dreamy quality that only manifested when the shit truly hit the fan. *"Trust me."*

Rather than wasting breath on further questions, Audrey refocused and sent the bank of silver mist careening ever faster toward the grassy park below.

"Almost there," he shouted. *"Almost there."*

"Almost where?" she screamed, the sun above blotted out by the mass of stone hurtling toward them.

"Okay." Steven ignored the question. "On three, send this thing flying out across the river, got it?"

"Got it," Audrey huffed.

"One." He kept his eyes focused over the edge.

The descending stone inched ever closer. "Steven?"

He didn't look up. "Two."

Audrey dropped to one knee to avoid the ever-encroaching granite. "Steven?!?"

"Three!" he shouted. "Go, Audrey! Across the water! Now!"

She threw her arms to one side, sending the misty bulwark holding them aloft from beneath the monstrous stony bludgeon and along a path perpendicular to their downward plummet. The sudden veer jerked Steven's head and neck with whiplash force, the dark mass of granite grazing his scalp as he and Audrey tore away from their spiral of death and out over the waters of the Mississippi River,

"My turn." The earsplitting declaration reverberated through the space as a giant of white marble with shoulders as wide as a Greyhound bus rose from the ground beneath the destroyed arch and caught the rushing mass of black rock like a demigod sculpted by none other than Michelangelo himself.

"Nik!" Audrey cried.

"Greetings, my Queen," came a voice like a rumble of thunder. "Everything okay on this end?"

"It is now." She looked to Steven. "What now?"

He raised a hand to block the suddenly bright sun and spotted one of his Pawn brothers standing at the center of the grass between the Arch's bases. "Take us there."

Moments later, Steven leaped down from the bank of cloud and clasped hands with his other self, merging together and regaining in an instant both the pouch and a modicum of hope. "New ballgame." He craned his neck upward and found a scene straight from Edith Hamilton's *Mythology.* Above him, Niklaus wrestled with the Black Rook's sixty story battering ram of stone like Heracles beating back the many heads of the Lernaean Hydra. He grew larger and stronger by the second, drawing mass from the surrounding ground, as the Arch itself continued its unbelievable transformation from stainless steel to glossy black granite. Soon, the White Rook had grown taller and more massive than he'd ever seen or dreamed possible, his legs like the largest trees he'd encountered along trails in the Great Smoky Mountains and his torso like the trunk of a California sequoia. Still, the battle of marble giant and granite serpent soon hit a stalemate as neither seemed able to gain the upper hand. Every few seconds, an arrow impacted the concrete at their feet, but even Wahnahtah's expert aim was limited from his sixty-story perch atop the remainder of St. Louis' most famous landmark.

"Any ideas?" Niklaus grunted as he struggled against the gigantic tentacle of stone, his voice like a rumble of thunder.

"*I have one.*"

Steven's breath caught with trepidation as Magdalene's distinctive lilt echoed across the makeshift battlefield as if amplified by a wall of speakers. The Black Queen floated down from the crimson sky atop her mystical square of ebon energy, her serpentine scepter held above her heads, a torch burning black in the midday light.

"It would appear, Steven, that one of our Rooks is rooted to the ground while the other, for all his strength and size, is not." She directed her gaze up at the six-hundred-foot stone serpent that moments before had been the Arch's northern leg. "Dearest Cynthia, perhaps a demonstration of the advantages of proper leverage?"

Before Niklaus could make a move, the enormous mass of granite split like a forked tongue and pinned his arms at his sides. In seconds, the divided tentacle of black rock held the White Rook aloft in a pair of helical stone coils, leaving the mighty stone giant as immobile as the statues he resembled.

"What now, my Queen?" came a rumbling voice from the mass of dark granite, the sound like a fracturing glacier breaking, and yet still feminine.

"Simple, my dear." Magdalene floated closer, the cold gleam in her eye sending a shiver up Steven's spine. "Crush them." The Black Queen threw back her head and laughed in triumph. "Crush them all."

4

ALICIAN

The earth shook as the Black Rook pounded Niklaus' ten-story form into the concrete bleachers at the Arch's base, the resulting shockwave hitting them with the force of a bomb. Though buffeted by the blast, Audrey didn't budge an inch, her mystical connection to the bank of mist beneath her feet as strong as her indomitable will.

Steven, whose position atop the bulwark of silver shimmer represented nothing but Earth's gravitational pull, wasn't as lucky. A grunt flew from his lips as the concussive force ripped the air from his lungs and sent him flailing out across the Mississippi's rippling surface.

"Steven!"

Audrey's scream barely registered through the ringing in his ears as Steven tumbled through the air at breakneck speed, the water rushing closer with each passing second. He braced for the hit, well aware the river's surface might as well be concrete at that speed.

Death on impact? Knocked unconscious to drown in Mississippi silt? He wasn't sure which was worse.

If this it, God, please watch over the others, especially—

His tumbling form came to a jarring stop, his hip screaming with sudden, searing pain. Upended and his head scant feet above the water, he stared up his body and found a tendril of silvery mist twined about his leg.

Audrey.

The palpable haze crept up his body and righted him even as it pulled him back toward the White Queen's bulwark of cloud. The briefest connection of their gazes took what remained of his breath.

Like an angel from Heaven.

Watching helpless from the end of his ephemeral lifeline, Steven's heart sank as the Black Rook sent Niklaus' massive form hurtling again into the ground, the second blast nearly sending even Audrey from her mystical perch. Ever defiant, she somehow kept her footing despite having her attention split between defending herself and reeling him in. As she again set the octet of silver spheres of energy in orbit around her graceful form, her birthright in every way that mattered, one thing became clear: in her every movement, the squaring of her shoulders, the planting of her feet, and even the set of her jaw, the White Queen had had enough.

One after another, she sent the balls of silver light flying at the sixty-story serpent of stone. Mystic grenades from another time and place, each exploded on contact with the Black Rook's rocky form, raining enormous hunks of granite onto the ground below and bringing the attack on Niklaus, at least momentarily, to a halt.

A few seconds later, Steven was back at Audrey's side, the two of them floating above the grand staircase that led from the Arch to the Mississippi's edge. No sooner had his feet touched down than the embattled Black Rook drew Niklaus' massive form thirty stories into the air and hurled the marble giant at the platform of mist holding them in the sky.

"Up," Steven shouted, "now!"

Audrey stretched both arms high and the bus-sized bank of cloud beneath their feet flew skyward. Despite her quick reflexes, however, something Niklaus' size proved impossible to dodge. His flailing arm passed through the bottom of the misty bulwark, a pair of massive fingers missing Steven by mere inches, and nearly cut the shimmering cloud in two, sending Audrey to one knee as if she herself had been struck. A breath later, the White Rook hit the river with an impact like a meteor strike. Twenty-foot waves surged in every direction as Niklaus' enormous form sank beneath the murky current.

"Audrey?" Steven knelt beside the White Queen and wrapped a still shaking arm around her. "You okay?"

"These mists I control are basically an extension of me. When I reach out and touch something, I can feel it. Looks like when something big enough hits back, I feel that too." She forced herself back to her feet and willed the halved mass of shimmering cloud whole again. "Can't worry about that right now, though. Nik needs our help."

They turned their shared attention to the river where the water was already resuming its normal turbulent flow. All that remained visible of the White Rook was a single bent knee rising above the silty water like a tiny island of colorless stone.

"Look. Nik's made of solid marble and tall as an office building." Steven steadied Audrey as she listed to one side. "I think he'll be okay."

As if in answer, Niklaus' massive head and torso emerged from the turbid water like an ancient river god waking from centuries of slumber.

And an angry river god at that.

"That the best you've got?" His voice echoed across the water as he scrambled to gain his footing in the rushing river. "Bring it, bitch. I can do this all day."

With Niklaus' taunts answered with nothing but silence, three things suddenly became very clear.

Not a single arrow had whizzed by their heads in a while.

The sixty-story mass of black granite attacking them had grown as still as a statue.

And Magdalene, the dark Queen of their Game, had disappeared.

"Phalanx." The word fell from Steven's lips as if by instinct. "Circle."

In a flash, his form was replaced by five doppelgangers, all dressed in the ivory tunic and tan pantaloons of the White Pawn. With pikes at their sides and shields held high, they surrounded Audrey, their five-fold gaze coalescing in Steven's mind. Flashes from the two Pawns he'd sent to Washington D.C. with Emilio, Lena, and Archie echoed across his subconscious as well as he stretched out his mind to encompass all his Pawn brethren.

Still, that made only seven.

Where was his eighth? The one he'd left with his father and Niklaus' ex?

Why couldn't Steven touch his mind?

A sudden flash from the incommunicado Pawn, of pain and heat and crimson, answered his question all too well.

"Are you looking for this?" The Black Queen appeared out of a swirl of velvet darkness, her feet resting on her shimmering square of obsidian energy, the missing White Pawn's throat held tight in her taloned grasp. "He's had better days." She released the Pawn and his unconscious form slumped at her feet. "My...apologies." She tilted her head to one side, the lilt in her voice heightened by the cruel mirth in her tone.

Steven's eyes narrowed. "What have you done with my father, Magdalene?"

"And Victoria?" Niklaus drew back up to his full ten-story height, the rushing water of the Mississippi hitting the giant mid-shin. "Where is she?"

"There." The Black Queen motioned to the shattered remnants of the Gateway Arch, the stainless-steel structure now completely transformed into dark granite. The cacophony of grinding stone again filled the air, though this time, the Arch's south leg was the one that folded and contorted as if alive. The sixty-story length of stone and steel bent down to the ground like the neck of some impossible dark creature of myth, the head of this rocky beast a wide cylinder the size of a small carnival carousel with granite bars making up its circumference. Within the enormous Venus flytrap of stone hung Deborah and Woody joined by Donald and Victoria, each bound to floor and ceiling by obsidian manacles.

"Careful, now," Magdalene purred. "Your loved ones are far more fragile than the cage that holds them."

"But how?" The old courthouse across the way had seemed the perfect hiding place and Steven had only left the Pawn as a precaution. "How could you have known where they were?"

"You're not nearly as smart as you'd like to believe, little Pawn. You arrived on this battlefield seconds after I did, and yet your father and your Rook's lover were nowhere to be found." Magdalene sent the point of her boot into the eighth Pawn's side. "There was no way you'd have left them behind, and you didn't have time to deliver them elsewhere." She took a mocking bow. "Didn't take much effort to sniff them out." She kicked the eighth Pawn in the ribcage again, the pain echoing along Steven's flank. "Along with their pathetic guardian."

"Leave them alone." Audrey sent the bank of cloud flying at the Black Queen and the rocky cage suspended above her head.

"Don't, Audrey," Steven shouted. "It's a trap."

A black arrow flew down from above, grazing her thigh and sending her again to one knee.

"Dammit," he muttered. "All right, close ranks." Steven drew the quintet of Pawns tight around their Queen, bringing their shields close as all five scanned for any sign of the Black Pawn. "Eyes open, all of you." He chanced a lone glance back at the White Rook who still struggled to free himself from the Mississippi's muddy bed. "Nik?"

"I'm coming, Steven." Niklaus pulled one foot from the muck and took one gigantic step forward. "But it's going to take a minute."

"So, for now, they're up a Rook." Steven allowed his mind to drift, the thoughts and perceptions of his two doppelgangers in Washington D.C. adding to the kaleidoscope of images in his head. The pair battled shoulder to shoulder with a dismounted Lena and Emilio to their left and Archie armed with his glowing crosier to their right. Despite his enemy's numerical advantage, the new Black Knight fought like a man possessed. It took everything the five gathered White had to keep him at bay while keeping Archie's great-grand-daughter and Lena's aunt from being hit in the crossfire. Meanwhile, in the Lincoln Memorial's famed reflecting pool, Rocinante and the Black Knight's dark steed reared at each other, their front hooves hammering together like rapid-fire thunderclaps.

One thing was clear: No help was coming from that quarter.

And God only knew where Grey might be.

"As usual," Steven muttered from five mouths at once, "it's up to us."

"Time enough later for cursing under your breath." Audrey drew herself shoulder-to-shoulder with the nearest Pawn. "What's the play?"

"The play, little girl, is surrender." Magdalene brought her dais of dark energy to rest at the bottom of the grand staircase to the east of the destroyed Gateway Arch. As she stepped across the unconscious Pawn and onto the Mississippi-soaked concrete, the Black Queen looked up from her stiletto-heeled boots to her opposite floating a story above her head. "Make no mistake. Like the mists at your command, the cage holding your loved ones is nothing but another aspect of our Rook. Should I give the word, she will crush them all like insects."

"Don't..." Audrey bit back her words, her fists trembling at her sides.

"Now," Magdalene continued, "though I'd honestly prefer the pleasure of immolating the both of you where you stand, my instructions are merely to acquire your icons and then leave you here in lovely St. Louis with your loved ones none the worse for wear. Hand them over along with that pouch at your waist and end this conflict before the three of us are forced to kill you all and everyone you care about in this world."

"As if I'd trust a single word that left your lips." Steven stepped forward, the remaining four Pawns closing ranks around their Queen.

"Whether you trust me or not matters little, Steven Bauer. In the end, you have but one choice if you want your father to see another sunrise."

"Don't listen to her," Donald shouted, his voice muffled by the Rook's stony prison. "She's not to be—arrh!" The rocky chains extending from the manacles at the senior Bauer's wrists and ankles grew taut, pulling at him from above and below like a medieval rack. The tortured scream was the first Steven had ever heard pass his father's lips.

"For the last time, your icons and the *Hvitr Kyll*." Ebon fire swirled around Magdalene's upraised scepter, the darkness reflected in her green eyes. "Now."

"Very well." Steven's hand dropped to his waist, his fingers deftly untying the silver cord holding Grey's mystic pouch to his belt. "Let's end this."

"What are you doing?" Audrey whispered. "If you give her what she wants, there's nothing stopping them from killing everyone in the cage a second later."

Steven sighed. "And if I don't, what makes you think the outcome will be any different?"

"God," she spat between clenched teeth, "I hate that bitch."

"Aye, watch your tongue, girlie." Magdalene's Irish lilt came out in spades. "I'd hate to have to burn it out of your mouth."

"Don't do it, Steven." A cacophony of shattering concrete filled the air as Niklaus arrived back at the riverbank and stepped onto dry land. "There's got to be another way."

Steven inhaled to speak, but found his answer preempted by the grinding of stone on stone as the Venus flytrap of granite surrounding the Rook's hostages drew tighter inch-by-inch, eliciting a collection of groans and screams from within.

"Last chance, Bauer." The Black Pawn appeared atop the granite prison and trained one of his barbed arrows on Steven's chest. "Do as the Queen demands, or your loved ones won't be the only ones that pay the price."

"She'll kill them all, no matter what we do." Audrey trembled as the stony prison surrounding her family and the others constricted another few inches, forcing all within save the unconscious Victoria to stoop. "If the cage gets any smaller, they'll barely have room to breathe."

"No room." Steven studied the cage with new eyes. Within, Audrey's mother and grandfather hunched arm-in-arm awaiting the end. Behind them, Donald looked on helpless as the rock continued to contract. Victoria's unconscious form lay at the senior Bauer's feet.

And between them all, no more than an arm's breadth of open air.

"Do you think my mists could break the bars?" Audrey brought up her octet of silver spheres of energy. "Or these, without killing everyone inside?"

"Breaking the bars isn't the answer." Steven held aloft the pouch, his shoulders squared. "And negotiations are over."

"What are you doing?" Her eyes grew wide with fear. "They'll—"

"We're out of time." He took a deep breath. "Watch your back and when it happens, link up with Nik."

"Nik? 'When it happens'? What are you talking about?"

"You'll know." He glanced up at their towering friend. "Hey, Nik, palms up." Before the White Rook could answer, Steven narrowed his gaze at the rocky cage suspended before them, the additional four Pawns vanishing into his singular form. "I'll be right back."

"But..."

Before Audrey could finish her thought, he crossed the air before him with the white leather pouch and let a single word fall from his lips.

"There."

In an instant, Steven's perspective changed, the crimson sky and open air replaced by the shadows inside the circular cell of dark stone, not to mention the forms of the people he'd come to save. Nose to nose with his father, Deborah and Woody stood to one side and Victoria lay sprawled at his feet.

He prayed the Arbiters of the Game, wherever they were, approved of this latest gambit.

"Axe." A shortened version of the White Pawn's signature spear-axe appeared in his hand. With a single spin, he broke the chains holding the hostages' wrists above their heads. Not wasting a second, he sent his weapon back into the ether and fell upon Victoria, hoping her unconscious state qualified as tacit acceptance of his plan. "Everyone grab hold. I'm getting you out of here."

Donald, Deborah, and Woody all fell to their knees and clutched his tunic.

"*Hvitr Kyll*, take us," Steven shouted as the walls closed in from above and below, "*all* of us, to the White Rook." He pulled in a quick breath, a pinch at his collarbone letting him know it was now or never. "Take us." The pouch let out a deafening pulse as the stony prison filled with silver light, the sonic boom followed by the ear-splitting crack of stone on stone as the cell's ceiling and floor crashed together.

"No!" Audrey cried. "Mom! Grandpa! Steven!"

"Here." Steven and the four hostages appeared in a silver shimmer atop Niklaus' gigantic outstretched hands. "All present and accounted for."

"Thank God." She sent the bulwark of cloud flying upward, stopped even with Niklaus' outstretched fingers, and leaped onto his gigantic marble palm to join the others. "Now, with all due respect, get us the hell out of here."

"Everybody hang on tight." Steven held the ancient pouch to the sky. "*Hvitr Kyll*, take us anywhere but here."

The Black Queen flew at them atop her dais of darkness as a trio of dark arrows whizzed past their heads and ricocheted off Niklaus' marble chest. The dark granite prison at the end of one half of the destroyed gateway bridge shifted into the head of gigantic serpent and flew at them as well, its fanged maw threatening to swallow them all whole.

"Steven!" Audrey screamed. "Do it!"

"*Hvitr Kyll*, now!"

The pouch answered with a deafening pulse that shook all their teeth.

A blink, and they were somewhere else.

From their vantage atop the White Rook's outstretched palms, an enormous cornfield stretched for miles in every direction. An old-timey barn and silo straight out of a Bob Timberlake painting rested to the west atop the only thing resembling a hill for as far as the eye could see. Below them by one of Niklaus' tree trunk ankles, a farmer sat atop a John Deere tractor gaping in disbelief at the giant of stone.

"Holy cow, Toto," Steven muttered. "I think we might actually be in Kansas."

Audrey dropped to her mother's side, her eyes welling with tears. "Mom." She stretched out an arm and pulled her grandfather into the embrace. "Grandpa. Thank God."

As Victoria slumped into the crevice between Niklaus' enormous fingers, Steven knelt by his father's side.

"You okay, old man?"

"None the worse for wear." His chin dropped to his chest. "Though the same can't be said for the stunt double of yours you left behind to guard us." Donald let out a pained sigh. "I've got to say, seeing you cut down like that, even if it was only one of your..."

"Pawns."

"Yeah." He shook his head. "A father shouldn't have to see that."

"Agreed." Steven passed his hands down his body. "But I'm fine, see?"

"But the part of you we left behind," Donald asked, "what happens to him?"

Steven took a breath and, with a quiet prayer, reached out for his eighth. Unlike the usual phenomenon of seeing through an extra set of eyes, he instead found a vivid nightmare of black fire and exquisite pain. "He's incapacitated, but alive." He sighed. "At least for now."

"And if that changes?" his father asked.

Before he could answer, Audrey touched his shoulder. "What about the others?" she asked, her brow furrowed. "Are they okay?"

Steven refocused, opening his mind to the remaining two absent aspects of himself. The scene that unfolded before his eyes took his breath. The pair of Pawns fireman-carried an unconscious Emilio between them as Archie and Lena ran alongside, their staff and mace at the ready. They raced en masse along the Lincoln Memorial's long reflecting pool for the Washington Monument, the thunder of hooves behind them louder with each gallop. Whether Rocinante or the Black Knight's dark mount, he hadn't the first clue. He tried to probe their memories further, but their chaotic thoughts made only one thing clear: their friends were in deep trouble.

"We have to go." Audrey declared once Steven relayed the situation. "Now."

"Without your eighth?" Donald asked. "Like you said, he's a part of you, not just some carbon copy to be discarded."

"You're right, Dad." The Black Pawn's shellshocked gape after losing seven of his eight beneath the White Rook's crumbling marble in Atlanta flitted through his mind. "He's a part of me, an important part, but for now, the others have priority."

"So, Black has taken their first Piece, then?" Donald shook his head sadly.

"And they're down seven Pawns and a Knight." Steven's mind's eye shifted to an image of the dark conquistador no doubt responsible for Emilio's current state. "Or at least they were." He rose from their Rook's enormous palm of marble and turned to Audrey. "Time to go." He looked up into Niklaus' gigantic stony eyes. "You ready?"

"Next stop," Niklaus' voice hit their ears like a cracking glacier, "Washington Monument."

"But what about us?" Deborah asked. "You can't just leave us here in the middle of nowhere." Her head dropped. "They'll simply come for us again."

"Don't worry." Audrey answered before Steven could say a word. "You're all coming with us."

"But, Audrey," he raised an eyebrow, "are you sure that's wise?"

"It's like Mom said." She crossed her arms. "We left them alone last jump, and you see what happened."

"I know." He looked away. "I failed them."

Audrey let out an impatient huff. "You didn't fail anyone, Steven. Your Pawn was simply overpowered, no doubt by surprise and superior force. We won't let that happen this time."

"We'll be fine." Woody offered a brave smile. "They've kept all of us locked up for weeks, but they fed us, let us sleep, basically left us alone. If they wanted us dead, wouldn't they have already done it?"

"Not sure if you were paying attention, Woody, but all of you were nearly crushed to death a few minutes ago."

"But we weren't," Donald said with a half-grin, "and we owe that to you."

"Glad everyone's getting a chance to share their feelings," Niklaus boomed, "but clock's ticking. Every second we wait..."

"I know, I know, I know." Steven took a breath and knelt again before his father. "What do you think, Dad? You taught me this game. What's the next move?"

"You know what to do." Donald beamed at him. "I've never been prouder to call you my son." He gestured to the pouch still resting in his son's hand. "Now, get that thing going. Let's go save your friends."

Steven looked on each of them: Woody Buchanan, Deborah Richards, Victoria Van Doren, Niklaus, Audrey, his father. All save Niklaus' unconscious ex looked on him with utter confidence, ready to follow him into yet another hell of the Game's making. Equal parts pride and dread filled his heart. Letting any of them down was not an option.

He held out his hand for Audrey. "Once more, then, my Queen? Into the breach?"

She took his hand and squeezed it tight. "Nowhere else I'd rather be."

5

TOMBOLA

In a flash of silver, Steven appeared hand-in-hand with Audrey inside a circular structure of marble, its Doric columns and domed roof like something straight from ancient Greece or a Led Zeppelin album cover. The *Hvitr Kyll* pulsed in his grip with an ear shattering drone.

"Definitely the right place." Exhausted and panting from the effort of their latest jaunt, he studied the interior of the bright marble edifice. "This is the D.C. War Memorial. A buddy of mine got married right here a few years back." His gaze came to rest on one column in particular. A shiver ran through his body. "Katherine and I stood right over there as they said their vows."

Audrey squeezed his hand anew. "I know remembering her is rough, but stay with us. We need you focused."

"Right." Steven forced his eyes away. To the north, the Lincoln Memorial Reflecting Pool sat still, the crimson sky above reflecting from its placid surface. Following the water to the west, he could just make out the Lincoln Memorial through the rows of trees. "Last I saw, everyone was running for the Washington Monument."

As Steven peered through the trees to the east at the enormous tower of white pointing up at the scarlet sky, Niklaus stepped from a mid-air shimmer carrying Victoria's still unconscious form, the White Rook returned to both flesh and his normal height. As he rested the woman's head and shoulders against the base of the nearest column, the remaining three appeared from the ether, Donald in the lead and Deborah arm-in-arm with her father close behind. As the last of them stepped through the breach in space from Kansas to Washington D.C. and the silver shimmer faded into nothingness, Steven returned the pouch to his belt and turned to Niklaus.

"Ready for round three?"

"As ready as I'm going to be." Niklaus trademark smile shifted into a look of concern. "You all right, Steven? You look like you just ran a marathon."

"Not so easy to do transcontinental jaunts when half of us aren't even part of the Game." He rested his hands on his knees to catch his breath. "Okay, Nik. Marble back up and be ready for anything."

"Right." Niklaus gestured to the bright white marble at his feet, his grin reappearing in a flash. "Talk about blending in with your surroundings."

"There he is." Steven answered the playful smirk in kind.

As Niklaus resumed his rocky state, Audrey drew close. "All right, Steven, what's the plan?"

"Yeah, Son." Donald pulled up on his other side. "What do you need us to do?"

He locked gazes with his father. "I need you to stay here with Woody and Deb and help keep Victoria safe till we can get the others out of hot water."

"And what's keeping them from coming and taking us again?" Deborah asked.

"Deb." Woody shot his daughter a stern look. "The boy's doing the best he can."

Boy. Steven's intestines tied themselves in knots. *Great.*

"We're not in the dark, you know." Deborah let go of Woody and came nose-to-nose with Steven. "We know Audrey almost died in Atlanta." Her eyes went cold. "The Black Queen seemed to take particular joy in making me aware of that little fact."

"I'm sorry," Steven stammered, "but—"

"My father and I have suffered for weeks in isolation only to come within seconds of being pulped by these terrorists or whatever you call them." Her arms crossed in anger. "We owe you big for saving us before, not to mention for saving Audrey back in Oregon, but I need to know your best is going to be good enough to keep my family alive through all of...whatever this is." Her gaze cut to Audrey. "*All* my family."

"Mom!" Audrey took Deborah by the shoulders. "Steven, all of us, we're doing everything we can here, but there are no guarantees with any of this. And right now, we don't have time to argue. Every second we stand here pointing fingers is another our friends are out there alone. Do you want their blood on your hands?"

Deborah considered her daughter's words. "Fine. Just don't leave us here all alone this time."

I didn't leave you alone. The twisting pain at Steven's core went ice cold. *I did my best.*

"Phalanx." Swallowing back angry words and a bit of his pride, he divided into his five remaining Pawns. Three took up a triangular formation around Donald, Deborah, Woody, and Victoria, summoning their pikes, shields, and cloaks. The fourth addition to their force gave a quick salute with his pike's glowing tip and took off through the trees to the west.

"Where's he going?" Donald asked.

"Last I saw, our friends were running for the Washington Monument with the enemy hot on their heels, but there was no sign of Lena's aunt or Archie's great-granddaughter with them. I'm sending him to the Lincoln Memorial to see if they're still there."

"Then I'm going with him."

"Dad," Steven fumed, "please, just stay here."

"Look, if either of the two of them are injured, your Pawn is going to need help bringing them back."

"Dad..."

"Son, don't tell me I have to watch you go off and fight for your life again while I sit here and wait." Donald lowered his chin, his eyes not leaving Steven's. "Let me help." A faint smile broke across his features. "Think about it. In a way, I'll be right with you the whole time, right?"

"Fine." He let out a resigned sigh. "Go."

As Donald took off after the Pawn, Steven turned to Audrey and Niklaus. "The Monument. Let's go."

STEVEN, Audrey, and Niklaus stepped to the edge of the reflecting pool. To the west, the Lincoln Memorial shone in the midday light, its marble columns reflected in the water like some impressionist's upside-down interpretation of the beautiful structure.

"Surprise, surprise," Steven murmured. "A national monument we didn't blow up today."

"Don't speak too soon," Niklaus grumbled, his voice like boulder on boulder. "The day is still young."

"Where is everybody?" Audrey gestured to the few shellshocked stragglers who remained around the Memorial and the Reflecting Pool. "A day like today? This place should be packed."

Steven raised a hand to his brow and shifted his gaze to the east where the Washington Monument waited in the distance, an alabaster finger pointing up at the blood red sky as if in warning. Squinting into the distance, he could just make out the dozens of people gathering beyond the circle of fifty flags surrounding the base of the marble obelisk, all of them no doubt witnessing the greatest spectacle most would ever see: a battle between light and dark, good and evil, to decide their very fate.

"None of the Black have bothered to cloak their actions today. That's how they were able to draw us out."

Audrey followed his gaze and pulled her own cloak of anonymity close about her. "So, if their Knight just tore through here after all our people, no doubt swinging a flail from atop an armored black horse..."

"Then everyone without the good sense to run for their lives followed." Steven shook his head. "Best show in town, I guess."

"If your lives aren't the ones on the line." The ground at Niklaus' feet groaned as he pulled mass from the earth, the Rook already almost half again his normal height. "Didn't Grey say the Game is supposed to be—what was it—a clandestine matter?"

"After today, the Black have pretty much turned it into a spectator sport." Steven touched Audrey's shoulder. "How fast can you get us there?"

Her gaze dropped to the pouch at his hip. "Not as fast as the *Hvitr Kyll*."

"If only." He let out an exhausted grunt. "I'm already drained from bringing everyone through from Kansas. If I try another jump now, I'll be worthless for the fight."

"In that case," Audrey's eyes flashed with a silver spark, "allow me."

Silver mist flowed from the ground at Audrey's feet, levitating the two of them several feet above the ground. Steven looked to his right and locked gazes with Niklaus, the Rook already twelve feet high and growing taller and more massive by the second, and gave the word to head out. At the White Queen's command, the bulwark of mist flew east for the Washington Monument with Niklaus close behind, his every footfall a piledriver striking unyielding earth.

"Do you think Mom and Grandpa will be okay?" Audrey asked.

"I left half the front line behind." Steven crouched at her side. "They'll have to be."

She swallowed. "Anything from your other two?"

"Nothing lately." He again cast out his thoughts for the two doppelgangers he'd sent with Emilio, Lena, and Archie and again came back with the telepathic equivalent of static. "No such luck. Unless something else I don't understand is keeping me from connecting with them, both my boots on the ground are out of commission."

"And with Emilio down for the count as well, that means Lena and Archie are facing that psycho alone?"

"We'll see." Steven peered ahead, but still could see nothing but the gathering crowd. "Where'd this new Knight come from anyway? Grey never said anything about replacing Pieces in previous iterations."

"He also made it clear it's never been like this." Audrey's hands balled into fists at her sides, and the cloud barge beneath their feet doubled in speed. "As I understand it, we shouldn't have even met the other side at this point, much less engaged them in mortal combat half a dozen times."

Steven shook his head. "All bets are off when it comes to the 'rules' of this Game."

"I wish Grey were here." Niklaus, twenty feet high and gaining, raced ahead of them, his every stride leaving a shallow crater in the grass along the reflecting pools periphery. "No offense, Steven, but I'd really like to hear what he has to say about all this. I know we're two for two so far today, but I can't help feeling we're being led down the proverbial cherry path."

"You and me both, Nik." As they approached the end of the Reflecting Pool, Steven willed pike to his hand and shield to his arm as his long white cloak billowed in the midday breeze. "But this close to the Game, we can't risk exposing our King."

"And I'm guessing that's exactly what they want." Audrey set the eight points of silver light hovering about her shoulders spinning in a tight orbit around her body. "I may not know much about chess or the ins and outs of this stupid Game, but if there's one thing I'm starting to understand, it's how Zed's mind works."

"How do you mean?" Steven asked.

"He's willing to do whatever it takes to win. First, it was killing us all before the Game could start. Then it was dispersing us through time so we'd die of old age years before we were even born. This time, he's put our families in the crosshairs to get us to spread ourselves thin. At best, I'm guessing he was hoping to pick at least a few of us off."

"And at worst?"

"As I understand it, when all the other pieces are occupied, a chess player sometimes has to bring their king out into the open to fight."

"It's not going to come to that." Steven stared up into those beautiful hazel eyes. "We've made it through worse before. We'll make it through this as well."

"Will we?" She pulled in a breath. "The way I see it, it's all traps within traps. If the mouse keeps going for the cheese, eventually he doesn't walk away."

Niklaus rushed past them, clearing the wreathed columns of the

World War II Memorial with a pair of bounding leaps, and stopped shy of the road on the other side. Two stories high, he peered into the distance at the gathered throngs beneath the Washington Monument and then looked back, concern etched in his marble features.

"Well, that can't be good." Audrey sent the bulwark of silver mist flying high over the World War II Memorial, the fountain below shining in the midday sun as if nothing were amiss. Steven's gaze had just fixed on the words of President Franklin D. Roosevelt carved into the granite below —THEY HAVE GIVEN THEIR SONS—when a flash from one the two Pawns hit him full force and sent him listing to one side.

From between half-open lids: a white obelisk viewed from its base, pointing up at the crimson sky, with a flash of star-spangled banner just visible at the corner of his vision.

The image quickly faded to black.

"Shit," Steven muttered, the sentiment multiplying exponentially as Audrey took them across the road to catch up to Niklaus. As she brought their misty transport to rest by the Rook's two-story-high shoulder, the carnage of this latest battlefield in a conflict that had spanned centuries finally came into view.

Atop the grassy knoll to the west of the ring of American flags surrounding the Monument's base, Rocinante charged the Black Knight's dark steed. The white stallion, covered head to toe in gleaming platinum, raced at his opposite, a black charger in barding the color of midnight, a foot-long spiral horn of dark metal protruding from the escutcheon of the horse's shaffron. As Rocinante drew close, both equines reared on their muscular hind legs and kicked mercilessly at each other with their powerful front hooves. At first, the dark horse seemed to be gaining the upper hand, but Rocinante quickly turned the tide and won this round of the ancient show of dominance. In defeat, the Black Knight's steed turned and fled to the far side of the Monument with the armored ivory stallion close behind.

"The Black Knight rides around on some kind of killer unicorn?" Audrey asked as they crested the still-growing crowd of onlookers. "Not that that's stranger than any other part of this insane Game."

"I just hope Rocinante can stay clear of that thing's spike." Steven brought his shield around to guard his front and flank and leveled the point of the pike straight ahead as if he held a jouster's lance. "I don't know if—"

"My God." Niklaus stopped dead in his tracks. "Look."

Steven followed Niklaus' outstretched finger to the northeast corner of the Monument where the last remnant of the White battled for her life. Midway between the Monument's foundation and the surrounding circle of flags, Lena stood alone against the Black Knight's vicious onslaught with only her gleaming mace to defend herself. At her feet sprawled an unconscious Archie and Emilio while the two Pawns' forms lay just yards away, crumpled against the foundation of the gleaming tower built to honor the nation's first president.

"Lena," Audrey shouted over the cacophony, "hang on!"

The White Queen sent the cloud that held her and Steven aloft hurtling straight for the circling pair of combatants. Niklaus followed as best he could, though the rushing mass of onlookers had transformed the area into a minefield of humanity. Steven gripped the pike and prepared to fight, a lone Pawn bereft of his front-line brethren for the first time since all this began.

Though the battle was joined, neither Lena nor her dark assailant dropped their focus for an instant.

The Knight pulled his flail's spiked ball up from the ground and set the lethal sphere of steel spinning at his side before sending the business end flying at Lena's head. Lena, in turn, swung her mace in a wide arc. The head of her bludgeon struck the spiked ball, sending silver and obsidian sparks flying in every direction and the Knight's weapon flying from his hand. The impact rocked Lena's body as well, sending her to one knee, but she was back on her feet in an instant, tenacity and rage all but radiating from her body. Still, the shaking of her legs as she rose from the stone, the heaving in her chest as she worked to catch her breath, and the weariness in her arms as she again raised the mace told the real story. For all her indomitable spirit, Lena was still a teenage girl facing an indefatigable foe, a David against her own dark-armored Goliath.

The Knight massaged the gauntleted hand that had held the flail. With a glance in the approaching White's direction, he summoned his shield from the ether where all their weapons rested when not required. The head of her mace shining like a magnesium flare, Lena stood before her enemy and did her best to hide the quivering of her legs as the Knight drew the basket-hilted rapier from the scabbard at his side. Though his face remained hidden within his dark helmet, Steven could feel the wicked smile from even a hundred yards away.

"Get us down there, Audrey."

"On it."

The Knight raised the blade above his head and flung its cruel point at Lena's heart. She somehow blocked the vicious sword strike, but the effort sent her again to the interlocking stone at her feet.

And this time, there wasn't going to be any getting up.

"Get away from her," Steven commanded as he leaped down from the barge of silver mist, "and face me."

"Patience, Pawn," the Knight grunted. "Your turn will come soon enough." He stepped across Lena's body, his feet coming to rest at either side of her waist, and rested the rapier's tip below her chin. "How ironic, little girl, that you, not even truly part of the Game, have outlasted the men who fought alongside you."

"Steven?" Audrey's voice trembled with anger and fear from atop her misty perch.

"Hold on." He motioned for her to stay back. "One false move and Lena's dead." He shot a glance at their collapsed Bishop. "And, barring a serious miracle, Archie's not going to be healing anyone today."

"Precisely." The Knight stared out from the darkness beneath his conquistador helmet, his only visible feature the sheen in his dark eyes. "The girl fought valiantly, but her cause was lost before the first swing of her mace."

That voice, Steven thought. *Where have I heard it before?*

"The 'girl' is right here, *pendejo*," Lena spat. "Let me up and I'll show you exactly what this mace can do."

"Let her go, Knight." Steven stepped in their direction. "As you said, Lena has no part in this."

"And yet, she carries a weapon of the Game." He glanced down at the shining mace still gripped in Lena's white-knuckled fist. "What an unfortunate decision, bringing innocents into our contest of wills." The Knight let out a sad chuckle. "And, of all people, a little girl. Truly a shame."

That accent. Muffled though the words were by his helmet, the Knight's voice again tickled neurons at the back of Steven's mind. Still, he couldn't quite remember from where. *Dammit, this is important.*

"And as for calling people *pendejo,* little girl," the Knight laughed, "a little more careful, *chica,* or someone might think you actually come from the street."

"Wait." Steven cursed himself for a fool. How could he have missed it? The accent. The conquistador armor. The unmistakable axe to grind. "But how?"

"Ah." The Knight shook his head in mock sadness. "Your Pawn has finally figured it out."

The fury in Lena's countenance dissipated, replaced first by shock, then understanding. "Vago?" Her eyes went wide as she stared up at the man who murdered Emilio's brother.

"The enemy of my enemy is my friend." Vago's head tilted mockingly to one side. "Isn't that the old saying?"

"But you're not a part of the Game either." Fingers of ice inched their way into Steven's chest. "The Black Knight, at least the one we fought in Oregon, is dead."

"Like all of creation, the Game apparently abhors a vacuum. As a result, I would argue that both I and the girl at my feet are well and fully indoctrinated into Zed and Grey's everlasting battle." Vago pulled his shield to his chest and tapped at his dark breastplate. "How unfortunate for her that, unlike my benefactor, your King didn't have the good sense to arm a new recruit with more than just a glorified baseball bat."

"If you value your life, Vago, step away from Lena." Audrey's eyes narrowed at the Knight, and in answer, tendrils of enchanted mist stretched from the wall of silvery shimmer holding her aloft and snaked toward her adversary. "Unlike Steven, I've never met you, but understand that I've already killed one Knight of the Black who threatened my life and the lives of those I care about. Don't think I won't do the same to you."

"Oh, I know exactly what you're capable of, Audrey Richards, just as I have no doubt you'd break my neck as you did my predecessor's without a second thought." Vago pressed the tip of his blade into the flesh between Lena's windpipe and jugular. "I don't, however, think you're willing to risk the life of this lovely girl."

Lena trembled at Vago's feet, though Steven suspected more in anger than fear. "Call me *girl* one more time, you piece of shit, and I'll—"

"Don't, Lena." Steven stretched out his hand in a plea for silence. "Please."

He admired the girl's courage but remembered all too well the ruthlessness of the man who stood before them.

The rival who killed Emilio's brother for the simple crime of wanting a better life.

The manipulator who started a gang war to cover his own crimes.

The coward who changed sides and stories at a whim to save his own skin.

And now, Steven's heart sank, *Zed has given him the power to do whatever the hell he wants.*

6

ZUGZWANG

I'm going to crush you and your little suit of armor like a can of sardines." Niklaus crossed to the Black Knight in two gigantic steps. His footfalls shook the ground like tiny earthquakes as his two-story marble form blocked out the sun hitting Lena and her adversary. "I hope it hurts."

"My, my." Vago straightened his spine in mock surprise as if shocked by the threat. "All of you among the White are so violent." He let out a quiet chuckle. "And here I thought you were supposed to be the 'good guys.'"

"Stop this." Steven peered up at Niklaus. "Both of you." He returned his attention to the man he'd prematurely let fade into the background of his memory, the proverbial chicken come home to roost. "Let her go, Vago. You know as well as I we're supposed to save it for the Game."

Vago scoffed. "That's funny, Bauer. In the last couple of minutes, both your Queen and Rook have threatened to end my life, and not a word from you. Also, were you not just arguing the girl isn't even a part of this?" He pressed the tip of his blade deeper into the flesh below Lena's jawbone. "Make up your mind, *pendejo*. You can't have it both ways."

"Look." Steven pointed his pike skyward and brought it to his side, an attempted show of goodwill. "We've already faced your Queen, Pawn, and Rook today and rescued the people you were using as bait to draw us out. Whatever Zed hoped to accomplish by dividing us, we're all here together now and ready for whatever you dish out."

"Together?" Vago threw his head back in laughter. "And ready?" With a flourish, the Black Knight retreated from Lena's supine form and sheathed his rapier. "Your Knight and Bishop lie unconscious at my feet, this pathetic girl you're so concerned about didn't last a minute against me, and your Pawns are scattered to the four winds."

"While you, Vago, are surrounded, outnumbered, and outclassed." Audrey willed one of the orbs of silver energy floating by her shoulder to fly at the Knight's chest. Vago reflexively brought his shield up to block the attack, his brave facade evaporating before their eyes. Rather than striking the man, however, the shimmering sphere merely fell into a slow orbit of his body as if awaiting further instructions.

"Nice trick," Vago mumbled. "What's next? A ride on your little cloud?"

Audrey fumed. "Understand this, you pathetic excuse for a human being. I understand all too well what's at stake if this whole thing doesn't go off at the right time and place, but if you don't shut that fool mouth of yours, I might see how far the rules of the Game, not to mention your little tin suit, can bend. *Comprendé?*"

"Things didn't go so well for you the last time we fought, Vago." Steven's gaze flicked to Lena then back to the Black Knight. "Walk away and live to fight another day. That's all we're asking."

"It's funny, you know." Vago shook his head, his swaggering laugh making a reappearance. "How you idiots just don't get it."

"Don't get what?" Niklaus' voice boomed down from above.

The Black Knight looked up at the White Rook and raised his arms skyward, sending Amaryllis aflutter in the pocket of Steven's tunic. "You're all acting like this is the end of our battle when it's only the beginning."

A rumble like distant cannon fire echoed down from above, soon followed by a rain of marble. Steven's gaze leaped upward as the pyramidion atop the tallest obelisk in the world tilted precipitously in their direction, the gleaming marble shifting to darkest granite.

"Shit," Steven groaned. "Not again."

"Don't worry, you guys." With a pair of bounding leaps, Niklaus landed next to the Monument and threw his hands against its marble base. "I've seen this trick before." All present, Vago included, looked on with bated breath as the White Rook poured his essence into the Washington Monument and drove back the darkness.

"What are you doing, Nik?" Steven shouted.

"Two can play this game." Niklaus barked out an earsplitting sarcastic laugh. "She's pushing one way, and I'm pushing back." In seconds, the rumbling ceased, and the Monument again stood plumb with the ground. "After keeping the entire Brooklyn Bridge out of the river for an hour, this should be a breeze."

Steven directed his pike at the Black Knight. "Looks like it's two on one, Vago."

"Make that three." With a deft roll, Lena sprang to her feet and fell in on Steven and Audrey, her mace gleaming at her side. "A decade of gymnastics for the win."

"You okay, Lena?" Audrey asked.

"Better than my man." She glanced at Emilio's unconscious form and sucked in a tremulous breath. "He's been out for a while. Archie too."

"What about your aunt," Steven asked, "and Archie's great-grand-daughter?"

Lena glanced across her shoulder in the direction from which they'd all come. "I haven't seen either of them since tall, dark, and gruesome chased us here from Honest Abe's big chair."

"Where are they, Vago?" Steven took a step in the Knight's direction. "What have you done with them?"

"Like you said, the hag and the brat were bait." Chuckling, Vago pointed a gauntleted finger first at Lena, then Audrey, then Steven. "And you all fell for it hook, line, and sinker."

Before Lena could respond, Rocinante and the Black Knight's dark steed returned to the fray. Racing through the Monument's wide shadow to the east, they sprinted neck and neck beyond the circle of

American flags, their thundering hooves sending earth and grass flying in parabolic arcs with every gallop. As his young mistress came into view, Rocinante arced in Lena's direction and stormed for her and Emilio with a loud whinny. The black charger, in turn, took advantage of the subtle course correction and flung its head into Rocinante's flank, plunging the faux unicorn horn into the white stallion's side.

The scream ripped from the depths of Rocinante's equine soul would haunt Steven till the day he died.

"No!" Lena cried as the horse she hand-picked from an isolated island off the North Carolina coast collapsed in a heap. "Rocinante!"

"And Sombra takes first blood." Vago looked on with glee. "Today just keeps getting better." He leered mockingly at Lena. "One by one, little girl. You're all going to fall. It's simply a matter of time."

"Don't listen to him, Steven," Niklaus shouted from his position at the Monument's base. "We've got this."

The Black Knight's steed circled his fallen opponent twice like a wary prizefighter and then cantered over to his master with a quiet nicker. Lena trembled in anger, but kept her tongue. Audrey took advantage of the moment to pull close to Steven who in turn busied himself fighting the urge to rip Vago's head from his shoulders.

"I know it looks bad," she whispered to Steven, "but we'll check on Rocinante as soon as we can." Her gaze flicked westward. "Any news from the Memorial?"

The quiet reminder as to why they were there in the first place brought him at least a modicum of calm. With a forced breath, he stretched his mind to the west, though his focus was soon shattered by the scream of sirens from every direction as a dozen police cars from the north, west, and east left the road and rocketed across the grass, all of them converging on their standoff with the Black Knight.

"Well, Vago." Steven kept his shield high and his pike at the ready. "Looks like a terrorist attack less than a mile from the White House wasn't Zed's best idea."

"Oh no, the *authorities*," Vago chuckled, stroking Sombra's broad flank. "What's that saying, Bauer? The jig is up?"

In seconds, the entire crowd with combatants from both sides at its center sat surrounded by patrol cars and police officers, each sidearm and rifle trained on a man wearing a dark version of conquistador armor none of them had likely seen outside of a textbook. Conversely, Steven, Audrey, and Niklaus remained cloaked and, by at least the D.C. police, unnoticed.

But Vago? He allowed all the world to see his every move. In fact, he relished in it.

"What do you suggest?" The Black Knight mounted Sombra and spread his arms wide in faux defeat, "Should we all just turn ourselves in?"

Steven narrowed his eyes at their enemy. "What are you playing at, Vago?"

"I'm not playing at anything. Simply waiting for the right moment." His head tilted to one side as if he were listening to someone, a mannerism Steven had seen before. Magdalene, moments before she unleashed a maelstrom of dark fire from atop the bar at a club named Corners back in Chicago and set his life down its current mad course, had done the same.

"Keep your eyes open," Steven whispered. "Something's about to go down."

"And that, Pawn, would be any hope you might have of victory." Magdalene floated down atop her dais of ebon energy with Wahnahtah, her scepter held close by her side and his bow drawn with arrow nocked.

"Now the party can really begin." Vago laughed from atop his dark steed. "You all have fun while I go take care of some business." The dark conquistador and his stallion retreated, leaving the White facing Black's Queen and Pawn alone as stalemate between their respective Rooks continued.

"You all have fought well today." Magdalene studied the fallen along their tiny battlefield. "How unfortunate that neither your Bishop nor your Knight and his poor horse fared as well as the rest of you." The Black Queen peered around at the dozen patrol cars surrounding the massive crowd and an all-too-familiar grin spread across her face. "Before we begin again, perhaps a little warmup." She held aloft her serpentine scepter and ebon fire tore down from the blood-red heavens above to meet its jeweled tip, a dark tornado of black flame at the Queen's command. "Just like old times, eh, Steven?"

"Magdalene!" Steven raised a pleading hand. "Don't!"

His shout lost in the deafening explosion of the Queen's cyclonic inferno of darkness, Steven forced Audrey and Lena to the ground and shielded them as best he could as black fire rained down all around. At first he thought Emilio and Archie were a lost cause, but in the end, they weren't the target of the Black Queen's assault.

Dark balls of fire rocketed at each of the patrol cars, half of the police cruisers detonating on contact and the rest bursting into flames. Most of the officers were cut down by the blast with only two to the west left alive after the initial assault, an oversight quickly addressed by a pair of Wahnahtah's arrows. The crowd as well bore the brunt of Magdalene's attack with dozens of bystanders running to and fro, their clothes and hair afire like a certain mob moll's had once burned in 1936, their screams ripped from the pages of Dante.

"Stop this, Magdalene!" Steven stared up at his nemesis, his mind returning to the night of their first fateful meeting. "These people are innocent. None of them had to die."

Magdalene pointed her scepter at Steven's head. "And their blood, Steven Bauer, is on your hands." She sent yet another dark fireball careening into the crowd of onlookers, and another dozen innocents disintegrated right before their eyes. "You have been given opportunity to surrender at every turn today, and instead of handing over your icons and returning safely home with your loved ones, you have chosen war."

"War it is, then." Niklaus pulled himself free from the Monument and swung an enormous fist at the Black Queen and Pawn. A flash of fear crossed Magdalene's features as she sent herself and Wahnahtah rocketing from the Rook's reach, the tips of his marble fingers brushing the edge of the shimmering square of darkness holding the pair aloft. A quick leap put Niklaus right on top of them, but again, the Black Queen managed to evade the Rook's blows by mere inches. The cat-and-mouse game continued with the Black Queen and Pawn remaining just out of Niklaus' reach. Only the staccato crash of falling rock clued Steven in as to what was really happening.

"No," he cried. "She's luring him away from the Monument."

"Bravo, Steven. Perceptive as always, but this time, you're too late." Magdalene returned her attention to Niklaus even as she pulled her and Wahnahtah to the opposite side of the enormous stone circle and far beyond the reach of White Rook. "You move quickly for one so big, Mr. Zamek, but not quickly enough." She looked up to the Monument's upper reaches, her trademark wicked smile returning in spades. "And since you've stupidly relinquished your influence over the stone at her command, perhaps it's time for Cynthia to teach you another lesson about proper application of force."

"No..." Niklaus dove at the Monument in a vain attempt to reassert control, but it was too little, too late as the pyramidion atop the tallest obelisk in the world shifted to black, ripped itself free from the marble tower, and fell point first at the gathered White below.

"Everybody take cover," Niklaus cried out, his voice like an avalanche, "now!"

Steven yanked Audrey and Lena to their feet, and the trio rushed over to cover Emilio and Archie with shield and mist and cloak. As the two-ton bomb of granite and marble hurtled at his friends, Niklaus pulled every bit of mass he could from the Monument's marble and the stone at his feet. Growing another story in height, the White Rook spun around and dove across his friends, his flailing arms cutting down a trio of the surrounding flagpoles as he fell face forward, each hand as big as a Volkswagen Beetle.

"Nik!" Steven screamed. "What are you doing?"

"What you would do, Steven." Niklaus arched his fifteen-foot-wide back, the marble muscles of arms and legs the size of tree trunks bulging as he braced for impact. "Taking one for the—"

The missile of dark granite hit Niklaus like a meteor, driving the marble giant to his knees. The shockwave sent the five of them—Steven, Audrey, and Lena, as well as Archie and Emilio's unconscious forms—sprawling like rag dolls in a hurricane. Deafened by the blast, blinded by the dust, and half-buried by the chunks of black granite and white marble raining down all around, Steven stared upward, powerless to save any of them as Niklaus' enormous form descended upon them.

"Audrey!" he cried out. "Nik's going to crush us!"

The only answer to Steven's frantic cry was a plume of shimmering white mist that shot upward from a spot not ten feet away and caught Niklaus' falling body mere seconds before it pulverized them all. He would never know what it cost Audrey to hold such weight aloft with nothing but the strength of her will, but as his friend's colossal form fell to one side, the silent prayer from his lips went out to the White Queen as much as God. The gust of wind from Niklaus' collapsing form as well as the sudden return of midday light blinded Steven even further, but as his eyes readjusted to the afternoon sun, his ears registered a sound that threatened to stop his heart.

The groan of a wounded Titan.

"Nik!" Lena leaped up from ground and ran for Niklaus' enormous marble face. "Nik!"

Steven forced himself to his feet, trudged over to Audrey's side, and pulled this miracle of a woman who had yet again saved them all to his side.

"Is Nik...?" She stopped her question mid-thought.

"I don't know." Steven squeezed her hand, and the pair walked to join Lena. "Come on."

As both the dust and his senses cleared, he made note of several things.

First, the Black had vacated the area, at least for the moment. Whether out of respect or merely to plot their next attack, he wasn't sure he wanted to know.

Second, Emilio and Archie appeared to still be breathing, though neither had yet to regain consciousness.

And third...

Niklaus' gargantuan form rested on its side, the mass of stone making up his torso cleaved in two at his waist. The usual light in even the marble version of his eyes grew dim.

"But he's pulled himself together before." Audrey's hand left Steven's and joined its opposite before her face as she fought to hold back tears. "Right?"

"Like I understand how any of this works." Steven bit down on his lip, fists clenched at his sides, as he did his best to keep himself from crying. "Come on. While he's still with us."

Lena stood before Niklaus' gargantuan head, her body wracked by sobbing. The White Rook looked on her with his gigantic eyes, his marble lips turned up in a pained half-smile.

"It's okay, Lena." His voice as quiet as a country stream, Niklaus fought for every word. "You're all okay."

"But we can't go on without you," Lena said, her own voice choked with tears. "Get up, Nik. Please."

"Won't be getting up from this one." As Steven and Audrey came into his line of sight, Niklaus forced his trademark grin into place. "Guess this is it for me, huh?"

"You're going to be okay, man." Steven fought to keep his voice even. "Everything's going to be okay."

"Don't bullshit a bullshitter, Steven." Niklaus let out an earsplitting cough. "My time is up. You know it as well as I do."

"We'll get Archie." Audrey rested a hand on his enormous chin. "We'll wake him up. He'll fix everything."

"No. Archie's down for the count, and I don't have much time left, so listen." He focused on Lena. "You keep swinging, Lena, and don't let anybody tell you what you can and can't do."

She ran her sleeve across her tear-filled eyes. "You've got it, Nik."

"And keep that macho shithead boyfriend of yours out of trouble, okay?"

"I will." Lena turned away, unable to look on her dying friend a second longer.

"Audrey," Niklaus grunted after another stony cough. "You've taught me more about kindness in the last few weeks than you can possibly imagine. Fight this fight to win, but don't you dare let this stupid Game change you."

"I will," she said, "and I won't."

"Steven," Niklaus said, his voice growing quieter with every word. "Two things."

"Of course."

"Lead them. Lead them well. Don't let the bad guys win."

"You've got it, Nik." He choked on the words. "What else?"

"Victoria." He forced the word from his lips. "Despite everything, I still love her." A sound like a fracturing boulder filled the air. "Save her, if you can."

"I swear it, Nik." Steven rested his hand atop Audrey's at the cleft in their friend's marble chin as his enormous stony eyes slid shut forever. "I swear it."

7

INCOGNITO

E nough with all this melodrama." In a burst of darkness, Magdalene, Wahnahtah, and Vago reappeared at the periphery of the stony circle at the Monument's base. The Black Queen stood proudly with her new Knight still atop his dark steed on one side and her last remaining Pawn on the other. "Observe, Steven. One of yours has now fallen, as have eight of ours, and still not a peep from the Arbiters of Old."

"We've lost a friend, Magdalene," Steven seethed, "not that such an emotion would register in that cold empty box you call a heart." He pushed down the rage simmering beneath his forced calm. "Do you really think any of us give a shit right now what the Arbiters of this stupid Game think of us?"

"Probably not, though your apathy is unwise." Magdalene directed her scepter at Steven. "You know as well as I that the only reason Zed has allowed the lot of you to continue breathing is his concern that killing you outright would bring the wrath of these so-called Arbiters down about our heads." She looked left and right before taking a step forward. "It would appear his fears are ill-founded, wouldn't you agree?"

"One more step, *puta*," Lena grumbled, "and I'll make damn sure you're the one taking their last breath."

"Such language, *chiquita*. Such fire." Vago crossed his arms, an intrigued smirk just visible from within the confines of his helmet. "I see why Emilio there keeps you around. Maybe when all this is over—"

"I'd rather die." Lena pulled the mace before her, its head shining like a magnesium flare.

"From your lips to God's ears, *chiquita*." Vago sent his flail spinning anew. "Round two?"

"Enough." Magdalene silenced her Knight with a stern glance before casting her gaze out along the shattered hunks of dark granite littering the battlefield. "Cynthia? Care to join us?"

Met first by silence, the Queen's request was soon answered by rumbling from all across the rocky battlefield. Pebbles, stones, boulders—all fragments of the granite missile that had shattered the White Rook—began to move of their own accord, each heading inexorably to the center of the Monument's north face where the various hunks of rock began to stack themselves, stone upon stone. At first barely recognizable as human in form, then misshapen like something from the paired imaginations of Stan Lee and Jack Kirby, the Black Rook eventually morphed into the three-story onyx goddess of myth they'd first seen striding across the urban Atlanta battlefield weeks before. Though beautiful as the work of the finest sculptors of ancient Greece, the cruelty of her actions poisoned whatever admiration or wonder Steven might have felt as he faced the latest in what seemed an endless parade of miracles.

Anything but endless, actually, Steven mused, seeing as how their own Rook had just breathed his last.

No. Not "Our Rook."

Niklaus.

"My opposite has been removed from the Board as commanded." Cynthia stepped across the White Rook's shattered form and joined the Black, a trio of gigantic steps delivering her to a spot directly behind Magdalene. "What now, my Queen?"

"That," Magdalene whispered, "depends on the outcome of the

next few minutes." She locked gazes with Steven. "We stand before you gathered—Queen, Rook, Knight, and Pawn of the Black. Meanwhile, your Rook has fallen, your own Pawns are scattered or beyond help, and your Bishop and Knight lie unconscious at the hands of my own armored cavalier, a man you should have ended when you had the chance."

"A mistake I won't make again," Steven muttered.

"What was that, Bauer?" Vago asked. "A little louder. I'd hate to misquote you on your tombstone."

"Quiet, Knight," Magdalene whispered. "Ah, Steven, after all we've been through, it's almost sad it's come down to this. To see your haughty pride after your pair of so-called victories this morning dashed so completely upon the rocks of one simple truth."

"And what truth is that?"

She laughed. "That we let you win." Any vestige of mirth left her face. "Now, however, you must surely understand the outcome of this day was never in doubt. In this Game, victory belongs to those who risk everything. By coming out of hiding to save your loved ones rather than focusing your energies on defeating a superior foe, you have shown weakness and therefore doomed both yourselves and your cause." Her gaze flicked to Audrey, then Lena, and then back to Steven. "Fully gathered, the White may have had a chance against us, but what hope have you now with but a lone Pawn, an isolated Queen, and a little girl completely out of her depth?"

"Come closer, *puta*." Lena pulled the mace close to her side, channeling Emilio's brazen defiance. "I'll show you who's out of her depth."

Using Lena's bravado as a cover, Steven whispered to Audrey, "There's the three of us, plus the four Pawns left guarding the others. I could—"

"Ah yes, Steven." Magdalene laughed. "The remainder of your much vaunted front line. Call them. Bring them here. Finish all of this. Then and only then will you see that our victory is already complete." She beckoned for him to take action, but met with only his dumbfounded stare, her hands dropped to her side in disgust. "Poor little Pawn. You still haven't figured out the last bit. The pièce de résistance." She raised the scepter high above her head. "Here. Allow me to help you."

The Queen's eyes slid closed, the serpentine scepter in her taloned hand swaying to and fro like a conductor's baton. A quiet murmur filled the space, as if a dozen whispered conversations rested at the edge of their shared consciousness. The Black Queen's dark crown shimmered with deep violet light that pulsed in time with the rise and fall of the murmuring. Then, as the whispering reached a fevered pitch, Wahnahtah stepped forward to take his place before his dark mistress as a single word fell from Magdalene's lips.

"Line."

In a shimmer of darkness, seven additional forms materialized before the Black Queen, Knight, and Rook, falling in on either side of Wahnahtah. The Black Pawn stood at the center before his Queen, menacing in his bizarre Plains warrior garb, with three of the dark-garbed newcomers to his right and four to his left. Of the seven new recruits to their enemy's front rank, four were women and three were men. Each wore a similar ensemble of black leather and chainmail across their upper bodies, dark pantaloons, and black leather boots, while each of their faces lay hidden beneath voluminous dark hoods. Unlike Wahnahtah and his combination of bow, arrow, and axe, each of the newcomers held one or another medieval implement of death in their gauntleted fists. Though he'd never seen any of them before, Steven had little doubt their shared proficiency with their various weapons rated at least on par with his first day as Pawn of the White. Regardless, the simple fact that Magdalene's front line stood, for the first time since Atlanta, reassembled and ready to fight left him wondering how their side could possibly survive the coming days, much less emerge victorious.

In sharp contrast, the remaining five of Steven's Pawn brethren, who had also appeared out of the midnight slash in the air, lay unconscious or worse at the feet of the newly formed Black front line, joining the two downed Pawns already present.

"The shoe truly rests on the other foot now, eh, Bauer?" Wahnahtah looked up and down his rank. "Now, you stand as the lone Pawn against my complete line. How does that make you feel?"

"Four of those at your feet were guarding our family and friends." Steven trembled with anger as he motioned to the fallen Pawns. "What have you done with our people?"

"How tragic." Magdalene sighed. "Even with all the evidence literally staring you in the face, you still don't understand." She shook her head in mock sadness. "Wahnahtah, direct your line to make introductions."

The Black Pawn looked left and right, making eye contact with the Pawns at either end of their front rank. "King's Rook's Pawn and Queen's Rook's Pawn, reveal yourselves and greet your opposite."

The two Pawns on either end pulled back their hoods, eliciting a gasp from Audrey.

"Mom." She barely choked out the word. "Grandpa."

On one end of Black's front row, Deborah Richards stood revealed, her face untouched by the years and worry that had taken their toll long before she first met Steven at the grand entrance of the Richards' home in Sisters, Oregon. Where before he'd found in those eyes a mother's exhausted love, he now found nothing but a reflection of the hate that radiated from the Black Queen's vindictive gaze. By her side, Deborah held a long black spear with a serrated hook at its business end reminiscent of a harpoon's. Steven had little doubt the woman who now stood before them would gut any of them without a second thought.

On the opposite end, Woody Buchanan looked on them with an expression just shy of disdain. With fifty years shorn from his visage, his chiseled features reflected the Vietnam era photo Steven had seen in their home in Oregon before it burned to the ground. If Deborah's gaze channeled Magdalene's, then Woody's channeled Zed's. Aloof and cold, he studied them as a butcher studies his day's work, a cruel battle-axe hefted across his shoulder.

In both their gazes, a gleeful zeal shone, as if part of them reveled in the White Queen's pain.

"What have you done to them?" Audrey screamed.

"Wait, wait, wait," Magdalene uttered in her most singsong lilt, "we're just getting started." She tapped Wahnahtah's bow with her scepter. "Pawn, please continue with the introductions."

"King's Knight's Pawn and Queen's Knight's Pawn," he said, "make yourselves known."

The second and seventh Pawns in the line pulled back their hoods.

"*Tía* Renata," Lena moaned. "No..."

A quarter century erased from her countenance, Lena's aunt looked on the remaining White with similar malice. Her previously salt-and-pepper locks now jet-black and pulled back in a ponytail, she favored her niece except in the only way that mattered. Even in the midst of her hottest anger, the goodness that embodied Lena Cervantes exuded from her every pore. Her aunt, conversely, held a dagger in each hand, flipping them in her nimble fingers and making all too clear in her stare and stance exactly what she'd do with her paired blades if any of them drew too close.

Opposite Renata along the Black's front line stood an unchanged Victoria still in her prime, though any semblance of the helpless socialite they'd already rescued not once but twice that day had evaporated, the unyielding terror previously found in the woman's eyes replaced with the cold sheen of a consummate killer. A bullwhip of black leather with shards of jagged metal embedded at its tip hung coiled at her side. A chill ran up Steven's spine as he met the merciless gaze of the woman he'd sworn to his dying friend he'd save at any cost. If it came down to it, and the choice was either the woman who broke his friend's heart or one of their own, oath or no oath, Steven knew exactly what he'd have to do.

"And now," Wahnahtah looked up and down his line, "King's Bishop's Pawn and Queen's Bishop's—"

"On second thought, Wahnahtah," the Black Queen rested a hand on her own Pawn's muscular shoulder, "let's save that particular revelation for later. We don't want to show all our cards." As the pair in question instead drew their weapons, a cruelly forged war hammer for the man and a long, wicked blade with a jeweled hilt for the woman, Magdalene's gaze locked with Steven's. "Besides, I'm eager to see the reaction of the White King's Pawn to his counterpart along the Black front line."

"No." The whispered word fell from Steven's lips, the horror of the moment about to unfold already building at the back of his mind. "Not him."

"Black King's Pawn," Wahnahtah shouted, "remove your hood."

The Pawn to Wahnahtah's left drew back the thick cloth concealing his features, revealing a face Steven knew at least as well as his own, a face he remembered from his childhood, from high school track meets and family movie nights and long hikes in the mountains of Virginia.

Donald Bauer, the lines carved into his face by both years and loss erased from his features, stood revealed as Zed's personal foot soldier. Steven had known the man in every season of life, in joy and sorrow, in peace and anger, contentment and fear, but never had he seen the mad gleam that now emanated from his father's eyes.

"Greetings, my son." Donald studied Steven with a cool contempt that chilled him to the bone, the pike in his hand a dark mirror to the one held in his only child's trembling fist. "I eagerly anticipate facing you again across the sixty-four squares." A wicked grin filled his father's face. "This day has been far too long in coming, though I did misspeak before." He motioned in the direction of Niklaus' fallen form. "It would appear that only now has Black truly taken their first Piece."

"Dad." Trembling with anger, Steven redirected his attention to the Black Queen. "With God as my witness, Magdalene, you're going to pay for this. Nothing any of us have ever done deserves such—"

"Stop." She silenced him with a furious glare. "You left me a scarred ruin of a human being for seventy-five years." She seethed, her anger radiating from her serpentine scepter in pulses of dark fire. "Seventy-five long years of pain and pity. My entire life has been nothing but stares and suffering, and all because of you, Steven Bauer." She drew herself up straight, collecting herself. "Of us all, no one is more deserving than me."

"Deserving?" Audrey asked. "Deserving of what?"

"Vengeance, child." Magdalene's eyes narrowed to slits. "Cold, satisfying vengeance."

"And yet..." Steven looked around at the seven unconscious Pawns laying scattered around the tiny battlefield. Though not one of them roused, each of them still took breath. "All my Pawns still breathe." He watched the Black Queen like a mouse watching a coiled serpent. "If it were within your power, I'm pretty sure they'd all be burned to a crisp already." He glanced in the direction of their fallen Knight and Bishop. "Emilio and Archie too. Not to mention, I doubt we'd be having this pleasant little conversation."

"And that, Bauer, is the true reason we find ourselves gathered here today."

Steven's heart skipped a beat. "What's that supposed to mean?"

Magdalene held aloft the *Svartr Kyll*. "Despite the lack of evidence that the Arbiters of this Game even exist, much less care about the outcome, Zed insists that those of us chosen by the Game continue to honor what rules there may be in order to avoid potentially forfeiting the spoils of his eventual victory. As I see it, your Queen took our first Knight, and nothing happened. The same when our Rook took yours. Two gross violations of the so-called rules of this Game, and yet both somehow fell short of currying the Arbiters' much vaunted wrath. Still, Zed is keen on not tempting fate, and thus, I stay my hand, at least for now." The Black Queen paused thoughtfully. "Our King believes, however, that these new Pieces we've indoctrinated into the Game are *anything* but chosen and therefore can likely skirt the rules with impunity." Magdalene flashed a vicious grin. "And the Game, after all, is his creation."

"In other words," Wahnahtah said, "we may not be able to kill you, at least not yet, but your friend from Baltimore here, not to mention the rest of my new line of Pawns, are not only willing, but able."

"What's the saying?" Vago laughed from atop Sombra, the sound cold and cruel. "You only hurt the ones you love?"

Steven's gaze ran the row of Black Pawns, his heart growing cold even as white-hot rage bubbled up from within.

"Oh, Steven. That look on your face." Magdalene studied his features with faux concern. "Is that confusion? Disbelief? Frustration? Anger?" Her laugh curdled his blood. "Grief hits us all a little differently."

"What have you done to my father?" Steven asked through gritted teeth.

"And my mother?" Audrey stepped forward, the billowing mists roiling about her feet like a simmering pot, a mirror of their mistress' soul.

"And my aunt?" Lena glowered at Magdalene, the mace at her side glowing like a shining star.

"All of you, calm yourselves." Magdalene's voice took on the dreamy cast of a nanny attempting to coax her wayward charges to sleep for the evening. "Your loved ones are fine. Unharmed, in fact. It is merely their allegiance that has shifted, a process I've been assured is more than reversible."

"Some kind of hypnosis?" Audrey whispered to Steven, her voice choking with emotion. "Or magic?"

"Does it matter?" He dismissed his pike but kept his shield front and center as he returned his attention to the Black Queen. "I assume this is yet another effort to force our surrender?"

"At least there's one thing today I don't have to explain to you with a diagram." Magdalene's words went cold. "Final chance, same terms, and we'll need your answer now. You've wasted quite enough of our time."

"Your icons and the *Hvitr Kyll*," Wahnahtah intoned. "Then walk away from all of this. Take your family and friends with the Black King's blessing." A smirk blossomed on his painted face. "Minus your Rook, of course."

"Honestly," Vago chuckled, "I hope you refuse." He motioned to Black's front line, his invisible sneer evident in his every word. "Watching you assholes cut your way through everyone you love just to take another shot at us would totally make my day."

"You bastard." Lena took a step forward, stopped only by a hand at her shoulder.

"Steady, Lena." Steven pulled her back. "Not now."

"What shall it be, Steven Bauer?" The Black Queen's voice resumed its singsong lilt. "Does your loyalty lie with your own flesh and blood? Or with an immortal who has already proven more than willing to sacrifice all in his charge simply to avoid losing his little Game?"

Steven stood gutted. If everything he'd been told about the Black King was true—a fact borne out by the very situation in which they currently found themselves—then allowing Zed to win remained unacceptable, no matter the cost. And yet, how could he, Audrey, and Lena fight, possibly to the death, against the very people they sought to save?

Do we save the world or do we save the people that are our world?

Magdalene tapped her foot impatiently. "Time's up, Pawn. What is your answer?"

"What do I do?" Steven's voice dropped to a mutter. "This decision, it's impossible."

"An impossible decision, indeed." This latest voice, one he'd only known for weeks and yet as familiar as his own, hit Steven with a bizarre one-two punch of relief and trepidation. "Not to mention a choice far beyond that which a Pawn, however proficient, should have to make."

8

MADRASI

A lone beat of Amaryllis' wings hit Steven's chest as Grey rounded the northwest corner of the Washington Monument, clad in his standard full-length duster, fedora, and sharkskin boots. Beyond his attire, however, Steven's esteemed mentor appeared a different man. Gone was the spring in his step, the spark in his eye, the temerity in his voice. As he stepped across a cracked hunk of marble that had previously been one of Niklaus' fingers, the last bit of vitality left the ancient wizard. With shoulders slumped, he trudged forward like a dead man walking, a convicted soul accepting his fate, the embodiment of inevitability. Though Steven had only spent the equivalent of a few weeks in Grey's presence, seeing this man who had literally dragged his ass out of the fire and set him on a nobler path in such a state left him devastated.

And if his suspicion about why Grey had chosen this moment to reveal himself was correct, the situation was about to turn even more sour.

"My, my, Grey," Magdalene murmured, her eyes wide with surprise, "if I may address the opposing King so informally." The Black Queen coiled like a snake preparing to strike. Even in this,

Black's moment of victory, she clearly expected the worst. "What an unexpected pleasure."

Both Wahnahtah and Vago drew close to their Queen as Grey approached. The dark horse, Sombra, lowered his head in deference. Even the Rook, for all her size, mass, and strength, crouched silently at the back of their huddle.

"Unexpected, indeed." Zed's voice echoed across the microcosmic battlefield. "A multitude of scenarios played across my imagination as I prepared for our confrontation, but this?" With a flourish of his long cape, the Black King, dressed in his customary armor and furs and the dark crown at his brow pulsing with violet light, stepped from the shelter at the base of the Washington Monument, sword in hand, and joined Magdalene and the remainder of the Black. "Both Kings in play rather than hiding behind their respective castles?" He gave a cursory glance in the fallen White Rook's direction. "Not to be insensitive, of course." His expression vacillating between amused and curious, Zed looked on quietly as Grey mirrored him and joined ranks with the remaining White.

"Greetings, Steven, Audrey, Lena." Grey studied what remained of the fallen marble giant they all called friend as if searching for even a hint of life. "My apologies for not arriving sooner." He peered all around, and at his silent command, a shimmering wall of golden shimmer appeared at the edge of the stone surrounding the Washington Monument and slowly began to move north, south, east, and west, pushing away the mass of humanity who bore witness to the strange events.

"What's happening?" Lena asked.

"As in Atlanta," Grey answered, "I have created a barrier around this site to protect those not involved so that we may continue this little tête-à-tête undisturbed by the general population."

"That's all fine and good, but what are you even doing here?" Steven drew close to his mysterious mentor and dropped his voice. "Everything we've gone through for weeks was done specifically to prevent this very situation."

"That is true, Steven." Grey scanned the tiny battlefield, his gaze pausing briefly on each of the fallen White. "And see what all of our best plans have wrought? Our Rook is destroyed while our Bishop and Knight hang on by but a thread—"

"His name is Emilio," Lena muttered, her hands immediately flying to her mouth when she realized she'd spoken aloud.

"I know their names, girl." Anger flared briefly in Grey's expression before fading back into defeated exhaustion. "I know the names of the fallen, both in this iteration of the great Game as well as the three that came before." In an uncharacteristic bit of emotion, his voice cracked. "Centuries have passed, and still I hear their voices, their laughter, their tears." The wizard's gaze ran the gamut of Black's new front line. "And now these innocents, your family and friends, all stand conscripted into a battle that was never theirs to fight." Though Grey looked on each of the new crop of Black Pawns with a mix of sadness, disappointment, and compassion, his stare lingered the longest on the two whose faces remained hidden beneath their hoods. "All of your lives, not to mention all whose came before, I carry on my soul."

"God, Grey." Lena's face lost all color. "I'm sorry."

"No, Lena." Grey forced a smile. "It is I who owe all of you the apology."

"Please," Magdalene spat. "This from the man responsible for the Antarctica massacre." She directed her scepter in Grey's direction. "Yes, Grey King, Zed has told us everything." Her nose crinkled in feigned disgust. "However do you sleep at night knowing such hypocrisy colors your every word?"

"But that, Queen of the Black, is precisely why I have come today." Grey pulled himself upright. "My charge to myself is to be a hypocrite no longer." He stepped around the remaining three representatives of the White and held his hands out before him. "Zed, my oldest friend, though it pains me to say it, I have come to offer myself in exchange for the lives of my various charges as well as those of their families and friends."

"You what?" Steven grabbed Grey's shoulder and swung him around. "Since the day you first dragged me and the others into this stupid mess, all we've heard about is the unthinkability of defeat. That we must win, no matter the cost. Each of us have had our own brushes with death and somehow lived to tell the tale. We've fought our way back from banishment to the past to fight in your war, all because the lives of a few don't matter when the fate of the entire world is at stake. That's what you sold us, and now you're going to surrender as if none of our sacrifices even matter?"

All present among both sides and even Zed himself remained silent as Grey considered his answer.

"Steven Bauer." Grey pulled in a deep breath through his aquiline nose. "This Game Zed and I created is indeed exactly that, a game. Games have winners and losers. I won the first iteration, and in the end, allowed the spoils of that victory to evaporate into the ether as he and I designed. After the opposing forces of the correction dissipated and everything returned to status quo, we continued onward. I was so proud of what we'd accomplished." He turned his attention on the Black King who stood blithely across the way. "My blindness to Zed's true intent coupled with that very pride has proven to be my undoing."

"Do we have to stand here and listen to this?" Vago grumbled under his breath.

"You will show respect for the opposing King, Knight." At Zed's sharp reprimand, all of the Black wisely kept their tongues as Grey continued.

"Zed's actions after his victory at the conclusion of the second iteration went against the very intent of the Game the two of us had created and wreaked havoc on the natural order. He incorporated the power inherent in that moment into his very being, an investment that nearly led to a second Black victory in Antarctica. In con man parlance, he had played the very definition of the long game. However, the greatest mistake that day was mine." Grey looked away, unable to bear any of their eyes. "More than refusing the boon of my initial victory or even trusting Zed's motives in the first place, my decision to abort the third iteration so that I might literally live to fight another day has irrevocably upset the universal balance and clearly allowed the travesty this fourth iteration has become."

"Grey," Steven whispered, "stop."

"No, Steven. You must all hear my confession." Grey glanced again in the direction of Niklaus' titanic fallen form. "At least all of you who remain."

The ancient wizard again met the gaze of his opposite, his questioning glance answered with a nod from the Black King. Grey spun his finger in a circle and a gentle rain of something resembling flower petals fell across the battlefield. The seven unconscious Pawns, sprawled across the star-spangled circle of stone, evaporated on the breeze, their essences coalescing back to their source leaving Steven feeling whole for the first time since they'd divided their forces in New York that morning. A moment later, both Emilio and Archie sat up from their spot on the grass as if awaking from a deep slumber. A bit further away, Rocinante stirred as well before rising gingerly to his feet.

"Emilio!" Lena ran to her love's side and cradled his injured body in her arms. "You're alive."

A groan from the bottom of Emilio's soul escaped the boy's lips. "Not so hard. I may be conscious, but a big part of me wishes I was still out."

"A sentiment I understand all too well." Archie rubbed at the back of his neck and peered around at the gathered Black and White. "It would appear we've missed quite a bit."

"Steven Bauer. Audrey Richards. Archibald Lacan. Emilio Cruz. Lena Cervantes. Listen to me carefully, all of you, for my time is limited." Grey pulled in a deep breath. "At the conclusion of the third iteration of this Game Zed and I created, I committed an act that at the time seemed the only conceivable option, an act that subsequently has become my deepest shame. I betrayed a group of people who trusted me enough to follow me to the most inhospitable place on the planet for a fight to the death. I wiped the Board clean when all seemed lost rather than leading from the front and inspiring them to continue the fight no matter the cost. I admit to all present, both sides included, that I was wrong."

"Steven," Archie asked, "what is Grey doing?"

"The only thing he can." Steven crossed his arms in a defensive posture. "The only thing *we* can."

"The choice before you all is impossible, so as the bearer of White's crown, and in an effort to honor both your sacrifices as well as the noble sacrifices made by three different generations before you, I choose to bear the weight of this decision and hereby absolve you all of any responsibility for its outcome."

"Grey." Steven rested a hand on his mentor's shoulder. "Don't do this. What happened all those years ago was simply you doing what you thought was best in the heat of the moment. Right or wrong, what's done is done. I know you still carry a lot of guilt over what you had to do, but that doesn't mean we let Zed win without a fight."

"Oh," a hint of Grey's usual swagger peeked through, "I never said there wouldn't be a fight."

"Come again?" Magdalene, uncharacteristically quiet for some time, chimed in. "I'm no grandmaster, but even I know the capture of the King is the end of any game of chess."

"And as Zed well knows, this iteration, for all our encounters up to this point, still has yet to truly begin." A faint smile invaded Grey's features as he again matched gazes with his opposite. "A question, old friend. Can a game truly end if it is never allowed to begin?"

Zed pondered the question. "What are you getting at, old man?"

"Like it or not, in a smattering of hours, this Game you and I created will summon all present to the Board. Then and only then will the battle unfold to decide who is the victor and who is lost."

"This is a trick." Magdalene took her King's hand. "We have the White at our mercy. Their King is capitulating as we speak. What else is there?"

"His train of logic is sound," Zed answered, "no matter how much it pains me to admit it."

Grey continued. "In matters of the Game and inherent in its very design, every rule and every aspect of play served one and only one function: to ensure the eventuality of each iteration, all in an effort to maintain the cosmic balance at any cost. As both sides have no doubt heard incessantly, the time of play is sacrosanct. At the fated juncture, no matter where on the planet a person may be, they will be summoned to the Board." He met the Black Queen's gaze. "Should either side be without their King when the moment arrives, however, there can be no Game."

"No Game," Steven whispered, "means no victor."

"Precisely." Grey nodded. "Without a Game into which to channel the incalculable forces of a correction, the gods only know what could occur. The razing of yet another continent? The latest in a long line of mass extinctions? Some other disaster beyond our imagining?" He licked his weathered lips. "One thing, however, I can guarantee will not occur."

"The power." Magdalene seethed. "It will elude us."

"And without that power, Mags," Audrey said with an uncharacteristically dark smile, "I'm guessing you're right back as 'Most Likely to Scare Small Children' at the nursing home."

"Says the woman fated to die no matter the outcome of the Game." Magdalene's eyes narrowed at her opposite. "Your broken form lying askance on a checkered battlefield or eaten from within by your own malignant blood. Quite the choice, Richards."

One of the silver balls of energy orbiting Audrey's shoulders flew at the Black Queen only to be shattered by a blast of ebon energy from Magdalene's serpentine scepter.

"Audrey." Steven's hand shot up in an effort to quell his Queen's anger. "Not now."

"Fine, but she'd better watch out once everything kicks off." The eighth ball of silver light immediately reformed before her, the octet of shimmering spheres slowly revolving around her trembling form. "Fire or no fire, she's going down."

"So, old friend, you can take me and do with me what you will." Grey continued his slow trudge toward the Black. "But regardless of what you do, all of us are still destined to appear on the Board at a pre-appointed time scant hours from now. In that moment, I suspect you will wish for me to still be among the living."

"Very well. As with the others before, killing you outright may be out of the question." Zed steepled his fingers before his chest. "But the remainder of your suppositions remain to be seen." His eyes cut to the armored dark conquistador at his side. "Knight, take him."

Before Vago could take a step in his direction, Grey held up a solitary finger. "Hold, Knight. As I said at the beginning, this arrangement between me and your King is not without conditions."

"Of course not." Zed stroked his dark beard, the faint smile that had occupied his features since he first appeared evaporating in an instant. "The lives of your Pieces."

"As well as their freedom to go about their business until such time as the Game summons us all."

"And why would I possibly acquiesce to this demand? My forces have already slain your Rook. The White may stand reassembled, but the advantage is mine."

Grey raised one bushy eyebrow. "There may be one other detail you have overlooked." He held his arms wide. "All of you may wear the raiment afforded you by the Game, but I stand before you wrapped in the color that is my namesake."

"The crown of the White." Zed studied the remainder of his foes, anger flashing in his dark eyes. "Which of your underlings is hiding your ace in the hole this time?"

"None of them." Grey gestured to his own line. "Not one of them even knows where it is. Left to their own devices, I suspect they should be able to locate it in time, but interfere or harm them in any way and you will find yourself right back in the situation we were just discussing."

"No King," Steven muttered, "no Game."

"Not just that, Steven. Without the crown, nothing tethers me to the Board. At the appointed time, even should all of you be pulled to the checkered battlefield to fight for your lives, still the violence of the correction will not be sated and disaster will follow." Grey returned his attention to Zed. "As we planned all those years ago, *old friend*, there must be two Kings. Otherwise, the rest of it is nothing but pomp and circumstance."

"We don't have to listen to this." Magdalene pulled close to Zed. "Even without the *Hvitr Kyll*, we were able to locate each of the White as easily as their Pawn did. If necessary, I'll find their crown and force the damned thing onto Grey's head myself."

"My dear Magdalene," Grey offered the Black Queen a smile just shy of condescending, "whatever advantage your side may have possessed in the beginning of all this in regards to discerning the location your enemy appears to have evaporated now that all the Pieces have been indoctrinated into the Game. Why else would you have needed to lure us to New York to disperse us through time or been forced to create such a trio of spectacles to get our attention today? Other than Zed's brief appearance after our return to the correct century, you and your compatriots seem to no longer possess the ability to ferret out your enemy." He let out a sad laugh. "And make no mistake: I've hidden the crown far beyond your taloned reach."

"So, *old friend*, you offer yourself as collateral on a loan of borrowed time," Zed mulled Grey's words, "knowing fully well that defaulting on such a loan will result in destruction on a scale unimaginable?"

Grey offered a single nod. "I have nothing but the utmost confidence my Pieces will rise to the occasion and obtain the crown by the appointed time."

Zed shook his head. Slowly. Deliberately. "Your faith in such a pitiable stable of the sad, sick, aged, and immature will be your downfall."

Grey studied the gathered back row of the Black. "If only the magicks of the Game had seen fit to surround me with the same quality of individuals as you have the pleasure of spending your time with these days."

Zed frowned. "Abject loyalty and driving ambition are nothing to denigrate."

"Perhaps," Grey intoned, "though I would argue the two are virtually antithetical, as you have proven time and again."

"You can't seriously be considering releasing these pathetic dregs back into the wild." Magdalene crossed her arms, defiant, her lips curled in a snarl. "After all the trouble we went through today to bring about this moment?"

"To the contrary." A smirk blossomed on Zed's lips. "They must be released, or else all our efforts have been for nothing. They will seek the crown not only to save their much-vaunted mentor but all their loved ones as well. Even more so than before, they have no choice but to succeed." Zed's brow furrowed, even as his smirk grew into a knowing smile. "Finally, after all these weeks, the error in my logic has been laid bare. To remove the opposite side from the Board before the Game truly begins—be it via their death, scattering them across time, or forcing their surrender—guarantees not victory, but defeat."

"But, boss," Vago said.

"In fact," Zed continued, ignoring his Knight, "as the Game is designed, as borne out over these last weeks and months, anything apart from allowing events to proceed according to the universe's clock may very well be impossible." The Black King strode out from behind his front line and met Grey alone in the no man's land between White and Black. "This Game we've built appears to be truly inescapable," his gaze leaped past Grey to meet Steven's, "as your charges are about to quite painfully discover."

"One other condition," Grey whispered without remotely the confidence he'd possessed moments before. "You must release my charges' loved ones among your front line from their forced conscription." A frustrated sigh fell from his lips. "I'm not certain what you've done to twist these people's thoughts and bend their will to yours, but such malfeasance is beyond the pale, even for you, Zed."

"I'd guessed you might make such a request." Zed paced before Grey, evincing consideration, but there was no doubt the dramatic pause was all for show. "But on that matter, you already know my answer."

"You refuse?" Grey asked. "And in what realm does the direct involvement of noncombatants in our Game seem in any way right or proper?"

Zed raised an eyebrow. "Has not the Cervantes girl struck down my Queen with her metal cudgel? Have I not been forced to replace my Knight secondary to the lethal actions of your Queen? While I would argue White is more than welcome to seek out a new Rook before our final confrontation, trust that I have no intention of releasing my front-line conscripts until they've fully served their purpose."

Grey's nose crinkled in disgust. "Participation in this Game is at the very least at some level voluntary, Zed. What you have done to these people, conversely, is inhumane and borders on perverse."

"Voluntary?" Zed laughed aloud. "Not one person standing with you volunteered to be any part of this madness. Given no other choice but to join you in your fool's errand, each drew their icon from your bag of tricks and has since played along to the best of their meager abilities, all the while trying to convince themselves they're doing the right thing. If you're suggesting, however, that even one would choose this life over the quiet boredom of their oh-so-average previous existence, you delude yourself." The Black King gestured to the Pieces among his rear rank. "To those loyal to me, I offer power, justice, vengeance, even immortality. The only thing those who stand with you can hope for is, at best, a return to mediocrity." He paused, his gaze shifting to Audrey. "Or worse, a guarantee of an early grave." He returned his attention to Wahnahtah and the seven newcomers to his vanguard. "Who knows? Wahnahtah remains so intrigued by what I have to offer that his loyalty has not faltered once despite the loss he suffered at the hands of your dearly departed Rook." He spread his arms in a magnanimous arc. "Perhaps, in the end, your family and friends will feel the same."

"Bullshit." Emilio, who'd been uncharacteristically quiet for longer than Steven had guessed possible, stepped forward. "You've got them all brainwashed. That's all this is."

"Ah, you poor misled boy. You follow a man who looked upon not only your predecessor but all who trusted in him along an icy Antarctic battlefield and wiped them out without a second thought, all to keep from losing." Zed looked on the young Knight with pity. "Who is the more brainwashed here, boy?"

As Emilio struggled with his answer, another of the White spoke up.

"Where is Clarissa?" Archie, all but forgotten in the scheme of things, took a brave step forward and joined Emilio in the precious few feet separating the opposing sides. "I can only surmise she is one of the two whose faces remain hidden."

"My dear Bishop," Zed answered, "for all the faults your esteemed mentor heaps onto me, placing children in harm's way is his sin, not mine." He glanced up at the Black Rook. "Cynthia, allow Mr. Lacan to see his assiduously safeguarded great-granddaughter, if you will."

The Black Rook rose to her full height, the midsection of her torso opening to reveal a compartment of sorts. Within, distraught but seemingly unharmed, Clarissa Lacan knelt weeping. The sudden onslaught of daylight blinded her temporarily, but as her vision cleared, she peered down onto the battlefield and locked gazes with Archie.

"Help me, PopPop," she cried, "help me!"

With a waggle of his finger, Zed signaled the woman turned mountain serving as their Rook to close Clarissa back inside her stony form. Archie stared with abject hate at the Black King. Rare tears streaked his cheeks.

"She is innocent, more than anyone else here." He leveled his glowing crosier at Zed. "Let her go."

"Put away your weapon, Bishop. You know as well as I your threat is empty, especially now that I hold someone you love dearly in such a precarious position. Should the lovely Cynthia bend the wrong way or even stoop to pick a flower..."

"Please." Archie took a step back, coming shoulder to shoulder with Steven. "Don't hurt her."

"You needn't worry, old man." Zed offered a congenial smile. "As I have shown you, she is safe."

"How does she even recognize Archie?" Audrey asked Steven in a hush. "He's dropped a few decades since she last saw him."

"Pictures?" he answered, shooting the priest a sidelong glance. "Instinct?"

"A mystery for another day," Archie whispered. "All that matters is saving her. All of them."

"Enough posturing." Zed sheathed his sword. "Surrender yourself, Grey, and your friends are free to go about their business completing this superfluous errand of your imagining. Should they succeed, we shall gather and fight one last time and for the third consecutive time, you shall lose. Should they fail, however, the consequences of allowing this correction to proceed unabated rests firmly upon your shoulders."

"I expected no more or less." Grey bowed his head. "I agree to your terms."

Zed matched Steven's gaze. "We will all be seeing each other again very soon, Pawn. When that moment arrives, the time for talking will be over."

"What of our family and friends?" Audrey asked. "My mother and grandfather?"

"And my aunt?" Lena added.

"And Clarissa?" Archie's words came out less question than declaration.

"As I said before," Zed answered, turning on one heel and walking away from the confrontation with Grey in tow, the grey-clad wizard's upper arm held firmly in the Black King's grip, "your loved ones will be coming with us, some more willingly than others, but all nonnegotiable."

"Not happening." Emilio willed the lance to his hand and then shifted his weapon into the shining battle-axe he used when fighting on foot as his injured steed limped to his side. "We're all back on our feet and ready to fight."

"To the bitter end," Lena stepped forward to join Emilio and Rocinante, "if that's what it takes."

"Children, children. So ready to fight. So ready to die." Zed stopped mid-stride and turned to study each of the White in turn. "Half of you can barely stand, and the rest wouldn't dare attack for fear of harming the very people you've spent the last several hours attempting to save." He turned his back on them a second time and continued his march toward the base of the Monument. "Fear not. You will have more than ample opportunity to exercise your collective death wish far sooner than any of you would care to imagine." He let out a quiet chuckle. "Go now and bring to our final battle the very element of your defeat."

"The element of our defeat?" Audrey asked. "What does that mean?"

"How can you all be so thick?" Magdalene leaned in with a conspiratorial whisper. "If you don't bring the crown, everyone, and I mean everyone, loses, but should you succeed and arrive in time to recrown your already captured King..."

As Audrey digested Magdalene's words, Vago slung his spiked flail across his shoulder and stared down the boy who had bested him on the streets of Baltimore.

"I still don't see why we don't just kill them all right here and let the cards fall where they may."

"Once, I would have agreed with you," the Black Queen chuckled, "but if my long life has proven anything, my dark Knight, it's that good things truly do come to those who wait."

The Black Knight turned to join his King, soon followed by Rook, Pawn, and the seven conscripts from among the White's family and friends, leaving only Magdalene to gloat in their victory.

"Oh, the irony," she whispered. "After all the trouble of the past few weeks, to have White's King surrender and leave the remainder of his forces all but required to bring our own King precisely what he needs to win the day. It almost brings a tear to my eye."

Not one among the White uttered another word, speechless as they looked on, the unfathomable becoming reality before their very eyes. Each face held a different emotion. In Audrey's, Steven found disappointment mixed with terror; in Emilio's, unbridled anger; in Lena's, unmitigated sadness; and in Archie's, a consigned melancholy, the usual madness and mischief he usually found in the man's gaze notably absent. He ran the scenario a thousand different ways, but in the end, he came to the same conclusion Grey arrived at in Antarctica.

"This sucks, but at least we live to fight another day."

"Not all of us," Emilio muttered, his gaze drifting to Niklaus' fallen form.

Steven took the comment in stride, pulling close to Audrey who appeared to be on the verge of a breakdown. "I'm sorry." His chin dropped to his chest. "I don't know what else to do."

"There is nothing else to do, you fools." Magdalene paced before them, her green eyes like a jungle cat's. "You have all watched far too many movies and are conditioned to think that just because you view yourselves the heroes of the story that you automatically win in the end. But allow me to offer another possibility." She stopped before Steven. "What if the heroes of *this* story are a man with shrewd intellect who, after centuries of toil, is about to achieve all he has ever dreamed of, and a woman, cruelly maimed in her prime, who has a second chance at life and will stop at nothing to finally find her happiness?" She spun on one heel and joined the gathered Black by the corner of the Monument. "My King," she whispered, "shall we take our leave?"

"Indeed." Zed took the *Svartr Kyll* from Magdalene and held aloft the dark leather pouch. "Gather close, my emissaries of the Black." The air filled with a tooth-shaking drone similar to that of its lighter-hued sister. "And you as well, my oldest friend." He held out his arm, and after a pregnant pause, Grey grasped the Black King's sleeve. "Tomorrow, we may fight for the glory and power, but tonight, we feast." A deafening pulse emanated from the King's dark pouch, and the entirety of his entourage, with Grey as their prisoner, vanished in a shimmer of darkness.

9

TEMPO

W hat now?" Audrey whispered, the hurt and disappointment and terror in her features twisting her face into a mask Steven barely recognized. "I mean..."

"I know." He wrapped his arm around her shoulders and found himself half-surprised she didn't pull away. "I'm so sorry."

"I can't believe we let them fucking walk." Emilio paced the stone at the base of the destroyed Washington Monument. "And with all our people."

Steven watched Emilio's ire through squinted eyes. The sun now rested in the crimson sky above the Lincoln Memorial to the west, the resulting golden shimmer from the reflecting pool blinding in its intensity. The unique view hit him as strangely beautiful, though being surrounded by the shattered marble corpse of one of his best friends transformed the moment into one of horror.

"And now, they've got Grey too." Emilio continued his rant. "This is all wrong. We should have gone down fighting. We should have—"

"We've been over this, Emilio." Steven worked to keep his tone even and the anger from his voice. "They used our people as living shields. What, were you planning on going through Lena's aunt to get to Zed?"

"Steven!" Audrey barked as Lena, already sitting on the ground crying, buried her face in her hands.

Emilio fumed. "And how's that going to be different when we face them all again in a few...what? Days? Hours? You don't think he's going to stick your dad and Audrey's mom and Lena's aunt right up front in our face the second we land wherever the hell this thing is going to go down?"

"I know, dammit, I know. I'm not sure what else you all wanted me to do. Even Grey said this was the only way."

"You mean the guy who just gave himself up to the bad guys?" Emilio's eyes narrowed. "Maybe if Grey was a little more like his buddy and took charge instead of leaving all the big decisions to..."

Steven stepped into the young man's space. "To who, Emilio?" Heat rose in his cheeks. "To the stupid Pawn?"

Emilio lowered his head. "I didn't say that."

Steven's head cocked to one side. "Then what were you going to say?"

"Stop!" Audrey leaped to her feet and separated them. "You two are not doing this."

The two men stood there, chests huffing with emotion, neither saying a word. In the end, Emilio was the one who offered the olive branch. "I'm sorry. I'm just so far beyond pissed." His entire body shook in anger. "I don't know what to say."

"I get it, Emilio." Steven allowed his shoulders to drop and reached out a hand. "Don't forget. That's my dad. You think I don't feel helpless right now?" He gestured around at Niklaus' rocky remains. "Here and now, in this place?"

As the conversational stalemate continued, Steven marveled that amidst the chaos of countless curious onlookers and the most robust police presence he'd ever seen, their cloaks of anonymity still somehow kept their presence veiled from the dozens surrounding them. Even Niklaus' titanic form remained all but ignored, a fact that left Steven cold.

Archie soon rejoined the group with a limping Rocinante in tow. Gored by Sombra's iron head-spike, the Knight's steed seemed in far better shape than Steven had dreamed possible. Whatever healing

Grey's rain of petals had done to bring Archie, Emilio, and Rocinante back from the brink, the priest's powers had served to bridge the remaining gap. Though the stallion appeared far from whole, Steven was grateful only one among the White had fallen in the battle.

"I was able to repair most of the damage done by the black charger's spike." Archie's knees appeared ready to buckle. "Does anyone else require healing?"

The priest's selfless question deescalated the tense situation, and Emilio finally took Steven's hand. Lena went to her young lover's side and wrapped her arms around his waist in her perennial role as yin to Emilio's yang. Audrey joined them as well, with Archie and Rocinante soon completing the circle.

"I've got to ask, Archie. Did you tend to yourself?" Steven did his best to keep any suspicion about the priest from his voice, a feat made far easier by the fact that nothing but the man's most earnest version had been present since Grey's enchantment had brought him and Emilio back to consciousness. "Save a little of your hocus pocus for our one and only Bishop."

"I'll be fine." Archie smiled, his expression free of the strange otherness that Steven often noted and always questioned. "I'll make my rounds with all of you as soon as I am able, but today, Rocinante had the most need of my services, and as you can see…"

The horse whinnied, appearing stronger and steadier with each passing second. The sound sent a wave of relief rolling through Steven's soul and brought a welcome smile to everyone's lips.

Of all the people brought into their fold, no one had poured more of themselves into the rest than Archibald Lacan, a fact made all the more apparent by his continued shunting of reparative energy into the stallion at his side even as he himself hobbled along with a leg that was clearly injured. How many times would he have to heal each of them before this madness was finished? Would there come a time when the Bishop's mercies were no longer sufficient? And what would happen to all of them if Archie were the next removed from the Board?

"Still," Steven continued, "you've got to take care of yourself. That limp—"

"Is nothing." Archie pulled in a cleansing breath. "Now, come. Let me tend to *you*."

Selfless. Generous. Noble.

And yet, the stirrings at the pit of Steven's stomach refused to go away.

The White Bishop took his hand, the man's touch both comforting and confounding, and began the low chant that summoned his restorative ability. Neither Greek nor Latin nor any other language either of them had ever heard, Steven often wondered how Archie reconciled his healing touch with the simple fact that its source was anything but a product of the Christian faith around which the man had built his life. The one time he'd so much as broached the subject, the priest answered simply, *"The Lord, Steven, moves in mysterious ways."*

At the White Bishop's shimmering touch, the pain pulsating through Steven's body from scalp to sole diminished to a dull ache. The sensation was anything but new, as Archie had given of himself to each of them more than once.

"Thanks, Archie." He let go the priest's hand. "Don't know what we'd do without you."

Archie smiled. "Just playing my part."

When everyone had tasted of the Bishop's power, the priest finally reached down to minister to his own injured leg, sending a silver glow that passed from fingertip to swollen ankle. With his next few steps, there was little doubt the healing had begun.

Archie had ministered to each of them before healing himself. Why couldn't Steven let go of his suspicions? Of all people, the healer of the team, the taker of their confessions, the truest man of God he'd ever met?

And yet, as always, something troubled him, something just below the surface.

The Game is upon us. Steven's eyes slipped closed. *For good or ill, I suspect we're about to find out.*

STEVEN STARED up at the stony visages of George Washington, Thomas Jefferson, Theodore Roosevelt, and Abraham Lincoln, and wished he could ask the advice of the four visionaries that led the United States through the most turbulent years of the preceding two centuries. Though he searched their craggy gazes for inspiration, for hope, for an inkling of what to do next, in the end, he was left even more lost than before.

More lost than when he ran for his life through the streets of Chicago. fleeing from a beautiful assassin who could bend fire itself to her will.

More lost than when he witnessed a man he only knew at the time as the White Rook fall from the King tower in Atlanta, his body riddled with the Black Pawn's barbed arrows.

Even more lost than when he pulled himself up from the ground in backwoods Florida almost a decade before his father was born and helped an injured Niklaus stumble back to civilization.

He purposefully avoided the fifth set of stony eyes, closed forever, that rested at the base of the mountain, not sure if his heart could handle even another ounce of guilt. Niklaus may have been the last Piece Steven brought into the fold, but their months together in the 1940s and after had left them as close as brothers. Now he stood at what had effectively become Niklaus' grave, and his heart ached as if he'd lost family.

And that was only the beginning of the pain.

His thoughts looped again and again, replaying the day's events. The loss of Grey to the Black. Niklaus' death at the hands of their Rook's stony assault. Watching everyone they loved not just willingly but cheerfully follow a man who wished each of them dead.

And the most painful? The words spoken to him by his own father, words that mixed gleeful cruelty with sadistic pleasure, inflicting an emotional wound no other could match.

Those words weren't Donald Bauer's.

And yet, they were.

How could he have been so stupid? Niklaus had called it early on, but Steven hadn't fully understood, and now his friend was dead.

"The proverbial cherry path," he murmured, echoing the White Rook's words. "Led by the nose, each and every one of us."

"No need to keep punishing yourself." Archie approached along the Avenue of Flags leading to the base of the breathtaking batholith of granite either immortalized or forever ruined nearly a century before, depending on your point of view, by sculptures of four of the greatest men from United States history. "Take it from someone who's talked to more than his fair share of monks over the years: self-flagellation isn't as helpful as you might think."

Steven let out a weak laugh. "With Nik gone, you taking over as the team comedian?"

"The group jester, eh?" A disquieting flash of amusement crossed Archie's features, the momentary dread punctuated by a tiny pinch at Steven's left collarbone. "I suppose I could give it a shot." Before Steven could ask what this latest cryptic comment was supposed to mean, Archie shifted the conversation in a different direction, the brief flicker of mischief in his eyes gone like breath on a window in winter. "I must say, you've chosen quite the fitting resting place for our marbled friend."

Steven pushed the unspoken question to the back of his mind and summoned a faint smile. "Mount Rushmore. Mom and Dad brought me here when I was a kid. The sculptures of the presidents were impressive, but I remember asking Dad about the big pile of rocks below. He said the rocks were what was left over after all the carving and blasting, and just like they never finished the four sculptures, they never bothered to cart off all the rock either." He pointed to the pile of boulders that crested below the space between the sixty-foot busts of Roosevelt and Lincoln. There, Niklaus' head and upper torso rested on its side surrounded by the remainder of his broken form. "It appears the power that cloaked Niklaus in life still keeps his form from being noticed, at least for now." He peered into the distance, daring to look again upon his fallen friend. Tears welled at the corners of his eyes. "When this is all over, though, Rushmore may have a new face for all the tourists to honor."

"Should this continent and everyone on it survive the next several hours, an extra countenance looking down from Rushmore will be the least of anyone's worries." Archie let out a quiet sigh. "In any case, you've left our friend Niklaus in good company."

"And you've finished your...business with him?"

"To the best of my abilities." Archie followed Steven's gaze to their friend's shattered form in the distance. "I've never before had to administer last rites to a three-story statue that once held a heartbeat."

Steven lowered his head. "What now?"

Archie shrugged. "We are far beyond any of the events revealed to me in my previous visions. All I can tell you is what I gleaned from Grey and Zed back in D.C."

"And that would be?"

"First, we seek the crown, so the Game can occur. Second, we seek a new Rook, so that we have a hope of winning. And then, we wait."

"Simple as that, huh?" Steven pulled in a breath of warm South Dakota air. "How is everyone doing, anyway? I've been giving all of you some space since Emilio and I got into it back in D.C. I thought we could all use some time to cool down and—"

"We're fine, Steven." Emilio's voice, close across his shoulder, no longer bore the edge of the young man's anger. "All of this still sucks, but we're fine."

Steven turned to find the remaining three of their party approaching from the tourist center to the southeast.

"Rocinante?" He shot Emilio a questioning glance. "Everything okay?"

Emilio shot a thumb back toward the parking decks to the south-east. "All chromed up and taking a break. Archie's mojo took care of most of the physical damage, but he's still a little skittish."

"We thought he could use some time alone." Lena stared past Steven and Archie at the pile of rubble at the base of the mountain. "Niklaus appears at peace." Her gaze filled with emotion and tears. "It still hurts my heart, though, seeing him broken like that."

"We couldn't just leave him there in D.C." Audrey stepped to Lena's side and wrapped an arm about the younger woman's shoulders. "And this is as good a place as any for him to rest." She looked to Steven, her expression resolute. "A place of honor."

"At least we showed up at a national monument today that didn't get destroyed within minutes of our arrival." Steven's attempt to lighten the mood was met with mixed results. Emilio's sad grin matched Archie's chuckle, while Audrey and Lena both crossed their arms and shook their heads. Undaunted, he gazed up at the scarlet sky, made all the more impressive by the sun setting in the west, and added, "There is still daylight, though."

"Perhaps," Archie gave Steven's ribcage a playful elbow, "you should leave the jokes to me?"

"Maybe so." Steven motioned for all of them to circle close. "So, we were talking about our next steps. Finding the crown of the White seems paramount if we don't want the whole damn continent to blow up when the Game doesn't go down as planned."

"Agreed." Lena's gaze dropped, her hands finding her pockets. "But after that, are we really going to try to replace Nik?"

"You want to go up against the Black without our own personal walking battering ram?" Emilio pulled Lena close. "That rocky bitch almost killed all of us twice today."

"Niklaus was more than a hunk of rock, *papi*. He was our friend." Lena brushed off Emilio's arm and pulled closer to Audrey. "It's not like we can go to a quarry and ask to buy a walking boulder with a quick sense of humor."

"Whoa, whoa, whoa, *mami*, I never said that." Emilio backed up, hands before him in mock surrender. "Just saying if we don't have a Rook, we're not going to last five seconds."

"Emilio's right, but I also agree with Lena." Audrey appeared very small in a simple t-shirt and jeans after sporting the raiment of the White Queen all day. "How are we going to find another Rook?" Her head tilted to one side as her eyebrows shot up in exasperation. "Not to mention, I may not know much about the game of chess, but unless I'm missing something, going into a game with your King already captured is a bit of a non-starter, right?"

"Each of the five of us remains free," Archie offered with as reassuring a smile as he could muster, "and with freedom, comes hope."

"Hope?" Emilio asked. "For what? It's not like we can wish away what's waiting for us. Any second now, we're all going to get zapped off to God knows where to fight everyone we know and love to try and get at Maggie and the others while they sit back and laugh their asses off. Is that what we're supposed to be hoping for?"

"With freedom, Emilio, we may not get to choose what is coming for us, but we can choose how we face the challenges that come our way. We can be bitter and angry about the cards we're dealt, or we can choose to rise to the occasion and do the best we can no matter what this world throws at us."

"Right." Emilio glared at the priest, arms crossed and chest pumping in frustration, before jamming his hands into his pockets and walking away from their circle. "We're all about to die, and you're spouting bullshit about adjusting sails during the storms of life."

"Emilio!" Lena called after him, her voice cracking with emotion. "Come back."

"You all finish writing your damn Hallmark cards," he grumbled. "I'm going to take a walk."

"Emilio has a point, you know." Audrey's words stopped the young man in his tracks. "In fact, Magdalene said it best. Just because we're the 'good guys' in this fight doesn't mean we win." She glanced in Niklaus' direction. "We've already lost one today, and no one among the White other than Grey has survived the last two iterations. Why should we think we've got a snowball's chance in hell, especially with Niklaus gone and Grey captured?" Her eyes fixated on a point in the distance, only her trembling lip betrayed her emotion. "I'm in this as much as anyone, but up till now, we've done everything right, fought the good fight, sacrificed everything, and still the bad guys walked away without a scratch with our families and our King. At this point, what are our chances realistically? Is this thing even winnable?"

Lena and Archie awaited Steven's response, the girl's earnest expression and the priest's beatific smile each firmly in place. Even Emilio, his back turned several feet away, seemed to perk up his ears.

Steven cleared his throat. "No matter what faces us, I refuse to believe our cause is without hope. The Game chose each of us for a reason, and that's not nothing. Things may look bleak, but at the end of the day we have each other, and that's what has brought us this far." He rested a hand on Lena's shoulder. "I wasn't sure if you, me, and Emilio would make it out of Baltimore alive, but look at how far we've come." He turned to Audrey, doing his best to quell the frantic beating of his heart. "When we first met back in Oregon, Magdalene and the original Black Knight had us dead to rights, and yet we somehow survived."

"Somehow?" A rueful grimace invaded Audrey's features. "I broke that bastard's neck."

"Yes, you did." Steven bore a grim smile. "On death's door from leukemia and then burned within an inch of your life, you still managed to hang on to the Black Knight's horse as he rode away and managed to save not only yourself, but me, a man you'd never set eyes on before that day." He looked on her with a mix of pride and passion. "You, Audrey Richards, are made of some stern stuff."

"Indeed, she is." Archie gazed at her with something approaching reverence. "God save the Queen."

"And you, Archie," Steven continued. "You've managed to keep us all alive, no matter what it cost you. I don't even want to know how much of your own soul you've poured out to get us to this point, not to mention all the others you've helped along the way."

"Thank you, Steven." The priest appeared genuinely surprised at the words of gratitude. "Like I said in D.C., I'm just trying to play my part."

Steven reflected in silence, thinking of the words he'd say to Niklaus Zamek, a man who'd proven himself again and again, and never more so than in his final sacrifice.

"The way I see it, the five of us have made it through everything thrown at us, whether all together or separated by hundreds of miles or even scattered across the decades. Today, we played Grey's Game valiantly, but in the end, the cards were stacked against us. The Black orchestrated every moment of their three-pronged attack today, like they've done at every turn since the very beginning, and this time, Zed's plans finally bore fruit. They divided us three ways and then sent our own family and friends to fight us, all of it designed to undermine our will and tie our hands. As a result, we lost the battle." Steven looked again in the direction of Niklaus' shattered form and swallowed back both fear and anger. "We haven't, however, lost the war."

10

SOMEONE ELSE'S STORY

Didn't think I'd be doing this again." Steven held aloft the *Hvitr Kyll*, its low drone permeating the area with an inescapable hum. "But here we are."

"Funny. Other than when we landed roadside in Oregon when the pouch sent us after Audrey, we've always landed in a major population center." Suddenly standing atop a mountain, Lena stared out upon a vista straight out of a storybook. "No surprise, but I prefer this."

"Where are we?" Emilio asked, a bit more discombobulated by their latest jaunt. "And why are we on top of a mountain?"

"Who cares?" Lena pulled in a deep breath of mountain air, grinning ear-to-ear and fished in her knapsack for an apple for Rocinante. The horse took the snack readily and whinnied in contentment. "If I had all the money in the world, this would be the view off my front porch."

"If you like this," Audrey said, "then we'll have to go hiking in old forest Oregon when this is all over."

"If we're still alive." Emilio shoved his hands in his pockets.

"Of course." Audrey's momentary ebullience deflated like a burst balloon at Emilio's comment. "So, Steven, this is the latest haystack?"

"Looks like it."

"Still think we should find Grey's crown first." Emilio studied the pouch in Steven's outstretched hand. "Why didn't that thing take us where you told it to like it usually does?"

Another pulse from the *Hvitr Kyll* shook all their teeth.

"You were there," Steven answered. "No matter how I said it, the pouch wouldn't do its thing when I asked for the crown." He shook his head, frustrated. "One request for a new Rook, however, and it was off to the races." He rubbed at his ears, still ringing from the deafening pulse, and let out a bitter chuckle. "It appears the *Hvitr Kyll* doesn't like being questioned."

"And to top it all off, we're actually worrying about hurting the feelings of some stitched together pieces of leather?"

At Emilio's snark, another drone from the pouch's cinched mouth sent all their hands to their ears and wrenched a pained whinny from Rocinante's equine lips. Though the blast of sound lasted but seconds, as the tooth-shaking sound faded into echo and silence again ruled the natural cathedral surrounding them all, one thing was clear: the *Hvitr Kyll* had spoken.

"What now, Steven?" Archie, who'd been quiet to that point, asked the question of the hour.

"We do what we always do." Steven's gaze followed along the well-worn trail that followed the top of the ridge to the southeast and into a sun rising into an already crimson sky. "We start walking."

THEY'D all rolled the dice the previous evening, checking into a Ramada in Keystone, South Dakota, a little town east of Mount Rushmore, rather than continuing to push forward despite their shared exhaustion. Lena and Emilio had both wanted to keep going at all costs, but Steven, with an assist from Audrey and Archie, had convinced the impetuous young couple of the wisdom in resting after such a tumultuous day. The three had bummed a ride into town with the two teens following behind on the gleaming-white Rocinante motorcycle.

No sooner had they eaten and found a suite for the five of them to crash together than Emilio curled up in a chair in the corner and began to snore. Lena lasted a couple minutes longer before falling unconscious beneath a thin blanket at the foot of one of the two queen-size beds. Archie excused himself to the bar upon their arrival for a well-deserved nightcap, leaving Steven and Audrey alone for the first time in two days.

"So," she asked, "how much of that speech you gave us earlier did you actually believe?"

"I don't know what you mean," he answered. "I meant every word."

"You're truly that confident we can still win this thing?"

"You're not?"

Audrey's downcast eyes answered the question before she uttered a word. "I'll admit that I felt better about it all when I thought we'd gained some kind of advantage." She sat on a corner of the unoccupied bed. "They were down a Knight, Niklaus had taken out their front line," she pulled in a long breath, "and then..."

"And then, today happened." Steven sat next to her, her nearness making his heart do somersaults. He wanted nothing more than to reach out for her, to draw her close to him, to make all the pain go away. But nothing he could do or say changed the fact that they would soon be fighting for their lives, and both her mother and his father would stand among their enemy's front line.

"I've heard you and Archie talking. You put on a brave front with us, but you're real when you talk with him."

"With Archie, it's different."

"How?" Audrey asked. "You let him see behind the curtain with all your talk about chessboards and pieces and what you really think, but with us? Sometimes it's like you're blowing smoke just to make us feel better."

"Look. I have doubts like all of you, but I'm never going to spout all the 'doom and gloom' running through my head when Emilio basically lives one stray comment from flying off the handle and getting himself killed. And you know as well as I do that Lena straddles the fence between unstoppable *muchacha* with a mace and scared teenage girl who just wants to run home to her mother."

"And me?" Audrey asked. "What are you protecting me from?"

"Do you really have to ask?"

She pulled close and rested her hand on Steven's knee. "Tell me."

Steven swallowed. "The thought of you not making it through this is beyond anything I can even bear to consider. I go to sleep thinking about it. I wake up thinking about it. It hits me every time I see you. Every time I hear your voice. Every time you cross my mind." He rested his hand atop Audrey's and gave it a gentle squeeze. "Which isn't a particularly uncommon occurrence, in case you were wondering."

"Steven," Audrey whispered, "I know how you feel about me, and I certainly hope by now that you know I feel the same way. When all this is over, you and me are going to talk." She shifted her hand and intertwined her fingers with his. "For now, though, we have to make it through this, and not just for the two of us, but the others as well, not to mention the rest of the world."

"Audrey," Steven said, "I've never said the words, but with all that's happened—"

She placed a single finger across his lips. "I told you. I know. Now, however, is not the time."

"And when all this is over," he asked, "are we going to talk about the other thing?" His shoulders dropped. "I saw how you were when we found you and Lena in Chicago. You have to know if that's what's coming, I'm going to stand beside you the whole way."

"I've already fought the good fight against the damn leukemia, twice even, and both times the leukemia won." She let out a sad laugh. "But one certain death scenario at a time is enough, right?"

"Audrey, I'm sorry."

"I'm kidding." As he looked away, she brought her fingers to his chin and brought his eyes back to hers. "Steven, look at me. If I'm not laughing, I'm crying. Do you understand?"

"I understand."

"When all this is over, I promise, we'll get to the good stuff."

"When all this is over..." Steven wrestled with his own emotions, doing his best to keep up the brave front he'd held for all the weeks and months since he'd first met this woman's captivating gaze. "But—"

She pulled his face to hers, gently but without hesitation, and planted a kiss as soft as silk on his trembling mouth. As light as a summer breeze, the sweet touch of her lips on his lasted but a second, but in that all too brief moment, a lone conviction crystallized in Steven's heart: he'd already lost the love of his life once, and he'd be damned if he was going to lose it again.

❀

"So," Steven muttered, "Montana." He studied the wooden sign before glancing back at the others clambering down the ridgeline trail. "Lena called it."

"I knew it." Lena arrived at the sign scant seconds before Emilio who was held up leading Rocinante along the rocky path. Audrey and Archie brought up the rear of their party, the priest helping Audrey navigate a particularly slick hunk of rock. "Glacier National Park." She turned to Emilio. "This one is on my list, *papi*."

Emilio shook his head and laughed. "Not long after we started dating, Lena's aunt and uncle drove the two of us into Virginia to Shenandoah National Park. Lena had always loved the outdoors, and once she wrapped her brain around the fact she had a brand-new continent to explore..."

Careful what you wish for. Steven considered all the places they'd seen together. *You might just get it.*

"I'll never forget that weekend." Lena grinned from ear to ear. "I've climbed my fair share of mountains, but seeing all that beauty and green with Emilio made it a whole new experience." Gone was the quiet trepidation that had been Lena's mask for days, replaced with the vibrant young woman Steven had encountered far too few times in the weeks and months since they'd first met in Baltimore. "I got one of those National Parks passports and started planning which one we were going to next. We were thinking about visiting the Great Smoky Mountains this summer until everything with Carlos started going south."

"Shenandoah *is* pretty." Steven worked to shift the conversation from the direction it was heading. "Mom, Dad, and I used to go every

108

year or two back when I was a kid." He locked eyes with the frightened young woman. "We'll get you there, Lena. I promise," he smiled, "and for now..."

"Montana." Lena traced the letters on the trail sign with an outstretched finger. "I knew I recognized the range of mountains from the last ridge. Lord knows I've stared at this place's website enough times." Her shoulders slumped slightly, as if someone had let the air out of her balloon. "I wish my first visit wasn't under such circumstances."

"We'll come back here someday, *mami*, when all this is done and enjoy the mountains."

At Rocinante's cautious whinny, Steven prayed Emilio's promise wasn't empty, a sentiment mirrored in all their faces, and in no one's more than Emilio himself.

"Any clue yet as to why we're all here, Steven?" Audrey eyed the pouch at his hip.

He pulled the *Hvitr Kyll* from his belt and spun around as if he held a mobile phone and was hunting for signal. "Still nothing," he muttered as the pouch continued its low but unchanging hum. "Do we keep walking?"

"What else would we do?" Archie took the lead and moved further along the trail. Lena and Emilio followed with Rocinante, leaving Steven alone with Audrey.

"You sure this is the right place?" she asked.

"As sure as I've been about any of this." He took her hand. "If I'd known we were hiking today, we could've packed some water or food or better shoes or—"

"We're all fine." She gave his fingers a gentle squeeze. "If things get bad, we'll have the pouch take us to the nearest town, right?"

"I don't know." Steven let go her hand and reattached the leather bag to his belt. "This thing is being a bit more 'mind of its own' today than I've seen before."

Audrey raised an eyebrow. "The mysterious Arbiters finally making their will known?"

"Maybe." He looked after the others, already a hundred feet down the trail. "Would be nice if something went our way. I feel like I'm letting all of you down."

"Hey, we've all got your back on this." She laughed. "Even Emilio with all his grumbling knows you're doing the best you can."

"The best I can." Steven shook his head. "What if it that isn't enough?"

"It's always been enough so far."

"Tell that to Nik."

Audrey's hands went to her hips. "Stop whipping yourself, Steven. We need you, all of us. You can't be letting guilt about things out of your control cloud your mind and judgment."

"But—"

"No buts. Look, I'm more than willing to be your shoulder to cry on after we have our new Rook, find Grey's crown, and are on the other side of kicking the shit out of Zed and his cronies, but here and now, we need the guy willing to jump off a building after a man to save his life, not the guy beating himself up because that same man's ticket finally came up." She pulled close and whispered in his ear. "This Game, it's dangerous, no doubt. Some of us aren't going to make it. I think each of us has had to make our own peace with that simple fact. But you? You're our leader. If you're not present, more of us are going to get hurt than necessary, and I don't think you want that on your soul." She wrapped an arm around his shoulders and squeezed. "So, get your shit together, get down that trail, and, like you've said to Grey and Archie a good dozen times, lead from the front."

"Yes, ma'am." Despite the scolding, Steven's lips turned up in a muted grin. Not since Katherine had a woman hit him with both barrels like that, simultaneously tearing him down and building him back up at the same time. Her impassioned speech left him both stung and spurred on, the words exactly what he'd needed to hear. "Shall we?"

He moved down the trail at a jog with Audrey close behind, and soon the six remaining White again faced together whatever lay ahead. As per his position on the Board, Steven took the lead with Lena and Emilio following behind and Audrey and Archie again bringing up the rear. One hour passed, then another, as they conquered peak after peak and made their way along the mountainous ridge, encountering vista after breathtaking vista on the challenging path. The peace was more than they'd known in weeks, but as the day wore on, both their dry throats and the soles of their feet began to burn.

"You sure we took off in the right direction?"

Steven wasn't sure if Emilio had asked the question six or seven times already, but he was on the verge of yelling at the poor boy when the pouch's low hum made its first warble since they'd first appeared in Montana.

"Looks like it." At the nadir of a spur between two peaks, they stopped and huddled. "What do you all think?" Steven asked. "Should we go up?"

"That's been the answer all day," Lena said as she passed the two men and started the next ascent. "Why should now be any different?"

With Lena in the lead and Rocinante scrambling up the incline behind her as best he could, the six of them headed for the summit of this latest peak as fast as they could. Despite Emilio and Lena's shared youth, the general health and vigor afforded Audrey and Archie by the Game, and Steven's runner's form, this steepest slope of the day proved challenging for all of them after such a physically and emotionally exhausting day. Half an hour passed before they finally arrived at the next summit, the pitch and rigor of the hike leaving each of them winded and parched. Over the last hundred feet, each step sent the pouch's drone louder, the pulsating wail hitting a fever pitch as the last of them reached the top.

"This is it." Steven cast his gaze left and right. "Someone or something here is making the pouch go nuts."

"Congratulations," came a male voice from beyond a small copse of trees to their left. "You've found me."

Steven followed the voice to a large outcropping of rock overlooking the valley below. Between a young spruce and a fir tree bent no doubt by years of whipping mountain winds sat a man facing away from them and staring into the distance, his long black hair pulled back into a braided ponytail. His well-muscled arms and broad neck were russet brown, the mark of a man who spent his days under the sun. He sat cross-legged as if communing with a higher power. A pair of faded cargo pants covered his legs. Catching Steven's attention more than any other detail, however, was the man's shirt.

The fabric a familiar blue embellished with gold stars and silver moons, the full-length sleeves and lower hem boasted a fringe reminiscent of the two evergreen trees that framed the man. As he rose and turned to face them, his chest puffed out with pride and the quartet of indigo birds decorating the front of the ornate shirt cemented a strange but simple fact. Steven had only seen one other shirt like this in his life, though not in this century or even the century of his birth.

The strange *déjà vu* at seeing the man's garment was eclipsed a moment later by the even more striking familiarity he found in the young man's gaze.

"Steven," Emilio whispered, "can that be who I think it is?"

"Normally," he answered, "I'd say what you're thinking is impossible, but if the last few months have proven anything, it's that nothing is—"

"*William Two Trees,*" came a voice amplified by loudspeaker, the all-too-familiar name echoing through the scant woods atop the ridge, "*stay right where you are, hands behind your head. We have you surrounded.*"

William froze in place as nearly a dozen law enforcement officers dressed in navy blue with FBI emblazoned in yellow across their ubiquitous bulletproof vests poured across the opposite end of the rocky peak. "Wait." He took a step in their direction. "I don't understand. You're not with them?"

"We're not," Steven said, "but like them, we *are* here for you." He raised his hands before him in a disarming gesture. "Can you *really* be Billy Two Trees?"

"Billy?" The man furrowed his brow. "Do I know you?"

Question of the century, Steven guessed. Or, at least, one from a couple centuries back. "Not sure, but if you'll come with us, we'll get it all figured out." Amaryllis fluttered at his chest, the tiny metallic blows answered by a flurry of beats from his racing heart.

"I'm not going anywhere with anyone." William scooped up a

backpack from the ground and held up something that looked like a jury-rigged cell phone with a foot-long antenna. "This backpack has enough C4 to blow all of us straight off this mountain," he shouted, spinning to address both Steven and FBI agents. "Now, all of you, disappear, or I swear I'll blow us all straight to hell."

11

DIFFICULT AND DANGEROUS TIMES

Yo, Steven." Emilio pulled close, his voice dropping to a low whisper. "Call me crazy, but is one of the job requirements for this stupid Game that the person has to already be in deep shit when you come along?"

"Says the young stud that was picking a fight with not one but two different Baltimore street gangs when we met?"

Emilio's nose crinkled. "Good point."

"*William Two Trees,*" came the megaphone-amplified voice again from an FBI agent who had yet to come out into the open. "*Surrender now, and you have my assurance you will be treated fairly.*"

"Fairly?" William laughed. "I know how your kind works with mine," he shouted in response. "Firehoses and rubber bullets, and that's if we're lucky."

"*This entire summit is cordoned off. There's no way down except with us. We can end this peacefully as long as you don't harm your hostages. You're in enough trouble as it is.*"

"Hostages?" Audrey whispered.

Last to join the circle, Archie drew close to the others. "I think they mean us."

"Well," Lena whispered, "If the shoe fits, I guess."

"Billy," Steven stopped mid-thought, "I mean William. What the hell is this? Why are you up here? What does the FBI want with you?"

William stared at him, incredulous. "Dude, in case you missed it, I'm holding a bag full of C4 here. You sure now is the time you want to play twenty questions?" His expression grew a shade more thoughtful. "Wait, if you don't know who I am or why I'm on this mountain, then what the hell are you even doing here in the first place? Why'd you bring a fucking horse?" His brow furrowed. "And why do you keep calling me Billy?"

Rocinante snorted and pawed the ground, his equine eyes clouded over with indignation.

"Seems there are a *lot* of unanswered questions." Steven gestured in the direction of the swarming government agents mustering for some kind of assault. "I have no idea why the FBI is after you, and for the most part, I don't care. My friends and I are here for you, regardless of what you've done, but we need you alive. Please, put down that backpack."

"I'm not putting down shit." William rested a thumb on the proverbial big red button of what could only be the detonation device for his backpack bomb. "If you people actually are with the feds, then this is the weirdest 'good cop/bad cop' routine I've ever seen; on the other hand, if you're not, then I've got a sneaking suspicion I'd be better off with those guys."

"Smart man." Emilio thumbed across his shoulder. "Except 'those guys' are the ones packing heat, and unless I'm missing something, I don't think rubber bullets are the order of the day."

William chewed on Emilio's words. "Who are you people?"

"Time for that later." Steven brought the pouch before him, its constant hum going up a few decibels as it drew near to William. "For now, we need to get you and the rest of us the hell out of here."

"What part of 'I'm not going anywhere with anyone' are you not getting? I am literally holding a fucking bomb here." William shook his head in a flurry of frustration. "After what I've already done, do you really think I'll hesitate to blow this thing and all of us straight to hell?"

Steven lowered his head. "Like I said before, I have no idea what it is you've done, much less what you would or wouldn't do. I'm simply here with an offer. I'll get you out of this, I swear, but once we're all free and clear, we need *your* help with something way bigger."

Before William could answer, the unseen wielder of the megaphone made his presence known again.

"William Two Trees, this is your last chance." In the distance, a collection of snipers took up positions while the remaining agents sought cover for the impending attack. *"Release your hostages and surrender."*

"Last chance?" Lena whispered. "What are they going to do? Shoot him?"

Emilio raised an eyebrow. "You watch the news in the last couple years, *mami?*"

"But we're all here with him." Her brow furrowed. "Are they going to risk our lives as well?"

"God only knows, Lena." Steven returned his attention to William. "Look, I don't know you from Adam, but based on that shirt you're wearing, you believe in what you're doing, your people, your cause. In a different time, another Billy Two Trees thought a similar shirt would protect him from harm, that a 'Ghost Dance' would call back the dead and bring justice to the continent, that the spirits of the slain would make him invincible. I'm here to tell you that all of those crazy stories you've ever heard and more can come true, but you have to come with us right now."

William's already incredulous stare doubled in intensity. "And I'm the one they want to lock up," he muttered with a sarcastic chuckle.

"He's not kidding, man." Emilio reached for the man's shoulder, but as William's eyes flicked to the button on his detonator, the White Knight raised his hands before him, palms out. "Not all that long ago, each of us stood in the exact same spot as you, facing one impossible situation or another, but then, as crazy as it all sounds, Steven came along and offered each of us a different path." He gestured to the *Hvitr Kyll.* "Looks like you could use the same."

"Steven, eh?" William trained his gaze on the pouch. "You've been holding that thing more carefully than I've been holding this backpack full of C4. This 'different path' of yours. Do you keep it in that bag?"

"The pouch has held an answer for every single one of us." He offered the open *Hvitr Kyll* to William, the low drone and the subtle silver incandescence pouring from its mouth pulsating in time with the heartbeat of the world. "Reach inside. Show me what you find."

William hesitated a moment before lowering the backpack to the ground, though he kept the trigger device gripped in his opposite hand. Carefully, he reached for the mouth of the groaning pouch of white leather and—

The crack of gunfire echoed across the peak, sending a flock of birds skyward from the tops of a few nearby trees. William's shoulder jerked forward with a dull thud, sending the cell phone trigger flying from his hand. Emilio backpedaled a few feet up the trail and yanked the device from the air before it could hit the ground while Steven and the others all dropped to a low crouch as they prepared for another gunshot.

As a suddenly skittish Rocinante vanished back down the trail, a wounded William toppled forward like a felled tree and landed flat on his face, a circle of red forming at the shoulder of the shirt that had left him anything but invulnerable. "Ow," he grunted as he rolled onto one side using his good arm. "They fucking shot me."

"What did you think they were going to do?" Emilio asked as Steven spun in the direction of FBI agents and waved his arms.

"Stand down!" he shouted. "We've got the detonator."

Wait. His thoughts raced. *As far as they're concerned, the person who caught the thing that could blow us all to kingdom come is just another kid with brown skin.*

"Emilio." Steven kept his voice calm but direct. "Put the detonator down. No sudden movements, but get the damn thing out of your hand and on the ground."

Half a second passed before the implications of Steven's words clicked in Emilio's head. He held the modified cell phone out to one side between thumb and forefinger and slowly lowered it to the rocky earth at his feet. Steven didn't say a word, but a glint from a scope in the distance let him know his young friend sat firmly in the crosshairs of at least one of the snipers across the way.

"All right," Emilio whispered. "It's down."

"Now what do we do?" Audrey asked. "They're fanning out to surround us."

Steven studied the movement at the far end of the summit and agreed. The agents would be on them in seconds, and though he knew full well he and the others had little to fear if they brought their full powers to bear, the thought of fighting and possibly hurting or killing government agents who were just doing their job didn't sit well.

"Hey, Mr. Life Changer." William clutched at his bleeding shoulder. "In case you forgot, man down over here. You got something in that bag for me?"

Steven's face broke into a rueful smile as images flashed across his memory.

Audrey's miraculous recovery back in Sisters, Oregon as she assumed the role of White Queen.

Archie's youthful transformation in the Roanoke hospital where Steven had years ago held his mother's hand as she fought the cancer that ate away at her.

Niklaus rising like a stony god from the rubble between the King and Queen towers in Atlanta, unscathed by a fall that should have left him broken and dead.

They'd come all this way to find their new Rook. He prayed the ancient magic would work yet again.

"Lena," Steven whispered, "cradle his head."

"You got it." Lena moved into position.

"Audrey, some cover, if you will?"

"Certainly." The icon in her hand disappeared, replaced by a crown atop her head and a shimmering cloak about her shoulders. The slightest of murmurs fell from her lips, and a thick fog of silvery mist poured from the ground at her feet, obscuring them all in seconds.

"Archie, a little help?"

The priest scooted close and brought a hand to the man's shoulder.

"Whoa, whoa, whoa." William pulled away. "You going to try to get the bullet out with your fingers?"

"The bullet will come, fear not." Archie smiled. "For the moment, though, I hope only to staunch the bleeding so you don't lose consciousness before Steven can introduce you to the *Hvitr Kyll*."

"The what?"

"The pouch," Steven said. "Now, hold on a minute and let Archie do his thing."

"Archie?" William peered around at all of them, his eyes growing wide as the priest's lips began to move, producing a low chant that drowned out all other sound. "What the hell is happening? Is this guy one of those crazy religious faith healers like on TV?"

"The only one I've ever met that could actually do what they say," Steven answered. "Not to mention, you're the one wearing the Ghost Dance shirt. Now, be quiet and let him do what he needs to do."

William inhaled to ask yet another indignant question, but stopped himself before the first word was out of his mouth and simply removed his hand from his wound. "Whatever it is can't be worse than this. Do it."

The strange syllables falling from Archie's mouth grew louder with each passing second. The priest's hands glowed like a pair of silver stars as he brought both to bear on William's wounded shoulder. William in turn let out a quiet grunt that was quickly followed by a metallic thunk as the slug fell from his shoulder and landed on the flat rock where Archie rested one knee. As the White Bishop's hands came away from the wound, the pain and fear in William's face evaporated, replaced with peace and wonder.

"But how?"

"Time for explanations later." Steven helped William to his feet. "For now, let's get out of—" Another flutter of Amaryllis' wings at his chest let him know that, yet again, moving on to the next square in this game of chess wasn't going to be as easy as he'd hoped.

"None of you are going anywhere." The tallest of a trio of FBI agents leveled his assault rifle at William and Steven while the pair of agents flanking him chose Archie and Emilio's crouching forms as their targets.

If they knew anything, Steven considered, *all three of them would have Audrey in their sights.*

"Step away from the fugitive." The lead agent, a man with dark, close-cropped hair motioned with his rifle. "We're only here for Mr. Two Trees. You'll all be coming with us, as we'll need your statements, but as long as none of you have any outstanding warrants, we should have everything cleared up before the end of the day."

"But—"

"Step *away* from the fugitive," the agent said, the borderline friendly tone in his voice diminishing with every word. "Now, sir. I won't ask a third time."

"Here we go again," Steven grumbled under his breath. "Why does it always have to be the hard way?"

12

MOUNTAIN DUET

What's that in your hand?" the shortest of the three agents asked as another five appeared out of the White Queen's misty obscuration. "Some kind of leather bag?"

"A little small," the second agent added, "but it could be another bomb."

Shit. Steven still held William's hand in his right, having helped the man up from the ground, and the *Hvitr Kyll* rested lightly in his left. Pulsing in time with the rhythm of the universe, the pouch's drone grew louder and louder. More than ever before, he was glad those outside the Game weren't privy to its secrets. The FBI agents had shot the last man on this mountaintop holding a suspicious satchel, and he had little doubt they'd shoot again without question.

"It's just a knapsack for food." Steven raised the pouch to shoulder height. "We were hiking and—"

"You people don't look like any hikers I've ever seen," the agent interrupted, "and last I checked, they don't sell smoke grenades at REI."

The lead agent raised his hand, silencing the two accompanying him, and then motioned for the more recently arrived agents to halt their advance. "You with the bag, what's your name?"

"Bauer." He locked gazes with the man. "Steven Bauer."

"In that case, Mr. Bauer, let go of Mr. Two Trees, carefully place your 'knapsack' or whatever it is on the ground, and put your hands behind your head."

Steven let go of William's hand and brought the bag before him. "Let me explain."

"I said put it on the ground." The lead agent's eyes narrowed at him. "Now."

Not since Baltimore had Steven experienced the peculiar rush of being outnumbered and surrounded by a mob armed to the teeth with guns rather than medieval weaponry. With the agents surrounding them having no knowledge of the Game or what was truly at stake in the coming hours, he and the others rested one itchy trigger finger away from disaster.

But, as he'd recognized moments before, the gathered White had one advantage they hadn't possessed back in Baltimore.

"Audrey." Steven smiled. "Help them understand."

As if she'd merely been awaiting the word, Audrey's eyes slid closed and the eight scintillating balls of energy that were her trademark began to orbit her shoulders. As her eyes reopened, gone was the hazel gentleness he'd always found there, replaced by a bright silver sheen straight out of an 80s Bonnie Tyler video.

At the White Queen's silent command, eight pillars of silver mist erupted from the shimmering murk that played about all their feet and seized first the agent's weapons and then the agents themselves. Like the eight arms of some mountain-roaming cousin of the mythical kraken, the misty tendrils of mist spun their way around the agent's legs, torsos, arms, and necks. Their eight weapons clattered to the ground with all but synchronous precision. The octet of FBI agents all stared bug-eyed at the young woman from Oregon, recognizing they faced power beyond anything any of them had ever experienced.

"What are you?" the lead agent choked out as he dangled several feet in the air. "What is this?"

"As I attempted to explain before—"

Before Steven could get out another word, a gunshot in the

distance shattered the quiet, and the air by his ear buzzed as if an angry bumblebee had flown by at Mach 2.

"Well, that was too close for comfort." His eyes narrowed. "The hard way it is." He inhaled. "Shield. Pike. Helm." He turned his body to face the direction of the sniper, all but the tops of the few mountaintop trees obscured by Audrey's bank of mystical fog, and brought his shield around. "Phalanx."

Where one Pawn had stood, now eight formed a file of anachronistic warriors. Interlocking their shields, they formed a tight arc around the gathered White, William Two Trees, and the mystically shackled agents. One Pawn broke away and stood beneath the agent in charge. Audrey brought the agent down to where he and the Pawn were all but nose to nose. As the remaining seven remained vigilant for attack, this eighth manifestation of Steven removed his helmet and squinted at the helpless man before him.

"For the last time, listen and listen well. William Two Trees is no longer your concern. Regardless of what he's done, he is needed for a higher cause, something beyond your understanding." He pointed skyward. "The red sky?" He gestured to the mountain beneath them. "All the earthquakes, floods, hurricanes of the last few months?" He pulled in a breath. "The man you're after and the rest of us represent the only thing standing between this continent and utter disaster."

"You're crazier than he is," the agent grunted.

"I wish I was." Steven again donned his helmet. "So, this is how it's going to go. My friend is going to release you and your men, and then, my associates and I, including Mr. Two Trees, are going to leave in a manner you aren't going to understand. You and your men will then head back to wherever you came from and report that your search came up empty and that you never found him. Do you understand?"

"One question. Do you actually know who it is you're helping to escape justice?" The agent shifted his glare from Steven to William who had stood strangely silent throughout their magical counterattack. "That man is a murderer and a terrorist."

Steven worked to keep the emotion from his face. "If that's truly the case, trust that when all this is over, my friends and I will turn him over to the appropriate authorities to face whatever judgment is coming his way." His eyes flicked to William who appeared shaken for the first time since their arrival. "Is that clear, Mr. Two Trees?" He asked, his voice continuing its shift into that mysterious tone only assumed when the Arbiters or even the Game itself—he wasn't sure which—lent his voice the gravitas of millennia.

"Yes, sir," William stammered, the bluster in his every word replaced by fearful reverence.

"So," Steven returned his attention to the lead agent, "if that will be all, we'll just—"

"You're not taking Two Trees anywhere."

This new voice, a woman's from somewhere beyond Audrey's misty smokescreen, came across infuriated, yet cool and in control. A glance down revealed a red laser that lit up the shimmering mist like a rock concert light show, its focus at the center of his chest. Steven had counted eleven agents before, though God only knew how many were standard on a manhunt for a crime that warranted federal attention.

"Now, have your friend put down Special Agent Alfiere and the rest of our team and then turn over Mr. Two Trees." A second beam of red laser pierced Audrey's bulwark of mist, this one terminating on the White Queen's own chest. "The lot of you are already guilty of interfering in a federal investigation of an international fugitive. Don't make it worse for yourselves by—"

The staccato rhythm of galloping hooves filled the air. The laser sights left Steven and Audrey and swept in the direction of the sound. The crack of a single round shattered the tension, followed a breath later by the twin sounds of stomping hooves and an equine roar that could only be one creature on the planet.

"Get 'em, Rocinante." Emilio, who had remained uncharacteristically quiet through the entire back-and-forth punched his fist into his opposite palm. "Good boy."

The unseen fight lasted but a few more seconds, and when it was done, the white stallion strode confidently through the mist to Emilio and Lena's side and lowered his head for a well-earned scratch.

"I think we've pressed our luck as far as we should." Archie grasped Steven's shoulder. "Let's take our leave."

The semi-circle of Pawns collapsed around the gathered White, bringing together Steven, Audrey, Archie, Emilio, Lena, Rocinante, and the man they hoped might be their new Rook.

"Hands in, everyone." Steven held aloft the *Hvitr Kyll* in one hand and shot out his other. Audrey grasped his fingers first, then Lena, then Emilio, and finally Archie. Lena took Rocinante's bridle in her hand as the entire group turned as one to gaze at William Two Trees.

"What?" William asked. "Are we doing some kind of huddle? A strange time and place to be doing a team-building exercise, don't you think?"

"We're leaving this place," Steven answered, the strange gravitas returning again to his voice, "and you're coming with us whether you like it or not."

William looked skyward. "You got a helicopter coming or something? I don't get it. What is it you want me to do?"

"Put in your hand," Lena said with no small amount of pique, "and we'll show you."

His gaze shot to his own bag, barely visible in the scintillating murk at their feet. "But, what about that?"

Steven matched glares with Special Agent Alfiere. "I'm sure these fine government agents know how to dispose of a bomb. Now, time is growing short. We need to go."

"I don't know about all this," William joined the circle, "but it looks like I don't have much of a choice."

"None of us do, my son." Archie rested his other hand atop William's and gave it a gentle squeeze. "Now, prepare yourself. The first time is always the worst."

"The first time for what?" William asked.

"*Hvitr Kyll*," Steven whispered, barely audible above the continued drone of the pouch. "Take us away from here, now."

ONE MOMENT the seven of them stood atop a mountain in northern Montana this side of the Canadian border, and the next they appeared in a flash of silver on a brick sidewalk alongside a city street. The shift of the sun's position in the crimson sky suggested a return to the eastern part of the continent.

"Lena," Steven asked, "what time have you got?'

Lena pulled out the lone burner phone the group kept for emergencies and flipped it on. "Wherever we are, it's 2:33."

His own watch showed just past 12:30 Mountain Time. "Like I thought. East Coast."

He peered around at the surrounding buildings. The architecture appeared northeastern and metropolitan, yet nothing in any of the surrounding signage gave him a clue as to what city they'd landed in this time.

Before anyone else could say a word, a car pulled up to the sidewalk by their circle and dropped off a woman in a pink top and denim mini-skirt.

"Jimmy," she shouted. "*Pahk* the *cah* around the *cornuh* while I get us a table."

Audrey met Steven's gaze as both dropped into half-amused smiles and as one said, "Boston."

"Boston?" William asked, incredulous. "You people expect me to believe we just," he stumbled on the word, "*teleported* across the entire country to Massachusetts?"

Emilio pulled up alongside him. "This look like a mountain range in Montana to you?"

William looked left and right before letting out a sigh, his shoulders slumping in acceptance of his impossible new reality. "I suppose not."

As if to add insult to injury, Rocinante let out a loud snort and transformed in a blink into his motorcycle form, the engine of the long ivory and chrome machine purring for a few seconds before its twin mufflers went silent.

"Steven." Archie studied the newest addition to their little band who in turn stared stupefied at the gleaming motorcycle in their midst. "Perhaps we should address the elephant in the room?"

More than one of those, he considered, though he knew exactly what the priest meant.

"Mr. Two Trees, before we go any further, I think you'd better explain to us exactly what Agent Alfiere meant when he said you were a murderer."

"Murderer." A storm of anger, guilt, and remorse raged on William's face, none of which touched the steely defiance in his brown eyes. "Terrorist." His tortured gaze swept them all, landing finally on Steven. "I suppose that's what they, and probably most of you, would call me."

"What the hell is that supposed to mean?" Emilio asked with his usual bluster. "What did you do?"

"Nobody was supposed to be there." Tears formed at the corners of William's eyes. "Nobody."

"Where, William?" If Emilio's voice moments before brimmed with anger, Audrey's now welled with compassion. "What happened?"

Both Audrey and Emilio, not to mention Lena and a strangely intrigued Archie, all waited for the answer.

This had better be good. Steven's mind flooded with images and memories of Niklaus. Their recently deceased Rook had been anything but a saint, but each member of the White loved and missed him like a lost brother. Filling his shoes wasn't going to be easy for anyone, much less someone with a checkered past and suspect motives.

Like spotless records were responsible for any of us getting chosen for our roles in this mess.

"Fine," William finally offered. "What do you all know about the Keystone Pipeline?"

"The oil pipeline?" Archie asked. "It's been on the news, I suppose," he grumbled, "in between all the coast-to-coast disasters and the sky turning red."

"Big Oil wants to bring crude oil from Alberta, Canada across three of your states and straight through protected indigenous lands." He glared at Steven. "Do you have any idea how many oil spills these stupid pipelines cause every year in this country?"

Steven sighed. "I'm pretty sure it's quite a few."

William's eyes narrowed in anger. "On average, one every other day."

"It's a problem, for sure." Steven pulled in a breath. "One of many, and that still doesn't answer the big question. What did you do that the FBI chased you straight up a mountain in the middle of a national park?"

"I wanted to show them that we weren't going to take it lying down anymore. Not like all the other times." His voice cracked. "I wanted to show them."

Audrey rested a hand on William's shoulder. "And?"

"One end of this new pipeline is supposed to connect in with existing pipe up in Alberta. They plan to cut across the big dog leg in the current line and bring the oil straight across Montana and South Dakota to hook up with the existing line down in this flyspeck called Steele City in southern Nebraska. Do you have any idea how much damage that's going to—"

"What the hell did you do?" Any semblance of patience in Steven's voice was gone.

"I blew it up." William's fists clenched at his sides and he began to pace. "Up in Alberta, a TC Energy field office. Leveled the place." He looked away, unable to meet any of their gazes. "Did it on a Sunday. Nobody was supposed to be there."

"But someone was?" Audrey squeezed the man's shoulder.

"A couple of IT guys were inside installing new computer equipment." William's voice lost all inflection. "One of them died in the explosion."

"And the other?"

"I saw on the news last night how his family is deciding whether or not to stop life support."

"You blew up an entire field office?" Lena asked, hands on her hips. "What is it with you and bombs? There are other ways to protest injustice that don't involve explosions."

"Don't talk to me about 'other ways,'" William spat, his voice growing sullener with each word. "At every turn for centuries, White people have used violence and genocide to get their way, and it's the indigenous people of this continent who have suffered. Two deaths the other direction, and suddenly I'm the 'fucking murderer'?"

"Those two men were innocent." Lena crossed her arms. "They

didn't bear you any ill will. They were just doing their jobs." She seethed with righteous anger. "And you killed them."

"Don't you think I know that?" William shoved his hands into his pockets and stalked down the brick sidewalk toward the corner.

As soon as Two Trees was out of earshot, Emilio turned to Steven. "I know we're desperate, but are we seriously going to team up with the Unabomber there?"

A pulse from Steven's hip, the first since Montana, answered the question all too well.

"I don't pick the Pieces, Emilio." He pulled the *Hvitr Kyll* from his belt and held it before him. "Here we go again."

13

LET'S WORK TOGETHER

W illiam!" Steven cried out as their potential Rook, half a block away, took off at a flat run. "Come back!"

"Let him go." Lena turned her back on the fleeing man. "Like the FBI agent said, the man's a murderer."

"But we need him."

"Are you sure of that?" She looked in Audrey's direction. "Back in Oregon, our Queen dispatched their Knight without breaking a sweat within seconds of coming into her power. In Baltimore, me, you, and Emilio fought the Black Queen and her eight Pawns to a standstill. Hell, you've survived everything they've thrown at you from the beginning." She glanced down the sidewalk in the direction William had fled. "He's made it clear he wants no part of this. Do we really want to bring someone like that into the fold?"

Heat rose in Steven's cheeks. "With all due respect, Lena, Audrey barely survived that first night, a night that nearly ended you as well. We made it out of Baltimore by the skin of our teeth and ended up creating a far worse Black Knight than the one we started with." His gaze dropped to the ground. "I'm not sure how many more times I can roll the dice before they come up snake eyes."

"And it's not like any of us truly want to be here." Audrey slipped her arm around Lena's shoulders and gave a squeeze. "We'd all rather be someplace else. He just hasn't had as much time to process as the rest of us."

"Audrey, Steven, there will be time for pontification later." Archie's eyes blazed. "Right now, our Rook is getting away."

"Don't worry, Archie." Steven inclined his head in Lena and Emilio's direction. "I chased these two all over Baltimore before I finally figured out what I was supposed to be doing. I can find William again." His eyes shot in the direction their Rook had gone. "Don't forget, we just hit him with a couple tons of hard-to-swallow reality. Like Audrey said, he's going to need some time to digest everything."

Archie glanced up at the red sky overhead. "Not a whole lot of time for navel-gazing these days."

"Let's give him a bit. He's seen a lot in the last hour."

"I don't know about you guys," Emilio pulled his wallet from his pocket, "but my mouth feels like I've been chewing on a tin can. You mind if Lena and I go find us all some drinks and snacks while you guys figure out the next step?"

"Be back in twenty." Steven's stomach rumbled. "I'll take anything that doesn't bite back."

As Lena and Emilio took off on Rocinante, Steven huddled with Audrey and Archie.

"So, Audrey, it's clear you think this guy deserves a shot."

"He did what he thought he had to do, and someone died." She bit her lip and looked away. "I hate to say it, but I can sort of relate."

The Black Knight, or at least the first one, had died at Audrey's hands, his tenure in their life so short, they'd never so much as learned his name. Lena's mention of their Queen's defeat of the dark samurai had clearly stirred something inside Audrey, but there would be time to work on that later.

He turned to Archie. "I'm guessing you're all for chasing William down and saying whatever is necessary to get him on board, pardon the pun."

"I'm sorry, Steven, but time grows short. What if we were called to the Board right now? We have no Rook, Lena and Emilio are off getting cheeseburgers and drinks, and the three of us are standing here in street clothes chewing the fat instead of preparing for war. We're not ready, and without a Rook of our own, the Black will pound us into pulp before you and that clever brain of yours can come up with a plan to keep us alive."

"What do you think we should do, then?" Steven asked. "For once, I'll ask you, Archie. What's the play?"

STEVEN AND ARCHIE stepped through the doorway of a nearby deli and appeared outside the open door of one of Boston's above ground subway elevators several blocks away. Directly ahead, past an ice cream vendor shielded from the sun by a large green umbrella marked as "Boston Parks & Recreation," lay a two-lane road bordered on the near side by a black wrought iron fence and on the far side by a row of seven-story brick buildings. The t-shirts and hats sold by the vendor to their right revealed their location.

"Boston Common." Steven looked around. "At least he's still outside."

A short walk to the west brought them to a twenty-foot-tall two-tier fountain of bronze surrounded by an octagonal pool. Topped with a metallic bird that appeared ready to take flight, the fountain boasted a base decorated with a quartet of figures that would have looked right at home amidst the ruins of the Acropolis, though Steven could have done without the serpentine detail of the lower bowl's dark metal.

A pair of children, to the apparent chagrin of a woman who was either their mother or a nanny with the patience of Job, played in the water's edge, their squeals of delight directly counter to the miserable man resting, face in his hands, on a wooden park bench just beyond.

William Two Trees, shoulders heaving with every breath, sat sobbing on the far side of the concrete. Steven and Archie opted to simply observe, unsure whether their presence might prompt him to bolt anew.

One of the children, a blonde girl no more than five, noticed

William was crying, stepped out of the fountain, and walked over to him. William didn't notice her at first, but as the girl tapped him on the knee, his head jerked up. His squinted, tear-filled eyes burned with pain. Steven and Archie were too far away to hear anything that was said, but as the girl offered him the plucked dandelion flower that rested in her hand, the anger in William's face melted into sad gratitude, and his tears flowed anew. The moment was short-lived, as the girl's mother rushed over, the only words audible being 'strangers' and 'you know better' as she dragged the curly-haired girl in the pink sundress away from a man who didn't appear capable of hurting a fly.

Steven scoffed. "This is the 'murderer and terrorist' that has entire teams of FBI agents climbing mountains to put away?"

"Not everyone is as they appear," Archie replied. "You'd do well to remember that."

Steven ignored the tingling at his scalp at the priest's words. "What now, then?"

William glanced over and saw the two of them standing there. Rather than running away, he rose and crossed to meet them.

"Are you two part bloodhound?"

Steven patted the pouch at his side. "This thing found you on top of a mountain in Montana. Tracking you a few city blocks was a piece of cake."

"I still don't know what you guys want with me, but I get the feeling you aren't the kind of people who take no for an answer."

"I hate to tell you this, but we need to fill a position on our team, and according to everything I understand, you're the man we're looking for."

"Me? On your team?" William studied the red sky, its crimson hue a bit darker than it had been earlier that day out west. "You people think you can fix all this?" He raised an eyebrow. "What, with your magic teleportation bag and your motorcycle-horse?"

Steven put on a congenial smile. "Says the man wearing a shirt commemorating a century-old ceremonial dance that's supposed to make you invincible."

William shook his head. "There's faith in a higher power and then there's whatever kind of serious juju you people are mainlining. What's this all about anyway?"

"Speaking of faith," Archie said, "how about a show of good faith on our part?" He shot Steven a sidelong glance. "What do you need to know?"

"A name." Steven nodded, following Archie's lead. "That should be enough."

"A name?" William asked. "What name?"

Steven locked gazes with the man. "The second person from the building you bombed, the one whose life is hanging on by a thread. What's his name?"

The scowl from before returned to William's face. "Why would you ask that? Don't you think I feel bad enough about the fact that man is dying?"

"That's just it." Steven stared into the distance. "If we can get there, we may be able to help." He patted the pouch at his side. "Give me a name, and I can get us there."

"You've said you're a man of faith," Archie added. "What would you say if I told you I can prove that miracles can indeed happen?"

With another bile-filled retort no doubt resting on the tip of his tongue, William swallowed back his anger and whispered, keeping his eyes focused on the ground at his feet.

"Edward," he said. "Edward Page."

"Okay." Steven unfastened the pouch from his belt and held it before the three of them. "Shall we?"

"Wait." William took a step back. "What do you think you're doing?"

"Just like we came here to Boston from Glacier National Park, we're going to go see this Mr. Page."

William's eyes went wide in disbelief. "And do what exactly?"

"You think cross continental teleportation and horses transfiguring into street choppers are impressive?" Archie cracked his knuckles. "You saw what I did for your shoulder back in Montana. Come with us, and I'll show you what I can really do."

"ANOTHER HOSPITAL," Steven muttered under his breath as they stepped from the doorway of the apartment building in Boston and into the cool antiseptic air of a fluorescent lit hallway in Alberta, Canada. "Seems to be our lot in life."

With yellow walls the color of sunflowers, the entire hall sparkled like new. Even the tile floor barely showed a scuff, though the wheels of countless hospital beds had left their mark.

"Where do you think he is?" Steven asked. "Intensive Care?"

"I'm guessing so," Archie said, "unless you know different, William."

"We're in Calgary?" His eyes cut left and right. "Unbelievable."

"We're only getting started." Archie wore a strangely mischievous smile. "You think the folks here would be so kind as to give us a room number?"

"Not if I show my face." William peered up and down the deserted hallway. "Surprisingly, I'm not too popular in these parts these days."

"No fixing that right now, but I've got an idea." Steven pulled the pawn icon from his pocket and held the hunk of marble before him. "Cloak." In an instant the ivory cloak of anonymity materialized about his shoulders.

William gazed at him in wonder. "What the hell happened? You didn't move an inch and yet the person standing before me isn't you anymore." He paused. "And yet, it *is* you."

"One of the many tricks in our arsenal. This is a cloak of anonymity." Steven unfastened the cloak at his neck, doffed the hooded length of cloth, and folded it across his arm. "Care to take it for a spin?"

"So, with this cloak on, I look like somebody else." The wonder in William's gaze faded into incredulous amusement. "Won't people start to wonder why I'm walking around a hospital in a superhero cape?"

"No one but Archie and I can see the cloak. To the rest of the world, you'll look like every other visitor to the hospital, both you and not you, just as you said."

"And I just put this on?" William asked as he slid into the cloak and pulled up the hood.

"Done." Steven glanced up at a sign above their heads and headed down the hall. "Let's go. Like Archie keeps reminding me, time is short."

A brief walk down a miniature maze of bright yellow walls and immaculately clean floors led to a double glass sliding door marked INTENSIVE CARE. A nurse with flaming red hair standing outside the door was finishing up with a family that sat in a semicircle in the ICU's open waiting room.

"Excuse me." Steven walked over to the nurse as she rose to return to her station. "Is this the ICU where you're taking care of Edward Page?"

She stiffened visibly. "I'm not allowed to discuss information about any of our patients without proper authorization."

Dammit, Steven mentally backpedaled. *They've got him on lock down because of the whole bombing thing.*

"Look, Nurse Tyler," he offered after a quick peek at her name tag. "My friend here is family and we road tripped here from Vancouver so he could see Mr. Page one last time."

"Family, huh?" She turned to William. "And what is your name, sir? I can go check and see if we have a Mr. Page in the hospital."

"William." He took in a deep breath. "Tell them it's William."

Steven and Archie shared a nervous glance.

"William. Got it." Nurse Tyler did a quick 180 and headed back into the unit.

"That's the best you've got?" Archie asked as soon as the glass doors slid shut. "Your actual name?"

"I'm sorry. Current predicament aside, I'm really not much of a liar." He raised an eyebrow in Steven's direction. "Though you all clearly left telling the truth in the rearview mirror a couple states back."

"I wish lying through my teeth at every turn was the worst thing I'd had to do since this insanity took over my life." He shook his head sadly. "We've all had to make difficult decisions. Do horrible things." The smell of Magdalene's burning flesh from seventy-five years ago wafted across his senses. "I know some of us in the group see things a little more black-and-white, if you'll pardon the pun, but know that Audrey, Archie, and I understand."

William furrowed his brow at Steven. "I don't understand half the shit that comes out of your mouth, but it sounds like you're cutting me some slack, so thanks."

The nurse strode back into the room with a slim woman about ten years Steven's senior. The first hints of grey highlighted her headful of deep brown hair pulled unceremoniously back in a ponytail. Though the bags under her eyes revealed a sleepless night or two, nothing in her shrewd gaze suggested the least bit of gullibility.

They were going to have to play this carefully.

"Which one of you is this 'William' person?" Her irate gaze swept over Archie and Steven and landed firmly on the newest member of their trio. "Is it you?"

William stepped back, unable to withstand the muted fury in the features of this woman who could be none other than Page's wife.

"Yes, ma'am," he said after a long pause. "I'm William. And you are?"

"Ed's wife, Jane." She studied the man before her, her mind clearly trying to pierce the veil of anonymity. "So, you know Ed?"

William offered a subtle shrug. "In a roundabout sort of way."

The emotion in her gaze shifted down the spectrum from irritation to confused fear. "Who are you people? What do you want with us?"

"I'll show you." As William reached to pull back his hood, Steven caught his arm.

"What are you doing?"

"This whole thing is my fault, and we're going to fix it my way." He shook off Steven's hand and grasped the front of his hood. "Ma'am, I apologize in advance for the shock."

Nurse Tyler, in a moment of self-preservation she would likely question for years, released Edward Page's wife and stepped back, too awestruck to even speak as William pulled back the covering of ivory cloth from his face.

The woman, on the other hand, stood her ground like an ancient oak in a hurricane. "Something told me it was you. What the hell do you want?"

"We're here to help," Steven got out before William quieted him with a raised hand.

"Ma'am, I need you to hear it from my own lips. I didn't know your husband or the other man were in that building. I didn't mean for anyone to be hurt that day. Words can never take back what I've done, but I've seen some wondrous things today and if you'll just let us see Edward, I think we can—"

The woman slapped William hard across the face, the sound drawing the attention of everyone in the waiting room. "Don't you say his name. You're not worthy."

"I deserve that," William's eyes dropped, "and a whole lot more, but that doesn't change the fact that like my friend here said, we've come to help."

"Or come to finish the job." She shot a glance at Nurse Tyler. "Call security."

"I didn't want to have to do this." Amaryllis fluttered at Steven's chest as William slid his hand into one of the cargo pockets of his pants and produced a snub-nosed revolver, keeping it low and close to his body. "Now, please, take us to your husband."

14

A TASTE OF PITY

rchie and Steven stood on either side of William, both of them dumbfounded by the unexpected turn. Page's wife and Nurse Tyler gasped in unison, gaping wide-eyed at the firearm in William's hand. Steven pondered briefly if that shared breath might be their last. He prepared himself to leap in front of the defenseless women and take the bullet himself, but half a second before his muscles fired, William turned the gun around and held it out, grip-first.

"I'm asking you to trust me, Ms. Page, even though you have no reason to." He pushed the revolver into her hands and took a step back. "You can end me right now, the man who put your husband in the hospital and left him at death's door, or you can let us go to him and try to help him. The choice is yours."

The woman wrapped her fingers around the handgun's grip, her index finger sliding into the trigger guard. "I've spent the last few days asking myself what I'd do if I ever came face to face with you." She brought her other hand up to keep the barrel from shaking in her trembling fingers. "What I'd say. What I'd do. What Ed would want me to do." She sucked in a deep breath and ran the sleeve of her blouse across her face to wipe away the twin trails of tears streaming down her face. "One thing has become very clear." She paused before handing the gun off to Nurse Tyler who accepted the weapon as if it were covered in maggots. "You don't fix violence with more violence."

"Ms. Page," William's voice shook, "we truly have come to help your husband." He gestured in Archie's direction. "This man can do things I can't begin to understand, things that appear for all the world like the miracles your Bible teaches as fact. When this is done, you can do what you want with me, but first, let this man try to help your husband."

Her quizzical gaze fell upon Archie. "What exactly is it you claim to be able to do?"

Archie lowered his head in a resolute nod. "Let us see your husband, ma'am, and I'll show you."

"We can't let any of you into the unit." The nurse's whispered words were punctuated by a sharp pinch at Steven's collarbone. "Not when you're bringing weapons into the hospital and threatening family members." Fleeting indecision flashed across her features before she herself brandished the revolver, pointing its business end directly at William's chest. "Now, you three stay right where you are while I call security."

"Please." Archie took a step forward. "This isn't necessary."

"Stay back," Nurse Tyler squeaked, shifting her aim from William to Archie. "I used to go to the range every week with my dad when I was a girl. I know how to use this—"

In a silver flash, Archie shifted into the attire of the White Bishop, his vestment, rochet, and soutane all gleaming in the hospital's fluo-rescent lights. The miter atop his head barely shifted as Archibald Lacan swept his poplar staff in an upward arc, the Celtic cross and crescent moon at its tip shining like a magnesium flare.

"Ow!" Nurse Tyler shouted as the wooden end of the White Bish-op's crosier struck the gun and sent it flying from her hand.

Archie snatched the gun from the air, depositing it in his volumi-nous robes, and then lowered the tip of his staff at Nurse Tyler. "All right, Steven. What's the next move?"

"We're about to get mobbed." Steven spun around to confront the throng of frightened hospital visitors from around the waiting room, all risen from their seats and ready to fight. "Why does it always have to be the hard way?" He again retrieved the pawn icon from his pocket and summoned shield, pike, and helm before offering a whispered "Phalanx" to the Arbiters of Old. Dividing into the White's front line of eight, he sent seven to form a perimeter around the door leading the ICU, while the eighth led Archie, Nurse Tyler, and Jane Page back into the recesses of the unit.

As they stepped through the doors, a half dozen nurses and doctors turned to face them, surprise and awe blossoming across each of their features. Having walked this particular walk before, Steven didn't bother slowing down, but instead prodded Jane to lead on. "Take us to your husband, quickly," he whispered, knowing all too well that the shock of a medieval foot soldier and a fully-arrayed bishop dressed in gleaming white storming through their ward of beeping machines and dripping lines would only buy them seconds. "We don't have much time."

On the opposite side of the half-circle of curtained bays, they crowded into the room; first him and Ms. Page, then William, then Archie leading a distraught Nurse Tyler by one arm. There, beneath the starched white sheets of the hospital bed, lay Edward Page. Even had Steven not already experienced his mother's long decline and eventual death, the preceding months had taught him much about the various tubes that go into and out of patients when their lives teeter on the edge: the NG tube protruding from the man's nose running to the suction on the wall; the endotracheal tube taped to the corner of his mouth that kept his chest rising and falling in regular rhythm; the catheter and clear plastic hose leading to the bag of yellow liquid that snaked from beneath the blankets that kept Jane Page's husband warm despite the cool IV fluids dripping into his left arm.

"Curious," Steven asked, motioning to Nurse Tyler, "why'd you bring her along?"

"This nurse risked her life valiantly in the defense of her patient." Archie released his grip on the nurse's arm. "She deserves to be a part of this."

"A part of what?" Nurse Tyler's voice cracked between sobs. "What are you going to do to him?"

"What every doctor and nurse in this hospital has trained their whole life to do." Archie's expression both sharpened with concentration and relaxed, as if his mind were suddenly somewhere else. "This, Nurse Tyler is the moment you've been awaiting your entire career." The priest stretched out the poplar staff until its gleaming tip rested mere inches above Edward Page's swollen face. He then passed the implement of his station down the man's dying form, pausing briefly above his neck, chest, and abdomen. "You've devoted your life to healing the sick as I have devoted mine to caring for the downtrodden, you with your faith in medicine, and I by my faith in God. Here, at the intersection of those two beliefs, you are about to see a miracle." He inclined his head in the direction of the man's head. "Now, if you will, please remove the tube from his throat."

"Take out his ET tube?" Nurse Tyler asked, incredulous. "You've got to be kidding."

Archie frowned. "If it remains, he will have significant difficulty breathing once I intervene."

"But it's the only thing keeping him alive," Jane whimpered. "The only thing."

"Have faith." Archie gazed deeply into each of their eyes: Jane Page, Nurse Tyler, and last of all, William Two Trees, who had remained silent since the five of them had entered the ICU. "You must all have faith. Know that I have come here today not as a rider upon a pale horse but as a bringer of new life." He locked gazes anew with Nurse Tyler. "Now, please remove the tube from this man's throat and stand aside."

The nurse looked to Jane for permission to do the insane. At the woman's fearful nod, she set to work.

As she carefully removed the tape holding the tube in place, Steven stretched out his mind to the other seven Pawns. Four remained outside the ICU doorway, keeping at bay both the mob from the waiting room as well as the more recently arrived hospital security. Closer in, on the other side of the curtain that separated them from the rest of the ward, the remaining three formed a tight circle that held back the frightened team of nurses and doctors. As intimidating as they were, Steven had no intention of harming any of the health care professionals whose shouts drove his heartrate higher with every passing second. He prayed none of them called his bluff. Twice now they'd been forced to invade a hospital to save a life, both times causing far more of a stir than Steven had intended. The first time had ended up working out for the best with no innocent casualties. He prayed this time would be the same. The last thing he wanted on his soul was the blood of one who'd sworn to "do no harm."

As Nurse Tyler shut off the ventilator and pulled the plastic tube from Edward Page's throat, Archie began to sway to and fro. The indecipherable chanting Steven had heard but a handful of times since first meeting the priest in a different hospital almost a continent away filled the space, the words evaporating into the ether as they fell from Archie's lips. The lights in the room alternatingly dimmed and flashed like torches in a windstorm as the silver crescent moon surrounding the knotted cross at the tip of the Bishop's crosier grew brighter and brighter with each whispered syllable offered to a forgotten god.

Electricity filled the room, the hair on the back of Steven's neck rising like a military regiment coming to attention. Jane Page fell to her knees at her husband's bedside, her hands clasped together in prayer. Nurse Tyler knelt beside her, wrapped the woman in her arms, and held her like a sister.

Minutes later—or was it hours?—the lights in the room ceased their flashing, the not-so-gentle breeze that had sent every loose slip of paper in the room flying settled, and the bizarre chanting fell silent. As one, Jane Page, Nurse Tyler, and William looked up at Archie.

"Is it done?" William asked.

"See for yourself." Archie stepped away from the bed to reveal Edward Page, no longer pale and unconscious, but awake and clearly annoyed at the NG tube occupying his left nostril.

"Jane?" He stared quizzically at his wife who was already scrambling up from the floor. "What's going on? Where are we? Why are we here?"

"Ed!" Jane dove upon her husband, covering his face in kisses, her sudden ardor only adding to his confusion.

"Sweetie, I'm fine," he said gazing around the room. "Now, who are all these people and why do I have a tube sticking out of my nose?"

His gaze drifted down his body, lingering a second on his nethers. "Not to mention...ummm...other places?"

"Doesn't matter. You're okay." She looked up at Archie and then Steven before allowing herself to meet William's gaze with unconflicted gratitude. "Thank you, Mr. Two Trees. God, thank you."

William stared back at Jane, unable to speak. The shared moment lasted for what seemed an eternity.

As Edward Page's wife returned her attention to her miraculously healed husband, William met Archie's gaze and mouthed the same two words to the priest who had undone, at least in part, the worst mistake of his life.

As the impassioned reunion of husband and wife continued, a paired river of memories flooded Steven's heart and mind: his far-too-short last moments with Katherine contrasted with the painful weeks-long process of saying goodbye to his mother. He struggled with the cosmic unfairness of it all, that the two most important women in his life both slipped through his fingers years before he first crossed paths with Archibald Lacan, a man who held in his hands the power over life and death.

And yet, as he met the gaze of each person in the room, he understood one thing above all others, a lesson driven home by the experiences of the preceding months.

Some things truly were just meant to be.

STEVEN, Archie, and William stepped from the silver shimmer onto the concrete at Brewer Fountain, not five steps from where they'd left Boston an hour before. Their egress from the Alberta hospital where they'd initiated yet another urban legend about miraculous healing from on high had gone without difficulty, courtesy of Steven and Archie's shared cloak of anonymity. As their eyes adjusted to the bright light of the soon to be setting sun in the crimson western sky, they noticed the trio of forms awaiting them by the fountain.

Astride the gleaming Rocinante motorcycle, Emilio sat impatiently with Lena close behind, her tan arms interlocked around his muscular torso. Sitting at the edge of the fountain in the shadow cast by the large lower bowl, Audrey looked on with a relieved smile as Steven, Archie, and William strode over.

"All taken care of?" she asked.

"Alberta and back," Steven said, "none the worse for wear."

"And the mission?" Audrey raised a questioning eyebrow.

He gestured in William's direction. "Ask the man himself."

William searched each of their eyes. "You saved him. All of you. I don't know how, but you saved that man."

Emilio nodded. "That's what we do."

"The other man is still dead." Lena refused to meet William's gaze. "I'm glad you got a do-over for one of the two people whose lives you interrupted," she fumed, "but what about the other, the one whose family will never see him again?"

"Lena," Archie raised a hand. "Please, my child. The events of the past few hours aside, what has been done cannot be undone. What we did today was an effort to balance the scales as much as we could, but at the end of the day, regardless of the outcome, Mr. Two Trees here will have to learn to live with what he's done. He admits what he did was wrong. He's repented and has agreed to help us. What more do you want from him?"

"I want him to..." Her voice trailed off. "I guess I just want him to be Niklaus."

William stepped forward. "Steven's told me a little bit about this Niklaus guy, the one I'm supposed to be replacing because he was..." His eyes shot in Steven's direction. "...killed doing the job you people are asking me now to take on. I didn't run, and I'm standing here now. Is that enough penance for you to be able to look me in the eye, girl?"

"I don't like you," Lena whispered, though she did deign to meet William's eyes, "but we need you." She let out a half-sigh, half-grunt. "I can set aside differences for now, but know that I'm going to be watching, do you understand?"

"I'm not the kind of man that typically backs down from a fight, but one thing that's become even clearer since I met all of you is that I've got a lot to atone for. The rest of your team here seems ready to give me a second chance, but it looks like I'm going to have to earn that from you." A rare smile invaded William's features. "I hope someday you'll be able to look on me with something other than disgust."

Lena's head tilted slightly to one side, her expression not shifting an iota. "We shall see."

The long silence that followed broke with a rumble of Emilio's stomach.

"Dinner time." Emilio offered a cautious smile. "Thoughts?"

"We passed by Chinatown on the way here." Audrey turned her head to look south. "Maybe Thai?"

The six of them took to the street, Emilio and Lena riding ahead atop Rocinante's ivory and chrome length to find a place while the remaining four took their time strolling south along the border of Boston Common, eventually zigzagging across the last couple blocks to the entrance to Boston's Chinatown. Half a block down the first street, they came upon Lena and Emilio taking advantage of one of their rare moments of privacy to catch up on a bit of nonverbal communication.

Steven cleared his throat as they drew close. "So, what did you two find?"

Disengaging from their passionate embrace, Emilio pointed to the Thai restaurant at the corner. "This place looks pretty decent. Cloth napkins and everything. I figure we deserve at least one more decent meal before the shit hits the fan."

Lena swatted his arm. "Emilio."

"What?" he said with a grin of false embarrassment. "You'd rather us hit a Mickey D's?"

"You know exactly what I'm talking about." Lena caught Audrey's eye. "Anyway, they've got that yellow curry you like."

"The hotter the better." Audrey shot Steven a questioning glance. "What do you think?"

Steven studied the restaurant's neon sign and shook his head, an amused smile breaking across his face. "We're right in the middle of the biggest game of chess the world has ever seen. One night in 'Bangkok' would seem more than appropriate, don't you think?"

15

WHERE I WANT TO BE

William stared incredulously across the pair of steaming cups of coffee at Steven. "So, you're saying you met my great-great-great-grandfather—the man I was named after—while you and the rest were all 'time traveling' in 1890 Wyoming?"

Steven sucked air in through his teeth. "To be fair, we didn't exactly travel to the past on purpose. Our enemy sent us there in an effort to get rid of us."

William gestured to the *Hvitr Kyll* which rested at the corner of the table. "Then I'm guessing they've got one of these as well."

"You catch on quick." Steven rested a hand on the pouch's warm leather, its low drone rising a decibel or two at his touch. "In this game of chess, we have one pouch—"

"And they've got the other. One black, the other white, I'm sure. Very yin and yang." William studied the droning satchel of aged hide, his eyes resting briefly on each of the ancient runes stamped at its neck. "Why a bag, though? You and Archie both said there's something inside waiting for me." He leaned back in his chair and crossed his arms. "I'm no fool. You've all made it clear from the start that you need something from me, that I'm a part of whatever this thing is you're all wrapped up in. So, why don't we skip to the part where you tell me exactly what it is you want?"

Steven swallowed down a gulp of scalding hot coffee. "I told you about Niklaus."

"You're not the only one." William let out a cautious chuckle. "From the way everybody talks, sounds like the man could walk on water."

"On his better days." An image of Niklaus trudging his way out of the muddy Mississippi flitted across his memory. "He was a good man, one of the best I've known."

"And he could do things, like the rest of you?"

Steven nodded. "He was our Rook."

"And you're the Pawn, Audrey the Queen, Archie the Bishop, and Emilio the Knight." William's brow furrowed. "Where's your King?"

"We'll get to that." Steven steepled his fingers beneath his chin. "We found Niklaus in Atlanta, about half a minute before our opposition did. They tried to kill him before we could bring him into the fold, but the Game foiled their efforts and saved him. Transformed him into a giant of stone. He was among the most powerful of us all."

"A giant of stone?" William took a sip from his own steaming mug. "What happened to him?"

"Their Rook dropped the Washington Monument on him. Broke him in half."

"Wait a minute. The Washington Monument?" William stared across the diner at the table where the other four waited. "That was you guys?"

"That was us," Steven muttered, "trying to rescue our families from the Black."

"But the news said it was some kind of terrorist attack."

"They're not too far off." He stared off into the distance. "We took his shattered body to the base of Mount Rushmore for as close to a burial as we could figure out. At least he rests in a place of honor."

"Rushmore." A dark scowl stole the earnestness from William's face. "I hate that place."

"Why?" Steven raised an eyebrow. "It's beautiful."

"It used to be." William peered out the window into the night. "The Lakota Sioux held as sacred ground the Black Hills of what is now known as South Dakota. Six Grandfathers took millennia to achieve its majestic beauty and only fourteen years for the White man to forever desecrate with their dynamite and drills and misplaced pride."

Heat rose in Steven's cheeks. "The men carved there are some of the greatest in the history of this nation."

"Your nation, maybe. As it's often said, history is written by the winners." William took another sip of coffee and placed his mug back on the Formica table. "To those of us who were here first, this mountain you call Rushmore is nothing but a monument to those who killed and conquered our people, all carved into one of our most sacred places." His lips pulled tight across his teeth. "A place, I might remind you, that was stolen from us by those very conquerors."

"But..." Steven considered William's words and decided anything he might say next was likely to fall squarely on the wrong side of history. "You know, to be honest, I'd never actually given it much thought."

"And that's the problem." William grunted out a resigned laugh. "All of us, White and Native alike, are born into a world made by those that came before. You bear me no ill will personally, Steven, nor I you, but that doesn't change the past. This is the world we live in. All we can do is try to do better going forward."

"No more bombs, then?"

"Those pipelines and the inevitable oil spills they'll bring will kill or destroy far more than any bomb I could put together. But sure, no more bombs." William pulled in a deep breath. "I'll find a better way." He returned his attention to the pouch of leather resting by Steven's elbow. "So, back to the business at hand?"

"The pouch brought us to you, much like it brought me to each of the others. This is the first time it's sought out a replacement, though, so I'm not certain exactly what to expect."

"From the sound of things, this man Niklaus doesn't sound easy to replace, but know that I shall do my best to fulfill his role in this Game, as you call it." William's eyes went out of focus, as if his mind

149

walked a different plane. "He was your Rook you say? And that's the spot I'm to fill?"

"Yes."

"I've only played chess once or twice." William smiled. "My grandfather John called that piece the tower."

"Rook, castle, tower." Steven studied William quizzically, "Whatever you want to call yourself, you're the big guy on the team."

"If I'm to be a Tower in this Game," William rose from the table, a strange confidence in his gaze, "then I know where we must go next."

"Back in Wyoming, eh?" Steven sighed. "At least it's warm this time." He turned to the east where the sky was beginning to pink. "And you can't beat the view."

He and William stood at the edge of the butte's flat top and looked straight down the eight-hundred-foot drop to the trees below.

"So this is Devil's Tower." Emilio joined them at the edge. "I'd never even heard of this place till Lena told me about it."

"My people call this place Bear's Lodge, the home of the bear." William crinkled his nose. "The name Devil's Tower is an offensive holdover from an inaccurate translation a century ago. The interpreter's command of the native language, unfortunately, left a lot to be desired."

"It's also been called Tree Rock, Great Gray Horn, and Brown Buffalo Horn by various tribes in the region." Lena left Rocinante with Audrey and Archie and joined the three men at their precarious perch, slipping her hand into Emilio's, their fingers interlocking instinctively. "Of all the stories, though, I like the bear story the best."

"You know the history," William asked, surprise coloring his words, "though your accent marks you as not from this continent?"

"Your ears do not deceive you. I am indeed from Spain, though my parents ensured I learned English as well as Spanish from the second they first started to teach me words." Lena gestured around the enormous flat circle of stone which held the seven of them. "I plan for Emilio and I to see every last one of the great wonders of North

America and the rest of the world together when this is all over. Trust me when I tell you I've done my research." She squeezed Emilio's hand. "Funny we ended up here. We currently stand atop the first national monument ever established by the United States government."

"I'm curious." Audrey took a step in their direction, stroking Rocinante's broad flank. "There's a bear story?"

"There are many." William's eyes drifted closed. "In one, a group of girls seeks refuge atop a rock from a giant bear with enormous claws, a rock left forever marked by those same claws as the Great Spirit sends their stony shelter growing ever skyward until the girls become the constellation you call the Pleiades. In another, two Sioux boys are the ones fleeing the bear and eventually make their way down from the great height and back to their village with the help of a majestic eagle. No doubt, there have been countless tales about this place, many no doubt forgotten." He shot a sidelong glance at Steven. "Now it's a tourist attraction for photographers and rock climbers and the like." His gaze wandered back to Lena. "No offense, of course. Your appreciation of the beauty of nature is quite refreshing."

"None taken." Lena pulled in a deep breath through her nose. "And I can see why the Native Americans would see this as a holy place. It's wondrous and pure."

"For the most part." Archie bent and picked up a half-emptied bottle of blue sports drink. "Humans, unfortunately, leave their mark wherever they go." He chucked the bottle off the edge with a strange twinkle in his eye and then returned his attention to Steven with laser-like focus. "I'm enjoying our latest field trip as much as any of us, but we've already rolled the dice with another night and still don't have our full complement. Perhaps we should get on with the day's necessary activities?"

"Of course." Steven shrugged off the transient glint in the priest's eye, unclear why no one but him ever seemed to notice the occasional oddity in the priest's behavior. "Shall we give this another try?"

"No time like the present." William swallowed and pulled himself up straight, somehow maintaining his composure though he likely sweated bullets on the inside. "How do we do this?"

"It's pretty simple actually." Steven pulled the pouch from his belt and worked at the silver cord holding it closed at the neck. The low drone that had pulsed in the background since they arrived doubled in volume. "The *Hvitr Kyll* has selected you out of 300 million or so to serve in this role, and all you need to do is reach into its mouth and bring forth the power that is already yours."

"Sounds like something you'd hear on Oprah."

"And yet here we are atop a sacred rock in Wyoming, about to determine your destiny in a legendary Game that will change the course of history." Steven held out the pouch, its now open mouth streaming with silver light, the tooth-shaking pulse coming in couplets like the beating of the heart of some invisible giant. "Ready?"

"No." William stepped back, the hesitancy in the motion in direct opposition to the curiosity that filled his gaze. "Yes."

He dove his hand and arm deep into the pouch's glowing mouth. Up to his elbow, then his shoulder, puzzlement filled his features as he searched the unseen void that lay beyond what Steven had come to understand as a gateway to another dimension, bound by nothing but centuries-old stamped leather and silver cord.

"There's nothing here." William's eyes flicked to each of them in turn. "When all of you did this, what happened? What did you feel?"

"I saw visions of the past," Steven whispered, the pouch shaking in his trembling hands, "both my own and the Game's."

"I mostly remember a sense of wonder." Lena watched expectantly as William continued to fish around in the silver shimmer. "Both during my own experience as well as Emilio's."

"Yeah," Emilio added. "Not to mention the electricity running through me like a live wire as my fingers found the tip of the lance."

"Warmth filled my body, leaving me well for the first time in months." Audrey brushed away a tear. "It was a miracle."

"A miracle indeed. While Audrey found healing, I found a second chance at youth." A smile invaded Archie's unwrinkled features. "The power of the pouch shaved almost half a century from this old mug."

"Seriously?" William stared quizzically at Archie's untouched face. "That would put you around...seventy-five?"

"A year or two shy, but yes. I've walked this earth for nearly three quarters of a century."

Two Trees shook his head in disbelief. "Anything else I need to know?"

Steven stepped in. "Just that the pouch wouldn't have led us to Montana if it didn't hold something similar for you inside."

"But there's nothing here." William's voice grew ragged and frustrated. "Nothing."

This is getting us nowhere. Steven pondered. *What would Grey do?*

As he searched his memories of the various encounters with his mysterious mentor for advice, the words of a different member of their team sprung to mind

"Emilio, remember when we were stuck on the island where we found Rocinante?"

"Yeah." Emilio raised an eyebrow. "What about it?"

"The door. You helped me find the door to get us back to the mainland. Now, help William find whatever it is he's looking for."

"How do I do that?" Emilio asked. "Niklaus found his icon when he reached inside the pouch, like you and Audrey and Archie, but what if it's like me and the lance, and he's trying to find something else?"

"That's why I'm asking you. You found what was meant for you in the *Hvitr Kyll* even though your experience was unlike the others', and you helped me find a door on an island when there wasn't one to find." Steven flicked his gaze in William's direction. "Now, help him, like only you can."

Emilio stood slack-jawed as he took in the words and then stood as straight as Steven had ever seen the teen and came shoulder-to-shoulder with William. "So, for each of us it's been different. Youth and health, awe and understanding, all from this little bag of wonders. But, unlike the rest of us, you're not making a connection. Something's holding you back."

"You think?" William grunted as beads of sweat formed at his brow. "I'm trying here. Really." He let out a frustrated snort. "What if this Game of yours gave up whatever it had to this Niklaus guy and doesn't have anything left for me?"

Emilio pulled in a breath, and when he spoke again, his words reverberated with a gravitas far beyond his few years. "Perhaps in your case, William Two Trees, it's not trying to figure out what the Game has for you, but what *you* bring to the Game." He grasped William's free shoulder. "Figure it out. What's wrong with all of this? What's holding you back?"

William peered around the top of Devil's Tower for several seconds, arm deep in mystic energy, and then glanced over the edge and down the side of the colossal column of stone.

"Not here." His whisper raised the hairs on Steven's neck. "For all its power, this hunk of rock is too barren." He raised a hand and pointed to a clearing in the stand of pines that surrounded the massive butte. "Take us there."

"But, your arm is still—"

"I'll be fine." William glanced across his shoulder at the remainder of the White. "Gather round, everyone. I think we have one more jaunt before this is going to work."

All of them drew close together, Lena leading a skittish Rocinante to the edge of the stony outcropping, and then, with a single whispered word from Steven, the seven of them vanished, only to reappear in a flash of silver and smoke at the center of the clearing William had spotted from atop the butte.

No sooner had his feet landed upon the dank earth of the pine stand, the carpet of orange-brown pine needles still wet with the morning dew, than William's entire demeanor changed. His previously tense form relaxed from head to toe and his expression adopted the same dreamy quality that overtook Emilio as he pulled the lance from the pouch what seemed years before.

"I feel it," William whispered. "Every fiber of my being singing as one, as if—"

He fell silent, his eyes growing wide with fear and wonder and surprise and rapture.

"What is it?" Steven asked, his fingers still clenched around the top of the *Hvitr Kyll.* "What's happening?"

"Stand back." And with those two quiet words of warning, William pulled his arm from the pouch, pushed Steven away with his opposite hand, and held both arms to the sky. "I've found what I was looking for."

Before anyone could say a word, the earth beneath their feet trembled, eliciting a quiet whinny of concern from Rocinante. A pinch at Steven's collarbone from Amaryllis prompted him to take another couple steps back.

And then, the latest in a long chain of impossibilities commenced before all their eyes.

With a cry ripped from the depth of his soul, William Two Trees screamed to the scarlet sky, whether in pain or in triumph, Steven couldn't tell. Roots erupted from his feet and calves and dove into the ground, splitting his shoes and pants as his legs became the twin trunks of a small but quickly growing tree. Grey bark flowed up his flesh, feet to ankles to knees to hips. His arms stretched outward like warm taffy, each finger extending into a willowy branch and each fingertip soon adorned with smoothly notched leaves and heavy with clumps of acorns.

All of them stood silent as the transformation continued. Thick rectangles of grey bark covered William's torso, neck, and face as his newly wooden body contorted left and right, twisting the massive tree into a spiral that doubled back upon itself like the double helix of life, the branches dividing a good twenty feet up into two mighty boughs. Higher and higher he grew until he stood as tall as the ponderosa pines that surrounded the enormous butte. And then, with a rending roar straight from a logger's nightmare, William's wooden form split in two from the ground up with his pair of massive legs becoming the trunks of a pair of gigantic twisted oaks.

"Unbelievable," Audrey whispered as they all continued to look on in wonder.

Like a cross between one of those stop-motion nature films Steven watched in high school biology class and one of the old Ray Harryhausen films he and his dad enjoyed together when he was a kid, the twin oaks grew not only larger with each passing second, but further apart as well. Each set of roots writhed like the tentacles of some landlocked sea monster, sending the ever-growing monstrosities of wood and leaf and acorn in opposite directions. In less time than he would have imagined possible, the pair of massive hardwoods rested on opposite ends of the clearing with Steven halfway between, the top of each tree swaying in the gentle morning wind.

"Two Trees, huh?" Steven studied first one and then the other of the pair of enormous oaks from his position at the center of the clearing before shooting Audrey a confused glance. "Funny, but I did *not* see that one coming."

16

YOU AND I

S teven put his hand to his forehead to block the still-rising sun as he looked on in wonder at the topmost branches of a tree that moments before had been a man. Though in awe for what seemed the thousandth time at the power and majesty of this Game that had taken over their lives, he couldn't help but ponder the unmitigated might of the Black Rook, a woman named Cynthia that none of them had ever so much as laid eyes upon outside her rocky form. She'd already bested and slain Niklaus, their own giant of stone, and while he had no doubt a century-old oak tree could knock you into next week, he couldn't quite fathom how a battle between wood and rock would end any other way but with another death on their side.

"I'm sorry," Audrey pulled close and dropped her voice, "but how exactly is a pair of trees supposed to help us?"

"I can hear you, you know." Niklaus' voice as the Rook had always hit like an avalanche; William's registered like the whistling of wind through the branches high above their head. "Every leaf along this strange new form is like an ear. Perceiving your whispers is no harder than capturing the sun's warmth as it streams down from above."

"Lord," Emilio muttered, "just when you thought it wasn't possible for this guy to get any preachier."

"My apologies, Emilio." Each of the giant oaks twisted in the boy's direction, the section of trunk where each tree divided into two boughs shifting into a pair of gigantic faces. "I had no idea my pointing out the inequities and injustices in this country everyone seems so proud of annoyed you so." Every few words, the strange whispering of wind between the leaves alternated from one mighty oak to the other. "That is something we will have to discuss."

"Damn, you *can* hear every word we say." Emilio raised a hand to block the sun and looked up into William's bark-covered face. "*Mea culpa*, all right? I was just making a joke."

"I see, hear, feel everything all around me." Both trees swayed in the morning breeze, the creak of bending branches adding substance to William's words. "The plants, the animals, the very air we share. All of this is truly a miracle."

"Hopefully, the first of many." Archie moved to stand in the mighty tree's shade. "A question, Mr. Two Trees. Can you move?"

"Let's see." With a thunderous crack, the trunk of each enormous oak split, and soon each of the pair of arboreal Rooks stood atop a set of massive legs that matched their mighty arms. As one, the pair took their shared first steps and within seconds, the pair of towering oaks stood before the remainder of the White.

"Not exactly what any of us were expecting, eh?" William's twin forms continued their singsong whispering, alternating from the branches of one tree to the other and back again. "I do hope all of you aren't disappointed."

"Disappointed?" Emilio stared up into the knotted burls making up William's twin faces. "Lena and I have watched all eleven and a half hours of the extended cut of *The Lord of the Rings*." He stroked Rocinante along his withers, a broad smile spreading across his features. "I know what happens when the Ents march on Isengard."

AT THE BACK corner of the latest of what seemed an endless succession of dives and diners, the gathered White sat quietly around a large round table filled with several plates of barely eaten breakfast.

They'd left Rocinante outside to rest, the chrome of his motorcycle manifestation reflecting the late morning sun. Each of their faces more haunted than Steven had ever seen, the impending Game clearly weighed upon them all.

"No matter how you slice it," Audrey rested her elbows on the table and her forehead in her palms, "we've got God knows how many hours and minutes or maybe even seconds left till we all get beamed to God knows where to fight for our lives, and still we have no idea where Grey is, no clue what he did with the crown…"

"And no hope of any of it getting better," Lena added. "I thought I'd feel better about everything once we had our Rook, but now it seems like we're back in the same holding pattern waiting to die."

"Hey." William let out a frustrated snort. "I'm right here."

"Fear not, Mr. Two Trees." Archie slipped into a placating smile. "Lena's comment has nothing to do with you in particular. She's simply voicing the anxieties we all feel."

"That's all fine and good, but this, all of this, is a load of bullshit." William rose from his chair, fuming. "You people went to all the trouble of dragging me off that mountain in Montana, chasing me around Boston, and gathering around me at Bear's Lodge only to sit here now all doom and gloom about how we have no hope of winning or even surviving?" He rested both fists on the table. "I know I'm the new guy and everything, but that kind of sucks."

"Truth be told, none of us asked to be a part of this." Archie rested his folded hands on the table. "Just like you, that decision was made for us long before we were born."

"You know, all of you talk a lot about fate and destiny and how things are meant to be in the big picture, but even in the middle of this Game we're all stuck in, I can't help but believe our strongest power is still our free will." William paced the back corner of the diner, his Ghost Dance shirt and the rest of his clothing mystically restored after his return to human form. "We could all choose to go our separate ways right now and simply wait for this thing to grab us and take us like cattle to the slaughter." He spun around and gripped the back of his chair. "Or we can choose to work on this together and try to survive this shitshow."

"Damn," Emilio chuckled, "didn't know we were getting a motivational speaker in the deal."

"William." Steven quieted Emilio with a raised hand. "I know we all sound pretty down and out, but this 'shitshow' as you call it has basically been our lives for the better part of a year. No matter how much we've fought and trained and prepared, we're all feeling like we're staring down the barrel of a loaded gun."

"And what else is new?" William's voice rose and fell with a politician's skill mixed with a master storyteller's flourish. "I know I've only heard the beginnings of each of your stories, but with all you've already overcome, don't you think it's a bit premature to throw in the towel now?"

"They have our King." Lena stood, eyes narrow and hands on her hips. "The Game is already won. All that remains to be seen is how many of us, if any, survive."

"If that were true," William asked, "then why would the Game have brought you to me? Why bother bringing a new Rook into the Game if the outcome is already decided?"

Lena inhaled to respond but said nothing. Nervously biting her lip, her eyes shot to Audrey who in turn looked to Steven, a new hope alight in her gaze. In the end, however, it was Archie who broke the silence.

"Prior to coming into the Game, I was able to see many aspects— be they past, present, or future—of this massive construct Grey and Zed created to save the world from the inevitable corrections that occur from time to time to maintain universal balance. I've often wondered why the visions deserted me once I became part of the Game, and I think I finally understand why. As William said, each of us possesses free will, the ability to change the outcome. Outside the Game, I am merely an observer, but as a full participant, my actions change the very events I would be perceiving." He placed his finger on the tip of his nose and chuckled. "Try as you might, you simply can't see the nose on your own face."

"At least not without a mirror." Emilio shot the priest a self-amused wink.

"Yes, boy." Archie's features grew dark. "*At least not without a mirror.*"

Steven inhaled to speak, curious about Archie's sudden change of tone, but before he could get a word out, William began anew.

"So, the other side—the Black—has your King, this man you call 'Grey'?"

"Yes," Steven answered.

"And this 'Grey' person has hidden the crown that makes him King."

"You've been paying attention."

"You all aren't the only ones afraid they might not come out of this still breathing." William sat back down at the table. "When I was a kid and would lose something, my mother would always ask the same question."

Lena's eyes flashed. "Where did you last see it?"

"Precisely." William met Steven's gaze across the table. "I don't think your King let himself be taken to buy you time only to send you on a wild goose chase. He must have left the crown in a place you'd be able to figure out. Where were you the last time you saw it?"

Steven pondered. "He's only worn it once. Back in Atlanta. He drew the crown from the *Hvitr Kyll*, placed it upon his brow, and shifted into the raiment of the White King, but ever since then, he's only come to us dressed in his usual—" He stopped mid-sentence. "Wait."

Steven had seen the White King in his full glory only one other time, but not the version of the man he met in Chicago what seemed an eternity ago. This other Grey hailed from a far older and darker time in his long existence. Steven's Grey had been there as well, forced to look on again and again as this previous version of himself from centuries before rained ice and pain and destruction down on friend and enemy alike, reliving hundreds or maybe even thousands of times his lowest moment, a decision that had haunted him for five centuries.

Could it be? Was that the clue as to the whereabouts of the White King's crown?

And if so, without the mystic protection of the Game in play to protect them this time, did they dare return to one of the most inhospitable places on the planet based on only a hunch?

"THIS IS THE PLACE." Though the icy terrain bore little resemblance to what Steven remembered from his brief glimpse of an Antarctic glacier five centuries gone, the crimson sky overhead notwithstanding, his every instinct screamed that he'd stood in that very spot with the man he knew as friend and mentor and King. Both the droning pouch at his side and a subtle flutter at his collarbone agreed with his assessment. "Now what?"

"I keep you and me from dying in this bone-chilling cold," Archie answered from a few feet behind, holding aloft his Bishop's staff that bathed them both in golden light, "and you get to work finding what we came for."

The helm, garb, and boots of the Pawn, regardless of their protective attributes in battle, had done little to keep Steven warm since their arrival on the seventh continent. Without Archie's abilities, even the short trek they'd already endured would have brought their quest to a swift and certain end. Lena's quick internet search before they left had revealed that the sun wouldn't set in Antarctica for months, though whatever light the sun overhead doled out did little to provide anything resembling warmth. Even knowing all of this, he found himself wishing he'd been able to achieve this particular mission solo.

He'd led the way through a couple hundred yards of thigh-deep snow and hadn't taken one step where he didn't feel Archie's eyes boring into his unprotected back. Few words had passed between them since their arrival, most of those directional and necessary. No matter how amiable Archie seemed, a bad feeling tugged at the back of Steven's mind and had since they stepped out of the Wyoming diner and initiated the ritual to return them to the barren wasteland beneath their feet, the same feeling of wrongness that had eaten at his subconscious for months.

"So, Archie," Steven did his best to keep a chipper tone in his voice, "what are your plans if we somehow manage to pull this thing off and win?"

"I beg your pardon?" Genuine surprise colored the priest's words. "My plans?"

"You know," he glanced back at the priest, "after all this is done. What's next for you?"

"I don't know." Archie let out a breath, the expelled moisture from his lungs half-frozen before it had so much as passed his pursed lips. "To be honest, I haven't really given it much thought, considering everything else we've had going on."

"That kind of thing has been on my mind a lot." Steven continued the verbal dance. "Especially Audrey."

"Poor girl." Archie shook his head. "I can only imagine."

"Things are likely to get ugly with the leukemia once the Game is all over." He sucked in an icy breath. "You know, like it did when she and Lena were stuck in Chicago biding their time till we arrived."

"But this time, she will be in her own time with all the advances of the modern era and the foreknowledge that leukemia is absolutely in the cards. I pray that if we all survive this, modern medicine and the Lord's healing touch will finally be able to cure her of that demon." Archie offered him a knowing smile. "For both your sakes."

"Then there's Magdalene." Steven pivoted, hoping a different angle might push Archie's buttons. "She's made no bones about why she's in this, her intense desire to burn me alive notwithstanding. She's finally free of the disfigurement we—or, I suppose—*I* caused when we ran into each other in 1936."

"And clearly wishes to remain that way."

"Young again, beautiful, returned to her prime." He locked gazes with Archie. "Do you think Zed truly has the power to keep her that way? You know, allow her to live forever?"

"I'm quite sure I don't know." Archie's brow furrowed. His puzzled expression deepened, his wheels clearly turning as he tried to figure out where exactly Steven's line of questions were taking them. "My many years of visions have indeed left me with intimate knowledge of this insanity in which we find ourselves embroiled, but what either of the two progenitors of the Game itself can accomplish with the powers in question once play is complete is well beyond even my understanding."

"It would be tempting, though, to try to hold onto newfound youth for as long as you could, wouldn't it?" Steven studied the priest's features with every carefully chosen word. "To get a second chance to do all the things you might've missed the first time around?"

"I must admit, I'm not quite certain what you're driving at, but a frozen desert of ice hundreds of miles from the next living person seems a strange place to launch into deep philosophical discourse, especially considering that all that's keeping us both from freezing to death is the power imbued this mystic crosier." Archie's head tilted subtly to one side. "To put it bluntly, Steven, is there something specific you're trying to ask me?"

Heat rose in Steven's already windburned cheeks, the blood rushing in his head a river that threatened to wash away his every thought. One thing was clear, though: now was not the time to fight.

If his suspicions were wrong, the accusation amounted to spitting in the face of an ally.

If they were right, the middle of Antarctica was indeed probably not the ideal location on the planet to call out a potential enemy.

"Sorry," he shifted gears, "I've just had a lot on my mind."

"As do we all." Archie's tone lightened a shade. "Anything in particular troubling you?"

"The way I see it, we all bring different things to the table, good and bad, independent of whatever gifts the Game has bestowed upon us. We all come at this thing a little differently, but when you get right down to it, each of us plays this Game because we have no other choice." Steven pulled in an icy breath. "For instance, Emilio is using all of this to work through some serious anger issues."

"Agreed." The whispered word echoed from the barren ice. "With some success, I might add."

"And Lena? I'm pretty sure she sticks around mainly to keep an eye on Emilio."

"That may have been the case at first," Archie countered, "but the young woman who has faced down the Black Queen more than once has come a long way since Baltimore."

"That's for sure." Steven looked out across the barren ice. "As for the others, Niklaus was running from heartache, God rest his soul, and now finally has some peace. William, on the other hand, is treating this nightmare as some kind of long shot toward redemption."

"And what of the lovely Miss Richards?" Archie's eyes twinkled. "I'm certain you've given her motivations more than a passing thought."

"Audrey." Steven shook his head. "I believe she's doing all this mostly because it's the right thing to do; however, though she'd never admit it, I have little doubt she's hoping against hope that somehow the leukemia won't come back when this is all over."

"After decades of taking confession, I couldn't agree more with your assessment of each of our little band." A hint of the dubious tone that always set Steven's hair on end invaded Archie's words accompanied by an unnerving glint in his eye as if the priest might at any second burst into laughter. "And what about you, Steven? After all this time and effort, what is it that you hope to glean from this experience? Like anyone would in your position, you've surely had your moments of self-doubt, but your devotion to Grey, a man you'd never met before a few months ago, has been impressive in its resolution. What is it that drives you so?"

Caught off guard by the sudden reversal, Steven kept his silence as he formulated an answer. Though he'd been planning the subtle interrogation for days, he'd prepared far more for asking questions than answering.

In the days, weeks, and months since Grey first saved his ass back in Chicago, Archie's question had crossed his mind more than once. Almost always, his answer to himself had been quite practical and basically some variation on one of his father's favorite sayings: *When you get thrown in the deep end, you swim or you drown.*

But there was something more. Something he'd never quite put into words before.

The sink or swim mentality had carried him far on this journey as well as his loyalty to a man who had literally pulled him out of the fire and set him on a new course.

Lena looked up to him, as did Emilio in his own way, but while living up to their admiration certainly helped motivate him, that wasn't exactly it either.

Then there was Audrey. Not a day passed that he didn't fall deeper in love with the freckled redhead from Oregon, but not even his barely concealed fondness for the girl fully explained what kept him going day after day.

"What I want, Archie, is to matter." Steven's eyes narrowed at the priest. "To make a difference. Hell, maybe even make the world a better place."

"And you don't think I want the same?" The inflection in Archie's words oscillated between amusement and genuine hurt. "Please, tell me, Steven. Your interpretations of everyone else's motives were all quite favorable and, I might even argue, generous. What could I have possibly done or said to make you doubt me or *my* intentions?"

Before Steven could utter another word, the pouch at his hip pulsed three times in rapid succession.

"I'm afraid we need to put a pin in this." The pouch erupted with another triplet of tooth-shaking sound. "The *Hvitr Kyll* is being pretty insistent about...something."

"Pin, *dagger*, whatever." Archie's words came out surprisingly bitter. "In the future, though, might I suggest you not wait until we're in the middle of the most inhospitable place on the planet to start throwing around baseless allegations?"

"Look, Archie, I'm sorry. There's just never seemed to be a good time to—*ow!*" The dragonfly clasp at his chest dug into his skin so deep that Steven feared she'd draw blood. "Great. Now, Amaryllis is freaking out too."

"And what, pray tell, could provoke such a violent reaction from your pair of talismans?" Zed stepped from a deep violet shimmer, covered head to toe in the dark furs and cloak of the Black King. "I have come but to help."

17

THE DEAL (NO DEAL)

"P ike." Steven summoned the weapon of the Pawn from the ether and directed its gleaming tip at the center of Zed's chest.

"Now, now." Zed rested the tip of one gloved finger at the axe-spear's tip. "I have come here unaccompanied," he said with a wicked grin, "and though I am far from foolish enough to appear before you unarmed, do I hold a weapon?" He raised both hands before his chest in mock surrender even as his snarling smile widened.

"What do you want?" Steven asked. "How did you find us here?"

"I had a hunch this might be the place." Lowering his hands, the Black King looked left and right, his nose crinkled in disgust. "Our mutual friend did have the misfortune of spending quite an inordinate amount of time in this, his least favorite place on the planet."

"Like you didn't have everything to do with that." Steven seethed, his breath misting in the frigid air. "I can't imagine anything crueler than what you put Grey through in this place. Weren't you two supposed to be friends at some point?"

"Far more than friends, Bauer." Zed pulled his fur-lined cloak close around him. "Grey and I were brothers of a fashion for centuries, bound to each other by decisions made in our foolhardy and overly optimistic youth. However, as my understanding of the world grew more cynical or, some might argue, more realistic, that's when the cracks in our relationship began to show."

"You mean when your hunger for power blocked out whatever part of you that used to be decent and kind." Steven narrowed his eyes at the Black King. "I saw what you did at Stonehenge."

"Just as you saw with your own eyes what your beloved mentor did in Antarctica on the very spot where we stand." Zed's smile faded, replaced with a look of cool contempt. "All of us—you, me, Grey, even the good Father Archibald Lacan here—are capable of far more darkness than any of us would like to admit. Have you not killed in service to your King and this Game he and I created? Has not your Queen, the woman you've done so little to hide your feelings for? Would not even your noble Knight and his paramour do the same, if given the need and opportunity?" He rested his hand on the pommel of his sword. "Bluster and preen all you want, but at the end of the day, don't delude yourself into thinking you're any better than me. We *all* do what we must to win."

"And that's why you've come here today?" Archie stepped forward and took his place at Steven's side. "To claim your victory?"

"To the contrary, priest." Zed offered the pair a subtle bow. "I am merely doing exactly what Grey would do in the same situation."

"And that would be?" Steven asked.

"Ensuring the Game comes to pass, little Pawn. Preventing the very disasters you and your little team of firefighters wasted weeks battling in your efforts to save a few paltry lives."

"Every life is worth saving." He raised the tip of his pike to an inch from Zed's throat. "Even yours."

"As I said, I've come here to help." Zed's smile vanished. "You should be thanking me for joining you today, here in this most inhospitable of places, not threatening me with violence." In a blur of motion, the Black King drew his broadsword, swung it before him, and knocked the pike from Steven's hand. The gleaming silver tip of the Pawn's weapon buried itself in the ice a few feet away. "There," Zed whispered, "much better."

"If you've truly come to help," Steven took a step back, his mind flashing through the myriad of ways Zed could finish both him and Archie right then and there, "then prove it."

Zed sucked at his teeth. "Put away your weapon, Pawn, and I'll put away mine."

"Fine." He focused his attention on the long poplar shaft protruding from the ice, and the archaic weapon evaporated into thin air. "You want to talk, let's talk."

"Finally." Zed sheathed his broadsword. "I know it has been weeks or, from your viewpoint, months since our first encounter, but time on both sides grows short. All this posturing is eating away at time better spent in rest and preparation for the battle to come."

"Says the man who has ambushed us at every turn, murdered one of my best friends, and brainwashed our families into trying to kill us."

"I told you I had come to help ensure that the Game went forward at its fated time and place. I said nothing about no longer desiring to win." Zed chuckled, the air steaming from his nostrils. "That being said, though I do have my own agenda, I have not forgotten the initial reason your mentor and I put this construct in place all those many years ago."

"So, you actually want to help us?" Steven shook his head. "Will wonders never cease?"

"Grey has made a rather brilliant move in this, our latest game of chess, albeit quite a risky one. Though he holds the position of White King, with no crown upon his brow the Game will not count him nor bring him to the Board at the appointed time." Zed stroked his beard as he mused. "No crown, no King. No King, no Game. And if the Game is not played, the return of catastrophe." Black King and White Pawn locked gazes. "The universe has been denied thrice in a row, Steven Bauer. I can only imagine the cataclysm to come should we fail in our task today."

"*Our* task?" Steven and Archie asked together.

"For the moment, the goals of White and Black align. You are free to reject my offer of assistance, though I may then be forced to search for the crown without you. Do you not agree it would certainly be easier if we combined our efforts?"

"At least, as you said, for the moment." Steven pulled the *Hvitr Kyll* from his belt. "It seems our two pouches agree, as each brought us here to this very spot. The crown cannot be far away."

"Nothing but ice for as far as the eye can see." Zed performed a full spin, his hand at his brow to block the glare coming off the ice and snow. "We seek the proverbial needle in a haystack."

"Thank you, Your Majesty." Archie leaned on his staff. "We hadn't figured that part out." He let out a sigh that literally froze in the air. "You've come quite a long way to help us, Zed. Surely you have some tidbit of advice on how to find a ring of platinum that's been on ice for five centuries."

"Your Bishop has grown bold, Pawn." Zed's brow furrowed in concentration. "No matter. One thing is clear. Your much vaunted mentor would not have left the crown here without some means of finding it." His gaze passed from the white leather pouch in Steven's hand to the dark one at his own waist. "I suspect, however, that neither the *Svartr Kyll* nor its bright sister will help us hone in on its location more than either already has. The same for any piece of weaponry or equipment afforded by the Game. The crown is the property of the White King, and while I could bring him here to aid in our search, I think I will keep my advantage and trust that the three of us can conceive an alternate means of divining its location." Zed clasped his gloved hands together beneath his chin. "For instance, do we not have in our collective possession an artifact of no small influence that has saved your skin multiple times and yet is in no way part of the greater Game we play?"

The throb overlying Steven's collarbone served as a more than sufficient reminder of exactly what item Zed referred to.

"Yes, Bauer," Zed continued, "the dragonfly clasp you wear at your chest, a gift from the Pedone woman who took in both you and Grey that first night." He smirked, his head tilting to one side. "Amaryllis, I believe she is called?"

Steven's stomach dropped. "How could you possibly know that?"

"You have your secrets, Pawn, as do I. Trust that in my centuries navigating the eternal chess game of immortality in a world that neither asks nor gives quarter that I have mastered the art of divining my opponent's weaknesses and strengths." Zed allowed himself a quiet chuckle. "As I understand it, this Amaryllis has kept you apprised of any and all dangers along your path—the most recent of which, my arrival here in Antarctica—since the old crone bestowed upon you the only thing she had worth giving."

"Crone..." Steven's mind filled with images of both the stunning Ruth Matheson he'd met in 1946, a girl who had offered him her very heart, and the even more beautiful soul, Ruth Pedone, who, along with her doting husband, had taken him into their home, fed him, and cared for him on the most terrifying night of his life.

"A second set of eyes and ears comes in handy, does it not?" Zed motioned to his own collarbone at the site where his fur-lined cloak met below his neck. There, a beetle of onyx and dark ceramic glistened in the blinding light reflecting off the ice. "Hellebore has served me well for centuries in much the same capacity as your Amaryllis." He crossed his arms, the amusement in his features fading into something like awe. "To deliver you safely to the ground after that leap in Atlanta, however. Now, *that* was really something."

Archie pulled close to Steven, his voice dropping to a whisper. "How does he know these things?"

"I have no idea," Steven murmured between clenched teeth, "but for the moment, he's not trying to kill us, and as much as I hate to say it, he's right. Amaryllis may be the key."

"In that case, let's get on with this." Archie stood upright and stretched out the golden glow of his crosier to include Zed. "Thus far, I've managed to keep the two of us from freezing to death, but I've learned all too well that both I and the Bishop's staff have our limits."

Steven studied the beetle at Zed's neck. "Are you sure your own little friend there can't help?"

Zed sighed. "If I thought Hellebore could locate the crown of the White and bring me what I desire, Steven Bauer, do you truly believe the two of you would still be breathing?"

"I suppose not." Steven plucked Amaryllis from his chest and held her bejeweled body before him. "All right, girl," he whispered, "show us what you've got."

For longer than he would have liked, Amaryllis rested unmoving in his palm.

"Come on," he murmured, his entire body shaking despite Archie's best efforts to stave off the cold. "You've never let me down before."

"Performance problems?" Zed snickered. "A bit of stage fright, perhaps, now that she has the limelight, so to speak?"

"Don't listen to him." Steven half-doubted his own sanity as he found himself addressing the mystical insect of metal and stone. "You've got this."

Another few seconds passed before the dragonfly of silver, emerald, and jade began to buzz atop his already trembling fingers. As fear and cold and dread and excitement all warred for supremacy in Steven's mind, Amaryllis finally turned in his palm and looked him straight in the eye before flying from his hand.

"Where'd she go?" Archie asked as a sudden wind whipped thousands of little razors of ice up from the ground, forcing them all to avert their eyes. "How will we ever find her in this mess?"

"Yes, Bauer," Zed added with a grunt, "how indeed?"

"She's only ever flown once before." Steven refastened the pouch to his belt. "I was standing somewhere close to this very spot before I rescued Grey from his own personal hell." He ground his teeth. "If this is how it's supposed to go, then it will happen, regardless of anything I say or do." Grey's words, seemingly from another time, flashed across his memory. "If not, we're in no worse shape than we are right now."

"I beg to differ, Pawn." Zed again rested his palm on the pommel of his sword. "If you and your Bishop are unable to provide me what I've come for, then your usefulness will have come to an end."

"Amaryllis will come through." Archie worked to keep a rare stammer from his deep baritone. "She hasn't let Steven down yet." He turned his attention back to the horizon, peering through the rising wind and ice for any sign of the tiny dragonfly of metal and jewel. "I have to admit, even I didn't know Amaryllis could do that."

That's because I never told you.

"It would seem," Steven kept his voice low, "that we're all full of surprises."

Even in that moment, with Archie by every measure unequivocally on his side, Steven still couldn't shake the voice at the back of his head that something wasn't quite right with the White Bishop. Despite his misgivings, but also because of them, he'd arranged for it to be just the two of them on this little expedition. He'd hoped to finally and conclusively bring the matter of Archie's inconsistent behavior to rest, but Zed's arrival had postponed yet again a talk that had already been far too long in coming.

The odd trio continued to stare out into the escalating blizzard for any sparkle of green or hint of light playing off Amaryllis' metallic wings even as the sky above turned grey, obscuring the crimson heavens as if the world were suddenly covered in a woolen blanket. The daylight dimmed more and more by the second as a rare Antarctic snow began to fall, dropping the already poor visibility to near zero. A frustrated Zed turned his head in Steven's direction, his ever-present scowl darkening along with the sky, but before he could speak again, Archie pointed into the distance.

"There," he shouted, "do you see?"

Steven and Zed both followed Archie's outstretched finger out into the blizzard to a barely visible rise a good hundred yards away. There, the falling snow swirled in a cyclonic pattern like a tiny tornado or one of those dust devils from the Middle East that helped give rise to myths of the Djinn. His high black boots completely enveloped in the knee-deep ice and snow, Zed stalked off toward the whirlwind of ice and snow with Archie close on his heels. Steven took up the rear, strangely hesitant to turn his back on either of his companions, a realization that chilled his heart more than the sub-zero temperature.

As they drew closer, the icy mini-tornado ahead brought memories of another time and place that had been anything but cold: the beach of one of the barrier islands along the Outer Banks of North Carolina where a swirling mass of fireflies had lit the night as if it were day.

This was magic and not only that.

As far as Steven could tell, this was Grey's magic.

With each step, the cyclone of ice and snow spun faster and the wind howled louder, the pitch just off from that of the droning pouch, the two sounds creating a dissonance that left Steven's teeth aching in his head. Then, with a high-pitched whir, barely audible above the warring cacophony, Amaryllis flew from the whirlwind of ice and stopped inches from the tip of his nose.

"Well, Bauer," Zed intoned, "what now?"

"I don't know." Steven studied the ever-growing mass of swirling white before them, his eyes eventually drifting downward to the ice at his feet. "Even if this is the spot, the crown has been buried for five centuries. How are we supposed to—"

With a couplet of loud buzzes from her wings, Amaryllis performed a series of aerial somersaults before flying headlong back into the icy cyclone. A clang of metal on metal provided a flash of intermingled green and silver revealing the object of their search floating at shoulder height at the whirlwind's frigid core.

"There." Zed rushed forward and dove his hand into the heart of the howling spiral of razor ice only to leap back in agony as if bitten.

"Argh!" The Black King drew his gloved hand close to his body. "So...cold..."

"Careful, Your Majesty." Archie spent little effort hiding the laughing derision in his tone. "Just because you joined us on our little field trip doesn't mean that crown is for you."

With a confused sidelong glance at Archie with his singsong mocking, Steven raised a hand to the Black King in continued truce. "With all due respect, Your Majesty, I think you'd best let me try."

"Very well." Zed tucked his injured hand into his fur-lined cloak and inclined his head in the direction of the crown. "Get to it, Pawn."

Steven approached the spiraling mass of snow and ice, never letting Zed or Archie out of his sight. He stared down at his bare hands which had nothing like the protection afforded by Zed's leather and no doubt fur-lined gloves.

"This is going to hurt," he muttered to himself.

"We don't have all day, Bauer." Zed grunted as he attempted to shake the warmth back into his hand. "And time is ticking. As you well know, the Game awaits."

Without another word, Steven pulled in a breath and stretched out his unprotected fingers for the ring of platinum at the cyclone's core.

The flying shards of ice cut at his hands, his arm, his face, and yet he continued to push forward despite the pain. Inch by frigid inch, he pressed on, though his every instinct screamed flight over fight. As his fingertips brushed the burnished platinum, the wind howled and the pouch screamed, but Amaryllis' insistent buzzing in his ear and a flashing memory of Audrey's smile gave him the impetus to push forward the last inch.

As Steven's fingers wrapped around the bitter cold platinum of the crown, three things, each stranger than the one before, occurred.

An electric charge ran up his arm, followed by a warmth that filled his entire body as if he sat in his family's backyard on a clear July afternoon soaking up the sun back at a time when he didn't have a care in the world.

A breath later, the cyclonic storm of ice fell silent as did the wind and snow from above as the entire continent as far as the eye could see became still and serene.

And then, with a booming pulse from the pouch, a brilliant flash of silver filled the air, leaving Steven both blind and deaf to the world around him. Amaryllis' familiar weight settled again at his collarbone, though even the reassuring presence of his metallic friend provided but the merest consolation.

As helpless as he'd been since this all began, Steven awaited the icy sting of betrayal, whether from either the ancient practitioner of magic whose Game he currently played or the man with whom he'd travelled and fought across an entire continent and three different centuries.

The fact that he even considered the latter left him colder than even the Antarctic chill surrounding the three men who stood at the bottom of the world.

18

QUARTET (A MODEL OF DECORUM AND TRANQUILITY)

As Steven's vision cleared, he found himself afforded a view that very few on the planet ever check off their bucket list and definitely one he never thought he'd see in his lifetime.

Day had turned to night in the few seconds he'd been sightless, but this night was like none he'd ever seen. Archie stood a few feet to his left and Zed a bit farther to his right, but none of them spoke or moved a muscle as they took in the spectacular light show that filled the heavens. After weeks of the ominous and ever-darkening red tinge of the sky above, the majestic curtain of green light that stretched from horizon to horizon represented a welcome change.

"What's this?" Steven clutched the crown close to his chest. "More magic?"

"As I understand it, the southern lights are more magnetism than magic," Archie answered without a hint of the biting sarcasm that permeated his tone before, "though after all we've seen the last few months, who's to say?"

"The aurora australis," Zed added, "a first, even for me." His wistful smile quickly faded. "Regardless of the matchless beauty, however, the fact that we can see this magnificent light show begs a far more important question."

"Like," Steven asked, "why is it suddenly night?"

"And why isn't the sky red anymore?" Archie added.

"I did the research." Steven stared up at the shimmering sheet of green. "The sun isn't supposed to set in Antarctica for a few months."

"What does that mean, then?" Archie held aloft his staff to hold at bay the freezing chill of the Antarctic night. "How can it be dark?"

"As disturbing as it may sound," Steven started, "we may not have moved in space..."

"But we've clearly moved in time," Zed finished. "Damn Grey and all his little fail-safes."

"Last I checked," Steven turned on Zed, "we're only here because you decided to remove our King from the Board before the Game could begin." He shivered, angry at showing even the slightest weakness in front of the Black King. "I'm curious. Have you even considered a strategy that doesn't involve circumventing the rules you yourself put in place, or do you truly have so little faith in your minions that you believe cheating is the only way you can win?"

"There's a bit of wisdom bandied about between professional athletes, politicians, military strategists, and many others that's far older than any of them know." Zed cleared his throat and, with a return of his wicked grin, spoke seven words as if he quoted the Bard himself. "If you're not cheating, you're not trying." He swept his arms wide, gesturing to the ice at their feet and the dark sky above. "Not to mention, you speak as if your own King sending the three of us skipping through time is a standard part of the Game."

"If we're talking about sending people 'skipping through time,' I'd argue that turnabout is fair play." Steven crossed his arms, keeping the crown close at all times. "Since we're down to throwing out platitudes."

"Touché, Bauer." Zed knelt to the ground, scooped up a bit of snow in his gloved hand, and put it to his tongue. "Arguments about which side has bent or broken the most rules this iteration aside, a far bigger question looms before the three of us."

Steven nodded. "When the hell is this?"

"And why has Grey sent us here?" Archie added. "If this is indeed Grey's doing."

"Oh, this is Grey." Zed ripped the glove from his injured hand and blew warm air on his frostbitten fingers. "This little sideways jaunt has his earmarks all over it." The Black King cast a questioning glance in the White Bishop's direction. "You know, since we're all stuck here together, perhaps you can spare a bit of your crosier's power so that I may participate fully in our little collective jaunt?"

"You want me to heal *you?*" Archie let out a quiet chuckle. "You must be kidding."

"Go ahead, Archie. We might need him." Steven studied his enemy. "Though your request does beg a question that's been on my mind for some time." He drew close, observing as Archie ministered to the Black King's hand, the golden glow from the Bishop's staff warming Zed's pale fingers like a ray of sunshine. "Every Piece from either side of our little Game has been brought out into the open. All, that is, except one." He held the crown close to his side. "The Black Bishop. Why have you held back one of your most powerful Pieces?"

Zed considered, his thoughtful silence shifting into mocking laughter. "As you've pointed out what seems an infinite number of times, Steven Bauer, the Game has yet to begin. Our minor skirmishes thus far are nothing compared with what is to come." His gaze flickered in Archie's direction before returning to Steven's. "Consider where you would be without your Bishop and his skills, little Pawn. Half your forces would already be dead, and the rest of you without hope. Still, you have placed Father Lacan here in the line of fire at almost every turn, a unique resource among the White who, if lost, may or may not be replaceable." As Archie completed his task, the Black King shoved his newly healed hand back into his glove. "I am obviously reluctant to share strategic insights with the opposition, as I'm sure you understand, but I will offer that perhaps you could learn a thing or two from my decision to hold back such a precious asset."

"Perhaps." Something in Zed's careful wording tickled the back of Steven's mind, something he couldn't quite put together. "So, Your Highness, you're the expert at zapping people back in time. How do you suggest we get out of here?"

"*Au contraire,* Pawn. You're the one who somehow regathered your forces after I banished the lot of you across both an entire continent and a dozen decades and even managed to deceive me into helping you a century before we were destined to meet, not to mention that you also rescued your King from a trap I designed to be inescapable." Zed pursed his lips in thought. "Wait. Could Grey have possibly sent us back that far? To the time of his entrapment? Such poetic justice, as he would no doubt view it, seems well within his wheelhouse."

"Except that Grey would have had no way to know you would be with me when we found the crown." Steven glanced down at the ring of platinum encircling his elbow. "I was the one he sent to retrieve it, so this little jaunt, whenever it is we've been sent, must be for me."

"I'd argue there's little else to see in Antarctica." Archie stepped forward and motioned to the pouch with a trembling hand. "By the way, I'm running a little low on gas. You think the *Hvitr Kyll* has enough juice to take us somewhere a bit warmer?"

"I suppose. This being the site of the third iteration, there should be enough ambient power floating around to send us from here." With one eye on the Black King and the other on Archie, Steven held tight to the crown and unfastened the pouch from his belt. "Gather close both of you. We may only have one shot at this."

"You expect me to trust you?" Zed asked.

"I could ask you the same." Steven held out his free arm. "Are you coming or not?"

First Zed, then Archie, took hold of his sleeve.

"*Hvitr Kyll,*" he commanded, "deliver us to wherever it is we're supposed to go next."

The pouch droned, its mouth shimmering with silver light, but in the end, nothing happened.

"We're still here." Steven focused on the ancient leather pouch that throbbed like a beating heart in his hand. "What are we doing wrong?"

"No doubt the repository of all things from your end of the Board has little use for the King of the Black." Zed let out a bitter laugh and reached inside his cloak.

"Hold it right there." Steven gripped the pouch tight in his fingers. "What are you—"

"Fear not, Bauer." Zed pulled the *Svartr Kyll* from inside his cloak.

"I am simply offering the services of your pouch's dark sister in an effort to get us off this block of ice."

With Archie at their center holding aloft his staff, its golden glow the only thing keeping the three men alive, the White Pawn and the Black King held aloft their respective artifacts of light and darkness and together murmured four words in unison as if they'd rehearsed the moment a thousand times.

"*Take us from here.*"

And with that, the twin pouches pulsed as one, the silver and violet scintillation of the *Hvitr* and *Svartr Kylls* intermingling with the light of the emerald aurora and the infinitude of stars above in a lightshow beyond the wildest dreams of the most accomplished pyrotechnician in history. When their eyes had again collectively cleared, they found a very different night sky above their heads, one interrupted by the yellow glow of mercury lights, the eerie silence of Antarctica replaced with the honking horns and squalling tires of inner-city America.

"Where is this?" Archie asked.

Steven cast about the empty alley for an answer, but before he could say a word, Zed sniffed the air and answered.

"Baltimore, Maryland." He crinkled his nose. "I'd hoped to never return to this corner of the continent."

"You weren't even there," Steven murmured.

"Wasn't I, Pawn?" Zed headed for the busy street at the alley's far end. "Just because you only faced my Pawn and Queen doesn't mean that I was absent." He laughed. "A successful general never strays too far from the front."

"But you leave all the unseemly business to your underlings?"

"I am King, Steven Bauer, and co-creator of this Game we all play. I've walked this world for centuries and watched countless genera-tions be born, grow old, and die. To such as Grey and I, the lot of you are nothing more than flowers in spring that have no sooner bloomed than begin to brown, wither, and perish."

"Like Sakura?" Steven asked.

"Speak her name again, and I will feed your tongue to my dogs." Zed's flash of anger dissipated as quickly as it appeared. "As I was saying, though the enchantment of the Game does indeed siphon away the energies that in the past led to many of the great disasters of legend—an arrangement that leaves the world unmolested for me to enjoy—I have also derived significant pleasure over the centuries watching the various puppets called to the Game dance on their strings." He studied Steven with a derisive smile. "In particular, I've enjoyed watching *you* flail against the machine, knowing all the while your efforts will amount to nothing."

Steven's free hand balled into a fist as he held tight to crown and pouch in the opposite arm. "I'll show you 'nothing,' you bastard."

"Stay calm," Archie whispered. "Don't let Zed get under your skin."

"A bit late for that," Steven answered.

"Ah." Zed seemed to lose interest in the conversation and instead peered off into the distance. "And speaking of generals staying close to the front," he spoke with mysterious inflection, "look who's arrived on the scene." The Black King walked to the mouth of the alley and stared silently across the busy street at the entrance to a fleabag motel. "If I'm not mistaken, I believe I've determined not only where we are, but when."

Steven and Archie joined Zed at the alley's narrow entrance and followed his gaze to another trio standing on the sidewalk opposite. Grey, dressed in his usual duster and fedora, leaned against a light pole, his face etched with a mix of pain and fatigue. The other two faced away as they conversed with the oddly dressed man, but Steven recognized the elderly couple in an instant.

"Ruth?" he whispered. "Arthur?"

Everything about the old couple was exactly as Steven remembered it. Arthur still wore the same faded jeans and flannel shirt from the night they met, and Ruth wore the same loose blouse, pants, and orthopedic shoes.

"It's the morning after everything started." He studied the motel sign. "This is the motel in Baltimore where we stayed after we got jumped coming out of the strip club."

"Strip club?" Archie asked.

"Any port in a storm, right?" Steven looked up, the sky still its native blue rather than the scarlet red that had permeated the stratosphere for days in what they knew as the present. "It's almost noon. I must have just left."

"And there is your King," Zed muttered blithely, "wasting time with a pair of pawns whose importance falls further down the food chain than even yours, Bauer."

Steven did his best to ignore the slight. "Why is Grey here?"

"My emissaries did destroy their humble home." Zed pointed in the direction of his opposite. "Perhaps my old friend has come to make amends."

As Steven, Archie, and Zed looked on, Grey produced an envelope from within his voluminous duster and handed it to Arthur before reaching into a pocket and pulling out a key which he gave to Ruth. The elderly couple looked deeply into each other's tear-filled eyes before turning back to Grey and nodding. Grey pulled the pair of them into a long embrace and then stepped back, pulled a skeleton key Steven had only seen once from his coat, and stepped to the door of the motel. A gentle hand on the frame and a turn of the lock and the door opened not on the dilapidated foyer Steven remembered, but a city street with a car on concrete blocks, all just visible past Grey's distinctive outline. With a glance in their direction and a subtle nod, the ancient wizard stepped across the threshold and the door closed behind him as if of its own accord, leaving Ruth and Arthur alone on the sidewalk.

Did he see us? Steven pondered. *Does he know?*

"I can't believe I've never gone to see them once since that first night." His cheeks warmed with something akin to shame. "Grey mentioned once that he'd checked on them, but we never discussed it again. We've just had so many other things to tackle."

"Pathetic, Bauer. What do you care about two who already have one shared foot in the grave?"

"Keep talking like that and maybe I don't wait for the Board to summon us."

"Your sentimentality is your weakness, one of many, in fact, if I may observe." Zed motioned at the elderly couple across the street. "Do you not understand, Bauer? You play the Game. What do these two lives matter in the grand scheme? The stakes we play for are far greater than the lives of two unfortunates for whom nothing awaits but the oblivion of a death that rushes at them on wings of night."

Steven took a long hard look at Ruth and Arthur, no more than a stone's throw away. The pair stood by the light pole where Grey had leaned, Ruth holding the key and Arthur the envelope. As the pair came together in a long embrace, he turned back to Zed with newfound strength.

"That's the one thing you don't get, Zed. *You* may play this Game for yourself, but *us*? We play for *them*. The Ruths and Arthurs of this world who can't fight for themselves, who can't even fathom the ideas behind this so-called Game. You've claimed more than once that you remember why you and Grey created this monstrosity, but I wonder." Steven locked gazes with the Black King. "Do you? Do you really?"

Zed pondered Steven's words. "The one thing I've learned over the centuries, Bauer, is that everything ends. Whatever efforts your mentor and I put forth in staving off the universal corrections that occur from time to time may have prevented the deaths of large swaths of humanity, but any benefit has been far outstripped time and again by the continued bloodshed perpetrated by these *people* you hold so dear, all in the name of religion, race, tribe or, worst of all, the twin sins of ignorance and greed."

Archie huffed. "Like your own greed doesn't fuel every decision you make."

Zed spat upon the ground. "I spent decade upon decade of my life in a vain attempt to save these ungrateful souls, but with each passing century, it became clear that the noble sacrifice themselves for the good of many and end up on the pyre of their own selflessness while the selfish simply survive." The Black King crossed his arms, confident in his command of the debate. "Continue to battle for the good of everyone else, Steven Bauer. In the end, however, who is it you believe will battle for you?"

"The others and I, we're all in this together, and no matter what hell you bring down on us, we're going to—"

Steven's train of thought completely derailed as yet another familiar, if not welcome, set of eyes appeared across the way. Archie followed his gaze and gasped as he too bore witness to the unexpected arrival.

"What's she doing here?" the priest whispered as Steven was too dumbstruck to speak.

"Precisely as I asked," Zed said. "Never forget with whom you play chess, children."

Her form covered in a long black duster, a dark cousin to Grey's own outer shell, Magdalene bore down on the elderly couple from half a block away. Instead of her usual snarl, however, she wore a congenial smile, though her emerald eyes still flashed with a danger Steven knew all too well.

It was over before he could make a move. One second Magdalene was there, chatting pleasantly with the elderly couple, and the next they were all gone in a shimmer of darkness as if they never were.

Steven turned on Zed, his cheeks hot with anger. "What have you done with them?" he shouted. "Where are they?"

"You're a smart lad." Zed smiled. "Figure it out."

Steven cast his mind back, desperate for any clue as to the meaning behind the Black King's mocking words. He hadn't seen Ruth and Arthur, at least in modern times, since this particular morning. Still, a half-formed question had dwelled at the back of his mind since their showdown beneath the Washington Monument. At the time, the revelation of his father's forced indoctrination into Black's front line had forced every other thought from his head, but now?

One by one, Zed had revealed the identities of his new line of Pawns, all conscripted into the Game to fill the spaces left vacant by Wahnahtah's brethren lost in battle in Atlanta.

All, that is, save two.

The identities of the pair of the hooded figures that comprised their enemy's bolstered front line had remained a mystery: a man bearing a war hammer like the one Steven had summoned in a house in Maine the first night he became a part of the Game and a woman bearing in one graceful hand an elegant rapier with a jeweled hilt.

"They're the last two Black Pawns." Heat grew in Steven's cheeks. "You bastard."

"We made certain to acquire at least one person each of you cared about as our cannon fodder, but in deference to both your King and Queen, Magdalene thought that doubling our insurance would be prudent."

Steven took a step toward Zed, his free hand raised in a fist. "With God as my witness—"

"Tut-tut, little Pawn. Time for oaths later." He gestured to the pouch. "It would appear your esteemed mentor has something else to show us."

Steven glanced down to find a silver tendril of energy from the *Hvitr Kyll* snaking in the direction of its dark sister. The *Svartr Kyll* answered in kind, sending forth its own ephemeral ribbon of deep violet. The diametrically opposed manifestations of light and darkness sniffed at each other like a pair of dogs meeting in the street and then flew together at the doorway where Grey disappeared. As the parallel trails of silver and violet reached the opposite side of the street, the door flew open, revealing the same street scene they'd seen before.

"What now?" Archie said.

"Hang on." Steven grasped the White Bishop's sleeve as the pouch grew hot in his hand. "Next stop, God knows where."

19

I KNOW HIM SO WELL

One second, the three men stood in the shadows of an alleyway four busy city lanes from a Baltimore motel that boasted hourly rates, and the next, they were street-side, miles away, in a part of Baltimore Steven remembered all too well.

In a section of the city best described as war-torn, a battle indeed brewed. Two rival gangs, each with a group of young men numbering as many as a small army platoon and armed at least as well, gathered to settle a disagreement that all started when, unbeknownst to most present, the leader of one side murdered one of their own in the name of loyalty and blamed it on the other.

The liar in this scenario was Vago, the man who would come to serve Zed as his Black Knight after Audrey ended the first holder of that title in the woods of Sisters, Oregon.

The young man who fell for this lie, at least right up to the very end, was Emilio, the White Knight and Vago's opposite.

Given the fearful symmetry of the moment, Vago's destiny as Knight of the Black could not have been plainer. At the time, however, the leader of the Blues had seemed no more than a speed bump on the way to the main event. More than once, Steven had kicked himself for leaving the traitorous Blue in the hands of the Black. Being conscripted into their enemy's ranks had given Vago exactly what he wanted: the means by which to exact revenge on the very people he held responsible for his status as a disgraced coward in the eyes of every banger in Baltimore, both from the rival gang in town as well as his own.

The latter, Steven considered, was likely the only family the man had ever known.

At the heart of the mass of Salvatruchas and Blues ahead, Steven knew all too well who and what awaited:

Vago, leader of the Blues, working every angle in an effort to get the brother of Carlos Cruz, dead by his hand, to commit suicide by gang justice.

Cortez, leader of the Salvatruchas, furious at having his turf invaded by Blues and unaware of Vago's lies.

And Emilio, desperate to avenge his dead brother the only way he knew how, as much a loaded gun as the various pistols he would hold in his trembling fist that day.

Steven remembered the events well. He peered down the block where another Steven Bauer raced for the heart of the mob and followed his doppelganger's agonized gaze up to the roofline where his opposite waited, arrow nocked and wicked grin firmly in place. As the dark archer, Wahnahtah, let fly his barbed arrow, everything came screeching to a halt. The entire throng, the Black Pawn, Lena, and even this other Steven became as still as statues.

"But the time warp didn't affect me." Steven shifted the crown to his other hand and kept his fingers firmly around the mouth of the *Hvitr Kyll*. "I drew the pawn icon and dove forward, and a second later, I was standing next to Emilio. Why is it different this—"

He stopped mid-sentence as the answer to his question became all too clear. Enveloped in his dark duster, Grey strode from the doorway of an abandoned hardware store across the way, walking amid the frozen mob like a child wandering through a graveyard at midday. He disappeared among the gathered throng and then ambled up the empty road to where the other Steven stood frozen mid-sprint, his icon held before him. Grey circled his White Pawn once, his expression that of a father trying to decide if it was time for the training wheels to come off. Another circle, and his decision was made. He launched into a stream of foreign syllables that disappeared on the breeze accompanied by a sequence of elaborate gestures, the end result of the arcane combination the release of this other Steven Bauer from the stoppage of time.

Steven looked on, heart racing, as the man he'd been months before contemplated the situation for all of half a second before thrusting the pawn icon forward and vanishing in a flash into the heart of the mob. Before time had opportunity to restart, as he remembered all too well it would, the Grey from this time turned fully in their direction, shooting Zed an angry glare before locking gazes with Steven, placing his hands together palm-to-palm, and offering him a humble bow. Steven raised a hand in answer, but his mysterious mentor already moved for the nearest alley and in another breath, had disappeared into the shadows.

"Grey was here." Steven's head dropped. "He never told me."

"It would appear he never told you a lot of things." Zed chuckled and gestured toward the silver and violet emanations from their respective pouches already intermingling for yet another jaunt. "Where do you think your absent King is sending us next?"

"I have no idea," Steven muttered, "and it appears he wasn't so absent after all."

In a blink, the three men jumped to yet another location: this time, the edge of a wood with the sound of rolling waves in the distance. Sand and twigs and scrub played beneath their feet, all barely visible in the dim light. The air smelled of sea salt and ozone and the unmistakable aroma of a herd of animals. A whinny in the distance, followed by a second and a third, confirmed exactly where they'd landed this time.

Through the scant trees that separated them from the sand that stretched to the ocean's edge, a twinkling campfire half a football field away revealed three forms seated in a circle keeping warm as a white stallion to one side stood guard. The crescent moon above shone off the undulating tide, the rhythmic back and forth of the waves hypnotic and serene.

"That's us." Steven pointed. "Me, Lena, Emilio. We're about to go search for the door to get us off this island."

As if directed by his words, the trio rose as one and began to scour the beach looking for something none of them could apparently see. On occasion, a bit of conversation colored by alternating laughter and frustration would carry on the wind to the woodline, and Steven found himself envying this younger and more innocent version of himself. How optimistic he'd been. How strangely happy at having found some purpose in life again.

How utterly naive.

A shout from Lena brought this other Steven and Emilio running. She'd found the spot. Soon, Emilio would be lecturing him on visualization, a lesson he'd taken to heart far more than the teen had ever realized.

Steven, Archie, and Zed all looked on in silence as the trio in the distance somehow managed to summon a door from nothing—an ornate double door floating in midair above an eight-pointed star of silver light—and then, in a brilliant flash, the beach was empty.

"Hmph," Steven grunted. "Guess we didn't need Grey's help for this one."

"No," came a familiar voice from behind them. "In fact, you did not."

Zed spun on one heel, sword out of its scabbard in a blur of motion despite the layers of fur and cloak. Archie turned as well to face this fourth in their party, his movement far more measured than the Black King's. Steven waited till last, apprehensive as the voice, though more than welcome, elicited a strange dread that permeated his very soul.

Behind their spot at the edge of the wood, not ten feet away, Grey sat atop an overturned tree picking his teeth with a twig.

"Hello, Steven." Grey's gaze went to Archie. "Archibald." With an exhausted sigh, his half-closed eyes fastened on his opposite. "Zed."

"Grey," the Black King answered. "Just so you know, we've already played several turns past this point. You have no idea what I have in store for you, old friend."

"More than you might think."

"How are you still here?" Steven asked. "You left long before we started looking for the door."

Grey cleared his throat, "It was important that you, Emilio, and Lena find the egress from this place without my assistance, but as I had no other business that evening—"

"You stuck around to watch?" Steven bristled. "I don't get it. After Ruth, Arthur, and I fled to Baltimore when the Black Rook destroyed their house, you were there. Then later, you helped me save Emilio, but left me to fight not one but two gangs, not to mention Maggie and Wahnahtah, all on my own. And now I find out that you just sat there and watched us flounder on the beach looking for a doorway off this island when you apparently, pouch or no pouch, have the power to come and go wherever and whenever you please?"

"Did you not see Ruth and Arthur to safety without me? Did you not save Emilio and Lena with but the slightest nudge in the right direction? Did you not find your way off this island with no assistance beyond the resources and intellects you had at hand?" Grey rose from the dead tree and swept his arms wide. "Has not learning to depend on yourself to find the solution at every turn served you well in the days, weeks, and months since?"

Steven raised a finger, a litany of harsh words resting on the tip of his tongue, but in the end, only four quiet syllables fell from his lips.

"We found the crown."

"Really." Grey raised an eyebrow, his lips pursed with concern. "Do tell."

"Right where you left it." Steven stroked the stubble at his chin. "Or, at least, where you're going to leave it."

"Yet again, you prove my point, Steven, though it's clear you have yet to see what that point is." Grey clapped his hands together once, the sound shattering the rhythmic tranquility of the incoming tide as pulsating sound and silver radiance spilled from the mouth of the *Hvitr Kyll*. "Very well, then. On your way. 'Miles to go before I sleep,' as my old friend, Robert Frost, once penned." He looked to the White Bishop and gave a subtle nod. "Archibald." The smile left his face as he trained his gaze on Zed. "See you soon, *old friend*."

A blinding flash and the trio found themselves in a very different wood at twilight, the dark earth at their feet a far cry from the bright sand of the North Carolina barrier islands.

"Where are we this time?" Archie asked. "This is no place we've been together that I can tell."

"I'm not certain, but unless I miss my guess—"

Steven's thought stopped short at the staccato beat of galloping hooves no more than a stone's throw away. An instant later, an armored stallion the color of night burst through the underbrush carrying a samurai in jet-black armor, the grimace of his kabuki mask fixing on the three of them for a split second before man and horse disappeared back into the forest.

But the Black Knight wasn't the only form atop his midnight charger.

Hanging on by her fingernails in more ways than one, a shriveled Audrey clung desperately to the horse's tack with one hand as she reached in vain for the white pouch hanging from its barding. Her ravaged body appeared ready to fly from the horse's side with each thunderous hoofbeat, but somehow she held on.

In no more time than it took to register their presence, Audrey and the Black Knight were gone, the steady sound of galloping hooves already fading into the night.

"I spoke to her that night, you know." Steven whispered to Archie. "Mind to mind, sort of like I do with the other Pawns, but different." His eyes followed the path the dark samurai had forged through the darkening wood. "It was the only time, but it was something special to hear another's thoughts inside your own head."

"Steven, Steven, Steven," Zed sighed, "to the trained ear, your mutterings may as well be shouted declarations." The Black King drew close. "Funny thing, mind-to-mind communication is not an ability your mentor and I granted the Pawn. Thought-speech remains the purview of the King." He studied Steven carefully. "And therefore, that means—"

"That I was here that night as well." Grey emerged from behind an oak that had seen at least a full century of scorching summers and frigid winters and fixed Steven with a knowing gaze. "Much like my little push in Baltimore that helped you save Emilio, all I've done here is open a channel so your past self and our soon to be White Queen can share necessary information."

"What about all that talk about not interfering?" Steven's face clouded over in confusion. "It looks like you were there at every step."

"As I have said in so many words before, Steven, desperate times call for desperate measures." His eyes cut to Zed. "And since even the flagrant disregard for the rules exhibited in attacking a dying girl in her own bed seemed to pass muster, I allowed myself a minor indiscretion as well."

"Ah, there's that infamous hypocrisy again, old friend. The same you've put forward for centuries." Zed's nose crinkled with disgust. "You wiped the entire Board clear in Antarctica, killing to a man both your side and mine, and all of you among the White collectively deem such action as not only fine, but necessary. Meanwhile, I simply tried to put out of her misery a girl resting quite literally on her deathbed— a girl I might add that you know all too well won't survive the year regardless of the Game's outcome—and I'm the villain?"

"Keep telling yourself such twisted versions of the truth, Zed." Grey crossed his arms. "Someday, you might actually convince yourself, if no one else."

"Stop." Steven stepped between the two ancient practitioners of magic. "The way I see it, you two have had centuries to sort out your differences, but we're out here in the middle of Oregon, weeks out of sync with time." He turned to Grey. "The Game could start at any moment back home, and yet the version of you from our time has sent us time-jumping through the last few months of our lives, eating up the time we have left."

"And?" Grey asked.

Steven lowered his head. "I guess I just want to know why."

"You still do not understand." Grey spun his finger by his head and the pouch at Steven's hip again answered with a pulse of sound and a burst of silver light. "Yet another lesson then."

In a blink, Steven, Archie, and Zed stood atop a skyscraper, a torrential downpour drenching them to the skin in seconds. Above their heads, the curved lattice work of a certain Queen tower's royal facade shone white in the deluge, the perfect complement to the King tower's angular lattice crown over a football field away, the only other thing visible in the storm-soaked darkness.

"Atlanta," Archie groaned. "I definitely remember this night." He shuddered. "All too well."

"And yet," came Grey's voice from the darkness, "there are aspects of this evening that none of you, not even Zed, have been aware of until now." A phantom in the darkness, the silhouette in grey duster and fedora peered from the building's edge at the all-but-invisible King tower in the distance.

"Grey?" Steven took a step in his direction. "What are you—"

"Silence." The ancient wizard's all-but-invisible hand shot up, admonishing him not to come any closer. "This is going to require a delicate touch."

"What is he—" Archie began.

"Now this makes sense." Zed snapped his fingers and the rain in his immediate vicinity diverted to a three-foot circle surrounding his body as if he stood beneath some invisible umbrella, a protection he didn't bother to share with Steven or Archie. "At every turn, your King has kept his finger on the pulse and provided just the right amount of electricity to keep the heart of your little group beating." The Black King laughed. "And here you thought, little Pawn, that you and you alone had been the lone force keeping the White together."

"You mark my words." Steven bristled, the falling rain doing little to dampen the fire raging at his core. "We're going to—"

"There!" Grey shouted, and a burst of green incandescence flew from between his outstretched hands toward the King tower in the distance. A moment later, a similar flare lit up the side of the other building approximately halfway down, briefly illuminating a pair of tiny figures tumbling in tandem toward the ground below. His body suddenly awash in a flash of emerald light, the first decelerated like a trained parachutist as a voluminous cloak flew out to either side of his body like the wings of an enormous moth. The first held onto the second as long as he could, and for a breath, it appeared the pair might drift safely to the ground. The fleeting miracle ended quickly, however, as a column of mist hurtled down the side of the skyscraper and caught the newly winged member of the duo around the torso, halting him midair. The sudden stop tore the two apart as a potent mix of gravity and momentum sent the other figure flailing into the darkness below.

"No!" Steven shouted, despite the knowledge that Niklaus not only survived this fall, but came out of this encounter the most physically powerful of them all and quickly became the deciding factor that led to their victory, however fleeting, this fateful night.

"Fear not, Steven." Grey stepped away from the edge and faced his Pawn. "Your appearance here and now changes nothing. Your past and my present will continue as you remember." A fatherly smile filled his drenched features. "Do you finally understand the reason why my future self has forced you to relive the events of these initial days of the Game?"

"All I've learned is that every last thing I thought I did on my own only happened because you were there, that my best efforts would have failed if it weren't for the fact that my own personal immortal wizard showed up to bail me out every single time." Steven did his best not to let his anger at Zed's mocking gaze show and failed. "That I'm nowhere near the leader I thought I was or, more importantly, that the others deserve."

"Your analysis of the facts does contain truth, Steven, though your conclusion is anything but correct." Grey shook his head, his fatigued smile fading. "Once more, then. A bit further back." He followed Steven's gaze to Zed who had remained uncharacteristically silent through the entire interchange. "Though my opposite's participation is no longer required for this particular leg of the journey."

"But—" Zed got out before Grey snapped his fingers, summoning a flare of silver from the crown in Steven's grasp that severed the tether between the sinuous energies of the *Hvitr* and *Svartr Kylls*. An instant later, the Black King disappeared in a shimmer of deepest amaranthine leaving the three men of the White alone atop the Queen tower.

"Steel yourself, Steven," Grey intoned, "for what you are about to experience is your darkest night."

"My darkest..." Steven began, his words trailing off as an answer began to dawn in his mind. "Further back, huh? Where is it you're sending me now? And when?" His lip trembled in anticipation. "What is it I have to see?"

"I told you the night we first met that I had known you longer than you could remember." Grey steepled his fingers beneath his chin, a quiet sigh parting his lips. "You're about to find out exactly how long that is."

20

DEFECTION

T he crown, if you please?" Grey gestured to the ring of
platinum. "I would prefer to handle this particular jaunt
through time and space a bit more personally."

Steven hesitated. His grip on the crown had left the metal warm
in his fingers, and its heft had become a welcome presence in his
hand.

"Steven?" Grey asked.

"Of course." He held the crown out to Grey who in turn doffed his
battered fedora, accepted the symbol of his station, and placed it to his
brow.

"Now." Grey stretched out his arms, taking Steven's and Archie's
hands in his. "If you will, hold aloft the pouch to empower our travel
as I bring us to our next destination."

Without hesitation, Steven held the *Hvitr Kyll* above his head.
Blinding silver shone from the pouch's mouth, its rhythmic pulsing so
loud, it shook his bones. This time, the resulting tendril of shimmering energy joined with the radiance of the crown resting atop
Grey's head. In a breath, they were somewhere and somewhen else: a
suburban intersection, late in the evening.

"Something about this place is familiar." Steven looked left and right as a lone pickup truck trundled by. "Where have you brought us?"

"To one last place where I can show you evidence of what you are refusing to see."

"Dammit," Steven grumbled, "this once, can you please just answer a question?"

"Patience." Grey exhaled through his nose. "Your answer is coming quicker than you might like."

"If I may," Archie cleared his throat, "what did you do with Zed?"

"I delivered him safely back to our own time. Unfortunately, he is correct in his assertion that each King must be both living and empowered at the time of the Game or the grand workings of our arrangement with the universe will fail, bringing the return of disaster and chaos." His eyes flicked to Steven. "Which brings us to the matter at hand." Grey pointed up the street to an approaching car. "There, Steven, do you see?"

In the barely lit darkness of the suburban neighborhood, a vehicle approached that Steven knew all too well.

A white Ford Mustang, just like the one he'd bought two years prior.

He'd planned to purchase something more reliable like a Honda or a Volvo as he and Katherine were planning their wedding and, more importantly, their life together. She'd convinced him, however, to get what he really wanted: the muscle car he'd dreamed of since he was a kid playing with Hot Wheels in his lakeside backyard at his family home in Virginia.

Both the girl and car of his dreams.

Steven had truly been flying high.

Which is exactly when, he'd learned, life likes to come along and bring you back to earth.

The Mustang decelerated as it approached the intersection, but as the light turned green, the driver hit the gas and rocketed into the intersection just as a Chevy Suburban as dark as the surrounding night tried far too late to make the light. Tires squalled as both drivers slammed on the brakes, but it was too little, too late. The black Suburban plowed headlong into the driver's side door of the Mustang, the cacophony of rending metal and shattering glass filling the air. The crash took less than a heartbeat, but Steven knew all too well the outcome.

"Why did you bring me here?" he asked, his eyes filling with tears. "I already lived through this the first time. Why make me experience it all again?"

"To show you this." Grey gestured to a tree that occupied the far corner of the street. From the shadows beneath its branches stepped a familiar figure. As always, cloaked in a full-length duster and fedora, yet another Grey stepped from the darkness and rushed to the car's passenger side. Ripping open the door, this Grey pulled an unconscious man from the wreckage and dragged him to the grass at the side of the road. Kneeling at the man's side, the shadowy figure rested a hand on the man's bloody forehead and with a few whispered words, surrounded the man in a cocoon of golden light.

Not wasting a moment, this other Grey returned to the pale sports car and climbed inside the open passenger door. A flash of silver filled the vehicle and the shadowy form pulled from the car the driver's limp body. The young woman, dressed in a pretty flower-print dress drenched in barely-visible crimson, draped like a broken doll in the wizard's arms. The sight of her lifeless limbs tore Steven's heart asunder all over again.

"Try as I might, Steven, I was unable to save your lovely Katherine that night." Grey rested a hand on his heartbroken protégé's shoulder. "Your injuries were well within my abilities to heal, but hers were beyond even the miracles our friend the White Bishop can perform." He lowered his head. "Though you have never known about my involvement, your understanding that Katherine was killed instantly has always been correct."

"I don't get it." Steven's voice choked. "Why didn't you intervene earlier? You could have saved her. She could still be alive."

"Her fate was sealed the moment you spoke to me of this night in 1946." Grey turned and walked down the sidewalk. "Contrary to countless books, movies, television shows, and the like, the past is not subject to change."

"But we've been to the past." He followed with Archie close behind. "All of us, changing things left and right."

"Truth be told, you all have changed nothing. Each action taken in the various pasts to which Zed banished you, each word, each confrontation, all became merely part of the tapestry leading to your present. Even now, I prepare to return to Atlanta on the night we bring our Rook into the fold and to return you to your present, never to speak of this until the time is right."

"But what if you did?" Steven asked. "If you told me about all of this, we could avoid so much pain, so much suffering."

"I suppose I could try, but the fact of the matter is this: your presence here and now demonstrates without a doubt that I did not." Grey stopped at the next intersection, turned to face Steven and Archie, and removed the crown from his brow. "I do find it ironic that I now return to my own time to draw from the *Hvitr Kyll* the very crown I now return to you."

"So, that's it?" Steven fumed. "You wanted me to watch Katherine die again? You weren't sure the hole in my heart was quite big enough?"

"Oh no." Grey smiled. "I merely wished for you to understand that I have watched over you for far longer than you can imagine, a fact far easier to show than tell."

"But why?"

"When next you see me, in your own time, I will tell you." Grey returned the crown to Steven's hand. "Your presence here means that the Game is nigh and just as I must return to my own time and place, so must you return to yours. Fear not, though. As some version of me further down the path clearly intended, I send you now to the aspect of me you know as a contemporary. Speak with him, and all will be made clear." He raised his hand before his face and snapped his fingers. "Fare thee well, Steven Bauer."

Again, the eldritch energies of crown and pouch intermingled in the air before them, filling the space with both brilliant light and jaw-shaking sound. Steven slammed his eyes shut but was unable to cover his ears, his hands encumbered with the two items at the root of the thundering display of power.

When he again opened his eyes, he could see nothing. The pouch suddenly dark and silent, opaque darkness and utter silence surrounded him even as gooseflesh rose along his body from the damp chill. A dank aroma filled his senses, and his taste buds registered the stale air of a place that hadn't seen the sun in years.

"Hello?" Steven perked his ears for so much as the sound of another's breath. "Is anyone here?"

"I'm here." Archie giggled nervously. "Wherever here is."

Nothing about the sudden giddiness comforted Steven in the least, and Amaryllis' pinch at his collarbone only sent his stomach further into knots.

"Steven." Grey's voice echoed from what seemed a hundred miles away. "At last." His ragged breathing washed away the quiet. "Please, bring the pouch. Allow its light to enter this darkest of places."

The *Hvitr Kyll* rested partially closed in Steven's hand. He pulled the crown up his arm to encircle his shoulder and then held the pouch high above his head. The characteristic silver glow that typically marked the pouch's power began to return, the dim glow nothing like the spectacular light shows that had marked the last hour of his life.

The muted light revealed that he and Archie stood at the center of an enormous room cubic in shape, the rugged floor of black granite measuring roughly the size of a basketball half-court. The walls were similarly fashioned of dark stone and windowless, while the ceiling consisted of countless stalactites pointing downward with razor tips. Several feet up the far wall and divested of his traditional fedora and duster, a half-naked Grey hung from wrists bound with dark chains, his hands enveloped in a ball of ebon fire that somehow didn't scorch his flesh.

"Grey." Steven crept across the room until he stood beneath the battered wizard. "Are you okay?"

"I still breathe," he grunted, "but the Knight's chains, the Rook's stone, and the Queen's fire in concert are more than even my magicks can overcome." Grey broke into a peal of coughing. "For days, even the slightest flicker of light from within my soul has been instantly doused by darkness."

"As if Antarctica wasn't torture enough." Steven looked up into the man's shadowy visage. "We're here to free you, exactly how the version of you we just left intended."

A wheezy laugh escaped Grey's trembling lips. "Seeing several moves ahead and predicting what is to come is what separates a simple player of chess from a grandmaster. A charm placed on your Amaryllis there along with a failsafe whispered into the depths of the *Hvitr Kyll* weeks ago, and here you are."

"How do we get you down from there?" Steven studied the ball of black fire surrounding Grey's hands. "Without killing you, that is."

"Though I cannot be certain, I have had more than ample time to contemplate this particular trap." Grey peered up at the ball of ebon fire surrounding his bound fists. "The light of the Bishop's staff should suffice to dispel the Queen's fiery bonds while the edge of your pike's blade should serve to sever the Knight's chains." His gaze returned to Steven. "Do catch me as I fall, though. I am not certain my legs will hold me in my current state."

"Of course," Steven stammered. "I won't let you fall."

Even in the midst of his time loop torture in Antarctica, Grey hadn't appeared so weak. Steven was accustomed to the Grey who was a force of nature, not one who reminded him of his poor grandfather in his hospital bed after his first heart attack all those years ago.

"All right, Archie." Steven summoned the pike. "Ready?"

"As ready as I'm going to be." Archie strode forward, holding aloft the crosier of the White Bishop, all the while uttering a series of syllables that vanished from memory the moment they were heard. The Celtic cross within the crescent moon shone like a silver flare, filling the room with blinding light. When the radiance finally abated, the dark flames encircling Grey's hands were no more. "Your turn, Steven."

"Phalanx." In a blink, Steven divided into his octet of doppelgangers. The seven additional Pawns quickly scrambled, four of them forming a human ladder to allow them enough height to work on Grey's chains while the remaining three held out their arms to catch his falling form once freed. In less time than he thought possible, he managed to cleave through one of the dark metal links with the spear point of his pike, freeing Grey's arms and allowing the wizard to slump forward into the arms of the waiting trio of Pawns. Shifting the pike briefly into its axe form, he dismantled each of the manacles surrounding Grey's bruised and bloodied wrists.

"Archie?" Steven asked. "A little healing hocus pocus?"

"Between keeping us alive on the seventh continent and dispelling the Queen's flames just now, both I and my implement are a little low on gas." Archie studied Grey's injured arms, his eyes showing no more than a flicker of compassion. "Perhaps in a few minutes."

"Save your strength, Archibald." Grey massaged his freed wrists and shifted in his rescuers' arms in an attempt to stand. "Once we have all had a meal and caught our collective breath, you can tend to my wounds."

The trio of Pawns lowered Grey to the ground, but their centuries-old mentor no sooner stood upright than his knees buckled and he fell back into their waiting arms.

"Not sure how much more this old body is going to take," Grey murmured with a quiet chuckle. "Now, Steven, please deliver us from this place."

"Do you even know where we are?" Steven asked.

"Likely the latest iteration of Zed's citadel, generated by his Rook." Grey shook his head. "Were Niklaus still with us, he would have generated a similar citadel for the White when the time for the Game proper was upon us, but seeing as how we have no Rook…"

"But we do." Archie took Grey's hand and helped him to his feet. "His name is William Two Trees."

Grey shot the priest a questioning glance and then looked on Steven with admiration. "So, you've already filled the position on the Board with no help or guidance from me." His laugh became a peal of coughing. "Surely you now see what I've been trying to show you."

"For once, I think I'm going to hold out for a second to hear an answer until we're all back to safety."

Steven peered around the twilit room. This was the moment when Magdalene typically would appear amid a lake of black fire to spout some cruel litany, or the ceiling full of razor stalactites of dark granite would begin to descend, or Wahnahtah would begin firing on them from some shadowy corner.

But not this time.

This once, was it possible that everything had gone according to plan?

Steven willed his seven Pawn brethren to dissipate, their essences returning to him, and then moved to help Archie support Grey's battered form. "All right, everyone, hold onto your hats." From his hunched position beneath Grey's arm, he held aloft the white pouch and whispered, "*Hvitr Kyll*, take us to the remainder of the White."

The latest in what seemed an endless succession of blinding lights and deafening sounds left the three men in what Steven hoped would be their final destination of the night. Fatigued by the series of translocations, he fought not to drop the pouch and crown upon their arrival.

As their senses cleared, Steven breathed a sigh of relief. The crimson sky confirmed they were back in their own time, while the cinderblock wall painted alternating daffodil yellow and sky blue placed them in the alleyway behind the Wyoming diner where the remaining four of their team had agreed to wait while he and Archie went to recover the crown. He had no idea how long they'd been gone, though the sun remained high in the sky. He hadn't counted on Grey sending him on a second tour through time and prayed the others had retained the good sense to hold on till they could get back. If all continued to go well, though, then William, Lena, Emilio, and Audrey all waited a few feet away.

"And now, let me see if these legs will hold me up." Grey pushed off first from Archie's shoulder and then Steven's, his trembling form held up, as far as Steven could tell, by sheer will alone. "Ah. Better than I expected."

"Should we get the others?" Steven asked.

"Not yet." Grey peered down at his barely covered form, his bare feet wet from what appeared to be discarded mop water on the broken asphalt behind the diner. "I do not wish for them to see me this way."

"Of course." Steven slid the crown down from its resting place at his shoulder and placed it in Grey's outstretched hands. "Take the crown. Its power should restore you, at least till Archie can finish the job."

The priest cleared his throat but maintained his silence as Grey studied the circle of platinum in his hands.

"You are right, Steven," Grey said. "It is well past the time that this crown should rest upon its master's brow."

"Then we agree." Steven stepped to Archie's side as Grey fell into a quiet reverie. "Well?" he said, breaking the silence. "What are you waiting for?"

"Waiting." Grey's laugh set off another fit of coughs. "That is precisely what I am doing. What I have been doing for centuries. But the wait is over."

"What are you talking about?" Steven stared quizzically at his mysterious mentor. "Put on the crown and get better so we can go see the others."

"But this crown is not for me." Grey brushed his fingers along the burnished platinum. "There was a time when I was worthy of its power, but that time ended the moment I brought an entire glacier of ice down upon those I considered friends and who considered me their trusted leader and King."

"But, you've worn the crown, the robes, everything." Steven trembled as much as Grey. "You're our King, and the Game could happen any minute. We need you." His eyes grew wide in desperation. "I need you."

"No, Steven. You and the White need a King. A King who is worthy. A King who has the respect of all under his command." Grey smiled. "A King who has proven time and again that he is up to the task."

Steven crossed his arms, sullen. "I'm not sure I understand what you're getting at."

"I think you do." Grey sighed. "Before your recent sojourn through the past, you often asked why I was absent so often as you collected the various Pieces of the White."

"I guess I'd come to understand that it's pretty basic strategy to send the Pawn forward to protect the King,"

"Almost there." Grey put his finger by his nose. "Now, your recent sojourns through the past have revealed that I was never truly absent, but merely working to aid you in becoming what you needed to be."

"Your foot soldier. Your lieutenant." Steven's eyes narrowed. "Your Pawn."

"No, Steven." Grey crept to a discarded milk crate and sat, his wobbly legs barely able to hold him upright. "A friend. A confidant. A leader." He smiled weakly. "In chess, the best players develop their various pieces in an effort to make them as effective as possible. In you, I have developed a Piece truly wondrous. My crowning achievement, if you'll pardon the pun."

Something clicked in Steven's mind. "Just say it."

"As you have said more than once to both me as well as the others, in chess, you safeguard the King at all costs."

"As we have."

"But neither my frequent perceived absences nor my behind-the-scenes maneuvering were ever meant to keep *me* from harm..."

"But to protect *me*." Steven locked gazes with Grey. "I'm the King."

Grey gave a solemn nod. "Disguised within the vestments of the Pawn."

Steven's brow furrowed in confusion. "And again, what about all that talk about oaths of noninterference? Was that all...a lie?"

"Another bit of prestidigitation, a sleight of hand to keep Black's focus on me and allow you to fulfill your role without raising suspicion." Grey chuckled. "Truth be told, though, with you assuming the role I'd abdicated, you could argue I was merely staying out of your way." The ancient wizard held the crown before him, his hands shaking. "The time for subterfuge, however, is over." His gaze leaped to Archie. "Archibald, I believe it is customary for coronation to be conducted by a holy man, is it not?"

"Indeed it is." Archie stepped forward, a broad smile plastered across his face. "Glad to be of service."

Steven's heart froze as Grey placed the crown in the priest's outstretched hand, but the moment was over before he could so much as utter a word.

"Steven, kneel before Father Lacan and accept not only this token of my utmost respect and honor, but also, if I may be a bit melodramatic, your destiny."

He paused, his every instinct begging him to jump Archie and take the crown, but Grey's smile was only outshone by the priest's ebullient grin.

"What's the matter, Steven?" Archie asked. "Cold feet?"

"Give me a second." Steven stepped forward, doing his best not to bristle at the subtle dig, and lowered one knee to the ground. "Okay. Ready." He tilted his head forward to accept the crown. Archie launched into one of those sing-song prayers in the dead language that evaporated from memory with every syllable. On and on the strange chanting went until it reached a fever pitch. Steven steeled himself, the idea of the crown's cool metal upon his forehead at once exhilarating and yet terrifying.

The crack of paired gunshots by his left ear sent Steven reeling to one side. His shoulder impacted the unforgiving asphalt, eliciting a grunt as the wind was knocked from his lungs.

The absence of any other pain, however, made one simple fact crystal clear.

He wasn't the one who'd been shot.

His gaze flicked to one side to find Grey lying on his side as well, the left side of his chest wet from a pair of tiny holes oozing crimson. Steven dragged his attention away from his downed mentor, his unbelieving gaze wandering up until his eyes met Archie's. The subdued hint of insanity he'd found in the priest's features time and again that he'd done his best to ignore for months was subdued no longer.

A mad gleam overtook the White Bishop's gaze as he whispered a quiet, "At last."

"What have you done?" Steven screamed. "Why?"

"You'll understand soon enough, boy." With a cackle, Archie fired one more round into Grey's chest and then trained the revolver's snub-nosed barrel directly between Steven's eyes. "Know that Grey there isn't the only one who's been waiting his entire life for this moment."

21

ONE MORE OPPONENT

ow many times, Steven?" Archie's voice went positively giddy. "How many times have I caught you staring at me, trying to figure out what the hell was going on up in old Archie's noggin?" The priest paced the asphalt, his steps simultaneously manic yet silent as if he were performing a well-rehearsed dance. Not once did the gun deviate an inch, its barrel trained like a laser directly between Steven's eyes, as Archie cradled the crown of the White King in his opposite arm like a newborn baby.

"Why are you doing this?" Steven pushed himself back to his knees though he didn't dare try to stand. "Even if you're with Zed—which makes absolutely no sense—why kill Grey? The man just told us both that *I'm* the King. Why not come for me?"

"If he's not King," Archie shrugged with a laugh just shy of a giggle, "then he's a waste of air as far as the Game is concerned." He checked the revolver's cylinder for a split second and then directed the business end again at Steven. "You, on the other hand, have just become a much bigger deal."

"Where'd you get the gun, anyway? You didn't have one when we sprung you from the hospital and that doesn't look like anything you would have picked up back in 1890."

"Think about it, boy." Archie chuckled, his manic tone the polar opposite of the customary calm Steven had come to expect from this man of the cloth over the better part of a year. "The weapon is familiar, right? I'm sure a young mind as clever as yours can figure it out."

Archie was right. He'd seen the snub-nosed revolver somewhere before, but where?

"William." Steven cursed himself for an idiot as he got one foot beneath him, his opposite knee throbbing as the rocky asphalt dug into his kneecap. How could he have forgotten? "That nurse in Alberta. She threatened us with William's revolver. You disarmed her."

"And held onto the gun since no one but me seemed to remember it even existed." He shot a derisive glance down at the man bleeding to death at his feet. "I thought it might come in handy on the off chance I needed to take care of business with something other than my usual Bishop razzle-dazzle."

"Who are you?" Steven attempted to get his other foot beneath him, but as Archie's head and weapon both tilted to one side, he froze in position. "I've had dozens of conversations with Father Archibald Lacan over the last several months. There's no way you're the same person."

"Your assertion is correct, yet flawed." Archie's head shook slowly from side to side in mock sadness. "Such insight would have served you well a few minutes ago or, hell, any time since the time you first noticed me."

"Noticed you?" Steven asked. "What the hell are you talking about?"

Archie laughed. "This is going to be fun." He crouched down closer to Steven's level, though he kept enough distance for the revolver to remain the deciding factor. "You're really going to hate yourself."

"Not as much as I hate you."

"Careful, Pawn. Don't forget which one of us is holding the gun." Archie brought the crown up to scratch the whiskers at his chin. "It's funny, you know. For all the wisdom you've gained over the last few months, you still looked Zed right in the eye when you asked the correct question and you didn't even realize it."

"Question?" Steven stared into the face of madness. "What question?"

"You asked him about the Black Bishop and why he'd never been brought into play. Do you remember?"

"I remember." Steven's heart went ice cold. "No. It can't be."

"Oh, but yes." Archie returned to his full height, the crown still cradled in one arm and the revolver pointed at Steven's head with the other. "When Zed first came to me, he said I represented a near impossibility: a man so perfectly suited to be Bishop in this Game that both the *Hvitr* and *Svartr Kyll* would claim me for their side." He ran a tongue across his teeth. "Guess who got to me first."

"You're the Black Bishop."

"The very same." Archie swept his arms out to either side, his gleaming white robes and miter shifting to midnight before Steven's eyes. In a blink, the Black Bishop's staff appeared in his hand. Far from the familiar length of light poplar beneath a gleaming Celtic cross and crescent moon in silver, this new piece of accoutrement was fashioned from six feet of polished ebony topped with the blackened skull of a ram. The revealed Black Bishop glanced up at the implement of his station where the platinum crown of the White King hung from its curved horns. "The pleasure, I'm afraid I must say, is all mine."

Steven ground his teeth. "And you've been playing us this entire time?"

"In a manner of speaking." Archie raised his shoulders in a sarcastic shrug. "In chess, the bishops represent duality. From *chaturanga*'s paired attendants to the *alfil* on each side of the king in *shatranj* to the modern bishop of the Western world, my station is and has always been dichotomous with one half restricted to the light and the other remanded to darkness. My unique nature allowed the binary nature of the bishop role to be taken to its ultimate extent." The priest pulled in a satisfied breath. "There were times, as I've allowed, when you've spoken with your friend, Father Archibald Lacan, and others when you spoke with me."

"You talk like you're two different people."

"Bingo, Steven. Did you not just say that yourself? I and the Archie you know are not the same." He pointed the gun to his own temple and then back at Steven. "We may share the three pounds of tofu jammed between these ears, but he would no more claim my thoughts and beliefs than I would claim his. In fact, he finds me so abhorrent that he's spent years walling me off and trying to pretend I don't exist." His voice dropped an octave for dramatic effect. "But that doesn't change the fact that I've been here a long time and that my roots are deep." A look of whimsy invaded Archie's features. "Tell me, Steven, do you remember a little boy you met at the end of your sojourn to 1946? Perhaps underfoot during your final visit to Rock Gate Park?"

Steven's mind leaped back to the night he and Niklaus finally found a way to escape Zed's initial time trap via the enormous revolving door of stone at the back wall of Edward Leedskalnin's Coral Castle. Only the three of them—he, Niklaus, and Mr. Leedskalnin—were there that night.

Except...

The family that was leaving as they arrived.

A black family.

And their middle child, a boy.

"You were there."

"Buried deep inside an eight-year-old boy's impressionable mind, but yes, I was there." Archie cracked his neck. "And all it took was him seeing nine tons of coral spinning like a blender and shining like a newborn sun to awaken me and give me purpose." He chuckled. "That and two men vanishing from the face of the earth right before his very eyes. Oh, the possibilities you showed me that night, of adventure, wonder, power beyond comprehension."

"Wait." Steven's mind worked overtime putting it all together. "Your visions. They're all because you saw Niklaus and me that night?" His wheels continued to turn. "Then, once you joined Zed's ranks, he knew everything you knew. That's how he and the rest of the Black kept finding us when I was trying to save you all at the beginning."

"I kept him apprised of your likely whereabouts right up to the hour you brought me into your fold." Archie crinkled his nose and sniffled. "The rest I left him in quite a long letter back in 1890." He let out an amused laugh. "A letter he allowed me to read days before you ever found me in that hospital in Roanoke."

Steven seethed. "You've known everything the whole time."

"And you thought Grey could keep a secret." Archie sighed with faux disappointment. "Perhaps if your mentor there weren't so tight-lipped about what he knows, he wouldn't be lying there in a pool of his own blood." He pulled back the hammer on the revolver. "Not that it would have mattered."

"So, what now?" Steven asked. "Are you going to kill me?"

"Unfortunately, no. As has been made imminently clear, both crown bearers must be among the living for the Game to begin, so, for now at least, I shall have to be happy with a good old maiming." Archie directed the snub-nosed barrel at Steven's bent knee. "You have no idea how long I've waited for this moment. You, with all your sanctimonious bullshit, now kneeling before me. It's a dream come true." An epiphany blossomed on the priest's face. "You know what just hit me?"

"Do tell," Steven grunted, saying whatever he could to keep Archie talking.

"For all his moralistic blithering, all along Grey has played a variation of the same deceitful game as his opposite. A King disguised as a Pawn is not all that different from a card-carrying member of the Black walking amidst the White for months. Funny how neither side had the first clue of the deception being perpetrated right before their eyes." Archie rested a hand on his hip. "Well, except you, Steven. You've known something was wrong since not long after we first met. How does it feel, knowing you never did anything about it, that you could have prevented so much pain and suffering?" He leaned in, a smug grin plastered across his face. "Bet you're wishing you'd forced our little South Pole *tête-à-tête* a long time ago, am I right?"

"You're not going to win," Steven grunted through clenched teeth. "I'll stop you. I swear."

"You can certainly try," Archie's grin melted into a scornful smirk, "though that bum knee of yours is going to make it quite difficult."

The gun's roar filled the alley as Archie pulled the trigger. Steven's eyes clenched shut reflexively as he steeled himself for the pain, but mysteriously, the agony of hot lead passed him by.

His eyes opened on a miracle.

Astride Rocinante's gleaming chrome body, Emilio held high the shield of the White Knight, blocking his view of the Black Bishop. To one side, Audrey stood surrounded by both her mists and the spheres of silver scintillation that were her trademark. Lena crouched on the other, the mace in her dual grip shining like a fledgling star. Above and behind them stood William, his arboreal form already twenty feet high and growing fast.

"Lena," Steven grunted as he forced himself to his feet, "check on Grey. See what you can do."

"Archie?" Audrey got out between choked sobs as Lena rushed to Grey's side. "What is this? What have you done?"

"In case you didn't catch the last bit of his big villain speech," Steven said, "he's been playing for the other side all this time."

"I kind of figured. The whole wardrobe change thing isn't particularly subtle." The White Queen narrowed her eyes at the priest who up until that moment would have been counted among her closest friends. "Hand over the crown, Archie."

"You're kidding, of course." The Black Bishop glanced up at the circle of platinum dangling from the ram skull's curved horns. "I've worked very hard for my prize." He tapped his staff on the wet asphalt and a swirl of violet opened up behind him. "I only regret that I take my leave of you all without my pound of flesh from your pedantic Pawn-King." He took a step backward across the threshold of the portal in space. "Trust, however, that I and the rest of the Black will be seeing all of you very soon."

Archie turned to vanish through the hole in space and nearly fell as the foot that remained on this side of the mystic doorway didn't budge a millimeter.

"What is this?" The Black Bishop glared down at his unmoving leg and every set of eyes followed his furious gaze. There, ripping through the asphalt, a trio of tree roots grew around Archie's jet-black boot and snaked up his leg.

"New Rook," came William's thundering voice, the sound like a falling redwood, "new tricks."

Before Archie could so much as take a breath, Audrey willed one of the eight spheres of silver energy floating about her shoulders to rocket at the revolver, reducing it in an instant to so much scrap metal. "The next one's coming for your head, you bastard."

For the first time since revealing both his true identity and intentions, an expression other than sheer arrogance overtook Archie's features. His eyes darted left and right, his nostrils flared with every breath, and every vestige of his patronizing smile dissolved into a rictus of panic.

"You're awfully quiet, Archibald." Steven stepped around Rocinante, summoning pike, shield, and helm from the ether as he approached the man who for months he'd considered both teammate and friend. "No more clever words? No more empty threats?"

Archie stabbed at the roots around his foot with the blunt end of his weapon, but they only grew thicker and longer with every grunted breath. Audrey reached out with a tendril of silver mist and retrieved the crown from the curved horns of Archie's staff as Emilio leaped from the back of Rocinante. The young Knight and Steven converged on the Black Bishop who in turn summoned a sphere of translucent deep purple force in an effort to defend himself from their attack even as William continued to tether him to the spot.

"Steven," Lena cried out, "Grey's coughing up blood over here. I don't know how much longer he's got."

Steven narrowed his eyes at Archie. "Heal him."

"And ruin my enjoyment of watching you look on as your beloved mentor bleeds out? Perish the thought."

"Do it." Emilio dismissed the shield and summoned the Knight's axe to his hands, the weapon held high above his shoulder like a batter preparing for a fastball. "Or you're the one who's going to need some magical healing."

"So violent, boy." Archie grinned. "I can't wait to see your end."

"You apparently think that little purple shield of yours will hold back this axe." Emilio tensed to swing on the priest. "Care to put it to the test?"

"Steven." The gurgled word was the first Grey had spoken since Archie shot him. "Let him go. There are things I must tell you, and my time is quickly approaching."

Archie laughed. "Not so tough without your magical 'combat medic' are you?"

"Tough enough." Lena shot up from the ground, the head of her mace blinding in its intensity, and rushed at Archie. "Go to hell, you bastard," she shouted as she ducked beneath Emilio's axe and swung at the priest's leg. Before he could utter another syllable, her bludgeon impacted his shackled ankle, shattering the bone and sending a boot-less Black Bishop flying through the doorway in space. No sooner had he passed from sight than the shimmering hole in space imploded, disappearing with a quiet crackle of electricity.

"Damn, Lena." Steven studied the young woman with new eyes. "That was—"

"No time for that." She dropped the mace to her side and collapsed into Emilio's arms. "Go to him."

Steven dismissed his weaponry and knelt beside Grey, taking the man's already cool hand in his. "Hang on," he whispered as he wadded the corner of the man's duster and pressed hard into the man's chest, trying to staunch the bleeding from the bloody triangle of wounds there. "We'll get you to a hospital. They can—"

"They can do nothing, Steven." Grey extended a pale hand. "Now, listen, for there my time grows short."

"I'm sorry." Steven shook from head to toe, his face burning with guilt and regret. "I didn't know." His gaze fled to the place where the injured Black Bishop had vanished moments before. "He fooled me."

"He fooled us all." Grey murmured as blood trailed from the corner of his mouth. "And from what he said, it would seem, himself more than anyone." He hawked a clotted hunk of deep red onto the asphalt. "But at least your enemy stands revealed before he can stab you in the back once you are all summoned to the Board."

"What am I supposed to do now?" Steven squeezed Grey's hand. "I need you."

"You have learned all you needed from me, Steven, and have surpassed even my greatest hopes. As it has been from the beginning, this collection of Pieces is yours to lead. With the *Hvitr Kyll* by your side, you have selected and prepared a most worthy group, and I could not be prouder to have stood among you." His tired gaze leaped from William to Lena to Emilio to Audrey. "Know this. Steven does not wear the crown in my absence. He is and always has been King." Grey descended into a peal of wet coughs that broke Steven's heart. "Follow him, defend him as he will undoubtedly defend you, and, above all, keep Zed from his prize. Another victory and—" A wet gurgle from deep within Grey's chest cut his admonition short.

Audrey dropped to one knee by Steven's side and took the ancient wizard's other hand. "But what about you, Grey? What happens now?"

"My dear, I have lived more lifetimes than most ever dream and buried more friends than I care to remember. I regret leaving all of you in such a time of upheaval, but even to one with the skill to bend the laws of nature to grant himself centuries on this world, there must eventually come an end." He let go of Audrey's hand and held out his trembling fingers. "The pouch, Steven. Give it to me."

Without a word, Steven placed the *Hvitr Kyll* in Grey's outstretched hand and the pouch answered with its customary drone.

"Now..." Grey's words stumbled out of his mouth two and three at a time, the pauses punctuated with ever longer spells of coughing. "As you did...a night...that now must seem...an eternity ago...reach inside the pouch...and show me...what you find there."

Steven met Audrey's gaze, the crown resting in her grasp. At her subtle nod, he released Grey's hand and dove his shaking fist into the shimmering mouth of the waiting *Hvitr Kyll*. When his hand again emerged, it held a far different marble icon than the one he'd drawn from the pouch months before.

Grey smiled weakly. "Do you finally believe..." he asked with another blood-tinged cough, "my King?"

22

ANTHEM

So, Lena." Steven spun on one heel to take in the surrounding forest of quaking aspen, the leafy canopy above the countless white trunks having begun its shift from summer green to autumn gold. "This is the place?"

Lena stepped to the nearest trunk and rested her hand on a dark knot in the shape of an eye. "This is it."

Rocinante, who munched on a shrub a few feet away, snorted in agreement.

Steven knelt and touched the compact earth at his feet. "And what in the world could have possibly led to you and Grey having a conversation about a forest in the middle of Utah?"

"It was a night not long after we all got back from our little 'all expenses paid vacation' to the past." Lena ran her fingers down the tree's smooth white bark. "I couldn't sleep, and Emilio was snoring like a chainsaw, so I wandered up to the roof of our hotel in Manhattan around three a.m. to get some fresh air. Imagine my surprise when Grey called out my name before my eyes could adjust to the dim."

"He did take special pleasure in doing that." Steven let out a quiet laugh. "I used to call that particular move the 'Reverse-Batman' but never told him. I wasn't sure if he'd get the joke."

"He always knew more than he let on." Audrey wrapped her arm around his shoulders and pulled him in tight. "You of all people should know that."

"He did like his secrets." Emilio knelt by the body wrapped in white sheets "borrowed" from the Wyoming motel where they'd hunkered down for a fretful evening of elusive sleep. "It's funny. Like most of us, I barely knew him, and yet, I really miss him." The young Knight rose, his demeanor uncharacteristically calm other than the shaking fist at his side. "It's like Carlos all over again."

"It's okay, *papi*." Lena stole to Emilio's side and took his hand. "We'll get justice. For Grey. For Carlos. For all of it."

"Justice?" A flash of anger crossed Emilio's features. "You think that's what I want?"

"I certainly hope so." Lena brought his face to hers, the passion in their shared gaze palpable. "If you let that bastard push your buttons, he'll be the one in control, and you and I both know he'd love nothing more than to kill us all, especially you. You have to go into this thing already knowing exactly what you're going to do when you see Vago again. You know it's coming as well as I do." Her eyes dropped. "If you don't..."

"If I don't, what?"

Lena's tear-filled gaze melted Emilio's glare. "I just can't stop replaying that old saying in my head about people seeking revenge needing to start by digging two graves."

"We're all in for the fight of our lives, *mami*." Emilio took Lena's shoulders in his hands to keep her from shaking. "What are you asking of me?"

"I can't lose you, Emilio." She placed a gentle kiss upon his lips and gently pulled his forehead to hers, holding him in the moment. "Promise me you won't do anything—"

"Stupid? Is that what you're going to say?"

"I was going to say foolish, dangerous, unnecessary, a hundred other words."

"But, Lena, Vago's gotta pay for what he—"

"Promise. Me."

A quiet nicker from Rocinante backed up Lena's words.

"Fine," Emilio murmured, "I promise."

"*Te quiero*, Emilio."

He pulled Lena tight to him, the two teens briefly becoming one. "I love you too, Lena."

As Steven looked on in wonder at the utter devotion between two teens not even out of high school, he prayed that no one else in their increasingly small circle would have to die in their fight to right the universe.

But his own words, spoken to Archie atop their Manhattan hotel the morning of Black's most recent assault, came back to haunt him.

"We've been lucky so far, but if there's one thing I know about chess, it's that no game ends with all the pieces on the board."

William, lost in quiet wonder amidst all the trees since their arrival, cleared his throat. "I'm curious, Lena. What was it about this place that Grey loved so much?"

"So many things. He may have been a practitioner of magic from the dawn of civilization, but Grey knew his science just as well." She flung her arm wide, gesturing to the surrounding wood. "These 'trees,' 50,000 strong, are all actually the same tree. Same genetic code, same root system, all bound together for centuries. Collectively, they're called Pando."

"That means 'I spread.'" Audrey grinned at Steven's questioning glance. "Mom made me take Latin in high school. Never dreamed it would come in handy."

Lena nodded. "Grey told me that the best estimates put Pando somewhere between a few thousand and 80,000 years old. It's considered among the oldest living things on the planet. He said the idea of all the different trunks and branches and leaves drawing sustenance from the same roots was a model of his dream for humanity, that someday we would all stand together and share in the sun and rain and nutrients of the earth, not fighting or arguing or killing each other, but reaching together for the stars." She wiped away a tear. "He also said he liked to come here to walk among these quaking aspens that were already ancient the day he was born. It was one of the few places on the planet where he still felt young."

"A most fitting place to bury such a man, with living trees rather than a tombstone to mark his place of rest." William looked to Steven. "I only regret that I didn't get to know him the way the rest of you did."

"Still, you honor him with your presence." Steven pointed to a hollow between two clumps of quaking aspens. "There. I believe that place will do." He shook his head. "I know we're all tempted to linger, but the Game could begin at any moment, and if we're not ready…"

"Say no more." William focused, his skin shifting into the grey bark of a white oak. "Stand back, everyone."

Steven, Audrey, Lena, and Emilio all stepped away from Grey's body as William raised his arms to the sky like a shaman of old. In answer, the massive root systems of the two groups of aspens pulled apart like some miracle from the Old Testament, creating a broad hollow and uncovering earth that hadn't seen the sun in millennia. Rocinante, usually calm during encounters with the unnatural, let out a concerned whinny. Lena slipped to his side and stroked the stallion's broad flank to calm him.

"Audrey," William whispered, "if you please."

The White Queen summoned the mists that obeyed her every command. The shimmering vapors played about her feet and then reached out for the shrouded form of their mentor and friend. With a gentleness only Audrey could impart, she lifted the body into the air and placed Grey's remains in the makeshift grave.

"Any last words, Steven?" William asked.

Steven pulled in a deep cleansing breath and let it out, praying his voice wouldn't crack. "This man we gather together to honor and lay to rest called himself Grey, Rex Caesius, and no doubt a hundred other names we will never learn and that will never be heard again. Like the thousands of white-barked aspens that surround us all, he was already ancient on the day each of us was born and still treated us with kindness and humility even in the midst of all the violence and destruction. My life—hell, all of our lives—would have been safer and more mundane had we never met, but I've got to say, without Grey I'd never have met any of you or learned how much of a difference one person or one group of people could make in the world around them." He looked to Emilio. "I'd never have learned about bravery in the face of insurmountable odds." His eyes shifted to Lena. "Or the power inherent in utter devotion to another." He met William's gaze. "Or the strength to stand up for what you believe in even when all the world stands against you." Finally, his eyes rested on Audrey, his voice cracking as a flood of images, some good and some painful, rushed past his mind's eye. "I never would have learned to love again." He returned his attention to the shrouded form resting between the uprooted aspens. "I owe this man everything, and with God as my witness, we will honor his last wish." Steven reached into the *Hvitr Kyll*, pulled forth the crown, and rested the circle of cool platinum at his brow. "Mr. Two Trees," he whispered as he gestured to Grey's still form, "if you please."

"It would be my honor." William brought his two upraised arms together and interlaced his woody fingers. In answer, the root systems of the two sets of aspen trunks writhed at his command, weaving together root and soil until the wound in the ground before them was healed as if it had never been. "This lone tree with thousands of faces will guard your friend until the day his body is a part of Pando itself." A smiling William met Steven's gaze. "Though already long-lived by any standard, Grey will now live on forever in this place he loved so much."

As they made their way to the lone boulder that marked the spot for both their arrival and exit, Audrey pulled close to Steven. "I'm trying to keep a brave face in front of Lena and Emilio," she whispered, "but there are only five of us now. We've lost Grey, Niklaus... Archie." Her voice choked. "I can't help but wonder who's next."

"We'll make it through, all of us." Steven stopped and brought Audrey's chin up to look deep into her despondent eyes. "I'm not losing any more of you to this madness." He forced a smile. "You believe me, right?"

"This horrible Game we play is a lot like this place. It's older than any of us and, as I understand it, will still be going strong long after all of us are gone." Audrey shook her head. "And even if we all do make it through, that doesn't change what's coming for me afterwards." Her gaze fell. "I want to believe, Steven, but our destinies are no longer in our own hands." She looked back at Grey's grave. "If they ever were."

"WHY DON'T we take the fight to them?" William stared across the makeshift table at Steven, the dim light of the abandoned warehouse in Nowhere, Iowa providing enough illumination to make out the righteous anger in his eyes. "It's stupid to wait for this Game to call us to some wide-open chessboard where they can slaughter us at will." His gaze flicked from Audrey to Emilio to Lena and back to Steven. "The way I see it, bullets seemed to work just fine against your man, Grey. I say we return the favor."

"You want us to gun up and try to kill the other side?" Steven looked on, incredulous. "While I appreciate the sentiment, William, I don't know if we're quite ready for that."

"Well, you'd better get ready, because I'm betting they show up loaded for bear. Meanwhile we're already down two people, and the fighting hasn't even started yet."

"I hate to say it, Steven," Emilio refused to meet his gaze, "but I've got to go with William on this one."

"After everything in Baltimore, Emilio?" Lena shook her head. "Really? Going in guns blazing is the way you want to play this?"

Emilio's lip trembled with a potent mix of anger and anxiety. "I don't know what you want me to say. They've already killed Nik and Grey, and like Archie made all too clear before he took off to join the bad guys, the days where we get fixed up when the battle doesn't go our way are *over*." He turned back to Lena, his expression fraught with emotion. "Don't you think we could use *some* kind of advantage?"

"Let's say you're both right." Steven rose from the overturned crate and paced the concrete floor. "Where are we supposed to get these weapons, William? Think we should knock over a local gun shop?

Maybe find a knife and gun show and walk out with as much as we can carry?"

William rested his elbows on the rough wood. "I was actually thinking we hit a National Guard armory or two with that magical door opener of yours and take what we need."

The room fell silent.

"You can't be serious," Steven said after a dumbfounded pause.

William's lips formed a thin line, devoid of emotion. "Have you ever known me to be anything but serious?"

"You want me to lead the five of us into an armed and guarded facility and steal from the U.S. Government?"

William's mouth curled into a hint of a smile. "Your tax dollars at work, right?"

"It's not just the ethics." Audrey broke her silence. "The whole thing sounds pretty dangerous."

"More dangerous than facing off against an immortal master swordsman, a human flamethrower, a psychotic priest, a crack shot with a bow, and a walking mountain?" William stared around at all of them. "Not to mention, as I understand it, you're all going to be pulling your punches because the enemy front line is currently made up of your family and friends."

"Another reason going in armed to the teeth may not be the best idea." Audrey steepled her trembling fingers before her face. "They've got my mother and grandfather, Steven's dad, Lena's aunt." Her hands dropped to her sides. "This is as much a rescue mission as it is a looming battle."

William gestured to Lena's mace resting head down and dormant next to her on the crate she and Audrey used as a bench. "Bullets or bludgeons, we have a big fight coming, and you're the only one of us who can attack from range." He shook his head. "I'm not much of a chess player, but I know all too well the priority of dispatching the enemy queen. They're going to be gunning for you, Audrey. Don't you want to be ready?"

"We'll be ready." She glanced in Steven's direction. "Our King will make sure of it."

"Our *King*." Emilio didn't try to hide the hint of contempt in his voice.

Steven bristled. "Do you have something to say, Emilio?"

"No." Emilio's entire body shook. "Actually, yes."

"Fine." Steven sat back at the table. "Let's hear it."

"I guess I still don't understand why we're only now hearing of your suspicions about Archie. I'd noticed you watching him like a hawk every now and then, but to find out you took him with you to Antarctica of all places to have it out. You played right into his hands. Hell, he almost got away with the crown." Emilio's eyes rolled. "Excuse me...*your* crown."

"What would you have had me do? Call him out in front of all of you? Embarrass the old man when I didn't have a shred of evidence to back up my suspicions?" Steven pounded a fist on the wooden crate that served as the meeting table. "What if I was wrong?"

"But you weren't wrong." Audrey covered his hand with hers. "I didn't suspect Archie, Emilio. Did you?" She turned to face Lena. "What about you, Lena? Did you see this coming?" She rose from the table. "From Archie's own lips, he made it clear he's been fooling us all right from the very beginning and Steven was the only one of us who even had a clue something was off." She crossed her arms before her and stared off into space, too angry to look anyone in the eye. "Look. Grey is gone, and there's nothing we can do about it. We're angry and hurt and afraid, but we've got to stick together or Nik and Grey won't be the last of us to fall." Her eyes went to Steven. "A man who was centuries old when each of us was born and had walked among dozens upon dozens of generations believed Steven was the best person to lead us. Unless any of you want to step up and take the job, I suggest we trust the man who has pulled each of our asses out of the literal fire and stop arguing amongst ourselves."

"I still say we ought to—"

"Mr. Two Trees, you're new here, and we'd be up shit creek if you hadn't stopped Archie from fleeing with the crown, but this isn't a battle we're going to win going in guns blazing like we're in a Stallone/Schwarzenegger double feature." Audrey turned to Emilio. "And you, Mr. Hothead. Check yourself. You and Lena both owe Steven your lives, same as me. He'd never say it himself, but don't you think he deserves some respect or, at the very least, the benefit of the doubt? None of the rest of us, Grey included, had the first clue anything was wrong."

"I suppose." Emilio studied the floor, sullen, and then stretched his hand across the table to Steven. "Look, I'm sorry. I'm just so mad, I want to start punching and, unfortunately, the only punching bag here is you."

"It's all right, Emilio." Steven took the young man's hand and shook it. "You've got to understand that no one here is angrier or more hurt about what went down than me."

All five took a collective moment of silence to allow the air to clear. In the end, Lena was the next to speak.

"So, Steven." Her voice was small. "What do we do now?"

"William's idea of going on the offense does seem to have some merit, don't you think?" Audrey's gaze flicked in the White Rook's direction. "Minus, of course, the heavy artillery."

"Agreed, except for the simple fact that we don't have any way of finding them." Steven pulled in a deep breath. "We finally know that the only way the Black kept locating us was Archie. The pouch can take me to any of you, but until the time of the Game, the same rules that keep Black from appearing here and attacking all of us protect them as well."

"At least while he's the lone Bishop of the Game, Archie doesn't get his visions," Emilio added. "That's one thing we've got going for us."

"We're back to waiting, then." Lena shook her head in frustration. "At least we've had a lot of practice."

"Actually…" William sat bolt upright on his section of crate. "I have a bad feeling the waiting is over."

"What do you mean?" Steven focused, curious if William was experiencing the bizarre pains that signified the presence of the Black. "What's happening?"

"The trees," William whispered. "I can sense them, always. Their presence. Their energy. During the day, when the sun is high in the sky, they all talk incessantly, and at night, they rest."

"What about now?" Steven asked. "What is it you feel?"

"Confusion. Outrage. Fear." He looked to Steven. "What you'd expect from a person struggling for air."

Steven rose from the table and walked to the warehouse's enormous sliding door. Pulling it open a foot, he peered up at the heavens, the sky no longer a light crimson but the deep red of an open wound.

"Guys, get ready." Amaryllis fluttered at his chest. "I think this is—"

23

OPENING CEREMONY

I t."

The roar of the pouch left Steven's ears ringing as the five of them appeared at the edge of a high cliff, bare rock the color of ochre beneath their feet. Half a breath later, Rocinante materialized between Emilio and Lena, a quiet whinny escaping his equine lips.

"Of all places, we're supposed to fight here?" Steven muttered under his breath.

The vista that filled his vision was of a place he'd always wanted to see, one to which he'd often dreamed of road tripping with Katherine and any children that might have come along by then.

One of the most famous and unmistakable locations in the entire world.

Directly ahead and across a mighty chasm, a vast formation of rock met the vermilion sky in a uniform straight line that stretched in either direction, the various strata of black and white and brown and orange trailing down to a winding river that snaked hundreds of feet below.

Steven never dreamed his first time laying eyes on the alternating layers of limestone formed millions of years before man walked the Earth might also be his last day on the planet.

"The Grand Canyon." Audrey slid her hand into his, their fingers intertwining. "Right?"

"Looks like it." Lena joined them at the edge, her hand at her forehead to block the rays of the sun sitting high in the blood red sky. "The eastern end of it, anyway. As I recall, this thing hits 18 miles across at its widest, but along here the other side can't be more than half a mile."

"If that." Steven pointed across the canyon at the colossal edifice that captivated all of their attentions. "Though the last time I checked, that monstrosity wasn't on any of the tourist websites."

He'd seen it all before, a fever dream that played across his subconscious as he dangled injured and dazed from the first Black Knight's charging steed the night he'd met Audrey.

The blood red sky.

The vast chasm punctuated by the meandering river that flowed at its bottom.

The black castle on the opposite side, its foundations flush with the limestone at the far edge as if it were just another part of the landscape.

Only one thing remained missing.

"There's supposed to be a bridge."

"What?" Audrey stared across the chasm. "A bridge?"

"I've seen this." Steven's eyes narrowed. "Our fortress on one side, theirs on the other, with a checkered bridge between us where both sides are supposed to stand and fight."

"No bridge here," Emilio stepped up, peering left and right, "and no castle, at least not one for us."

"Unless I miss my guess, our shelter falls under the purview of the Rook." William stepped forward, his skin again taking on the dull white of the mighty oaks that would soon represent him on a checkered battlefield imagined centuries before. "If you all will give me a moment..."

At the center of their party of five, William Two Trees knelt and placed both palms flat on the stone beneath their feet. Nothing happened at first, but Steven waited. He'd seen one too many miracles in the preceding months to count their new Rook out so quickly.

He wasn't disappointed.

The rumbling started quietly, but soon the earth rocked beneath their feet. The limestone on which they stood cracked and split, the miniature earthquake radiating backward from the canyon edge and fracturing the rocky surface for a hundred yards in every direction. In a blink, the ochre rock beneath them went green as thousands of tiny shoots and leaves sprouted through the splintered stone. Another breath, and the entire area burgeoned with a multitude of saplings that grew taller and broader by the second, achieving in minutes what would normally take years.

"Slow down, William," Steven shouted to the White Rook who had disappeared behind a rapidly growing group of tree trunks. "At this rate, we're going to be crushed."

"Have faith, Steven Bauer," came a voice from the quickly growing canopy above their heads. "The same faith we all have in you."

In less time than seemed possible, the area stood transformed from barren rock to a forest fortress complete with oaken walls, beech buttresses, and poplar spires. The ground beneath their feet erupted in a thick carpet of moss, while above their heads, a dense canopy of leaves blocked out the sun, leaving them in near total darkness.

"Great," Emilio muttered with an ironic laugh, "now we can't see."

Rocinante answered his master's grumble with a frustrated snort.

Before Steven could say a word, a tiny spot of phosphorescence appeared above Emilio's head, then another, and another. Soon, the entire area was lit up with the roving spots of light. For the first time since their arrival, he smiled, his turn in mood punctuated by a quick flutter of Amaryllis' wings against his chest.

"Huh," he whispered, "fireflies."

Lena marched over to Steven, her beaming grin just visible in the dim but growing light. "Like Grey said back east on the island where we found Rocinante, 'Nature's little lamps.'"

"Good memory." He peered around. "William," he called out, "I'm curious. Did *you* summon the fireflies?"

"Like I know how any of this works." William stepped around an enormous trunk that served as one of the columns of their newly formed tower of trees, his russet skin returned to its normal state.

"Though I am glad you all can see now." His brow furrowed. "Why do you ask?"

"No reason." Steven pulled in a breath. "Just trying to put it all together."

William led them all through the arboreal maze to a massive arched doorway formed from twisted ironwood that looked out upon the canyon and the dark keep of their enemies.

"What's happening there?" Lena pointed into the distance. "Are they attacking us already?"

Steven followed Lena's finger and focused his vision on the base of Zed's fortress. There, an outcropping of black granite stretched across the chasm, the rushing mass of stone rocketing in their direction like a giant's fist.

"Clearly the work of the Black Rook," he scratched his chin, "but what's she doing?"

"You said there's supposed to be a bridge, right?" William stretched out his muscular arm, his skin shifting yet again to the rough grey-white bark of his oaken form. "Here it comes."

Woody tendrils sprang forth from the broken rock at their feet, and soon, the roots of their castle of trunk and branch and twig and leaf stretched across the expanse at a furious pace.

Audrey shook her head. "I keep thinking that all of this will stop amazing me at some point."

"And yet," Lena whispered, "it never does."

The enormous arm of black stone and the mass of ivory roots raced at each other like lovers desperate to embrace after years apart. In less time than Steven thought possible, the two sides met in the middle with a deafening thunderclap. Then, with a rumble felt more than heard, the conglomerations of alabaster wood and black stone began to intercalate, the tendrils of woody growth forcing their way between the cracks in the rock and the dark granite filling the spaces all along the outgrowth of William's fortress of trees. This dance of wood and stone, all set to a tune of impossible physics, played out over several minutes. The outcome, however, was never in doubt.

"One checkered battlefield," Emilio murmured, "no waiting."

A hundred feet wide, the half-mile bridge stretched from forest fortress to granite keep, the entire structure divided into alternating ten-foot squares of tightly packed oaken roots and smooth black stone. Braided wood and rock formed the parapets at either side of the mighty expanse, while three columns of spiral oak and granite stretched down into the canyon below.

"Without the energies of the Game, you couldn't build something like this in a thousand years." Lena returned from her exploration of the north and south edges of their end of the massive bridge and knelt between the white and black squares at the center of their back row. In wonder, she ran a finger along the tiny crevice separating root and rock and looked up at Steven. "When this is done—if the bridge survives the next twenty-four hours, of course—the park rangers, the tourists—hell, anybody—they're not going to know what to think.

"A problem for another day." Steven stepped to Lena's side and onto the middle black square. "Now it's time to fight for our lives."

"Not to mention the lives of everyone we love." Audrey stepped to Lena's other side and onto the white square to Steven's left. Taking his hand for what could possibly be the last time, she gave it a squeeze, and then the two of them moved to the centers of their respective squares. "Ready?"

Steven reached into the *Hvitr Kyll*, retrieved the crown, and placed the simple circle of platinum at his brow. "As ready as I'm going to be."

Surrounded by the ebon stone of the White King's square, Steven did his best to maintain his brave facade before the others. Months of preparing to stand on this battlefield as a small army of eight had done little to prepare him mentally for the reality of being not only the leader, but the main target of an entire force of superhuman enemies that could attack at any moment. He'd been prepared, as a mere Pawn, to lose aspects of himself in defense of the others and had prayed that at least one would remain in the end to escort home the woman he'd come to love.

Now, standing beside Audrey on the nightmare chessboard with he as King and her as Queen, he wondered at the symmetry of it even while swallowing back the fear that neither of them would see the next morning.

Emilio and Lena went next, stepping together onto a square of dark granite two to Steven's right. Rocinante followed, moving between the pair, his equine eyes never leaving the dark castle in the distance.

"Are you sure about this Lena?" Steven already knew what she was going to say. "Technically, this isn't your fight."

"The truth, Steven? If I didn't already know your heart so well, I'd be a bit insulted." Lena glanced at the love of her life before returning her resigned gaze to Steven. "At this point, I thought it would go without saying that till all of this is over, I'm sticking to Emilio like glue."

"Yeah." Emilio took her hand in his. "Me and Lena, we're in this together, to the end."

Rocinante let out a defiant whinny, muting the dread at Steven's core, though the last word in Emilio's brave declaration stuck with him.

"In that case, make sure to watch each other's backs." Steven glanced back at their Rook with a hopeful smile. "Care to join us, William?"

"I stand ready to fight." William's chin dropped to his chest in concentration as again his body commenced the miraculous transformation from ordinary man to his twofold namesake. The change occurred more quickly this time as William seemed able to draw mass and power from the arboreal fortress he'd brought forth from the stone. In less time than seemed possible, a pair of fifty-foot twisted white oaks lumbered in opposite directions to assume the outer two squares of White's back row. "I await your command, my King."

As Steven tried to process the sudden respect from their Rook. Audrey stole to the edge of her square. "I feel bad saying it out loud, but we're looking a little sparse." She peered up and down their line. "And the last time we fought the forces of the Black on a bridge, if you recall, didn't go so well."

"We're all we've got, Audrey." Steven's eyes slid closed as he summoned for the first time the garb and accoutrements of the White King. Flowing down from the crown of burnished platinum, the glyphs along its surface glowing with an inner light, a shimmer passed over his body, transforming his ordinary street clothes into raiment more appropriate for battle. Plates of dull white metal appeared at his chest, abdomen, and back, rushing past his nethers and down his extremities until he stood completely encased in an intricate suit of armor befitting royalty. In a flash of blinding brilliance, an open-faced helm materialized about his head, the platinum crown incorporated into its very substance. A white cape edged with embroidery of silver thread flowed from his shoulders to his knees even as a sudden weight at his hip let him know the weapon of the King now rested at his side.

He reached one gauntleted hand down to the side opposite from where the *Hvitr Kyll* hung and drew forth his blade, a gleaming silver broadsword with a handle wrapped in white silk. The heft felt natural in his hand, as if he'd held the sword before, as if it belonged there in his armored grip.

Grey's last words echoed through his mind.

In an alleyway behind a diner in the middle of Wyoming, his friend and mentor had lain bleeding and pale, his head lying askance in Lena's lap. Steven knelt at one side and Audrey the other as Emilio and William looked on from a few feet away.

"*The crown.*" Grey had whispered between wet gurgles, his eyes never leaving Steven's. "*I'd like to see it upon your brow at least once before I pass beyond the veil.*"

Steven nodded and reached out to Audrey who held the crown in her trembling fingers. She placed the circle of platinum in his hand, its already familiar weight somehow different now that he knew who would truly be leading them all into battle.

"*You're sure I'm the one?*" Steven asked.

"*You always did ask too many questions.*" Grey chuckled, his lips parting in one last smile. "*Did you not draw the King icon from the pouch?*" His weak laugh descended into a peal of coughing. "*Don the crown. I'm sure you'll find it fits quite nicely.*"

And in that moment where Steven had finally accepted his destiny, he'd found that the crown did indeed fit, as if custom made for him and him alone.

"What now?" Audrey asked, bringing him back to the present. "Do we wait? Advance?"

"Hang on a sec." Steven glanced left and right, the new helm interfering a bit with his peripheral vision, and made a strange discovery. Just as his mind's eye somehow integrated the disparate input from eight sets of eyes and ears when he was divided into the octet of Pawns, now he saw not only with his own eyes, but with a grander vision that allowed him to perceive the Board as if from above.

"So," he muttered, "not just the King, it seems, but the player as well."

I may die today. Emilio's voice sounded in Steven's head. *But not before I make that motherfucker pay for what he did to Carlos.*

"Emilio?"

"Yeah?" The White Knight looked at him quizzically.

I'm made of wood, came William's deep baritone, *and the Queen of the bad guys is a walking flamethrower.*

Emilio needs you, Lena. The girl's voice floated next through his subconscious. *Don't let him see that you're scared out of your mind.*

Steven focused, lowering the trio of voices in his head to a whisper. Even as he asked himself the obvious question, it came to him. As both King and player, he'd need to know what his various Pieces were thinking, feeling, and doing even as he'd need to be able to communicate with them in an instant. The phenomenon had happened only once before, the night Audrey's life rested in the hands of the original Black Knight.

That's when a few things clicked.

First, if this ability to communicate mind-to-mind with the other Pieces was indeed a power of the King, then Zed's ease at tracking them down time and time again no longer seemed strange at all.

Second, Grey had never once used such an ability with him or the others.

And most importantly, any doubt that he'd been King from the beginning was swept away like a grain of sand in a hurricane.

Audrey? He reached out with his thoughts to the first mind that he'd ever touched in this way. At first, he heard nothing, but then, even as the other three voices continued their low murmur at the back of his head, the voice of the White Queen came through loud and clear.

It doesn't matter what happens to me today.

Audrey's words struck him like a physical blow.

When this is over, whether Zed and the others get me or not, I'm dead.

Matter-of-fact. Without emotion. A mental exercise she'd clearly performed a thousand times.

So get in there and fight.

Audrey? Steven tried again. *Can you hear me?*

Steven? At the mental invocation of his name, the stonewalls around her emotions fell to the ground. *Are you doing this?*

He projected a mental laugh. *Comes with the crown, I guess.*

And the others?

I can hear them too.

Can they hear me?

I hear you both. William's rough tones filled Steven's mind. *So, in addition to everything else, you all can speak mind-to-mind?*

We can now. Emilio glared at Steven. *I guess that means privacy's out the window.*

Come on, Emilio. Lena squeezed Emilio's hand even as she reached out with her mind. *Anything that helps keep us alive is a good thing, right?*

After a healthy pause, Emilio grumbled with both mouth and mind, "I suppose."

"Sorry to break up whatever powwow this is you have going on..." The familiar voice, spoken calmly at normal volume and yet amplified so they could all hear it, emanated from further along the bridge. "But the day isn't getting any shorter."

Even before he looked up, that old familiar sensation at the core of Steven's being let him know they were no longer alone, a pinch at his collarbone and the nervous whinny hitting his ears together confirming their respite from the realities of Zed and Grey's Game was over.

Some sixty feet away on a square of alabaster wood one column to the left of Steven's own square stood Wahnahtah, dressed in his ceremonial Blackfoot armor, bow in hand and arrow nocked.

The enemy front line took their squares, one after another, each in a flash of deepest violet, wearing various iterations of armor fashioned from black leather and dark chainmail. One by one, the seven

Pawns pulled back their hoods, each with a sneer across their features and a taunt for their five adversaries.

"I see you've replaced my once lover with a pair of trundling trees." Victoria cracked her dark whip, the shards of metal at its tip popping with ebon electricity. "I look forward to watching our Rook smash yours a second time."

"If the back row even needs to come out." Woody, from his corner far to Steven's left, hefted his ebony-handled battle-axe before his chest. "I suspect this axe of mine can make short work of a couple of oaks."

"Hello, Lena." Renata crossed her pair of daggers before her and studied her niece with a cruel grin. "I've looked forward to this moment when I can end the imposition of your presence in my life." She studied Emilio with cold eyes. "And to think, it was all so you could stay on the same side of the ocean with this orphaned rat."

"At least you haven't had to play nursemaid to a dying child, Renata." Deborah locked eyes with Audrey. "Oh, my darling daughter, your horrible suffering, along with your endless mewling, will both soon be over."

"Silence, all of you." The Black King's Pawn directed the tip of his pike at Steven, the pole fashioned from dark walnut and the head forged from metal of deepest grey. "We face a solemn duty, to serve the Black King and defend him at all costs." Donald narrowed his eyes at his son. "I don't relish the thought of slaying my own flesh and blood, but he now stands before us as the enemy King."

"You may not bear the Bauer-King any ill will, Donald, but with God as my witness, I hope it's me who gets to crush his damned skull." Pulling back his hood, Arthur Pedone glared at Steven, the seventh Black Pawn's face beet red with anger and animosity. "The only woman I've ever loved has carried a torch for him every minute of our sixty-five years together and for that humiliation, he's going to pay."

Not the old man who had welcomed Steven into his home in Maine months before, the Arthur that stood before them bore the youthful features of the young man he'd met in the New York City of 1946, recently back from war and well on his way toward falling in love with the first woman he'd seen since his return. Any kindness that had resided in the young man's eyes, however, had evaporated, replaced with a level of hate he hadn't thought Arthur capable of.

Only one of the Black Pawns remained unrevealed, but Steven knew all too well whose dark eyes awaited beneath that last hood.

With a dancer's grace, the final Pawn pulled back the cloth from her head of voluminous blond curls. Those eyes that had sent his heart racing on many an occasion during his exile to the past looked on him with a potent mix of anger and pain and hunger and lust.

"Hello, lover." Ruth Matheson Pedone ran her tongue along her teeth like a predator preparing to lunge for the jugular. "It's been a while."

24

NO CONTEST

Both sides stood in silence atop the checkered bridge, each taking the other's measure. Steven took advantage of the momentary ceasefire to communicate mind-to-mind with each of the Pieces in his charge. He nursed Audrey's wounded feelings, assuaged Emilio's anger, reined in Lena's defiance, calmed William's fears, and kept a skittish Rocinante from charging to his death.

When it became clear that none among the White would allow themselves to be baited, his father broke the silence.

"The only question now, I suppose," Donald paused mid-sentence, his cold gaze running along the seven figures that represented all that remained of Black's opposition, "is which side is going to go first?"

"It is customary for White to initiate the battle, is it not?" William's voice echoed in stereo from the pair of gigantic oaks at either end of their back row. "What's our opening move, Steven?"

A little something to even the odds. He racked his brain for anything that might turn this situation into something other than a bloodbath. Literally anything.

And then, a word popped into his head, a word all but foreign to him the first time he spoke it, but now one that flowed off his tongue as easily as his own name.

"Phalanx."

In a blink, the row before the gathered White sat empty no longer. Eight doppelgangers of Steven, each dressed in the tunic, pantaloons, and boots of the White Pawn, filled the octet of squares, increasing by eight the sets of perceptions roiling through his mind. "Shield," the Pawns shouted in unison, then "Helm," their two-part command summoning eight long ovals of marbled platinum to their collective left arm and eight gleaming helmets atop their identical heads. "Pike," came their eightfold cry as each brought their shield to the front, the call answered by eight flashes of blinding silver light. When all gathered could again see, the row of foot soldiers waited toothless no longer as an eight-foot pole arm of poplar crowned with gleaming silver now rested in each Pawn's hand.

"Your move, Wahnahtah." Steven forced confidence into his words, though he didn't forget for a moment exactly who and what they were up against. "Last chance to release your hostages. Let's leave the fighting to those of us who are actually supposed to be here."

"While you keep your full complement of Pawns, of course." Wahnahtah sneered. "Thank you, Bauer, but I think we'll retain these conscripts to our front line. After all, fair is fair, and, as you can see, none of them seems to be chomping at the bit to leave."

"I don't know what you've done to brainwash them into acting this way, but let my mother and grandfather go." Audrey summoned the silver mists of the White Queen from the ether. "They have no part in this."

"To the contrary, Miss Richards. While neither your family nor the others were actually chosen by the *Svartr Kyll*, they are no less a part of the Game than any of you. Do they not stand on the Board like you, armed, armored, and ready to fight for their lives?" Wahnahtah retreated to the rear of his square. "But enough with your stalling. You do nothing but delay the inevitable." The Blackfoot warrior dismissed his bow and summoned his axe, holding it high above his head. "Pawns of the Black, attack!"

A tiny part of Steven had dared hope that once the Game proper began and they all stood atop the Board, the full-on battle that had been their reality for months might shift to something more resembling the actual game of chess, a flicker of hope snuffed as the collective war cry of Black's front line filled the air.

Wahnahtah led the charge, his axe high above his head and his own full-length shield held before him, the only one among the charging enemy with any defense beyond the dark leather and chainmail each of the remaining seven wore. The next part of Zed's foul plan crystallized in Steven's mind: Black's line of Pawns could maim and kill at the whim of their master; meanwhile, none among the White dared bring anything approaching their full power against any of them save Wahnahtah without risking injury of an innocent loved one.

One thing was certain: The bloodthirst blazing in each set of eyes among the rushing Pawns guaranteed the same quarter would not be granted.

"He's sent everyone we love on a suicide mission to kill us," Steven muttered to himself. "Bastard."

"Steven," Audrey's voice trembled, "what do we do?"

"The only thing we can." He drew his sword. "We defend ourselves."

At Steven's mental command, the line of White Pawns drew in close, forming a half-circle in front of his and Audrey's squares. Shoulder to shoulder and shield to shield, they leveled the tips of their pikes at chest level, their formation resembling an armored porcupine with not nearly enough quills. Lena, Emilio, and Rocinante mustered between their King and Queen while the twin oaks that comprised William Two Trees' split consciousness formed up on either end of the arc of Pawns.

"*Ready or not,*" Steven broadcast mentally to the others, "*here they come.*"

Wahnahtah's brainwashed foot soldiers broke on White's front line like a dark wave crashing against a marble cliff. As the eight Pawns held their loved ones at bay with shield and pike, Steven kept a close eye on Wahnahtah who had stopped halfway through the ululating charge and now stood twenty feet away at the intersection of four squares.

"Bow," the Blackfoot whispered, the movement of his lips barely visible due to his dark face paint, though the white line that stretched from temple to temple accentuated the gleam in his dark eyes as he summoned his favored weapon. "Shaft."

"Incoming," Steven shouted. "Watch him."

Wahnahtah raised his bow, scanning White's front line with a mix of focus and glee as he searched for any weakness to exploit. His arrows had penetrated Steven's defense before, hitting one of Vago's boys back in Baltimore and nearly ending Audrey in Atlanta. But that was with the Black Pawn using the brute force of eight archers, each firing faster than humanly possible. Defending against a lone archer seemed a less daunting task, though Steven knew all too well that Wahnahtah wouldn't let fly a single arrow unless he planned to make it count.

Donald and Deborah, armed respectively with pike and spear, posed the biggest threat as their weapons allowed them to probe the wall of shields without getting too close. The remaining five, however, pressed the attack with a furor bordering on madness. Woody and Arthur, armed with battle-axe and war hammer, punched at Steven's line without fatigue, leaving little doubt that, given time, they would make their way to White's final rank. Victoria lashed out time and again with her whip, working to open up a chink in White's defense to allow the Black Pawn on either side of her to land a blow. Ruth with her rapier and Renata with her paired daggers also probed side-by-side at the Pawn's wall of shields, two vipers taking turns striking in an effort to land one venomous bite.

"What now, Steven?" Emilio grunted. "I don't dare bring out either lance or axe, not against them."

"Leave it to me." Audrey pulled the silver mists that were her destiny close around her and set the octet of floating balls of energy orbiting about her shoulders. "I should be able to incapacitate them without hurting them."

A rumble from either end of the row filled the air as both mighty oaks took a step forward. "I can try to stop them as well." William's words hit their ears like a whisper of wind through ten thousand leaves. "Let me try."

"No." Steven shook his head. "Stay put, all of you. Our loved ones may be all juiced up with whatever Zed is using to make them attack us, but they're still only human." He narrowed his eyes. "No one can go on like this forever."

"Indeed, Bauer." Wahnahtah's words hit their ears as if amplified as the Black Pawn let fly his first arrow. A Pawn to Steven's forward left easily blocked the bolt but paid the price as the tip of Ruth's rapier found his thigh.

Steven winced in pain at his doppelganger's wound, but held fast in his square, his mind racing for a different tactic or strategy to bring them all through the next few minutes alive.

Wahnahtah threw his head back in laughter. "At last, I see the folly in my tactics." He nocked another arrow and again studied Steven's line. "I've always attacked en masse with bow or axe but never considered how difficult it might be to defend against both at once." And with that, the Blackfoot warrior let fly his second shaft.

A Pawn to Steven's right blocked the lethal missile as easily as the first, but the brief distraction proved his undoing. A flick of Victoria's wrist sent her whip flying at his neck, and in less than a blink, barbed leather the color of night dug at the Pawn's windpipe. Like a spider drawing a fly into her web, she pulled the Pawn hand over hand from his rank, never once letting up on the leather's choking tension, until he was out in the open and defenseless, at which point Arthur and Deborah finished the task with war hammer and spear.

Taking advantage of the break in Steven's line, Wahnahtah let fly another barbed missile which impacted the next Pawn's suddenly defenseless flank, imbedding itself in his hip with a horrifying thunk of stone on bone.

Steven's knees threatened to buckle at the triplicate pain of one Pawn's fall and the other two's injuries, but he refused to give Wahnahtah the pleasure of seeing him falter.

"Steven!" Audrey rushed to his side. "Are you all right?"

He shot his Queen an agonized glance. "I'm keeping the pain from the others so they can keep up the defense, but—"

A third arrow, its shaft an inch in diameter, struck Steven center chest. The bolt ricocheted off his plate armor, though the force of the impact nearly sent him reeling from the Board.

"Difficult to concentrate, is it not, Bauer-King?" hissed Ruth to his left. "When your emotions are running high and your entire world is coming down around your ears?"

"This isn't you, Ruth." Steven summoned the King's shield to his arm and swore to himself to keep at least one eye on Wahnahtah until the battle was over. "Whatever it is they've done to you, fight it."

"All Zed has done is free my mind from your poison." She laughed as she stabbed again at one of the Pawns with her rapier. "The memory of you has haunted me for decades, but after today, I will finally be free."

"You must know that you will fall," Arthur grunted as he struck with his war hammer again and again at the remaining two Pawns to Steven's right. "Surrender now and perhaps Zed will be merciful with your deaths."

"No matter what you choose, however, it's only a matter of time," shouted Woody from the far left, his axe, inches from a Pawn's neck, blocked by an upraised shield. "Lay down your arms and accept your fate."

"Or don't," Donald shouted as his pike found the calf of his opponent. "The outcome will be no different."

"Dad…" Steven ground his teeth to hold back the tears that blurred his vision. "No…"

What has Zed done to them?

No sooner did the question flicker through his mind, than Wahnahtah offered an answer.

"I suspect you'd like to think I speak through them, that it's my words coming from their lips." The Black Pawn fired another arrow, this one impacting the shield of the newly-wounded White King's Pawn. "Zed may have found a way to unlock their darker nature, but know that every word and thought is genuine and unfiltered, straight from the source." He laughed as he loosed another arrow, this one missing Audrey's head by mere inches. "How does it feel, hearing such hate and resentment from the ones you love?"

Steven forced the pain and nausea broadcast by the trio of

wounded Pawns from his mind as well as his anguish at Wahnahtah's words and surveyed their tiny battlefield. The pair of uninjured Pawns to his right held their own against Donald, Arthur, Victoria, and Deborah, though the two-to-one odds forced them to remain completely on the defensive. Meanwhile, the pair to his left fought valiantly to hold Woody, Renata, and Ruth at bay. All split their attention between the melee directly before them as well as the archer to the enemy's rear, a factor sure to end with another mistake, another injury, another fall. The three wounded Pawns who had tasted Ruth's blade, Donald's pike, and Wahnahtah's flint worked together to pull themselves back and regroup, their every movement sending excruciating pain back through their link with the White King, yet another distraction that might end up getting them all killed.

He did his best not to think about the part of himself that lay unmoving at Victoria's feet, a part of himself that was gone forever.

"Audrey," Steven grunted through the pain as he pointed to their right forward line. "Do what you can to plug up our defenses over there."

"On it." Audrey sent four of the eight spheres of silver energy flying at Donald, Arthur, Victoria, and Deborah in an effort to give the duo of fatiguing Pawns a momentary respite.

"William," he shouted aloud. "Push forward and help guard the flanks.

"Done." The pair of giant oaks strode forward, their lowest branches deploying to bolster the ends of White's struggling defense.

"The rest of you, pull together and hold the line."

A mental message to the three wounded Pawns directed them to stay down and out of the battle, though Steven knew it wouldn't be long till they would have to fight again. Their circle had grown tight, and their loved ones conscripted into darkness showed no sign of slowing down their vicious assault.

"Why do you fight, Bauer?" Wahnahtah's whispered question filled the space. "Our victory, as it has been from the beginning, remains inevitable." His painted face turned up in a wicked grin. "Can you see the symmetry in your fall from grace? You may have risen from the lowliest position on the Board to King of the White, but minutes or even seconds from now, it will be a mere Pawn that brings you low."

"You haven't won yet." Steven's mind leaped between each of the remaining four Pawns in his line and found each more fatigued than the one before. "We'll find a way."

"In the beginning," Wahnahtah continued, "I assumed the first stage would come down to a battle of wills between you and me, a true Blackfoot warrior versus yet another White plunderer." He let fly another pair of arrows, each embedding in one of the twin oaks that made up White's pair of Rooks. "To know that I, the lone Black Pawn, will defeat you without even the most meager assistance from Zed's back row brings me joy beyond compare."

"To the contrary, my brother." The tandem voice of William Two Trees echoed from the pair of gigantic oaks and down into the canyon below. "It is you who have allied yourself with the aggressor."

From either end of White's ever-shrinking line, the pair of enormous oaks let fly with a shower of fist-sized acorns that pelted the Black Pawn like a thousand bullets, knocking him flat to the bridge's surface.

"You, Wahnahtah of the Blackfoot, have dishonored yourself, your family, and our people with your choices."

Another shower of acorns flew at the Black Pawn who quickly dismissed bow in favor of his shield.

"So, 'brother.'" Wahnahtah forced himself to his feet. "You stand before me, a pair of unassailable giants, and still you hide behind the White man's defenses?" He dropped his shield to the Board and summoned his axe. "This is not the warrior's way, but the way of the coward."

"Coward?" William's voice, still a whisper of wind through a canopy of leaves, grew cold and angry. "I'll show you a coward." The fifty-foot oaken combatants stepped forward as one and with their shared second step, converged on the Black Pawn.

"William," Steven shouted. "No!"

"Yes," Wahnahtah taunted. "Come to me, Rook. Show me what you're made of."

William had closed nearly half the distance between himself and

Wahnahtah when a shimmer in the air next to the Black Pawn sent Steven's intestines into knots.

For all the power inherent in Black's newly formed front row, the true heavy hitters along Zed's back row remained far more dangerous. Kept out of sight and, therefore, out of mind, even Steven had allowed himself to be lulled into a tragic false sense of security.

The time for such games, however, was over.

Stepping from the dark ripple in space, Magdalene took her square and wasted no time sending a stream of dark fire hurtling at the rushing oak to her left. Within seconds, the tree's entire canopy had burst into flames, leaving that half of William in agony, the screams of the White Rook simultaneously assaulting Steven's ears and mind.

"Tsk, tsk, Steven." Magdalene stepped forward a square and fixed the White King with her emerald gaze. "Sending out both Rooks to take care of a mere Pawn? It's like you've never played this game."

Before any of them could say another word, the gigantic tree set aflame rushed to the edge of the bridge and hurtled itself over the side, leaving the checkered bridge silent.

"One down," Magdalene sneered, "one to go."

Wahnahtah gestured to the remaining oaken Rook who paused halfway between White's front line and the Black Pawn and Queen. "Woody, Arthur, bring your axe and hammer and help me bring down that damned tree." He again summoned his bow. "As well as the *coward* at its heart."

As the two summoned Pawns joined Wahnahtah in a three-pronged assault of the remaining Rook, Magdalene brought forth her customary dais of dark energy beneath her feet and floated up into the sky.

"I must say," she crinkled her nose in disgust, "I'm not sure the switch from rocky colossus to a pair of old trees ready for a bonfire was the most inspired strategy."

Audrey, Lena, and Emilio atop Rocinante rushed forward to aid the four uninjured Pawns of the White in their continued struggle against the diminished but still formidable Black front line as Wahnahtah, Woody, and Arthur surrounded William. The White Rook had the advantage of size, but he was outnumbered, and Steven knew all too well that, in chess, a single Pawn could all too easily bring down a Rook.

Or even a King.

"How does it feel Bauer?" Wahnahtah shouted as he lopped off one of William's low hanging branches with his hand-axe. "To know that your great victory over me in Atlanta has cost you the Game, everyone you love, and even your own life?"

Steven ground his teeth. "The Game isn't over yet, Wahnahtah."

But wasn't it?

No matter how long they fought, nothing would change the fact that they'd have to pull every punch for the rest of this battle for fear of maiming or killing someone they cared about while those same loved ones clearly shared no such reservations. And Black's Knight, Bishop, Rook, and King all waited in the wings, fresh for the fight.

Barring a miracle, Zed's victory was inevitable.

And it was all Steven's fault.

Though seemingly a brilliant ploy at the time, by wiping out seven of the eight Black Pawns in Atlanta, he and Niklaus had left seven spots vacant along the enemy front line, and with nowhere else to go, the energies of those squares were free to invade and control the minds of others, leaving their loved ones, as far as Steven could understand, possessed by darkness.

And the only priest alive with the power to perform an exorcism in this particular Game apparently had defected to the other side long before they'd ever met. Without Archie, there was no way to heal their thoughts, to push the darkness from their minds.

But, Steven gasped at the sudden inspiration, *perhaps it could be...pulled?*

A vigorous flutter at his chest confirmed the merit in his mustard seed of an idea.

Audrey, he broadcast his thoughts, *I've got to step away for a moment.*

Now? The panic in Audrey's mental question was audible. *Where the hell are you going?*

To get help. He sucked in a breath, sheathed his sword, and freed the pouch from his belt.

From where? she asked.

The last place you'd ever imagine. Steven held aloft the *Hvitr Kyll*, its mouth shining with blinding light and its deafening pulse drowning out the din of battle. *Keep them all safe until I return.*

A pause.

I will.

Another pause.

Do you know what you're doing? Audrey asked.

I certainly hope so, Steven answered as he disappeared in a flash of silver. *No matter what happens, never forget that—*

25

THE ARBITER

I love you."

The words steamed in the frigid air as Steven appeared atop an icy glacier. His body, encased head-to-toe in metal armor, immediately began to shiver.

He prayed this latest jaunt had gone as planned. Any deviation from either the intended time or place would likely assure not only his death from exposure but the death of everyone he'd just left fighting for their lives.

William. Emilio. Lena. Rocinante.

Audrey.

Focus, Steven. He pulled in a frigid breath. *You only get one shot at this.*

He knelt behind an outcropping of ice and listened, hoping against hope to catch fragments of a conversation both centuries old and still relatively fresh in his mind. At first, he heard only the whistle of the wind and the occasional crack of ancient ice shifting under its own weight, but then, a voice.

A very familiar voice. One he'd feared he'd never hear again.

"Do you honestly believe any of them would follow me again after seeing

that?" Grey's words, despondent and filled with regret, tugged at Steven's heartstrings.

"*Any broken trust will take time to heal, of course, but that's beside the point.*" Hearing his own voice, not within his thoughts, but with his own ears, hit him as one of the more disconcerting experiences of Steven's life. "*As you've told me a thousand times, like it or not, the Game is happening. When it does, we will either emerge victorious or be found wanting, but we don't have the first hope of even beginning if we don't have our King to lead us.*"

"*Truer words were never spoken.*" As the memory of Grey's sad smile washed over him, the true meaning of his mentor's answer filled Steven with awe.

"He knew," he murmured to himself. "Even then, he knew."

"*Then,*" came the other Steven's voice from beyond the bend in this crack in the glacier, "*shall we?*"

Steven remembered the moment from the final seconds of their shared banishment to the past weeks ago as if it had happened moments before. Far below but unseen from where he crouched, the sixty-four squares of light and dark stood empty. The Grey whose exhausted voice he listened to along with a previous version of himself stood together in Zed's cruel time prison moments before the latest loop of chronicity was scheduled to force the ancient wizard to again watch his lowest moment of failure and shame. Just beyond the wall of ice stood a Steven Bauer blissfully unaware of his true destiny and a Grey who had yet to redeem himself by surrendering his own life to save the lives of charges who had become more than just friends, but family.

As Steven recalled, however, the Board below would remain unoccupied but a few seconds longer. In fact, he was counting on it.

As if listening to a movie he'd seen a thousand times, Grey's despondent voice repeated the words that had broken Steven's heart in the moment and now broke it all over again.

"*Now that you are here, I cannot bear to watch another moment.*"

Get ready. Steven prepared to execute his mad plan. *They're about to leave.*

"Take us from this place." Grey's words grew quieter with each sylla-ble. *"Far away from this...tragedy."*

And then, Steven's own voice again, the last words he'd spoken in this terrible moment and the cue for Steven, once Pawn and now King, to begin his latest gambit in earnest.

"One ticket out of here, coming up."

As this other Steven commanded the *Hvitr Kyll* to deliver him and Grey to their rendezvous with the others atop a South Dakota mesa several centuries hence, a single earthshaking pulse sounded, ending the overheard conversation.

"Time to get to work." Steven rose to his feet. "Going to have to time this just right."

Above his head, a blizzard raged, but there in the tiny blemish of the otherwise pristine landscape of ice and snow, the air remained imbued with just enough warmth to prevent one's death from exposure.

"Zed certainly knows how to build a prison." He rounded the corner into the tiny space where Grey had spent countless hours, months, maybe even years watching his greatest failure again and again and again. "Complete with torture."

He stepped to the edge and looked down into the valley upon the checkered battlefield below. As he remembered, the thirty-two Pieces of the Game's third iteration stood newly in their places, preparing for the battle to come, with Grey leading one faction and Zed the other. The blizzard above stilled, the screaming wind and blinding snow vanishing in an instant, though Steven knew the silence was but harbinger for the slaughter about to unfold. From this height, he couldn't hear any of the voices from below, but the simultaneous raised swords of both Kings meant only one thing: the battle had begun.

As he remembered from their last sojourn to this corner of the past, the Pawns went first. The two lines of foot soldiers charged across the checkered ice for each other, shields held high and spears directed toward the hearts of their enemy. Their battle soon became a disjointed free-for-all occupying four small areas of the Board, but leaving the rest up for grabs.

A breath later, each pair of Knights leaped from their positions along their respective back rows, all heading toward one edge of the enormous chessboard to battle. One pair wore jet-black plate armor, each riding a gigantic black horse that would dwarf a Clydesdale, while the other pair, covered head-to-toe in armor of shining silver, rode a pair of polar bears in golden barding like something out of a summer blockbuster. Soon, the clang of dark flails impacting silver shields and glowing maces thundering off dark armor echoed up from the valley.

Next came the titanic Rooks, one side of ice and the other of onyx. They hammered at each other stories above the others, sending rain of mixed sleet and snow down onto the Pieces below. Each blow a sonic boom, Steven remembered all too well the tragic outcome of this four-way battle of giants.

Finally, out came the Queens. The White Queen, her dark brown skin in sharp contrast to both the stark white of her loose tribal robes and the surrounding ice, faced off against her counterpart, a woman with tawny skin dressed in ceremonial Incan garb the color of midnight. They circled each other like two seasoned prize fighters, each guarded by a pair of Bishops wielding ornately carved staves of poplar and ebony respectively. The entire spectacle appeared all but choreographed like some ballet of old, but Steven knew better, the grace and poise of the moment destined to be fleeting. As each of the Queens manifested their power, the White Queen's hands surrounded in silver lightning and the Black Queen's with spheres of crackling darkness, the four Bishops lowered their staves at their opposites and their ritualistic dance devolved into a battle to the death.

"Lena said it." Steven swallowed back the lump in his throat. "This is carnage."

At the rear of each microcosmic army waited the Kings. Though the distance left their expressions indistinct to Steven's eye, he could almost see the broad smile occupying Zed's face and the horror-stricken determination that no doubt filled Grey's.

Steven looked down on his own raiment, the shimmering white and silver of the King that mirrored his ancient mentor's garb below, and a realization came to him: for his gambit to work, he would need to change his appearance. Running his fingers along the crown's cool metal, he held the aged sack of leather before him.

"*Hvitr Kyll*, disguise me as you did your previous master." He pulled in a breath. "In robes of grey."

A slow shimmer of silver started at Steven's brow and flowed down his body, the magical energies replacing his radiant armor with a simple grey robe, gloves, and boots. The thick cloth blocked the cold and held onto his body heat in a way the armor couldn't, and as he pulled up the hood to hide the evidence of his station on the Board below, he immediately stopped shivering as if by magic.

Silent since his arrival in this Antarctica of centuries gone, Amaryllis climbed his chest and clasped together the top of the voluminous grey robes above his heart. He stroked the metallic insect and then peered back down into the valley.

Memories of the first time he'd watched this battle washed over him: the fear, the carnage, the hopelessness, but above all, one fact: Archie, the man who knew literally everything about the Game, didn't know how this battle ended and, more importantly, didn't know why he didn't know.

Almost as if someone was keeping it from him, someone inside his own mind.

But was the secret keeper the Black Bishop or the White?

As Archie had laughed and preened over Grey's dying form, Steven's heart had hardened toward a man he called friend, all based on what seemed an irrefutable fact: he'd been playing them since day one.

In that moment, however, he wondered if the truth was far more complicated.

"What else is new?" he muttered.

The battle played out as it had before.

The pair of Black Rooks each defeated their opposite, sending one stumbling from the Board and shattering the other, the latter's fractured form thundering down on the combatants below like an airborne avalanche. Both lines of Pawns fell prey to the raining boulders of ice, as did one Knight from each side and the nearest White Bishop. One of the Black Bishops moved to engage his opposite atop the dark squares while his compatriot continued to watch his Queen's back. The Queens, in turn, continued to circle beneath a shimmering dome of swirling black and shining silver, their intermingled powers working in concert to protect them even as each of their mistresses fought to end the other. Though captivated by the strange manifestation of yin and yang, Steven knew all too well what lay ahead.

The endgame.

The two remaining Knights continued their skirmish on one end of the Board, the battle of the Bishops raged on from a pair of black squares on the opposite end, and the Queen's continued their dance of attack and defense at the Board's center. Pawns of both stripes pulled their injured forms from beneath the icy debris even as the pair of gigantic Black Rooks reentered the battle at large.

One bludgeoning kick from an onyx giant's enormous foot sent the remaining White Bishop hurtling into a rocky outcropping, the crunch of her snapping bones audible despite the distance, while the other Black Rook directed a titanic fist at the last White Pawn still standing and crushed him beneath a shower of dark stone. Without mercy, the remaining Black Knight dispatched his opposite with a spiked flail to the chest.

Steven fought off a wave of nausea as the gathered Black descended upon the White Queen. He'd felt every blow, every broken bone, every last breath: all strange phantom pains that echoed through his mind thanks to the empathic connection he held with the forces of the White. And yet, all had to transpire as it had before. Grey had been emphatic in his answer.

"*Possible to go back, perhaps,*" he'd said. "*To change the past, however, is impossible.*"

Steven prayed the bit of wiggle room in Grey's sweeping proclamation would be enough.

The Black Bishops zigzagged around each other in a grand sweep of the Board, each staying on their respective color, as they converged on the fallen White Bishop. Broken and bloody from the Black Rook's kick, the robed woman limped away leaving a trail of scarlet along her diagonal path of white squares. Her two dark counterparts showed surprising restraint as they drove her from the Board, though their crossed staves made clear the alternative would be far worse.

As the melee went on, both Kings looked on from their respective squares, one with chin held high in triumph and the other with head hung low in defeat. The time of Grey's inexorable decision approached as his enemy's Rooks, Bishops, Knight, and Queen isolated the last standing Piece of the White. With no path forward to attack the enemy King nor possibility of retreat to join her own, the White Queen stood her ground as her opposite unleashed barrage after barrage of dark energies in a never-ending assault. Though her mystic defenses withstood every attack, her response time grew a split second longer with every hastily formed shield, and the silver shimmer surrounding her balled fists dimmed with every blocked strike. This iteration's White Queen fought more valiantly than Steven dreamed possible, but in the end, as he'd seen previously, her inevitable defeat was merely a matter of time and fatigue.

As Audrey's predecessor glanced back at her King, the man known five centuries hence as Grey, Steven steeled himself for the precise point in time he'd been awaiting since his arrival.

His mentor's moment of truth was about to become his own.

The White King stepped forward within his own square, gazed one last time upon the checkered battlefield he and his opposite had conceived centuries before, and shook his head. The defeated drop of the White Queen's shoulders, visible even from the high perch, told a story all its own.

As Steven had witnessed before, Grey raised both his arms, the pouch in one hand glowing like a magnesium flare and droning like a hundred foghorns, and unleashed every iota of mystical force at the surrounding cliffs of ice. As the teeth-shaking drone of the pouch below was drowned out by the countless tons of shattering ice violently cascading down from every side, the self-same *Hvitr Kyll* that rested at Steven's hip began to throb with an otherworldly heartbeat. Steven pulled open the mouth of the pouch, retrieved the King icon, and waited.

Zed truly had picked the best vantage point from which to torture Grey, for despite the destruction and the avalanche that seemed to come from everywhere and nowhere at once, Steven could see and hear it all.

The Queens' shared scream.

Grey's brief hesitation before holding aloft the *Hvitr Kyll* once more, disappearing from the battle at hand in a concerted effort to literally fight another day.

Zed following suit, vanishing a breath later in a shimmer of darkness.

Both Kings gone. Steven's fingers gripped the marble figure in his hand. *Showtime.*

With an action he'd only employed once since the Game began, and that time based solely on instinct, Steven moved the hand holding the King icon forward as if advancing the piece over an invisible chessboard. Time ground to a halt, leaving the tons of snow and ice rushing to demolish the third iteration's Board and everyone remaining atop its sixty-four squares literally frozen in space and time. Like Shrödinger's Cat, the Pieces below were both dead and alive in that halted moment, their shared fate dependent solely on the next words spoken by a man who wouldn't be born for five centuries.

"*Hvitr Kyll,*" Steven proclaimed, "take me to the White Queen below."

In a blink, he stood in near darkness, the temporarily halted avalanche blocking out most of the Antarctic light. Before him, barely visible in the dim, awaited a sight he could hardly believe. The Queens, embroiled before in mortal combat, now stood frozen together in a terrified embrace, their gazes directed upward at the icy doom that awaited all who still resided on the Board. His mad plan had included White's Queen alone, but this unexpected union represented the first hopeful omen since they'd lost Niklaus to Black's assault in D.C.

Steven drew close, rested a hand on each of the women's shoulders, and willed time to restart, praying the entire time the "universal translator" ability that had allowed him to speak with the first Black Knight back in Oregon was still a thing. An instant before time resumed its lethal course, Amaryllis buzzed at his chest, flooding the space with her trademark green incandescence. The two women, their voices intertwined in one final shared scream, went instantly silent as Steven poured every ounce of gravitas into both word and thought.

"Dome!" he screamed over the deafening cacophony. "Cover everyone!" He raised his shield above his head in an instinctive yet futile gesture as he braced for impact. "Now!"

The horror in both women's eyes transformed instantly into bold defiance. As one, they clasped hands and raised their opposite arms to the sky with both furor and majesty that would rival that of the women who would wear those very crowns nearly five hundred years hence.

"Dome," they cried out in unison to whatever gods they worshipped, the words hitting Steven's ears as strangely as the original Black Knight's speech had all those months before. "Protect us all."

In an instant, the silver and black dome of swirling energy that had previously served to keep all other combatants from the battling Queens swept upward and outward in every direction and soon encompassed the entire Board. A breath later, the incalculable tons of ice hit the hastily formed defense, sending both Queens to their knees.

The White Queen cried out in agony while the Black Queen fell listless to one side, blood dripping from her nose onto the mirror-like ice beneath her shoulder.

And yet, miraculously, the barrier formed from their shared power held.

"You did it!" Steven's eyes went wide in wonder, his voice on the verge of giddy. "We're not dead."

"Clearly." The woman wearing the dark garb of Incan royalty rose from the ground weakly, her brown eyes appearing as green as Magdalene's in the viridescent light pouring from Amaryllis. "Who might you be, stranger?"

The dark-skinned woman clothed in white came to her feet as well, her head tilted to one side as she stared quizzically at their grey-robed savior. "And what is that object on your chest that banishes the darkness?"

"Dearest Queens of White and Black," Steven reigned in his joy at not having been flattened by countless tons of ice and snow, "fear not, for I have come to rescue you from this woeful catastrophe." He swept his arms wide. "All of you."

"All of us?" The Black Queen's eyes narrowed, reminiscent of the next woman to wear her crown. "Perhaps you should start by answering our questions."

"But of course. The dragonfly that rests above my heart is called Amaryllis, an ancient artifact of untold power, while I am the Great and Powerful Arbiter who has decided that those of you who have survived to this point deserve to see the rest of your days." He offered both women a deep bow and then locked gazes with the two most powerful women on the entire planet as the other remaining Pieces gathered close. "You and your associates, however, may simply refer to me as Grey."

26

ENDGAME

here the hell is he? Audrey ran a sleeve across her brow to wipe the sweat and blood from her eyes. *We're getting massacred here.*

To her left, Emilio and a rearing Rocinante fought in tandem, driving back Renata's glinting daggers and the quick blade of this woman Steven had called Ruth. To her right, Lena and the last of Steven's eight doppelgangers stood among the bodies of the fallen White Pawns as they battled to keep Donald's bloody pike, Victoria's cruel whip, and Deborah's serrated spearhead from penetrating their defense, the pair doing their best to aid their beleaguered Rook. William, who had fought three-to-one odds for far longer than Audrey had dreamed possible, stood directly ahead, the previous wild thrashing of his mighty oaken boughs slowing and slowing until they finally, pitifully, stopped.

With an exhausted cry, Audrey let fly what seemed the hundredth barrage of the shining silver orbs that were the focus of her power, trying in vain to drive Wahnahtah, her entranced grandfather, and the man Steven knew as Arthur Pedone from William's wounded form. Her efforts, however, proved futile as Magdalene's dark flames yet again blocked her attack. The three Black Pawns, armed with a pair of

258

tree-ready axes and a war hammer straight out of a Lord of the Rings movie, had proven more than a match for their Rook. After felling the mighty oak that held the soul of William Two Trees, the three of them worked to make sure the wooden giant would never rise again. Repeated strikes from Arthur's war hammer splintered the twin trunks that served as the White Rook's legs. Wahnahtah hacked at the upper branches with his axe, leaving the clear lifeblood of the tree running onto the wood and stone bridge. All the while, Audrey's grandfather struck at the main trunk of the tree, swinging again and again until he reached the heartwood, the literal heart of this man William who had so quickly become a friend.

"It is done." Woody grunted, winded but grimly satisfied with his efforts.

"Grandpa…" Audrey whispered, her heart breaking at seeing him so young and virile and yet so full of hate. "No…"

"What now?" Arthur asked Wahnahtah, the cadence of his voice disjointed as if he were waking from a daze.

"Rejoin the line." Wahnahtah dismissed his axe in favor of his bow and rapid-fired another pair of arrows, the second whizzing so close by Audrey's ear the fletching caught her hair. "Finish them."

Arthur and Woody raced back to join the five Pawns of the Black who continued their attack on the remnants of the White line without mercy, without fatigue, without conscience. The momentary distraction as Arthur stepped back within range and swung his war hammer at Lena's head was all it took for Deborah to find an opening. Thrusting her spear's serrated point at the girl's midsection, her cruel smile twisted into a frustrated frown as Steven's last remaining Pawn shoved her out of the way, taking the blow himself. Gutted, the final Pawn dropped to his knees, his empty eyes staring up into the eyes of the young woman Steven had first met on the war-torn streets of Baltimore. An unheard word bubbled from between his bloodied lips as Deborah planted a foot on his hip and ripped free the head of her spear.

Seeing the last vestige of the man she'd come to love more than she knew possible slump lifeless to the ground before her all but extinguished the hope that had burned at Audrey's core since Steven vanished on his mysterious errand. Seven of the eight dark Pawns drew tight around the four of them, their weapons held high and ready to strike. One rank away, Wahnahtah rested the fletching of his latest arrow against his cheek as he maintained aim on the center of her chest, a shot he'd made once before with near lethal effect. Magdalene smiled silently from atop her dais of darkness, the wicked grin of a jackal waiting for the antelope to breathe its last so it can finally feed.

Steven, she sent her thoughts out into the ether, *wherever you are, it's now or never.*

"In that case," Steven stepped from a shimmer in the air and onto the King's square to Audrey's right, his hooded form clothed in voluminous grey robes that seemed more appropriate for the former wearer of White's crown, "I choose now."

"Steven!" Audrey cried out, her voice brimming with newfound hope. "Thank God."

"Stop this," he commanded, ignoring his Queen. "All of you."

Though his crown remained hidden beneath this strange new hood and cloak, Steven had never been more King. Black and White alike stopped their fighting at once, as if everyone were waiting for the other proverbial shoe to drop. The various Pawns among the enemy took turns glancing back at Wahnahtah as if awaiting instructions, the one true Black Pawn looking in turn to his Queen for guidance. Magdalene simply glared at Steven, curiosity and impatience and vexation all warring across her features.

"Why, Steven, where in the world have you been?" The Black Queen's diamond of shimmering darkness drew her forward until she hovered directly behind her line of Pawns. "We all thought you had turned tail and run." A wide sweeping gesture included Audrey and the remaining White. "And I do mean *all* of us."

"Don't listen to her." Lena glanced back at Steven, her glowing mace held before her chest. "Just tell us you found something while you were away."

"Yes, Bauer," came Magdalene's mocking lilt, "we're all waiting with bated breath."

"Unfortunately," Steven let out a long sigh, "I have nothing." He hung his head. "No cavalry, no silver bullet, nothing." He held his hands before him, palms up. "I've led us as far as I can, and I refuse to lead you all to your deaths."

All among the remaining White, as well as the majority of the Black, looked on in utter disbelief.

"You're giving up?" Emilio's lance shook in his trembling grip. "Now?"

Rocinante let out a frustrated snort.

"We held the line." Lena fought back the anger in her voice. "Just like you asked."

"Steven," Audrey whispered, "I know this looks bleak, but you can't give in. They've already killed William. They'll kill us too."

"You'll all die whether you fight or not." The Black Queen's shrewd gaze dissected her opposite, filling Audrey with a potent mix of rage and fear. "Still, we shall spare you all for at least another moment as I simply must hear the story of your fearless leader's ridiculous garb." Her gaze shifted to the cloaked King. "Did you skip out on the fight to join a monastery?"

Steven held his hooded head high. "I left you wearing the armor of the White King, but return to you as my predecessor first came to me, a simple wanderer in grey." He gestured around to his fallen Pawn brethren. "Enough blood has been spilled this day. I come before you, unarmed, to offer a deal."

"Don't trust him, my Queen," Wahnahtah's eyes, demarcated by the pale stripe painted from temple to temple, narrowed at the White King. "Bauer has proven to be nothing if not cunning."

"Cunning, yes," Magdalene intoned, "but even his resources are not limitless." The Black Queen considered. "His Pawns lie strewn before us, he has no Bishop or Rook, his Knight and that pathetic girl approach the end of their youthful endurance, and his Queen stands before us exhausted and wounded." She let out an amused sigh. "I would hear the terms of this 'deal' of his, if for no other reason than to learn what he might possibly offer that would be more enticing than the pleasure of slowly killing everyone he loves right before his very eyes."

Audrey waited, barely able to breathe, for Steven to speak.

261

"What I offer," Steven whispered, dropping to one knee, "is our complete and utter surrender."

"You can't be serious." Magdalene descended from her dais of darkness, her feet coming to rest on the centermost black square behind her front line. "You honestly believe we'll accept your surrender now? In our moment of victory?"

"Magdalene." Steven raised his gaze to meet the Black Queen's. "You've hated me for the better part of a century, and I admit to my part in that."

"Your 'part'?" she seethed. "You burned me alive and left me to suffer without a backward glance."

"And yet, you survived. And now look at you, in your prime, with the wisdom of almost a hundred years and the ruthlessness to get whatever you want. Did you come here today to win a Game or to exact revenge?"

"Don't let him play you, Magdalene." Wahnahtah shifted his aim from Audrey to Steven. "He's trying to screw with your head."

The Black Queen let out a low grunt. "I'm well aware, Wahnahtah."

"So, which is it, Magdalene?" Steven asked. "Victory? Or revenge?" He pulled back his hood, removed his crown, and placed it on the ground before him. "I'm well aware of what Zed is offering you. Accept our capitulation and this second chance at life is yours to keep."

"Or," Magdalene raised her serpentine scepter, dark fire coalescing around its bejeweled tip, "I could set you all aflame one by one, letting the rest hear the screams of those who went before." Her nose crinkled into a snarl. "Fear not, my dearest Steven. I'd save you for last."

"You could, but you won't." Steven lowered his head. "Audrey, Emilio, Lena, even Rocinante," he pulled in a deep breath before uttering the final words, "all of you, kneel."

"Kneel?" Emilio's entire form shook with rage. "You want me to fucking kneel to these assholes?"

"This is not a request, Emilio." Steven's eyes bored into his young friend. "No one else is dying today, do you hear me? Dismount and kneel."

"But—"

"No buts. Just do it." A part of Audrey died hearing Steven speak more decisively in submission than at any time since their first meeting. "All of you."

Like Superman II, came a whisper through the ether. *Kneel before Zod.*

Audrey's gaze shot in Steven's direction, but for the first time in recent memory, she didn't find the eyes of the man she loved looking back in return.

His gaze, unblinking, remained riveted on the Black Queen.

Without another thought, she dropped to her knees and lowered her head.

I'm all in, Steven, she broadcast back, hoping he could hear. *No matter what, I trust you.*

Lena followed suit, releasing her mace and kneeling before the line of Black Pawns.

Rocinante went next, lowering his head in deference and taking a knee.

Having caught all of this from the periphery of her vision, Audrey chanced a glance up at the final member of their party. As expected, he hadn't budged an inch.

Emilio, still astride his kneeling white stallion and angrier than she'd had ever seen him, glared around the battlefield, refusing to yield. Whether courage or pride or sheer obstinance fueled his defiance, Audrey knew good and well that Magdalene would need little excuse to joyfully make an example of him.

"Emilio," she said, "I know this sucks, but you've got to do it."

From the corner of her vision, she took in Steven's nod as he added, "It's the only way."

"Fine." Emilio dismounted and found himself nose-to-nose with Lena's aunt. Renata held her daggers at her side, but didn't make a move on Emilio, nor he on her.

"Now," she sneered, "on your knees, like the street rat you are."

Emilio's entire body tensed, but in the end, he capitulated, as much to his friends as his enemies. "Never in a million years did I see it going this way." He dismissed both lance and shield and dropped to his knees. "See you all in hell."

"So," Magdalene asked, "that's it? Your grand plan? You're going to kneel before us and beg for mercy?"

"You know, Magdalene," Steven glared at the Black Queen, "I've always hated the way you have to have the last word, but I guess if that's how the chips are going to fall today, then I have but one more thing to say."

"And what might that be," Magdalene scoffed, "little Pawn?"

He locked gazes with this woman who'd been his mortal enemy longer than he'd been alive, his teeth bared like a cornered animal.

"Phalanx."

All along and between White's kneeling front line appeared six swirls of grey that pulsed with the heartbeat of the universe.

"What is this, Steven?" Donald broke the silence of his relentless assault, addressing his son with a mix of curiosity and concern. "What are you—"

In a blink, the six miniature maelstroms collapsed upon themselves revealing two trios of identical hooded warriors, their cloaks the color of sky before snow. Each armed with only a simple spear of ironwood and steel, they attacked as one. The element of surprise firmly on their side, the newcomers in grey skewered the six attacking Pawns of Black's front line and then stepped back in concert and tore the heads of their spears from their enemies' bodies. The brutal assault sent the six conscripted Pawns falling to the wood and stone bridge like marionettes with their strings cut. Before anyone could take a breath, swirling darkness poured from the fallen Black Pawns like a swarm of ephemeral rats fleeing a sinking ship and flowed into the attacking warriors, shifting their collective grey garb to a deep charcoal.

Almost black, Audrey noted, *but not quite.*

"Mom!" Audrey screamed, her mother's lifeblood seeping from a ragged gash across her midsection. "No!"

"*Tía* Renata!" Lena cried out as she watched her aunt sink to ground. "Why, Steven?"

Before he could answer, a third voice, the shrillest of the three, joined the others.

"No!" shrieked Ruth, the only Black Pawn other than Wahnahtah left standing. "Arthur! No, no, no!"

Audrey shot Steven a look of confused anger. "We're supposed to be saving them, Steven, not killing them."

"I had no other choice." Steven rose from his low crouch, crown back in his hand. "There's no other way out of this."

Trust me, he added through their mental connection. *All of you, please.*

"You've tricked me for the last time, Steven Bauer." Magdalene directed her serpentine scepter at Steven's head and unleashed a maelstrom of black flame. "Now, die."

"No." Audrey raised both hands before her face in the shape of an inverted bowl, the gesture summoning a concave column of silver mist that caught the flying inferno like an infielder's mitt catching a line drive. "No matter what he's had to do to save us, I trust Steven to the end."

"That end, girlie, is coming far sooner than you would care to know." Magdalene looked to her Pawn. "Wahnahtah, open fire." Her lips twisted into a venomous grimace. "I shall bring the others." The Black Queen disappeared in a flash of deep violet, leaving Wahnahtah and Ruth alone to face the White.

Despite the rush from their momentary victory, Audrey knew all too well how short this respite would be and prayed Steven knew what the hell he was doing.

As the Black Pawn opened up with another rapid-fire deluge of arrows, the six warriors in charcoal grey summoned shields and formed a defensive perimeter around Audrey, Lena, Emilio, and Rocinante.

"Emilio, take Rocinante and do your best to subdue Ruth." Steven returned the crown to his brow, his grey robes shifting back to the gleaming armor of the White King even as Amaryllis flew up to attach herself to his left breastplate above his heart. "Try not to hurt her."

"Try not to hurt her?" Sarcasm dripped from Emilio's words as he leaped onto Rocinante's back. "You just dropped your own father with a spear to the gut."

"Don't you think I know that?" Hurt anger filled Steven's words. "Now, do what I say, or we're all going to die."

"All right, Steven, I'll follow your orders." Emilio pulled Rocinante around to charge at Ruth, his lengthy lance against her lone blade. "For now."

"Lena," Steven commanded, "watch Audrey's back. I'm trying to keep Wahnahtah at bay, but an extra set of eyes can't hurt."

"On it." She swept up her mace and rushed to their Queen's side.

"And what about me?" Audrey's voice choked out the question, her tear-filled eyes unable to shift from her mother's writhing form. "What do you need me to do?"

"Get all the wounded to William's fortress as quickly as you can." Steven summoned a shield to his arm a split second before Wahnahtah's latest arrow hit, the impact nearly knocking him to the ground. "And be careful."

"The fortress?" Her brow furrowed. "But why?"

Just do it, Audrey. Even Steven's mental voice sounded exhausted. *I'll make all of this right, I swear.*

"Okay." At Audrey's silent command, the mists playing about her feet shot out six ephemeral arms, one for each of their downed loved ones. Gently, the tendrils of mystic fog drew their wounded forms up from the ground and pulled them to her as, to her forward left, Ruth performed a deadly dance of lance, sword, and steed with Emilio and Rocinante. She couldn't help but think Emilio could use Lena's mace more than her.

That was until the girl batted away an arrow meant for the White Queen's heart.

"Thank you, Lena," she whispered as she focused on bringing the six wounded forms in black closer without dropping any of them or jostling their fragile bodies.

"Save them, Audrey," Lena answered. "I'm begging you."

Audrey shot Steven a glance as he fell in at Lena's side, his shield raised high. "That's up to Steven and whatever plan he's working."

In seconds, the six wounded levitated side by side, held aloft by Audrey's mists and protected from Wahnahtah's missiles by the six warriors in grey. She spun to race for their fortress of trees, but found her way blocked by a ten-foot wall of ebon flame.

"So close, Richards," came Magdalene's malicious lilt, "but not nearly close enough." The woman's quiet laugh raised the hairs on Audrey's neck. "Now, turn and face your fate."

Audrey turned and looked past the six forms in black under her control; past Steven, Lena, and the six strange warriors in grey their King had summoned from God knows where; past Emilio and Rocinante who still faced off against the last of the conscripted Black Pawns, the woman called Ruth; and met the cold green gaze of her opposite.

As she'd promised her Pawn, the Black Queen had not returned alone.

The sight of Zed's pantheon of darkness, gathered in force for the first time since all of this had begun, filled Audrey's heart with dread.

Wahnahtah remained out front, pacing in the square before his Queen, his errant aim roving among them as he searched for a vulnerable target. Defending against the Black Pawn alone had been difficult enough, and with the remainder of Zed's forces now gathered, their archer would be even more dangerous with White's focus split between multiple adversaries. Audrey remembered all too well how both accurate and deadly a single arrow from that bow could be when unleashed in the heat of battle.

On either end of Black's back rank towered twin behemoths of dark granite several stories high, the shape of each gigantic form vaguely feminine. Zed's Rooks, both aspects of a mysterious woman they knew only as Cynthia, stood impassive as they awaited their master's command, a force in her own right. Without William, Audrey had no idea how they would be able to withstand such a paired onslaught of sheer power.

One square in from the Rook on Magdalene's side, Vago sat astride a fiery black stallion in midnight barding, the cruel unicorn horn of the dark metal shaffron glinting in the light. He studied the remaining forces of the White from beneath his dark steel conquistador helmet, though Audrey guessed his wrath revolved mostly around their own

Knight. Humiliation, she'd learned a long time ago, is rarely forgotten or forgiven.

Standing one square to Zed's left, Archie looked on, his face filled with a strange glee. A far cry from the wise old man wearing a young man's features she thought she'd known and come to respect, the creature before them now teetered on the verge of madness. His usual implement of power notably absent, he held in his hands instead a chain of beads that terminated on the same blackened ram skull that served as the head of the Black Bishop's staff.

No. Not a chain. A rosary.

Archie seemed oblivious to them all as he ran the metallic beads through his fingers, his lips moving all the while with words Audrey could neither hear nor understand. As he glanced in her direction, a maniacal smile erased any memory of the man she thought she knew. How could he have fooled them all for so long?

Everyone but Steven, of course. She'd caught him giving Archie the side-eye on more than one occasion but never quite understood why. *Grey chose his replacement wisely, not that it changes anything about our current situation.*

To Zed's right, Magdalene glared ahead, the malice in her eyes matched only by her boredom. Her serpentine scepter coruscating with scintillation of deep violet, a sphere of black flame the size of a medicine ball hovered above her head awaiting its mistress' command. Of them all, the Black Queen had the least compunction about ending anyone for whom she had no use, and Audrey was well aware of what they faced when Zed finally removed the muzzle from his most powerful attack dog.

And lastly, the Black King himself. Zed stood, feet apart, with the point of his broadsword resting between his toes on the alabaster wood beneath him. His dark helm held beneath his left arm, his right hand rested on the pommel of his weapon as he took their measure. He acquitted himself as a man who'd already won, the sheen in his gaze beyond mere confidence and verging on certainty.

"Magdalene discussed with me your proposal of surrender, Steven Bauer." Zed raised his sword and directed it toward the half-circle of grey-armored warriors surrounding the remaining White and the levitating forms of their various loved ones. "A proposal I might have considered had you not already proven yourself as ruthless as your predecessor."

"Ruthless? From the man who tried to have me killed before I even knew I was a part of this insanity you and Grey created?" Steven's voice echoed across the Board as if amplified from within his shining helmet. "Grey was forced to do things of which he wasn't proud, but if it weren't for your twisting of the Game for your own ends, none of those actions would have been necessary."

"Keep telling yourself that, Bauer." Zed's eyes narrowed at the six warriors in grey. "I'm curious about one thing, though. Where did you find such capable volunteers to your cause?"

"I didn't have all that far to search, actually." Steven raised his visor. "Pawns of the Grey, reveal yourselves."

In concert, all six grey-clad warriors pulled back their hoods and stood revealed. Zed let out a surprised gasp, his eyes growing wide as the color left his face.

"How is this possible?" the Black King asked. "They're all dead."

"Not all who fell that day in Antarctica lost their lives," Steven answered. "Three Pawns from each side had yet to succumb when you and Grey left the board." He smiled. "Black and White alike, they were all more than interested in what I had to offer, and far more suitable hosts for the energies of Black's front line than your collection of replacement Pawns."

"You went back." The connections in Zed's mind played out across his features "You saved them." His eyes went cold. "Brought my very own Pawns to bear against me."

"Seemed only fair since you conscripted everyone we loved to your side." Steven took a step forward. "And, by the way, any offer of surrender is off."

"As if such were ever truly on the table." Archie crept close to the edge of his dark square to speak with his King, his gait a bit more halting than at their last encounter. "Don't worry, Your Majesty. Bauer there isn't the only one who showed up today with a trick up his sleeve."

"Wow, Archie," Lena taunted, "I must have really done a number on that ankle if *you're* still limping."

He shot Lena a sidelong glance, his lips turned down in a frown. "An insult that will be repaid a thousand-fold, I assure you."

"Ignore the girl, my Bishop." A hint of smile reappeared across Zed's shaken mien. "What latest machination do you bring to bear against Bauer and his soon-to-be-dead cause?"

"Oh, I thought we'd start with a change in management." With one fluid motion, Archie flung the weighted end of his faux rosary at Zed, the chain stretching the few feet between them and encircling the Black King's neck. "Shall we discuss terms, *Your Majesty?*"

Both Wahnahtah and Magdalene rushed to aid their King, but a simple wave of Archie's hand generated a translucent bubble of tremulous darkness that held at bay both the Pawn's arrows and the Queen's fire.

With a strength beyond anything Audrey would have guessed possible, Archie yanked Zed's armored form to the ground and dragged him choking and kicking from his alabaster square and onto the dark stone of his own. All other fighting stopped as the battle for the crown of the Black ensued. The outcome, however, remained in question for but a moment as, with a booted foot, Archie kicked the Black King onto his back, summoned his staff from the ether, and plunged its tapered tip of ebony through Zed's neck with a horrific sound that would haunt Audrey the rest of her days.

"No!" Magdalene screamed. "What have you done?"

Ignoring the Black Queen's cries, Archie knelt by Zed's side, removed the crown from the Black King's brow, and placed it at his own. "Ah, my *fianchetto*, long in place, has finally borne fruit." A plume of blood from Zed's severed carotid left a diagonal line of crimson gore across Archie's deranged grimace. From the crimson sky above, a bolt of violet lightning split the sky with a deafening roar, the violent discharge knocking the Black Bishop to his knees and shattering the dome of energy that had kept the others at bay.

"You'll pay for this, Lacan," Magdalene hissed. "You've ruined everything."

"Ruined, little Magda?" Archie grinned, the partly bared teeth the snarl of a hyena about to feed. "I beg to differ." He yanked his staff from the Black King's unmoving form and directed his weapon across the Board at Steven. "In fact, for all his assurances, it is only now that the things Zed promised you all can be made real."

"What do you know of Zed's promises?" Wahnahtah asked.

"Only everything." Archie scoffed. "You must know that Zed was never going to do any of those things. Give up one iota of power to reward you all for a job well done? A *fool's* dream."

"And *you* will?" Magdalene asked.

"Perhaps. Perhaps not." Archie giggled. Actually giggled. "We all have a Game to win first."

"With God as my witness, Archie," Steven spoke from across the Board, his words reverberating throughout the deep canyon that served as their final battlefield, "I will end your madness today."

"Oh, Steven, so brave, so sure of yourself, so perfect for the role you've assumed in this grand conflict, but no, I'm afraid, you won't be ending anything." Archie stepped across Zed's corpse and swept an arm in a wide arc, gesturing to the various Pieces on both sides. "You see, from the beginning, you and all the others have made this entire thing so unnecessarily black and white. Only one among us ever truly understood the grey in between, and I made sure to finish him first." He ran a finger along the crown that rested at his brow as if it belonged there. "Now that both of the original Kings of this Game are no more, it's down to just us, my friend. At last, the endgame can truly begin." His tongue slid from his mouth to sample the blood working its way down his face. "And believe me, I've been planning for this moment a very long time."

27

NOBODY'S SIDE

At the center of the King's Bishop's square, Archie reveled in his moment of triumph. Bishop's staff in one hand, lethal rosary in the other, and Zed's crown upon his head, his face bore not the slightest concern, as if he'd already seen the outcome of their battle and knew without a doubt victory was his.

Who knows? Steven pondered. *Maybe that's exactly what he's done.*

As Steven considered his next words, his thoughts were cut off by Magdalene's screaming lilt.

"Traitor!" The Black Queen rushed the self-coronated Bishop. "Do you have any idea how long I've waited for this day? How long I've suffered? How much I need what Zed had to offer?"

"Oh, I'm well aware of all those things." Archie spun in her direction, dropping into a low martial stance and directing his staff in her direction. "For instance, I think Miss Richards across the way would be quite interested to find out she wasn't the only Queen plucked from her deathbed."

Magdalene raised her scepter and hurled a ball of dark fire at Archie. "You bastard, I—"

Archie tapped his staff on the black stone at his feet. The resulting flash of scintillating darkness extinguished Magdalene's flames, banished her scepter to the ether, and sent the Black Queen's suddenly frail form to the alabaster wood at her feet. Her long dark tresses fell from her suddenly scarred head, leaving only a few straggly shocks of grey. Her voluptuous form atrophied to skin and bones before their eyes, her black-bodiced dress hanging off her in as ungainly a fashion as her newly pallid flesh.

For a woman so wrapped up in her own vanity, the revelation of her true nature before ally and enemy alike represented the ultimate in cruelty.

His mouth open in shock and awe, Wahnahtah raised his bow to fire on the Black Bishop, but Archie's waggling finger convinced him to hold his fire.

"Now, now, Wahnahtah," he taunted, "or, should I say...*John Small?*"

Wahnahtah's entire body tensed. "How do you know that name?"

"Have you not put it together by now?" Archie cackled. "I know all of your secrets, White, Black, and now, Grey. All of your lives are an open book to me, and since each of you has already played your necessary part in my imminent victory, the need for secrecy is over." He directed his staff at the Black Pawn. "The only question that remains, 'Wahnahtah,' is will you remain 'He Who Charges His Enemies' and fight for me as you did for the prior wearer of this crown, or will you force me to take back that oh-so-muscular leg you received from the *Svartr Kyll?*" Archie rested the tip of his staff by his foot. "Rumor has it you weren't doing too much charging before Zed brought you into the fold, isn't that right, *John?*"

Wahnahtah considered for all of two seconds. "My life in your service, Lacan."

Archie looked to his right at Vago who had observed the entire interchange in silence. "And you, Miguel Fausto Vasquez? Do you stand with me?"

"Do I still get to kill the Cruz kid?" he answered without hesitation.

"With my blessing." The Black Bishop held aloft the bizarre rosary that had served as garrote in his violent coup d'etat and turned his attention on the dark granite behemoth two squares to his left. "And you, Cynthia? I stand by the arrangement you held with Zed, but only if you agree to stand with me, here and now."

The towering woman of stone looked down on Archie as if she considered squashing him like a bug, but in the end, her only answer was a solemn nod.

"It's settled then." The Black Bishop directed his staff again at Magdalene, a burst of darkness restoring her to her previous glory, and returned his attention to the remaining White. "Last chance to reconsider that surrender, Steven."

"Not a chance, Archie," he hissed through clenched teeth. "And, in case you missed it, it's just us now."

The dark flames blocking their egress from the Board had dissipated the second Archie severed Magdalene's connection with the Game. Steven had directed the sextet of Grey Pawns to retreat with their downed loved ones to the relative safety of White's fortress of trees. This left him, Audrey, and Lena standing together at their end of the checkered bridge while Emilio astride Rocinante and Ruth continued to circle to their forward left, their momentary truce following Zed's death already a distant memory.

Despite their dwindling forces, Steven raised his sword and directed its tip at Archie's dark heart. "I'll die before I give you that satisfaction."

Archie answered with yet another knowing grin. "As epitaphs go, my friend, that one's not half bad."

"You were never our friend," Steven spat. "Deep down, I always knew something about you smelled wrong. I just hate that it took the deaths of Grey and both our Rooks for us to see you for what you really are."

"And yet, you still don't quite know the answer to that one, do you?" Archie asked. "What it is that really makes old Archie tick?"

"Not yet," from beneath the bridge came a voice like a wind whispering through countless leaves. "But if you want to know what makes a watch tick, you open it up and take a look at its gears." An enormous bough of branches, its scorched bark smoldering like wet kindling, appeared at the side of the bridge where Emilio and Ruth continued their impasse. The mighty oaken hand secured purchase on the edge of the checkered expanse, shaking the entire structure. His arboreal musculature creaking with every move, William pulled himself back onto the wood and granite bridge, the crown of his massive oaken form smoking and mostly devoid of leaves and the bark that served as his skin charred black as coal. "I'd be more than happy to oblige."

Shaken, Archie directed his staff at the smoldering Rook. "So, you still have your walking tree. How unfortunate that I employ both a human flamethrower and twin towers of unstoppable granite. My only decision point is whether to burn or pulp your pathetic Rook at my whim." He raised a brow. "Is this all you bring to our final battle, Steven Bauer?"

"There is one more," came a voice before Steven could answer, a voice like a rain of boulders. "Time for a little blast from the past."

"No." The word escaped Archie's lips, no doubt to the Black Bishop's chagrin. "It's not possible."

"If there's one thing I've learned in my time as a part of this Game, it's that anything is possible." The stony voice seemed to reverberate from everywhere at once. "A quick study of the Board shows that White is down a Rook." With an air-rending roar, the center of their arboreal fortress exploded upward like a nascent volcano, sending a shower of dirt and broken limbs in every direction. As the dust cleared, an imposing figure stood at the center of the destroyed castle of trunk and branch and leaf: a titan of bright marble, stark against the crimson sky.

"Nik!" Steven cried out, unable to contain his joy. "But how?"

Growing taller and more massive by the second, Niklaus took one gigantic step forward onto the edge of the Board and turned to occupy the King's Rook's square. "There will be time for hows and whys later," came the Rook's craggy voice. "Right now, as Archie put it oh so well, we have a Game to win." He raised his rippled arm of marble to point at the crowned Bishop of the Black. "And a friend to avenge."

From his place at the center of White's back rank, flanked by Audrey and William to his left and Lena and Niklaus to his right,

Steven met Archie's gaze and found there something he hadn't moments before.

Doubt.

"Now that we're all gathered, Archie," he shot the Black Bishop a sarcastic grin, "shall we begin?"

Archie hesitated, his eyes dancing as he no doubt struggled to recalibrate the strategy of such a meticulously planned day. "Wahnah-tah," he grumbled, "you and Vago go help your remaining Pawn bring down the boy and his wretched steed." He directed his staff at Steven. "Cynthia, Magdalene, guard my life with yours." He pulled his staff to his side and adjusted the crown at his brow. "If any of Bauer's brood so much as look in this direction, kill them."

"Not exactly sure how that would be different from the last several months of our lives," Audrey mumbled under her breath. "Should we pull Emilio back?"

"Not without Ruth," Steven answered. "We need all the innocents off the battlefield before we attack."

Audrey's brow furrowed. "She's not looking so innocent at the moment."

Done with taking Ruth's measure, Emilio spurred Rocinante into action, the horse and rider rushing the lone Black Pawn with her curved blade. A split second before being trampled by Rocinante's thundering hooves, she leaped into the air with both a dancer's grace and a gymnast's power. At the apex of an impossible aerial flip, she slashed Rocinante's side with her blade even as her booted foot shot out and knocked Emilio from his saddle. His armored form impacted the dark granite below, knocking the breath out of him and sending the lance flying from his hand. A second later, Vago arrived atop Sombra at the square to Ruth's right and Wahnahtah, bow drawn, at her left.

"Time to die, boy," came Vago's guttural grunt.

"Emilio!" Lena's cry melded with Rocinante's scream of pain. Before Steven could stop her, she darted from her relative place of safety next to him and raced to Emilio's side with her mace, shining like a fledgling star, held high above her head in her gauntleted fist.

"Lena!" Audrey cried after her, but it was too little, too late. A disarmed and dismounted Emilio, a wounded Rocinante, and a terrified Lena now faced off against two confirmed killers and, possibly even more dangerous, a brainwashed Ruth whose martial skills seemed without compare.

Help them, Steven broadcast at Audrey via thought-speech. *William, Nik, and I will deal with Archie.*

Without hesitation, Audrey raised her arms, sending a bulwark of mist and her full octet of shimmering spheres of silver flying at the trio of Black converging on their friends.

Trusting that the most powerful Piece on the Board could handle herself, Steven turned his attention on Archie, Magdalene, and the pair of granite behemoths flanking the crowned pair.

William, Nik, he broadcast, *I'm not sure how either of you are back, but if Audrey is going to have a shot at pulling the others out of the fire, we've got to handle the heavy hitters.*

We're with you, Steven, came William's voice of whispering leaves through the ether. *Just point us in the right direction.*

I must say, came Niklaus' far more gravelly tones, *I like this upgrade. It's like getting texts in my head, and without all the stupid emojis.*

Steven took comfort in his Polish friend's distinctive laugh, even chuckling himself. Even as the world burned around them, Nik was still Nik.

William, we can't risk the Black Queen setting you afire again, so you work on neutralizing Cynthia while Nik goes after Magdalene. Steven stepped forward, sword and shield held high. *As for Archie, leave him to me.*

The Board descended into chaos. Steven and the two Rooks charged ahead, converging halfway across, as Audrey floated up into a swirling cone of mist to fly at her trio of enemies. While keeping track of the shared minds of eight Pawn doppelgangers had proven challenging, mentally guiding Queen, Knight, and both Rooks while simultaneously keeping himself alive and kicking seemed nigh impossible. And yet, in the midst of the mental chaos, a strange order overtook Steven's thoughts, a grid in his mind formed from sixty-four squares where everything had always made sense. Both moment-to-moment tactics as well as overall strategy translated differently with the involvement of actual combat as well as Pieces who lived and breathed and loved and dreamed, but the basics, well-ingrained over years of countless mock battles with his father at their scratched coffee table remained the same.

Enough pontification. Steven rushed at Archie with sword held high as the crowned Bishop sequestered himself behind the Black Queen and both his Rooks. *Time to fight.*

Flanked on either side by a giant of walking wood and a titan of rushing stone, he fought to stay focused despite the danger and adrenalin and dread, the last of which permeated his every thought, though not for any danger he and his two Rooks were about to face.

Trust Audrey to keep herself and the others safe. He forced image after image of her broken form from his mind's eye. *She's never let you down before.*

With a snarl, Magdalene leveled her scepter at Steven and summoned a maelstrom of black fire, sending it flying at the White King. At the staccato beat of Amaryllis' metal wings against his breastplate, he dove to the dark granite and brought his shield around to defend himself from instant immolation.

He needn't have bothered.

With the grace and power of the Olympic athletes his chiseled body resembled, Niklaus dove in front of Steven, caught the spherical inferno in one gigantic hand, and in one fluid movement spun like an expert discus thrower and sent the dark fireball flying at the towering mass of black granite before him.

"No!" Magdalene screamed as the Black Rook to her right took the brunt of her redirected attack mid-torso, sending a mixture of dark stone and darker fire raining down like Old Testament judgment from on high. She leaped into Archie's square to avoid being crushed as this nearer half of the woman they knew only as Cynthia stumbled backwards into the next square and fell to one side, the impact sending a tremor through the entire bridge.

"Nik," Steven asked, "how the hell—"

"You're not the only one who did track in high school," came Niklaus' craggy voice with a stony laugh.

Steven rose from the Board and directed the tip of his sword at the

Black Bishop as the Black Queen rose from her embarrassing leap and the remaining Black Rook stared solemnly at her injured twin.

"Down to three on three, Archie," he shouted. "Care to dance?"

For once, Archie didn't let fly with the usual verbal barbs but instead brought his Bishop's staff before him and set his unholy rosary spinning like a sling of old.

Nik, Steven broadcast, *take Maggie down a peg or two.*

Done. Niklaus stepped forward into a two-story crouch and swept an arm at the Black Queen, his outstretched backhand missing Magdalene by inches. Before he could come around for another swing, she fired a second fireball up into his rocky abdomen, the explosion sending a shower of marble rocketing in every direction. The stone shrapnel peppered Steven though his armor served him well.

Wounded, Niklaus dropped to one knee, an ear-splitting groan escaping his stony lips as the impact again rocked the checkered bridge.

"Such a muscular lad," came Magdalene's chilling lilt. "A shame to have to break you again so soon. We might've had a little fun when this was all over, don't you—" The Black Queen's taunt cut short by Niklaus' flying fist, she fled up the diagonal away from both Steven's blade and William's swooping branches to avoid the White Rook's blow, again escaping a crushing death by the slimmest of margins.

What about me, Steven? came William's mental voice in the half-second respite. *What would you have me do?*

"Take down the other Rook," Steven answered aloud as he charged the Black Bishop. "Archie is all mine."

With Black's right flank suddenly exposed after Niklaus' dispatching of their Rook and Magdalene's flight, Steven rushed to take advantage, keeping one eye, as always, on the Black Queen. William, however with his gigantic strides, made it to the remaining enemy Rook first. The charred white oak planted one of his twin trunks in Cynthia's square, one formed from the roots of William's forest fortress rather than the Black Rook's stone, and melded with the alabaster wood beneath his gigantic foot.

"You may best me in brute force, woman of stone," Woody tendrils erupted from the square and encircled Cynthia's dark granite legs, "but how will you fare when you cannot move?"

Cynthia briefly struggled to free herself from William's trap, and then went on the offensive, lashing out with a flailing punch, her enormous rocky fist taking out a quarter of William's smoldering canopy in a single blow. A second stony haymaker took out another bough of smoking branches.

"Steven," William cried out as the Black Rook gathered her strength for a third blow, the terror in his voice coming through loud and clear. "She's too strong."

"I've got this." Despite the smoking crater at his midsection, Niklaus leaped at the second Black Rook, three stories of pure marble impacting the humanoid mountain of dark granite like a bomb dropped from altitude. The two giants of stone fell sprawling to the checkered bridge with a roar so thunderous that Steven's ears rang.

Deafened with Archie to his front and Magdalene sweeping up his suddenly unguarded flank, Steven dropped into a low defensive stance and braced for attack from either direction. If he defended himself from Magdalene's flames, Archie would no doubt end him as quickly as he had Zed, but if he kept his focus on Black's crowned Bishop, he knew good and well what their Queen would do.

Perhaps another dip into the Lena Cervantes playbook.

"William," he shouted, spinning in Magdalene's direction. "Time to switch partners."

"I thought you'd never ask." The gigantic oak stepped fully onto the light square vacated by the Black Rook and turned to face Archie. "Let's see how you fare against someone who's prepared for your treachery."

As Archie faced off against the attacking oak, Steven spun around just in time to bring up his shield, deflecting a plume of black flame from Magdalene's scepter. His attention already divided, he did his best to keep track of Niklaus and Cynthia's wrestling match and William's standoff with Archie while keeping himself alive.

He didn't dare spare a thought for Audrey, Lena, and Emilio, though a quick glance revealed their battle with Ruth, Wahnahtah, and Vago continued with no quarter given on either side. He brought his attention back to Magdalene, cursing himself for even the brief distraction, but her inevitable follow up attack was far less inevitable than Steven would have dreamed.

Though her guard remained up, the Black Queen's focus, for once since this all began, wasn't on roasting Steven alive. Instead, she looked on aghast as William stepped into Archie's square. The ivory tendrils of wood at the Rook's command leaped from the coiled roots that formed the alabaster square beneath his colossal feet and swept across the dark granite for the Black Bishop. Archie dove to one side, but the oaken roots followed him like heat-seeking missiles and ensnared him from ankle to knee. In a blink, the woody tendrils bound both his legs as they had the Black Rook's before, leaving him frozen to the spot.

But unlike Cynthia, Archibald Lacan was anything but an unstoppable giant of stone.

Like an angler pulling in a fighting fish, William willed the writhing roots to drag Archie toward the light square to face what remained of his thrashing limbs. For the first time since the battle had begun, Steven got a glimpse of real fear in his former friend's face. Neither his flashing sword nor Niklaus' marbled might had elicited so much as a flinch, but William's inexorable pull left him terrified.

"Magdalene," Archie shouted through gritted teeth, doing his best to keep a measure of composure in his voice and failing miserably, "there's no point in attacking their King if yours has already fallen." A sheen of anger, fear, and hatred flashed in the priest's eyes. "Free me now, or everything you desire is lost."

With an urgency borne of desperation, Magdalene redirected the aim of her serpentine scepter at the wooden tentacles drawing Archie's clawing form into William's square. Like a surgeon's scalpel cutting away a tenacious cancer, Magdalene's scythe of black flame severed tendril after tendril until he was again free, the Black Queen's fiery efforts eliciting a cry of agony that welled up from the bottom of William's oaken soul.

Steven never dreamed he'd hear the heart-rending scream of a tree, much less hear it twice. He hoped it was a sound he'd never hear again.

Left inches from the edge of his own square of dark granite, Archie scrambled backward to the center of the stone on hands and heels as if the devil himself would take his soul should he cross that line.

"Take us from here," the Black Bishop bellowed, Zed's crown askance atop his head. "Now."

"But the others..." Magdalene glanced back with trepidation at where her Knight and Pawn still battled Steven's Queen and Knight. "They're—"

"Now, woman, or when all is said and done, you'll be left as Zed found you."

"Very well." Her eyes narrowed into slits as she raised her scepter above her head in a gross mockery of Lady Liberty, shot down the dark diagonal to Archie's square, and took the Black Bishop by the arm. "To the castle."

In a shimmer of darkness, Black's Queen and Bishop vanished, leaving Steven the victor of this round.

Whatever thrill he might have felt, however, was cut short an instant later by a high-pitched scream from the opposite end of the Board accompanied by a second frantic beat of metallic wings above his heart. Steven spun around and found Vago dragging a limp and bloodied Lena up onto his horse. Her mace lay on the dark stone beneath the Black Knight's rearing steed, its inner light snuffed out like a torch dropped into a deep well.

"You cannot save them, Bauer," Vago shouted as he turned Sombra to race for the dark castle in the distance. "Try as you might, this is the day you finally lose." He flashed a wicked grin from beneath his conquistador helmet. "And not only the Game, Pawn-King, but everyone you've ever loved."

28

HEAVEN HELP MY HEART

"L ena!" Emilio screamed as he leaped onto a wounded Rocinante, commanded the horse to shift into his mechanical form of chrome, rubber, and steel, and rocketed down the checkered expanse in pursuit of the Black Knight. "Let her go, you bastard!"

"Emilio, no!" Audrey levitated into the air in preparation to follow the White Knight only to suffer a flying roundhouse kick to the side of her head that sent her crashing back to the mist-obscured bridge.

"Hold up, Queenie." Ruth lit by her sprawled form before leaping backwards, the reverse handspring landing her back in her own square of black granite. "You aren't going anywhere."

"Divide and conquer is, after all, the order of the day." Wahnahtah fired an arrow at Audrey's left flank, an attack that nearly made it past her mystic defenses. As one of the eight orbs of silver intercepted and shattered the incoming missile, the mists lifted the White Queen from the Board and deposited her one square to her left, a position where she could better defend against both remaining Black Pawns.

"No, Audrey!" Steven raced down the diagonal, a sense of dread blossoming at his core. "Anywhere but there."

In a normal battle or fight, her move would have been prudent, keeping both her opponents in front of her. With a chessboard as their battlefield, however, she'd just stepped into the shared kill zone of two Pawns.

"You should guide your Pieces more carefully, Bauer." Wahnahtah's ebon bow shifted into his tomahawk as he rushed the White Queen, his ululating scream freezing her to the spot.

"So falls the mighty Queen." Ruth charged as well, her rapier brandished at Audrey's unprotected heart.

Audrey set the orbs of energy spinning about her torso even as the mists at her feet rose like a pack of dogs in defense of their mistress. Still, Steven could see the fear in her visage even from several squares away.

I'm coming. No reply whatsoever came to his broadcasted thought. *Hang on.*

After dodging Wahnahtah's axe and ducking Ruth's blade, Audrey sent flying a silver grenade of eldritch energy at both her opponents. Wahnahtah cleaved the one meant for him in two with his tomahawk while Ruth leaped over hers with a flying somersault and landed within striking range of the White Queen.

"How does it feel," Ruth taunted, "knowing you're about to be brought low by—"

The silver ball of energy boomeranged and struck Ruth full in the back, knocking her two squares forward and well past Audrey's position on the Board, leaving the White Queen alone to face the remaining Black Pawn.

"Don't count your chickens before they're—" This time it was Audrey's retort that was cut short. Her focus on taking Ruth out of action left her open to Wahnahtah's attack. A lucky strike of the butt of his tomahawk to her temple sent a reeling White Queen to her knees. As the spheres of light surrounding faded from view, the hope in Steven's heart flickered as well.

"Audrey!" Still twenty feet out, he closed on Wahnahtah, racing square by seemingly infinite square and feeling all the while like he was wading through molasses. His eyes narrowed as the Blackfoot warrior pulled her up from the ground by her auburn locks, his tomahawk held high in his opposite hand. Behind them, Ruth retrieved her rapier amid a skilled forward somersault and popped up on the White Queen's other side.

A familiar block of ice formed around Steven's heart.

Nothing in his bag of tricks was going to be enough to turn this around.

"Allow me." Rushing up his right flank, William leaped along the straightaway to Steven's right with an agility that belied his massive form. In two enormous bounds, he landed before the trio of friend and enemy and sent Ruth flying yet again with a swat of branch and leaf straight out of Tolkien. "One down, one to—"

"Stay back." Wahnahtah brought the edge of his axe to Audrey's throat as Steven finally caught up with William, coming to rest in the giant oak's shadow scant feet from the Black Pawn.

"Let her go," Steven said. "Your King is dead, a madman wears Black's crown, and no one is coming to bail you out this time." He sheathed his sword. "Free Audrey, and we'll allow you to return to the others."

"And if I do that, what's to keep your friend from sending me flying like he did my protege there?" He gestured to Ruth who lay sprawled at the edge of the checkered bridge.

"Sorry." William's voice was surprisingly quiet. "I was just trying to help."

"It's all right, William." Steven returned his attention to the Black Pawn, doing his best to keep his concern for Ruth from his face. "It definitely helped with negotiations."

"Not that it matters, Bauer. When all of this is over, some of us will live, and others will not." His eyes flicked downward at Audrey's struggling form. "But Richards here? You've made no secret of the fact you love this woman. Therefore, I believe I'll keep her right here with me."

"Listen, Wahnahtah…" Steven cast his memory back a few minutes to Archie's revelatory rant and dismissed his helmet so he could look on the man with his unguarded eyes. "Or, would you prefer John?"

"Do *not* call me that." A rivulet of blood ran from beneath Audrey's chin and down her slender neck. "So, what now? Will you sacrifice your Queen to remove a lone Pawn from the Board, or will you finally concede, save the life of this woman you love, and let us all be done with this madness?"

"Don't listen to him, Steven." Audrey's words, broken by a peal of coughing, came out slurred. Whatever fight was left in her currently sat at a low ebb. "Just finish this. For me." She hawked a mouthful of blood onto the pale wood at her feet. "For Grey."

"Yes. Sacrifice the woman you love to continue this painful struggle. And for what? Do you truly believe you know what will happen at the end of all this?" Wahnahtah's muscles loosened, if only slightly. "Grey and Zed are gone. It's a contest between us mere mortals now. Hand over your crown to me. Then you and your once-Bishop can discuss our places in his new world order."

"No way." Steven's grip tightened on the hilt of his still-sheathed sword. "It's you who are surrounded, John Small. Harm her and I swear William and I will make sure it's the last thing you ever do."

"Such talk, Bauer." Wahnahtah's eyes, from behind the simple line of white that split the black face paint that obscured his features, focused on the circle of platinum atop Steven's head. "The time for negotiations is over. Remove your crown, agree to bow before Lacan, and perhaps you and your beautiful Queen here will be allowed to live happily ever after. Hesitate, however, and she dies." Audrey sucked in a breath as Wahnahtah rested the razor-edge of his axe at her jugular. "Make your move, Pawn-King."

"Don't listen to him." William shook at Steven's side. "I know his kind. No way this snake will let her live."

"Are you quite certain of that, *brother*?" Wahnahtah shot a smarmy gaze up into William's smoky upper canopy. "I could have killed her a dozen times already, and yet, here we are, still talking." His attention returned to Steven. "The crown, Bauer. Hand it over, and the girl lives."

Steven pulled in a breath and released the hilt of his sword. Slowly and deliberately he brought his hands to his temples, his fingertips resting on the ring of cool metal that encircled his brown curls.

Audrey, he reached out with his mind, *can you hear me?*

Yes. Feebly at first, but stronger with each word, she answered. *I hear you.*

Good. Steven quickly relayed the plan, all the while praying he wasn't signing Audrey's death warrant. *We'll only get one chance at this. Are you ready?*

Somehow she choked out a quiet laugh as she mentally broadcast six simple words.

Do you even have to ask?

"A trade." Steven removed the crown. "This symbol of power for the life of the White Queen."

"Agreed."

"Your word?"

"As if you trust me one iota, Bauer." He tilted his head forward in a subtle nod. "But yes, my word."

"Very well." Steven flung the crown sidearm at Wahnahtah's head. The muscles of the Black Pawn's forearm tensed, but before he could break his hastily given promise, intentionally or otherwise, a thick tendril of mist shot up from the lake of fog at Audrey's feet and surrounded her neck forming a gorget forged of mystic fog and the White Queen's indomitable will.

Before the Black Pawn could react, the ephemeral tentacle of mist encircled the handle of his tomahawk and hurled the weapon from the bridge and into the chasm below. Another breath and a second tendril of fog shot up from the ground and caught the crown mid-air inches from Wahnahtah's outstretched fingers. With a snarl, Audrey took a more hands-on approach to battle than was her standard, launching backwards with all the force her legs could muster as she flung her elbow into her captor's unguarded stomach. The air driven from his lungs, Wahnahtah stumbled backward, and he and his captive fell in a tangle of arms and legs, her long hair still wound around his clenched fingers. Flush with renewed vigor, Audrey gave as good as she got, trading blow after blow with the dark-clad Plains warrior even as she returned to Steven his crown atop a tiny bank of shimmering cloud that appeared to move of its own accord.

One thing became clear very quickly.

Audrey's raging fists represented far more than simple self-defense or even her giving her all in the day's battle for the fate of the world. Wahnahtah's arrow had nearly ended her life at the climax of their rain-soaked first encounter in Atlanta months before, and his axe very nearly again that day.

This was personal.

This was payback.

This was revenge.

And all Steven could do was watch.

A weaponless Wahnahtah discovered quickly that having a Queen by the scalp was very much akin to having a tiger by the tail as she buffeted his form with fists and fog and spheres of magical energy, his own blows barely slowing her relentless onslaught. Finally, mercifully, he released his hold on her curly locks, and the pair sprung to their feet like the veritable cobra and mongoose of Kipling fame and began to circle.

"Damn you, Bauer." Wahnahtah addressed Steven, though he kept his attention focused solely on the White Queen. "You and yours think you're so superior, that I and the others among the Black represent the 'bad guys' in your myopic view of the Game, but know this: You're no better than Zed or even Lacan. You've lied and cheated as much as he did, if not more, to get where you are now, the bearer of your side's crown." He shot a finger in Steven's direction, never letting his eyes drop from Audrey's enraged gaze. "Just because your side wears white doesn't mean that you're beyond reproach or that your actions don't have consequences." A smile broke across his battered face. "At least your master was honest enough to clothe himself in grey."

Don't let him get in your head, Steven. Audrey's voice, spoken directly into his thoughts, filled him with hope. *He's trying to sow doubt in your mind, win the battle of words since he's currently toothless. Don't let him. You of all people know the truth.*

And what truth is that? Steven asked.

That you are our King. Not Grey. You. Her eyes cut in his direction even as she continued to broadcast her deepest thoughts. *Would Emilio stand by you if you were no better than Zed? Would Lena? Nik? William?* A pause. *Would I?*

I suppose not. Heartened, Steven returned the crown to his brow and spoke aloud. "Now, as promised, John Small, you may go." He ground his teeth. "Tell Archie we're coming for him next, and this time—"

"Steven," Audrey gasped, her eyes suddenly focused like lasers across his shoulder. "Look out!"

Steven spun around, his gaze lighting briefly on the continued battle between Niklaus and Cynthia in the distance, the two titans of marble and granite trading blows that would level city blocks, when something from behind hit him like a speeding Mack truck. In seconds, he found himself beneath an enormous tongue of black granite, the malleable yet unyielding rock pinning him firmly, arms, legs, and torso, to the Board. Only his head remained free, no doubt so he could watch his own demise.

"It would appear our second Rook has recovered from our Queen's fireball." Wahnahtah laughed. "Correct me if I'm wrong, Bauer, but I believe you're in check."

A tendril of silver mist shot out from Audrey's feet and encircled Wahnahtah at the waist. "That's quite enough of your mouth, Pawn." She hurled him down the bridge in the direction of the dark castle in the distance and then turned to face the ever-shifting blob of granite that was the Black Rook. "Let him up, Cynthia."

"Last I checked, a Rook can't bring down a King alone." William stepped forward, his tree trunk legs melding with the wood at his feet even as the remaining boughs of limbs that served as his arms and hands grasped his opponent's rocky mass on either side. "Now, like Audrey said, get off him."

William shifted the strength of his oaken form to one side, his irresistible force meeting his opposite's immovable object. Limbs snapped, rock crumbled, but in the end, their fight was an impasse.

"I'm sorry," came William's defeated voice. "I can't move her. I just can't—"

"Enough." Audrey pulled every last bit of the mist covering the Board to her and infused it with the eight points of light orbiting her shoulders. "You may be a mountain of stone, Rook, but the Queen remains the most powerful Piece on the Board." This new energy pulsed about her fists, twin orbs of purest light. As the White Queen pulled her arms above her head, Steven's eyes reflexively shut to block out the blinding light, though her words came through loud and clear. "Now, for the last time, get the *hell* off my man."

With the roar of a thousand cannons, Audrey unleashed her full might on the Black Rook. The crushing weight bearing down on Steven's chest disappeared and he could breathe again. As he raised his head and opened his eyes, he discovered why.

Hovering thirty feet in the air and surrounded by a nimbus of silver scintillation, the Black Rook shifted form again and again in an effort to escape the White Queen's power. More than once, a rocky tongue flew at the White Queen from the ever-changing mass of stone only to be held at bay by another ray of tangible silver light.

Seeing Audrey so radiant and full of life, an Old Testament angel armed with the wrath of God and the knowledge of eternity, made Steven fall in love with her all over again. Amaryllis fluttered above his heart, and for a moment, he allowed himself to believe the metallic beats represented victory. The next, however, his heart went colder than Grey's Antarctic prison as the White Queen fell forward to the checkered bridge's unforgiving stone.

Behind her stood Ruth, rapier wet and dripping with crimson, a wicked smile upon her face.

"Technically, Steven..." The last of the conscripted Black Pawns stepped across Audrey's body and wiped the tip of her blade on the White Queen's dress, the bodice already soaked through with blood from a wound above her left breast. "In every way that counts, I saw you first."

"Audrey!" Steven's shout echoed in the space between the Rook's enormous mass hovering above him and the Board beneath his supine form. "No!"

The several tons of living black granite held aloft by Audrey's sheer will began to fall. Steven rolled to one side in an effort to get out of the way, but it was too little, too late.

This is it. The words ran through his mind in a flash. *This is how it ends.*

"Move." William leaped forward and forced what remained of his oaken canopy beneath the falling rock like a gigantic broom, sweeping the White King from the kill zone.

Steven missed being crushed by inches.

William wasn't so lucky.

"No." Steven ground his teeth. "William…"

The pair of massive trunks that served as his legs writhed as the White Rook fought to free himself, but only for a disquieting few seconds before going as still and silent as the aged tree he embodied.

"So, Steven." Ruth drew closer. "Here we are."

"It would seem you are surrounded." Wahnahtah strode up from the opposite side, returned from his brief banishment from the battle.

"Please, Steven Bauer." The mass of black stone atop William's still form folded itself into a roughly humanoid shape. "Concede."

"And why would he do that?" came a voice from the remains of White's forest fortress. "The battle has just begun."

At the center of White's back row stood a woman dressed in the robes of a healer, a simple headdress obscuring all but her eyes. In one hand she gripped a gnarled staff that terminated in a glowing star fashioned of quartz while the other held only a chain of simple prayer beads.

"First an extra Rook, now an extra Bishop?" Wahnahtah puffed up his chest. "We'll dispatch her as easily as we did your girlfriend and the walking tree."

"Except for one thing." A grim smile invaded Steven's features. "If she's finally making her appearance, it means she's done."

"Done?" Wahnahtah asked. "With what?"

"With this." Steven motioned to the White's second row and uttered a word that had become all but battle cry over the previous months. "Phalanx."

The six center squares all flashed with a blinding light and when all present could again see, the battlefield had again become very different. Before the remaining combatants stood six of the seven Pawns conscripted into the Black, their wounds healed and their raiment shifted from hooded dark leather and chainmail to a uniform garb of shimmering white with elements of gleaming silver. From left to right, Woody Buchanan, Renata Garcia, Donald Bauer, Arthur Pedone, Victoria Van Doren, and Deborah Richards stood restored and ready to fight.

"Please excuse my tardiness," spoke the White Bishop, five centuries out of her time. "Healing both your loved ones' wounds as well as the stain left on their minds by Black's influence took longer than I anticipated."

"Better late than never." Steven drew his sword and directed its point at Wahnahtah. "Pawns of the White, attack!"

Before the first could so much as take a step, however, the Black Queen reappeared in a swirl of darkness.

"You three, with me." She turned her head to look upon Niklaus and the other half of the woman known as Cynthia in the distance, their literal clash of titans still going strong, and let out an exasperated sigh. "The bearer of Black's crown demands an immediate audience with us all."

With a snap, the remaining forces of the Black—both aspects of Cynthia, Wahnahtah, Ruth, and Magdalene—disappeared from the Board, though Steven suspected they would be seeing all of them again and far too soon.

He rushed to Audrey's side, her impaled chest gushing blood front and back, and fought to keep his voice from choking. "Heal her," he asked desperately of the out-of-her-time Bishop. "Bring her back to us." He swallowed back the bile in his throat. "Bring her back to me."

"My apologies." The Bishop knelt by his side. "It took all I had and more to bring these six back to you. I won't have the strength again to help her until it's far too late."

"Then stay with her," his voice dropped to a whisper, "and do what you can."

He brought his gaze up to inspect his new line of Pawns. One by one, he studied their faces, tears welling in his eyes at the determination and steel in their gazes where minutes before he'd found only anger and madness.

Woody, his youthful hands grasping a gleaming battle-axe, and Deborah, brandishing a long spear of smooth poplar and shining steel, rushed together from opposite ends of the line to converge on Audrey.

"My baby," Deborah choked out, falling into her father's chest. "We're too late."

"Not yet." Donald strode over from the center of the line of newly rechristened Pawns. "If our friend the Bishop here can somehow keep her alive while we finish this."

"Hey, Dad." Steven swallowed back the emotion. "Good to have you back."

As Donald offered his son a solemn nod, Deborah shot an accusing finger at him. "This is your fault. You were supposed to protect my little girl." She dropped to her knees and buried her face in Audrey's bloodied bodice. "My baby…"

Steven pulled in a breath. "One of the enemy I'd counted down struck her from behind." His head dropped. "I swear, Ms. Richards, I did all I could."

"That he did." Niklaus, his every step sending a tremor through the checkered bridge, approached from the far side. "We all did."

Woody rested a hand on Deborah's shoulder. "You stay here with Audrey, sweetheart. The rest of us are going to go end this once and for all." He met Steven's gaze. "And then, if I have to drag his half-dead ass back here, I'll make that weasel of a Bishop bring our little girl back." He raised an eyebrow. "Isn't that right, my King?"

"Let's go." Steven and this latest iteration of the forces of the White circled round Audrey's form as Deborah and the Bishop from the previous iteration tended to the White Queen's wounds and did everything in their power to keep her alive. "I'm going to need you all."

He looked each one in the eye.

Niklaus, three stories high and as angry as Steven had seen him, towered over them all, his marble features pulled back in an enraged grimace.

Woody with his battle-axe and Arthur with his war hammer forged of iron and hickory, both veterans of war, stood ready to fight yet again.

Renata, her fists wrapped around one of two twin daggers, the grip and guard of each forming a Catholic cross that flowed into a razor-sharp two-edged blade, chomped at the bit, more than ready to avenge herself for being made a literal pawn of the enemy.

Victoria, her no-longer-barbed whip held loosely in her hand, stood distracted and confused as she stared up into the features of the marble giant standing across the circle.

Donald, dressed in the garb of a Pawn and carrying a pike identical to Steven's, looked on him with a pride his son might have seen a handful of times in his life.

With a quick study of William's still inert form and one last protracted gaze at Audrey's closed eyes, Steven held aloft the *Hvitr Kyll*.

"Take us to the White Knight."

In an instant, King, Rook, and five Pawns vanished from one end of the bridge and appeared at the other. Before them, the walls of Zed's-now-Archie's dark keep rose steeply before them, the unscalable black granite filling their vision like the darkness of night. Far more terrifying than the imposing fortress, however, was the sight of a lone girl on her knees, herself bloodied and broken, hunched over a fallen figure in silver armor, his conquistador helmet crushed, lance broken, and breastplate crumpled as their shared enemy mocked from atop his black steed.

"So long, Cruz," Vago taunted as Sombra circled what remained of Rocinante' s demolished chassis of crumpled chrome, bent steel, and burst rubber tires, bringing the Black Knight around to face the newcomers in white. "Tell your brother I said hello."

29

LAMENT

God, not Emilio too." Niklaus' words, booming down from above like a boulder rolling down a rocky hillside, echoed Steven's thoughts.

"Too?" Vago studied the gathered White, his barely visible smile growing wider beneath his dark conquistador helmet. "Only one Rook?" He laughed. "And no Queen either?" He directed the business end of his flail at Steven. "Things aren't looking good for the home team, huh, Bauer?"

"Give the word, Steven," Niklaus took one thundering step forward, "and I'll wipe that smug grin off his face."

"I think not," came Magdalene's distinctive lilt. Sombra reared as the Black Queen stepped from a dark fold in space and gestured to the Black Knight. "Come, Miguel. We are summoned."

Before any of them could so much as take a breath, Magdalene, Vago, and Sombra all vanished in a shimmer of night, leaving Steven and the others to face the latest in a seemingly endless cascade of horrors.

Though, with so few Pieces remaining on his side, the end seemed closer than ever before.

"Why is Archie pulling all his Pieces back," Steven muttered to himself, "when he currently has the clear advantage?" Filing the question away, he crept to Lena's side. "Lena," he whispered, "is he…"

"Steven…" Barely audible, Emilio's whisper cut him like a blade. "I saved her. I saved Lena." A wet cough left a spatter of scarlet on the smooth wood beneath his wounded form. "But you're gonna have to take it from here."

"Come on, Emilio. You've got this." His mind raced for anything, any miracle, that could save the young man's life. The eyes of the White Bishop from the opposite end of the bridge flashed across his memory, but she'd already made it clear her battery was running on empty. Meanwhile, the only other person in a hundred miles who could possibly help currently sat inside the black behemoth of stone at the bridge's other extent waiting to end them all.

"Look, I know I don't have long. No time for bullshit." Another wet cough sent a chill up Steven's spine. "Two things."

"Tell me."

"Make sure Lena makes it through this."

He nodded. "I promise."

Emilio shifted his attention from the face of the only woman he'd ever loved, his eyes narrowing to slits as Knight and King locked gazes. "And make sure Vago doesn't."

"You've got it." Steven considered his dwindling forces and prayed he could keep either of those promises and even more so that any of them might survive the day. "I swear."

"Win this thing. For me. For Grey." Another heartbreaking peal of coughs left Emilio's voice a quiet croak. "For the world."

Steven lowered his head in a grim nod. "With all that I have."

Donald rested a hand on his son's shoulder. "With all that *we* have."

Emilio's gaze returned to Lena. "Rocinante?"

"He kept them off me, *papi*." Her eyes flicked briefly in the direction of the destroyed ivory and chrome machine that held the heart of a wild Carolina bank pony. "He kept me safe."

"*Gracias a Dios.*" Emilio's eyes took on a dreamy cast, one Steven had seen far too many times in his life. "Lena…" Another blood-tinged cough forced the air from his lungs. "*Mi amor, mi corazón, te quiero…por siempre.*"

"*Siempre...*" The word, delivered so softly that Steven almost wondered if he'd imagined it, was all Lena said, her lips barely moving to allow the whisper to pass.

As Emilio breathed his last, his eyes mercifully closed and lips turned up in that half-cocked smirk Steven had grown to not just tolerate, but admire.

"Lena," he asked, without a clue of what he was supposed to say, "are you...okay?"

Lena Cervantes didn't move, didn't blink, didn't utter another sound. Only the tears that slowly worked their way down her flushed cheeks and the staccato rise and fall of her chest betrayed the war brewing within the young woman's body, mind, and soul.

"We have to go." His father motioned to the vast monstrosity of black stone that rose before them. "Every passing second is another they have to plot how to kill us all."

"Are you coming, Lena?" Steven hated himself for asking the question. "We're down to nothing here and if we don't have every—"

His words cut short by the sudden fury in Lena's eyes, the rage punctuated by a diagonal smear of blood from temple to chin that divided her features, he turned to Niklaus and his new set of Pawns. "It's just us, then."

"We're ready." Donald took stock of the situation, bowing his head in deference to his son who better than a decade before had defeated him on a much smaller version of the checkered battlefield. "What's the plan?"

"The only plan left," Steven said. "We take the fight to them, on their own turf, and make damn sure we win." He motioned to his left. "Dad, Woody, over here."

With a simultaneous nod, Donald raised his pike and Woody his battle-axe and formed up back-to-back on Steven's left flank.

"Victoria, Arthur, on my right."

"Roger." Arthur fell in on his opposite flank, every bit the young soldier to which the Game had reverted the elderly man. "We're going to save Ruth, right?"

"We're going to do all we can to save everyone, Arthur." Steven stared down at Emilio's lifeless body. "Everyone that's left, at least." He shifted his attention to Victoria who couldn't keep her despondent eyes off the three-story giant that in another lifetime offered her not only a ring of gold but everything that went with it. "Victoria—Miss Van Doren—are you in?"

Shaken by the mention of her name, she shifted her focus to Steven, her gaze the wide-eyed stare of a deer facing a semi on the interstate. "Of course." She glanced down at the whip resting in her hands. "What would you have me do?"

"Fight, Victoria," came Niklaus' granite voice from above, "fight for what's right and good and true."

After a thoughtful pause, she cracked her whip, the miniature sonic boom shaking some of the cobwebs from her thoughts, and wound her weapon around her hand. "I'm in."

Steven looked to Renata who knelt by Lena's side, her arm around her niece's heaving shoulders. "Renata, we could certainly use you inside, but I think it's best you stay with Lena."

"But—"

"She's in no shape to take care of herself." He swallowed back his fear. "Guard her with all you have, and if we don't make it back, get her out of here as fast as you can." He lowered his head. "One favor?"

"Of course," Renata whispered.

"Tell Audrey—or Deborah, if it comes to that—that I love her."

"You can tell her yourself when this is over," she lowered her head, "my King."

First William, then Woody, and now Renata had deferred to him as "King." With each repetition, his awe at their utter faith in him had bolstered his confidence even as the worms of self-doubt continued to chew at his core.

But the time for reflection was over.

The moment called for decisive action.

"Niklaus," he pointed to the enormous double door of darkened steel and black wood that blocked the entrance of Black's refuge. "Would you be so kind as to knock?"

"With pleasure." With three bounding leaps, Niklaus charged the dark castle and leveled a haymaker to end all haymakers at the center of the colossal double door, only to be hurled backward by the force of his own blow. His three-story form ricocheted backwards onto the black square adjacent to where Steven and the others were gathered. The impact shook the bridge like a biblical earthquake, sending half the gathered White to their knees while the rest struggled to remain standing.

"Nik?" Steven got back to his feet. "Are you hurt?"

"I'm fine." Niklaus scrambled back to his full height. "But those doors aren't going anywhere. I hit them dead center with everything I had and didn't even leave a dent."

Steven stepped back and studied the structure he'd first seen in his mind's eye the night they rescued Audrey from the Black Queen's fiery clutches. The prophetic vision, courtesy of the concussed haze that left him hanging helpless from the original Black Knight's horse as he raced through the darkened forest of Sisters, Oregon, didn't do justice to the enormous edifice of black stone. The grand double doors appeared unassailable, at least with brute force, while the walls rose far too high and sheer to consider climbing.

Not to mention his guess that anyone who tried would likely meet an untimely end.

"This is their stronghold, Son." Donald stepped up. "Their King, or at least the maniac wearing Black's crown, has castled. While your own Rook may indeed be the most powerful Piece you have left..."

"The straight-ahead approach plays to *their* Rook's strengths." Steven lowered his voice as his gaze wandered to Emilio's still form. "And we've lost our teleporter."

"What about the pouch?" Arthur asked. "It brought us clear across the bridge. Can't it take us inside?"

"I doubt it." Steven pondered. "They didn't raid our fortress of trees, but waited for us to make our way out onto the bridge."

"So we can't get to them, and they won't come out to us." Woody rested the head of his battle axe on the smooth white at his feet. "It's almost like after all this, Archie doesn't want to fight."

"Or he's afraid to." Victoria's first contribution to the conversation triggered a memory inside Steven's head. The only time in the entire battle when Archie had seemed afraid.

The moment when he was inches from being pulled by William onto a white square.

"That's it." Steven looked up at the White Rook. "Nik, it's all on you."

Niklaus balled his gigantic marble hands into fists, the sound like boulders splitting. "I already tried, Steven." He motioned to the gigantic doorway. "Remember? Not even a scratch."

Steven smiled. "You may be a Rook, but right now, I need you to think like a Bishop."

Niklaus' features softened, his defeated grimace transforming into a half-smile. "You mean, hit them from a different angle."

"Exactly." Steven pointed to the opposite end of the bridge where the ruins of the stronghold rested and did his best not to think about the young woman who lay there bleeding. "When we first appeared here, William willed into being that fortress of trees as our defense just as Cynthia created Black's. Each gave of their own form and essence to provide their side with shelter and defense."

"Okay." Niklaus' marble brow furrowed as he tried to follow Steven's logic. "So?"

"You too are a Rook, but one that has yet to create his castle."

"You want me to create a castle?" He motioned to the bridge. "Here?"

"Not exactly." Steven eyed the dark monstrosity that rose before them all. "We can't enter here, as this place is clearly reserved for the Black, but perhaps if it were a bit more...grey?"

His mind flashed back to the Brooklyn Bridge, where Niklaus melded with the uprights of the enormous expanse and, with the force of his will alone, kept the fractured bridge from falling into the East River.

Niklaus processed Steven's hypothesis and without another word, took two gigantic steps toward the castle, positioned himself by the stone wall, and pressed his titanic marble hands to the dark granite.

"What's he doing?" Victoria asked.

"Every chess game begins with an opening." Donald rested a hand on her shoulder. "God willing, this is ours."

At first, nothing happened. A brisk wind howled by the newly formed bridge and whipped around Niklaus' enormous legs. As the moment stretched on, Steven's hope began to sour to despair, and his heart froze in fearful anticipation at the next words to hit his ears.

"Steven," came Niklaus' pained groan, "I don't feel so good." His back arched in pain, the sound like an avalanche. His gigantic form writhed as if he'd grabbed a live wire. Before their eyes, the White Rook began to shrink, his outstretched hands sliding down the dark castle's stony wall as faster and faster he approached his normal height.

And yet, everywhere his hand touched, a miracle occurred.

Flowing from Niklaus' fingertips, ripples of white flowed through the black granite, left and right and up and down and through, though the end result was not the proverbial grey castle Steven guessed his mentor had hinted at with his chosen appellation, but something else entirely.

The white marble flowed from Niklaus' essence, leaving him again a being of simple flesh and blood, small and fragile in a battle populated by mortals with the powers of gods, but their gambit had worked, for the dark castle of the Black was dark no more. Alternating squares of black and white, like the bridge beneath their feet, now formed the imposing walls, the interlocking squares of dark granite and bright marble transforming the enormous edifice into their final checkered battleground.

No longer able to stand, Niklaus slumped to the ground at the base of the castle, his eyes half-closed but his trademark grin still in place.

"Nik!" Victoria's scream surprised Steven as much as anyone as the woman rushed to the side of the man she'd unceremoniously dumped months before. "What's wrong with him?"

"I'm fine." Niklaus ignored her and stared up at Steven's armored form with a weary smile. "Is this what you had in mind," he raised a sarcastic brow, "my King?"

"Close enough." He offered the man a hand and helped him to his feet. "Did it work?"

"Time to find out." Niklaus cracked his neck as if preparing for a fistfight. "You might want to stand back." He took a few steps back from the massive door with Steven to his right and a trepidatious

Victoria on his left. When they were all a full square from the castle entrance, Niklaus slid into his characteristic grin and uttered the only two words most people know from *One Thousand and One Nights*.

"Open sesame."

The magic words of Ali Baba were met with silence, followed by the interwoven sounds of clinking chains and grinding gears. Both doors sprang open, and Steven raised his shield, fully expecting a dark fireball or midnight shaft or tongue of granite to fly at them from within.

Instead, they were greeted only by a long empty corridor full of shadows that danced on the checkered floor, walls, and ceiling. Along both sides of the passageway, torches burned with black flames that Steven had little doubt would perform Magdalene's dark bidding in an instant.

"We're in." He met Niklaus' gaze, the first time he'd seen his eyes of flesh and blood since he'd fallen to the Black Rook's attack back in Washington D.C. "Unless I miss my guess, you just poured all you had into that castle. You got anything left?"

Niklaus closed his eyes, his brow furrowed in concentration.

Visualize. Emilio's favorite word crept through Steven's mind. *Be the stone.* He focused the same thought and will it took to summon his phalanx of Pawns through the ether to Niklaus, but to no avail.

His last remaining Rook had given his all simply to allow the battle to begin.

Steven gazed around at the forces he had remaining.

A shirtless Niklaus stood next to him, depowered and shivering, avoiding the gaze of the woman whose scorn had left him distraught, drunk, and suicidal atop a skyscraper in a hurricane months before. His friend had opened the door for them, but much beyond that seemed an impossibility.

Victoria, as much a pawn as anyone in Zed and Grey's little Game, seemed to have little more to offer than a bit of remorse over treating a man for whom she clearly still had strong feelings so poorly. Against Archie's guile, Magdalene's flames, Cynthia's power, Vago's cruelty, Wahnahtah's skill with a bow, or even Ruth's athleticism, he didn't see how she'd survive long in the upcoming fight.

Woody, the little old man they'd met at the festival back in Sisters, Oregon, now leaned on a battle-axe, young again for what would likely be the last few minutes of his long life. With his daughter and granddaughter at the far end of the bridge, his attention might be split, but this man had been to war. Steven hoped with all his heart he'd survive this battlefield as well as his last.

Arthur, the kind elderly gentleman he'd met in Maine the first night of this madness wearing the face of the young soldier he'd met in 1946, stood swinging his war hammer like Babe Ruth preparing to face a fast ball. Inside, his wife of sixty-four years waited, her eighteen-year-old face likely twisted into a grotesque mask he'd barely recognize. Would he have what it took if it came down to the two of them? Was that even something to hope for?

And last, the man who taught him how to play this Game in the first place when he was just a boy. His father, returned to his prime and armed with the same pike that had seen Steven through so many battles. But there was only one of him. No phalanx of doppelgangers waited to come to his aid with eight sets of eyes to monitor the enemy. Just Donald Bauer, armed with naught but a pole arm, a shield, and a son's prayer that his father hadn't come all this way only to die because he'd trusted the wrong man.

"No time like the present," Steven said as he stepped across the castle's dark threshold. "Shall we?"

His father stepped to his side and rested his shield against his knee. "Emanuel Lasker once said, 'The laws of chess do not permit a free choice.'" Donald wrapped an arm around his son's shoulders and pulled him in tight. "'You have to move whether you like it or not.'"

30

PITY THE CHILD

Forty feet wide with high vaulted ceilings straight out of a Gothic cathedral, the passageway stretched into a murky dim Steven's keen vision couldn't penetrate. The torches along either wall produced both light and shadow, making it possible to see, but only so far and only so much. The checkered squares that surrounded them on all sides formed a surreal pattern like something from the mind of M. C. Escher, and Steven understood for the first time why so many grandmasters ended up going mad.

Interlocking squares of black and white formed the floor beneath their feet, eight across from wall to wall. The gleaming marble between each hunk of dark granite was all that brought any semblance of hope to the otherwise oppressive darkness.

The four Pawns assembled before Steven from left to right, with Donald and Woody on either end and Arthur and Victoria occupying the center. Having the weakest link directly in front of him left him feeling a bit exposed, but Steven wanted to keep Victoria close in case things went sideways. He'd promised Niklaus he'd look after her, a promise he'd kept when they'd believed him among the fallen, and a promise he planned to keep now that the White Rook had poured all he had into their last hope at victory.

Niklaus crept forward up the gloomy corridor at the White King's left flank, quieter than Steven had ever seen him. Resurrected from what seemed his final rest? Suddenly powerless in the heart of enemy territory? Confronted with not only the woman who broke his heart months before but the warring feelings they were both clearly experiencing? He actually found himself surprised his friend was doing as well as he seemed.

Especially considering the varied fates of the others.

Images flashed across his memory.

The burned bark and crushed knots of William's oaken face.

Lena's tear-filled blank stare as she wept over the body of her first love.

Audrey's pained grimace as she fought to stay alive at the far end of the bridge.

Emilio's sharp eyes, closed forever.

Stop it, Steven. He forced the images from his mind. *Or else the others will be dead too.*

As they proceeded down the hallway, his Pawns four across, Steven couldn't help but imagine the scene from the *Wizard of Oz* where Dorothy and her three friends tread warily down the hallway leading to the chamber of the titular Wizard.

Except in this case, he knew all too well the identity of the man behind the curtain.

Not to mention, in this version, the Wizard and the Wicked Witch had decided to join forces and were no doubt anticipating killing each and every one of them.

No harmless charlatan with a heart of gold awaited them at the end of this particular hallway. No poignant gifts burdened with meaning. No more inane quests meant to stave off the resolution. No promise of a passage home back to a world that again made sense.

Only pain and suffering.

"This passage seems to go on forever." Niklaus pulled to the edge of his square and whispered. "How big is this place, anyway?"

"I have no idea." Steven squinted, trying to pierce the tenebrous darkness ahead. "You've seen what we can do. We've traveled to the past. Hell, you basically came back from the dead." A blue box with a glowing bulb above its door, a relic from his dad's favorite sci-fi show, filled his mind. "Is it so hard to believe this place could be bigger on the inside?"

"This place is half me." Niklaus peered around at the dim. "When my body became the tower back in Atlanta, I could feel every brick, every stone, just like you know where your hands and feet rest even when your eyes are closed. But here, with Cynthia's essence forming every other square, it's like I'm flying blind."

Steven shook his head. "Here's hoping Archie and the rest of the Black are blind to us as well."

"I hate to be the bearer of bad news," Victoria said, clearly having followed the whispered back-and-forth, "but I'm pretty sure they know we're here."

She pointed straight ahead, her finger trembling. Standing in the dim, one foot on white and one on black, waited Ruth. Her long blond curls coruscated in the violet light coming off the torches on either side.

"Two suitors, each come to see who gets to claim their prize." Her piercing dark eyes skewered Steven to the spot. "The one that got away," her gaze shifted to Arthur, "and the one I settled for."

"Steven?" came Arthur's voice, full of pain and anger and uncertainty.

"That's not her talking, Arthur, but Wahnahtah's cruelty mixed with Archie's madness." Steven pulled his shield up to defend his heart. "No offense, but less than an hour ago, you all sounded like that."

"You really want me to fight Ruth?" Arthur asked.

"You'd best fight, lover," Ruth directed the tip of her blade at his chest, "or else you'll be the first to fall." Her head tilted to one side as she raised her shoulders in a subtle shrug. "Not that the order of your demise matters a whit to me or the others." She turned and sprinted off into the darkness. "Come along, quickly now." Her voice faded as she disappeared into the dim. "The master awaits."

"So much for the element of surprise." Donald peered back at Steven. "What now, Son?"

"What Pawns do, Dad." He pointed in the direction Ruth had run. "Keep moving forward."

The six of them pressed on. Donald and Woody monitored the periphery to ensure no one sneaked past them, Arthur and Victoria kept their eyes up and forward for any evidence of the enemy, while Niklaus all but crept up the hall backwards to safeguard all their backs. Their enemy still had someone who could jump around from square to square unseen, and Steven knew all too well Vago's penchant for backstabbing.

After what seemed an eternity, they came to a large antechamber, the circular space forming a dome of intermingled black-and-white stone above their heads. At the opposite end, carved into the stone, awaited yet another portal, a tall double door fashioned of solid ebony and darkest steel. Not a hint of Niklaus' essence invaded the makeup of this latest barrier, leaving the shadow-filled space even darker than the previous corridor. Feeling his way across the murky room, the powerless White Rook crept over to the half oval break in the wall and stood before the black doorway. With a snap of his fingers and a quiet request of the universe, he attempted again to force his will on the castle of their enemy, but this time, the door remained closed.

"This must be their stronghold." Niklaus shook his head. "I'm afraid I'm past the point where I can be useful anymore. Sorry."

"You've stood by me, Nik." Steven patted his friend's shoulder. "That's all that—"

His words were cut short by the rapid-fire beating of metallic wings at his chest.

"No, Bauer." Archie's voice hung in the air as both doors sprung open and the shadows throughout the large antechamber sprang to life, obscuring their vision as the nebulous darkness surrounded them. "All that matters is which of us, at the end of the day, is the winner." The shadows, not nearly as ephemeral as they appeared, dragged the six of them through the door and deposited them just beyond the threshold along the near wall of an enormous room, the floor sectioned off into sixty-four squares of alternating granite and marble.

The final checkered battleground of this fourth and likely final iteration of Grey and Zed's immortal Game lay before them.

"God help us," Steven murmured.

At the far end of the Board, atop a throne of dark iron fashioned to represent a pair of intertwined dragons, Archie occupied the center black square, normally the Black Queen's spot. To his left, in the King's square where Zed no doubt thought he'd be standing when this moment arrived, Magdalene waited, dark flames swirling about her feet like a pack of ravenous dogs awaiting their mistress' command to rush, to attack, to feed. Two squares to Archie's right, Vago sat astride his midnight steed, Sombra, his spiked flail hanging loose in his gauntleted grip. The split stony essence of the woman known as Cynthia sat at either end of Black's back row, formed into two identical towers that stretched halfway to the impossibly high vaulted ceiling of their enemy's stronghold. Before Archie and Magdalene stood the only two Pawns remaining of the enemy's front row: Ruth, leaning on the hilt of her rapier, and Wahnahtah, bow drawn and arrow trained on Steven's heart.

With only four Pawns, a powerless Rook, and himself with which to continue the fight, Steven fought to envision any way forward, any path that could possibly lead to victory, but every scenario ended the same. His mind flirted briefly with resigning and throwing themselves on the mercy of their enemy, but any search for such mercy in the eyes of the gathered Black came up just as empty.

Numerically, materially, positionally, they had every advantage.

Black had won.

Archie knew it. As did everyone in the room.

And yet, as painful and devastating as it would be, nothing remained but to play it through.

How would each of them meet their end? Magdalene's flames? Trampled beneath Sombra's hooves? Skewered by Wahnahtah's barbed arrows? Pounded into oblivion by Cynthia's gargantuan fists? Or something far crueler, from the warped mind of the architect of all this madness?

"You've come all this way only to stall out here at the end?" Archie studied him from atop his draconic throne. "How pathetic."

"No bearded wizard in grey is coming to drag you from the fire this time, Steven." Magdalene stepped forward within her square. "I'd promise you a painless death, but you know I'm a woman who keeps my promises."

"Once we're done with you six," Vago sneered from atop Sombra's barded form, "I'll make sure the Cervantes girl and her aunt go the way of your Knight."

"While I promise to finally put your poor cancer-ridden Queen and her grief-stricken mother out of their shared misery." Wahnahtah smiled. "It's the least I can do for a fellow *Pawn*."

The pair of Black Rooks kept their silent vigil as Ruth drew up the point of her blade and directed it at Arthur. "Oh, my husband, how it pains me to see you taking up arms against us, allied with the very man I've favored since long before we ever met." She let out a quiet giggle. "How mortifying that must be."

"That's not Ruth." Where before Arthur had seemed all but destroyed by his wife's taunts, this time he remained firm, reserving his comments for Archie alone. "Let go of the woman I love, you bastard."

Archie rested his cruel rosary on the arm of his throne and beckoned Arthur with a waggling finger. "Come and get her, Pawn."

"My thoughts exactly." Steven brandished the broadsword of the White King. "Forces of the White, attack!"

The six of them raced across the Board, a microcosm of the valiant charge from every action and war movie Steven had ever seen. Shields held high and weapons at the ready, the four Pawns sent his heart swelling with pride at their bravery even in the face of certain doom.

And then, the first fell.

One second, Woody raced up the right side of their charge, and the next, he lay sprawled face down and contorted at the intersection of four squares, one of Wahnahtah's arrows protruding from his thigh.

Before Steven could even process the loss, his father's scream from the opposite end of their charge captured his attention. Donald's brave run, his shield and pike held bravely before him, proved impotent against a single blow from the Black Rook that sent him flying into the nearest wall.

Victoria was the next to fall as Vago disappeared into a dark fold in space only to reappear in the reluctant Pawn's path. His whirling flail impacted her shield and sent her flying unconscious into Niklaus' arms.

"Nik!" Steven shouted. "Is she?"

"Breathing," he whispered, "but barely."

Steven's eyes danced between Arthur and Niklaus, the only two besides himself remaining of their failed last-ditch assault.

"Get her out of here," he grunted at Niklaus as cold certainty mounted in his chest. "Try to save her."

"But—"

"Do it."

With one last imploring look, Niklaus turned and rushed for the door with Victoria's crumpled form draped across his shoulder.

"My dear, Cynthia," Archie commanded with a caustic laugh. "Crush them."

And...nothing. For the first time in Steven's recollection, an enemy Piece hesitated.

"But they're fleeing," came a voice from the two-story tower of dark stone. "Powerless."

The four words represented only the fourth time Steven had heard the Black Rook speak in all their confrontations. The first had been a few words in deference to Zed in Atlanta, the second asking Magdalene for further instructions after she'd attacked and shattered Niklaus back in D.C., and the third begging him to concede less than an hour before.

Something had always seemed different about the Black Rook and her participation in the Game. More than the quiet competence he'd assumed at first, this woman they knew only as Cynthia seemed to always perform exactly as commanded and yet remained the only one among their enemy who hadn't shown even a hint of glee in her actions, only submission to the will of whomever wore Black's crown.

Unfortunately, her joy in serving their enemy or lack thereof didn't change the lethality of her blows one iota.

"Defiant as ever, I see." Archie groaned. "For the thousandth time, my Queen, show her."

Magdalene raised a hand as if commanding an orchestra to play. In answer, the flames at her feet rose before her and formed an oval of black fire. Within the oblong curve of crackling flame appeared an image of a child. A dark-skinned boy no more than six years of age sat in a corner of a dark cell, the walls and floor similarly checkered black and white, hugging his knees and rocking himself as tears poured from his swollen eyes.

"Oscar!"

"You've come so far, Cynthia, since this all began." Archie's words took on a hypnotic sing-song quality. "Help me win this, and you and your son will be reunited along with more wealth than you can possibly imagine." His voice dropped to a guttural growl. "All you have to do is *exactly* what I say with *no further hesitation*."

"Very well." With a rumble like an oncoming locomotive, the mighty tower swept up the vertical file after Niklaus and Victoria, catching them a few steps from the enormous door leading back to the antechamber and sending the pair flying. The upright battering ram collided with the arch of the massive doorway, sealing the only exit with several tons of stone.

"It is done, my lord." The dark tower turned away from the pile of rubble, and then, as one, both the attacking Rook as well as her other aspect remaining at the far corner of the Board shifted into their shared humanoid form, a pair of titanic goddesses carved from darkest stone. "Only Bauer and Pedone remain."

"Not for long." Ruth swept up the Board, taking the squares one at a time with a dancer's grace. "Time, I think, for a little game within a Game." A seductive sashay past Vago brought her to the intersection of the four squares before Steven and Arthur with Woody writhing to her left, blood oozing from his arrow-pierced leg, and Donald's unmoving form to her right. "The name of this particular game is 'Who Loves Me More?' The winner shall be granted a kiss, while the loser of this simple competition," her eyes dropped to the rapier in her hand, "will undoubtedly wish his heart had made wiser decisions."

"Don't do this, Ruth." Steven kept his shield high as he implored with both eyes and words for her to renege. "The outcome here is already decided. We both know that. But when all this is over, what about then? How will you live with yourself if you strike me down, or worse, the man you've loved for decades?"

"Why, Steven." A hint of genuine emotion flashed across Ruth's features. "Are you offering up your own heart to save his?"

"No." Arthur dropped both shield and war hammer to the ground. "It has to be me."

"Arthur," Steven whispered, "what are you doing?"

"Look, Steven," he answered. "I appreciate everything you've said, but this is the moment of truth of the most important day of my life, and therefore, the next move is mine to make." His gaze flicked in Ruth's direction. "Not only do I believe in my wife's love more than anything else on this planet, but I'll be damned before I let anything happen to you, the King and last Piece standing in a chess game that will decide the fate of the world"

"Arthur," Steven grunted, the heat rising in his cheeks, "it's over. The Game? We lost." He pointed to Ruth whose shoulders heaved in anger and frustration. "That may look like the woman you married, but this person standing before you now will kill you without a thought."

"But that's just it." He turned toward Ruth, arms at his sides, palms up, his chest exposed. "Long before you were born, I gave this woman my heart. As far as I'm concerned, it's still hers to do with as she pleases." He took a step forward. "Knowing she met someone like you first and still chose me to be her husband and the father of our children tells me everything I need to know about my Ruthie." His eyes locked with his wife's. "Ruth, your words right now aren't your own. Somehow, they've filled you with hate and resentment and cruelty, but that's not you. That's never been you. I know you're in there, just as I was still present when my mind was clouded by the Black. But my mind is now free, and yours can be as well." He held his arms out in invitation. "You can come back to me, no questions asked, but you have to put down that sword."

"Arthur?" she asked.

"Put down that sword, now, and come to me so that we can be together, here at the end."

Indecision warred across her features. No one, not even Archie, spoke as Ruth battled the mystic brainwashing eating at her soul. In the end, however, the darkness proved too strong, as the cold sneer returned to her face.

"Or, husband, I could end both this farce of a marriage and you with a single flick of my wrist." She brandished her rapier and sent its tip flying at Arthur's heart. "Now."

"No!" Steven cried out, the word amplified as it flew not only from his mouth, but Ruth's as well. The blade's tip stopped an inch short of Arthur's ribcage, Ruth struggled with one arm to force the rapier forward even as the other held her wrist.

"My lord?" She called out, angry and confused and frightened. "My blade. It—"

"Finish him!" Archie commanded.

"I can't." Tears pooled at the corners of Ruth's eyes. "I...*can't*."

"Then you've proven too weak to be of any further use to me." Archie tilted his head toward Magdalene. "My Queen, if you will, show her how it's done."

"Gladly." Magdalene raised her serpentine scepter and sent a sphere of black fire rocketing at Ruth's back, the explosive impact sending the woman flying and the blade of her weapon straight through the center of Arthur's chest.

As Ruth's flailing form flew past him and Arthur sank to his knees, Archie finally rose from his draconic throne and smiled.

"Just as I envisioned it, Steven Bauer." He tapped his Bishop's staff on the dark stone and set his cruel rosary to whirling. "Here at the end, a crowned Bishop with Queen, Rook, Knight, and Pawn at my beck and call, and you all alone with no friends, no wizened mentor to whisk you away, no hope."

"There's always hope." Steven raised his chin. "And you know what they say about going up against a man with nothing to lose."

"Ah, but that's where you're oh-so-very wrong." Archie studied him from the confines of his dark square. "The power you would gain as winner of the Game could give you everything you'd need to fix all of this, everything you've have ever desired, everything you believe a man who has fought as long and hard as you deserves." The Black Bishop let out a long, satisfied sigh. "Know as I pound the final nail in the coffin of your pathetic existence that you are a man who literally has everything to lose."

31

ECHEC

"S hould it be me?" Magdalene asked, all but licking her lips like a hyena over a wounded antelope. "Such delicious symmetry it would be were I the one to finally finish this."

"As long as I get a piece of him." Vago circled Steven atop Sombra. "I haven't forgotten what went down in Baltimore."

"Where you were a treacherous, murdering, lying chickenshit?" Steven kept his shield held high, one eye on the enemy Knight, and the other on Black's back row. "I hate to be the one to break it to you, Miguel, but that pretty much still seems to be the status quo."

"Let me kill him, Lacan." Vago seethed from his mount. "One swing of this flail upside his fool head, and he won't be mouthing off to any of us again."

"*Fool*, you say." Archie snickered. "Listen, everyone. As much as I know how fervently each of you would love to be the one to feed Bauer his own entrails, this must be handled, as I understand it, delicately." He returned to his iron throne of intertwined dragons. "The rest of the Pieces can fall in whatever order or manner that occurs, but the King must be placed in true checkmate for the Game to end." The Black Bishop released his staff and interlaced his fingers around the cruel rosary beads dangling in his grip. "After that, however, you may all feel free to exact your various pounds of flesh."

Steven took advantage of the distraction and lunged at the Black Knight with his broadsword. The point of his weapon, however, encountered only open air as his mounted opponent vanished from view only to reappear in the square behind him. With an ear-piercing whinny, Vago's steed reared and knocked Steven flat on his face with his flailing forelegs.

"Ha!" Vago laughed triumphantly. "After all our bluster, it is Sombra that draws first blood."

Steven forced himself back to his feet and cursed himself for an idiot. Vago's move left him penned in with enemies on either side. To retreat would mean facing a mounted foe who had little compunction about bashing in his skull, while going forward meant facing Wahnah-tah's martial skill, be it bow or axe. In either case, a single lapse in his focus could mean death by rushing stone or exploding fireball.

And yet, the most dangerous enemy remained the mastermind behind it all.

"You know, Archie, I've finally put it all together." Steven stood tall, doing his best to watch Vago from the corner of one eye while keeping the remainder of the Black firmly in his field of vision. "How you played this Game as well as all of us from the very beginning."

"I would certainly hope so, Bauer." Archie laughed from atop his grand throne of iron. "I'd hate to think the man who nearly played me to a stalemate was an imbecile."

"You may not have known all along that we were going to be sent to the past, but once we were there, it was you who set all this in motion: you who summoned Victor Brenin to the middle of nowhere, Wyoming; you who hired and then killed those men to blow up the train; you who told him how to find you years later when the time came."

"Very good," Archie sneered. "Do go on."

"You've already admitted that you were indoctrinated as the Black Bishop long before I came along and found you in that hospital bed. From that point on every word from your mouth has been lie after lie."

"Not quite a bullseye," the Black Bishop slid into a wicked grin, "but close enough."

"With your visions providing foreknowledge of the Game, you knew exactly what to say and how much of the truth to reveal to get both sides to bring you to a point where you could betray both Kings and take all the power for yourself."

"Bravo, Steven. Your discovery comes a bit late, but I do take strange pleasure in knowing you'll take the evidence of my brilliance to your grave."

"All that being said," Steven rested the tip of his sword on the marble between his feet. "Even *you* don't know everything."

Archie's smile diminished ever so slightly. "Do tell, Bauer-King."

"You didn't know that I'd be able to rescue the various Pieces from the Antarctic iteration." He allowed himself a slight grin. "That move clearly took you by surprise."

Archie motioned around the room. "And your recovered Pawns have accomplished oh so much."

"You didn't see that Ruth would be able to overcome whatever brainwashing you and Wahnahtah performed on our friends and family."

The Black Bishop let out an exasperated sigh. "And yet, both Pedone and his wife now lie among the fallen."

"All those months plotting your betrayal of Grey, and you didn't know that, in the end, the crown was meant for me." Steven narrowed his eyes at his enemy. "That I was King all along."

Archie did his best to hide the wince that overtook his features. "It would appear that I've adapted quite nicely."

"Lastly, you didn't know that I'd figure out your lone weakness."

Archie straightened up on his throne. "And what might that be, Bauer?"

"Grey didn't choose me for this job because I was an expert combatant or a master tactician. He selected me for this Game of his and Zed's for one reason and one reason alone: because I'm an excellent judge of character."

With a chuckle, Archie shook his head in amusement. "The fact that you welcomed a man into your ranks that now sits upon the enemy throne would seem evidence to the contrary."

"Actually, the fact that all of us accepted you so readily only confirms what I've suspected for a while."

Vago spurred Sombra an inch in Steven's direction, but a single stern glance from the newly confident White King convinced them to back off.

"If there was one thing about Emilio," he continued, "it was that he could smell bullshit a mile away, and yet he stuck by you not only in the here and now, but for months when it was just the two of you stuck in Wyoming in 1890. Lena can spot a liar like an eagle in the sky hunting its next meal, and yet, she defended you time and again. Niklaus may have always been the jokester of the group, but his heart was pure, and there's no way he would have given his confession to someone he didn't trust inherently." Steven choked back the emotion. "Lastly, Audrey may be the finest human being I've ever met, and she never blinked once in your direction until the day you shot Grey." He smiled a victor's smile. "You may have been there all along, whoever or whatever you are, but you aren't my friend, Archie, anymore than that was Ruth before, trying to impale the husband she's loved with all her heart for the better part of a century."

The Black Bishop sat silent atop his throne, studying him with renewed interest for the first time since the one-sided melee began. "And if you are correct, Steven Bauer, what of it?"

"For all your machinations, the man we know as Archibald Lacan is clearly still in there and maintains far more control than you'd like to admit." Steven pulled in a deep breath and lowered his chin. "I may die today with the others, and our loss of this contest may cause the world a ton of suffering I wish I could prevent, but I just wanted my friend to understand unequivocally that I know the truth, and that I forgive him." He raised his gaze to meet the Black Bishop's. "A warning, whoever you are: you may have the upper hand for now, but the good man shackled at your core will undoubtedly win in the end." His lips spread in a grim smile. "I'm betting the world on it."

Flabbergasted, Archie leaned back in his throne, his entire body shaking with rage.

"Boss?" Vago turned Sombra about and set his flail whirling. "What do you want us to do?"

"Simple." Archie's gaze wandered among the gathered Black, his voice getting louder and more exasperated with every syllable. "Perform on this simple grid of sixty-four squares what I have already done over the many months since all this began. Force the White King into a position where he cannot escape and end this." His fist closed tight around his dark rosary. "And then, *end him.*"

"At last." Magdalene pulled herself up straight, the dark flames that danced around her feet growing visibly excited as she approached the forward edge of her square. "I've waited a long time for—"

THOOM.

The entire room shook, as if a legion of cannons had fired upon the castle walls.

Vago's eyes shifted left and right. "What the hell was—"

THOOM.

A mix of marble and granite rubble rained down from above, the perfect interplay of alternating black-and-white geometry above their heads marred by the unseen force.

"Cynthia," Archie hissed, "did you not dispatch their Rook?"

THOOM.

The checkered wall adjacent to the pile of rubble left by the Black Rook's attack on Niklaus and Victoria exploded inward. Through the jagged opening in the stone poured white light as blinding as the midday sun, forcing all present to shield their eyes. When the fledgling star that had torn its way into the room finally diminished enough that they could again see, a collective gasp overtook the Black.

There, at the far end of the Board, atop a fully-barded and rearing Rocinante sat the White Knight, her armor pristine and new, her conquistador helmet allowing her flowing brown locks to cascade down her back, and her mace gripped loosely in one hand, ready to smite anyone who stood in her way.

"Lena?" Steven looked on in wonder. "But how?'

"Defend yourself, my King," Lena and Rocinante disappeared in a flash of silver only to reappear in the square next to Vago and Sombra, "while I rid the Board of this garbage."

"Cervantes." Vago's wicked smile gleamed from the shadow of his own conquistador helm. "I was actually hungry for some dessert. Prepare to meet your—"

Lena's mace hit Vago center chest like a meteor strike, sending the dark-armored Knight flying from his saddle to the periphery of the Board. Sombra lunged forward to attack both horse and rider with his spiked escutcheon. Failing that, he spun around in a vain attempt to land a kick to Rocinante's side. The ivory steed, however, proved far too quick for either of the dark stallion's attacks.

"Run to your master," Lena growled, "and keep your distance unless you'd care to try my mercy."

Rocinante backed up his rider's words with a rare roar of his own, their shared message all too clear.

As Sombra trotted, head down, to Vago's side, another rumble filled the room as the quartet of squares that formed the center of the Board buckled upward like a volcano about to erupt. At the apex of this growing mound of shattered marble and granite, a single shoot of green burst forth. A blink later, the tiny branch had tripled in both height and diameter and sprouted leaves. Another second and an oak sapling occupied the center of the Board, growing before all their eyes like something out of myth until a mighty tree filled the space, its branches stretching as high as the two towering figures of stone at either end of the Board.

"But you were destroyed." Archie's scowl grew darker from atop his throne of iron. "I saw it with my own eyes."

"Funny thing about trees," William answered, his voice the sound of a gale wind howling through an old hardwood stand, "if you don't get the root, they grow right back."

"Rest assured that when we are done today, I will leave nothing but ash." Archie shook atop his throne. "Cynthia, my dear, time again to earn your keep." He motioned to the aspect of the Black Rook positioned at the opposite end of the Board. "You, destroy that damned walking tree." He shifted his attention to Cynthia's other half, still waiting at the end of his back row. "And you can join Magdalene and Wahnahtah against the White King while Vago occupies their newly minted Knight." The Black Bishop's voice dropped to a low growl. "Bring Bauer to me."

As William and Lena each faced off against their respective opponents, the Black Queen, Rook, and Pawn rushed Steven from three sides. Like a team of spiders maneuvering a fly deeper and deeper into their web, the trio forced him square by square toward a waiting Archie, the Black Bishop's lethal rosary already spinning in his hand as he awaited the precise moment to strike.

Back atop Sombra, Vago proved far more cautious against Lena the second time around. Similarly, Cynthia chose a mainly defensive posture against William. With neither Piece playing the aggressor, any hope for prompt aid from Knight or Rook seemed remote. Steven reached out with his mind for Niklaus, for Audrey, even for Emilio, and was met each time with only crushing silence. With no more rabbits in his metaphorical hat, one simple fact ruled the day: if he wanted to survive, it was down to him and him alone.

In the least surprising turn of the day, Archie stayed atop his seat of power. Contending with Magdalene, Cynthia, and Wahnahtah together, however, proved more than challenging enough. Steven ducked one dark fireball after another, blocked multiple arrow strikes, and stayed out of the reach of punch after punch of sweeping granite fists, losing ground with every move, backed further and further into the corner with each defensive move. As he leaped back to avoid a river of black fire, he fell into the wall at the edge of the Board's seventh rank. Turning, he made his stand as the enemy Pawn, Rook, and Queen closed on him.

"Bring it on," With shield before him and sword held high, he motioned for his enemies to attack. "But know that I'll be taking some of you with me."

"Oh, for God's sake, Bauer, give up already." Archie let out a disgusted sigh from atop his iron throne. "You have no more surprises up your sleeve and are hopelessly outnumbered, pathetic Pawn-King." The Black Bishop's nose crinkled in disgust. "Drop your useless weapons and surrender now, and perhaps I won't make you suffer in death as you have in life."

Pawn-King. Amaryllis fluttered at his heart at the paired words and

Steven's scalp tingled as an image of his dead mentor's knowing smile flashed across his memory.

Thank you, Grey.

"Very well." Steven dropped his sword to the black granite at his feet. "You're right." He turned to face his attackers. "You've got me."

Wahnahtah stood midway across the Board, eyes narrowed and barbed shaft nocked and drawn.

The Rook gazed down silently from two squares away along the seventh rank, a true check if this were but a simple game of chess.

Magdalene crouched by the disrupted stone at the room's center, her face the shrewd look of someone who has already been fooled one too many times.

"You've backed the King into a corner, given him no avenue of escape, attacked him with superior force and numbers, but there's one thing you've forgotten." Steven stepped backwards onto the marble square that formed the corner of the Board's eighth rank. "As you've all made certain to endlessly remind me since this all began, at the core of this particular King beats the heart of a Pawn." A wicked grin spread across his face. "Remind me, Archibald. What happens in chess when a pawn reaches the opponent's back row?"

Archie's eyes, previously amused and complacent, went wide with fear. "No! Stop him!"

A vortex of silver energy surrounded Steven like a cyclone of starlight and power and ancient secrets. The room filled with palpable electricity, setting the hairs atop his head on end, as the previously still air began to churn. Wahnahtah and Magdalene let fly a volley of arrows and ebon spheres of fire that all dissipated into nothingness as they touched the maelstrom of swirling light. And then, as suddenly as it appeared, the mystical tornado of radiance exploded like a thousand flashbulbs, and the White Pawn-King was no longer alone.

A low mist of silver coalescing at her feet and eight spheres of shining force orbiting her shoulders, Audrey Richards stood restored, her form again arrayed in the resplendent regalia of the White Queen.

The cold fury in her gaze communicated all too well that she was no longer in the mood for games.

"Audrey," Steven gasped, "you're okay."

"Never better," she answered, never once taking her eyes off her dark opposite. "All right, Mags. You've been flexing your muscles as the Big Bad Wolf since all this began." Audrey swept up the Board at her opposite like a hurricane dressed to the nines. "Time to settle once and for all who rules this Board."

Magdalene summoned yet another sphere of ebon flame and sent it flying at the White Queen. "My name, bitch, is—"

Audrey sent all but one of her silver spheres of power flying at Magdalene's head, cutting off the Black Queen's retort before catching the hastily cast fireball in a swath of glimmering mist and redirecting it at the Black Rook. Cynthia, having tasted her Queen's fire already that day, dove to the Board's stony surface. Magdalene, on the other hand, took the full brunt of Audrey's assault, the seven glowing balls of energy flying around her like a hive of angry hornets before converging on their target in an explosion of silver and sound that sent the Black Queen flying to the Board's opposite corner.

"What a one-trick pony." With Magdalene temporarily neutralized and Cynthia's nearer aspect sent to ground, Audrey turned to Wahnahtah, the mists churning at her feet like a sentient storm as the final sphere of silver orbited her lithe form.

"I'd lower that bow if I were you." Her voice echoed in the space like a rock star angel fallen from heaven. "Unless you'd like me to make it three for three."

Wahnahtah considered for all of a second before dropping his bow to his side and returning the arrow to his quiver. "As you wish," came his harsh whisper.

With the Black Pawn's capitulation, all fighting across the Board ceased. Cynthia's struggle with William came to a standstill. The furious battle of Knights went silent as both Vago and Lena brought their steeds around to bear witness. The Black Queen, not saying another word, rose to her feet and, along with Black's Pawn and Rook, turned to watch White's King and the usurper of Black's crown discuss terms.

Silent as his Queen brought the White back from the precipice of defeat, Steven now strode purposefully down the eighth rank to face the Black Bishop atop his iron throne of enmeshed dragons.

"So, Archie, in the end, after all you've done, all the lies and treachery and murder, it comes down to a simple conversation." Steven retrieved his sword from where he'd dropped it, but rather than threatening his opponent with steel, he opted to return his weapon to its sheath. "It would appear your best laid plans haven't borne the fruit you anticipated."

"This battle is far from over." Archie coiled on the iron throne like a viper readying to strike. "My forces—"

"Are matched by mine." Steven swept his arm wide to indicate the sixty-four squares that had come to define all their lives. "We can keep on fighting if you want, and in the end, you might even emerge the winner, but both sides will suffer losses."

"Like that matters to me."

Steven gazed around at all the Pieces, both Black and White. "It matters to *them*."

"I suppose it does." Archie's eyes gleamed as he considered Steven's words. "You've played this Game well, Bauer, and come further than I would ever have dreamed possible."

"I offer you a stalemate." Steven held out his hands, palms up, in a gesture of cooperation. "Let all this end. Allow the energies of the Game to return whence they came like Grey and Zed first designed, and we can work out everything else."

"You're asking me to resign?" Archie asked. "You can't be serious."

"I'm asking you to agree that the Game is over." Steven pulled in a breath. "Haven't we all suffered enough?"

"Perhaps." Archie scratched his chin. "A generous offer indeed." The Black Bishop's wicked grin returned in spades. "But there is one card I still hold that trumps all you can bring to bear." His gaze shot to his Rook. "A mother's love."

At Archie's silent command, the two aspects of the woman known as Cynthia melted into the dark granite beneath their respective feet only for a singular tower to emerge at the Board's center where William had before made his dramatic reappearance.

"I'm sorry," came a voice like boulder grinding on boulder as the pinnacle of the structure rushed at the checkered ceiling like a battering ram. "He has my son."

With a force like a bomb, the tower struck the stone above their heads, sending a shower of marble and granite down upon them all. Without warning, the Board split in two and the individual squares pulled away from each other as the castle surrounding them began to tear itself apart.

"You bastard!" Magdalene flew at Archie.

"You'll kill us all!" Vago spurred Sombra into a mad dash for the iron throne.

"Not if I can help it," Wahnahtah added, nocking an arrow and firing at Archie's dark heart.

"No, no, and no." Archie blocked the dark shaft with a wave of his hand and then directed his ebony staff at his Queen, Knight, and Pawn in order. With a trio of dark bursts of violet from his implement's horned headpiece, the Black Bishop pulled from each of them every last iota of power granted by the great Game.

Magdalene fell flat to the stone beneath her, her body again withered and old, her hair thin and colorless, and her face scarred by the very fire that moments before had been her willing servant.

Vago and Sombra, suddenly naked of any protection other than street clothes and saddle, collapsed in a heap as the crumbling stone beneath them tangled the black stallion's feet.

Wahnahtah fell to one side, the leg granted him by the Game's energies suddenly missing even as the rising rock beneath his remaining foot hurled him to the unforgiving floor.

"The price, Magdalene Byrne, Miguel Fausto Vasquez, and John Small," Archie's voice dropped to a low growl, "for betrayal most foul."

"You'd rather all of us die than admit defeat?" Steven rushed the Black Bishop's throne.

"Not all of us." Archie let fly with his rosary, the wide arc meant to catch him at the throat as it had Zed. "Just everyone but me."

"Not happening." The White King blocked the mystical garrote with his gauntleted forearm, but rather than the disappointment he expected to find in his enemy's mad gaze, he found only manic delight.

"Perfect." Hand over hand, Archie drew Steven closer, the metaphor of spider and fly becoming all the more evident with each passing second. "Cynthia, my dear," he all but giggled, "I feel a bit exposed. Also, a little assistance would be *most* appreciated."

As the castle continued to fragment around the gathered Pieces, a bunker of dark granite grew from the wall behind the Black Bishop's throne to shield him from falling debris even as a tongue of dark stone rose from the square beneath Archie's feet like a snake charmer's cobra and lashed out at Steven, binding the White King's opposite arm and lifting him from the floor like a child's toy.

"This wasn't how I foresaw the events of this day resolving," Archie continued, "but I suppose taking a page from your much beloved mentor's book seems almost poetic." Any mirth left the Black Bishop's voice. "Though, unlike him, I intend to stick around and receive my just desserts."

"Like you know what happens next," Steven grunted as dark rosary and rocky shackle threatened to pull both his arms from their sockets. "You talk a big game, but even you're in the dark about how all this ends."

"Neither Grey nor Zed could possibly have planned for such an eventuality in their original design." Archie flashed him a vindictive smile. "But with both of them dead and the rest of you soon to follow, I'm willing to wager everything that the last man standing, not to mention in possession of both crowns, can pretty much write his own ticket."

"Hang on, Steven," Audrey cried out. "We're coming."

Time and again, she, Lena, and William all moved to rescue their King only to have their way blocked by wall after wall of black stone erupting through the rapidly disintegrating floor.

"Too little, too late." Archie stared up at Steven, the White King's sword arm trapped within unyielding stone and his opposite limb rendered immobile by the Black Bishop's rosary chain.

"Don't do this, Archie," Steven implored, "There's got to be another way for this to end."

"But this is precisely how I want it to end, with all of you dead and me with the power of the universe at my beck and call." Archie rose from his throne and strode over to stand directly beneath Steven's dangling form. "Now, lower your head and let that damned crown of yours fall, unless you'd prefer I take it myself from your dismembered body." He brought his staff around and raised its darkened ram skull head to his enemy's face. "The Bishop's implement can give life, Steven Bauer. Did you never consider it might also be capable of taking it away?"

The eye sockets of the long dead ram glowed a pulsating purple that rose and fell in time with an audible throbbing like a demented version of the *Hvitr Kyll's* drone. The strange incandescence grew brighter and the undulating sound louder with every cycle, as the Bishop's staff drew the very warmth and vigor from Steven's body.

"Now, do you see? Your cause was lost before you ever learned of this Game that has defined and now ends your worthless existence."

"Not...dead...yet." Steven's head lolled to one side where from the corner of his vision he could see William vaulting yet another wall in an effort to get to him, Lena atop Rocinante leaping and dodging the various bulwarks of rushing stone and falling rock, and Audrey atop a cloud of silver mist flying at him like a runaway train.

William, who had risen from utter destruction to fight for him more than once that day.

Lena, who had overcome defeat and despair to accept the mantle of Knight.

Audrey, who had answered his call despite mortal wounds that left her on oblivion's door.

Each of them fought against hopeless odds and even death itself to save the world from Archie's madness.

Could he do any less?

The White King summoned all his remaining strength, bringing everything he had left to bear against Archie's cruel rosary chain, and grabbed his enemy's staff. Though his strength poured from him no less than if he were bleeding out on a frigid battlefield in one of the world's many wars, he somehow pushed the staff away as he wrestled to free it from its master's grip.

"Damn you, Bauer," Archie growled. "Why won't you just die?"

"Where there's life," Steven grunted, "there's hope."

"Stop!" came an unfamiliar female voice from across the room. "Stop all of this."

The distraction coupled with Steven's failing strength allowed Archie to wrench his staff free, but rather than renew his assault, the ever-wary Bishop stepped back to appraise this latest arrival to their checkered battlefield. With the last dregs of will he had remaining, Steven craned his neck to the right and followed Archie's hate-filled gaze to the opposite end of the Board. There, framed by the interlocking hunks of uneven marble and granite in the enormous gap left by Lena's explosive entrance, stood Victoria Van Doren.

"Cannot one of you damned people stay dead?" Archie considered and then released his rosary's hold on Steven's arm. "On second thought, perhaps you'd like to see me end each of your friends one-by-one while you hang there helpless."

"The only ending today," Niklaus joined Victoria beneath the jagged arch, "will be yours."

"Enough!" Archie's eyes shot to the lone Piece remaining on his side. "My Rook, bring this place down upon all their heads."

"No." The enormous tower at the room's center again took on the form of a giant woman of stone. The Black Rook's head turned her attention on Niklaus and Victoria. "Did you find him?"

Without a word, the pair stepped into the room and parted, revealing a pair of children. The first, a young girl with dark brown skin and knotted braids dressed in a tattered and stained school uniform, held a hand to her eyes as if even the relatively dim light of the room was the brightest she'd seen in days.

"Clarissa?" Something akin to worried kindness flashed across Archie's face like a break in the clouds, only to vanish again behind the Black Bishop's perpetual sneer.

The second child, a first-grader with brown skin and close-cropped natural curls, looked on the scene with wonder, the terror in his gaze washed away in an instant by the miraculous sight before his eyes.

"Oscar!" The word, delivered by the colossal Black Rook, shook the room like a sonic boom.

Despite the gravelly delivery of his given name, the boy looked several stories up into the granite eyes of the woman called Cynthia, a look of recognition blossoming on his face, and uttered one simple word.

"Mom?"

"Watch him," was all Cynthia said as her three-story form spun around to confront the Black Bishop.

Archie raised his staff, no doubt in preparation to expunge the Black Rook's powers as he had the others', only to have it batted away by a tongue of stone from the wall behind him. In a blink, the granite shelter that had shielded him from falling rock became an enormous stony fist that seized the Black Bishop and lifted him breathless from the ground. Cynthia dissolved into the dark granite beneath her feet, her disappearance bringing the rumbling tremors, falling rock, and crumbling walls all to a halt. Another breath, and she emerged anew from the dark granite beneath the Black Bishop, the giant fist holding Archie's struggling form elongating into an arm, a shoulder, a head, a torso, and finally legs. Every hunk and fragment of dark stone in the destroyed room, including the one holding Steven, flowed into the Rook's still growing form like jet-black mercury, increasing her mass with every passing second until her form grew so titanic, she had to hunch to keep her head from tearing through the room's high ceiling.

Audrey and Lena, no longer blocked by the Rook's obstacles, rushed to Steven's side. William pulled up behind the three of them and was soon joined by Niklaus, Victoria, and the two children. As Audrey helped him to his feet, Steven shot Niklaus a sidelong glance. "How?"

"Tall, dark, and rocky may have hurled us from the room, but she didn't hurt us." Niklaus rested his hands on the boy's shoulders. "She made us a deal. Find the children and she'd be free to do what was right."

"But this place is basically her. She couldn't free her own son. How could you?"

Niklaus knelt and picked up a hunk of marble the size of his fist. "Cynthia may have built this place, but I poured all I had into its walls and floors and hallways and doors." He let the jagged rock fall to the ground. "I may have given up what made me the Rook, but this place is half me now, and I'll come and go as I please."

"Yeah, he will." Victoria looked on Niklaus with admiration, and, even more surprisingly, he seemed to reciprocate. Steven might never know what words the two had shared as they searched the castle to find the kidnapped children, but for the first time, in the presence of the woman who broke his heart, the White Rook's walls were down.

Cynthia, so huge she basically held Archie between her thumb and forefinger, brought his comparatively tiny body before her enormous stone face.

"You. Threatened. My. Child." The sheer force of the words exiting Cynthia's colossal lips shook Archie like a leaf on a tornado-torn tree. "Made me do unspeakable things."

"Technically..." Archie forced the words from his breathless lungs. "Zed is the one who took your child."

"At your recommendation, coward." She gave the Black Bishop a firm shake that Steven was half-surprised didn't break the man's neck. "And now, Archibald Lacan," she wrapped her remaining fingers around his body and squeezed, "you shall pay for what you've done."

Niklaus and Victoria covered the children's eyes as the sound of breaking bones shattered the strange quiet.

"Don't," Steven shouted, his gaze fixed on Archie's bulging eyes. "Not like this."

"Not like this?" Bitter sarcasm filled Cynthia's tone. "You and I both know he deserves so much worse."

"Agreed, Cynthia, but more than darkness fills this man whose life you literally hold in your hand."

"If there is," she glared down at him through angry granite eyes, "I've not seen it."

"No one on this Board has more of a right to wish this man dead than you, but there's another way."

She squeezed harder, the sound like green wood popping in a campfire. "What other way?"

"A variation of checkmate." Steven motioned to the marble square waiting empty between Cynthia's gigantic knees. "Make the Black Bishop stand upon a square of white, and I suspect you'll find all the justice you're looking for."

"Justice? I don't want justice." Cynthia squeezed Archie even tighter, and Steven honestly wondered if his insides might squirt out like a tube of toothpaste. "For what he's done to me and my son, to all of us, he deserves nothing but cold vengeance."

"Wait." Steven pulled in a breath, desperate for the words that would allow this to end without seeing Archie crushed like an aluminum can. "What about Oscar?" He motioned to where Niklaus and Victoria stood with her son and Archie's great-granddaughter. "Don't listen to me. Listen to your heart. What would Oscar have you do?"

Cynthia pondered his words, and with a huff like a collapsing mine, plonked Archie's breathless form onto the Board, his upper torso, arms, and head resting on black granite, but his lower half positioned exactly where Steven had intended.

On cool, white marble.

"Thank you, Steven Bauer." The Black Rook's titanic form folded in upon itself again and again until Cynthia arrived at what Steven guessed was her normal height. "And my apologies for all I was forced to do." With a sigh, she transformed from stone to flesh and stood revealed, a black woman just old enough to have a boy Oscar's age. She ran a suspicious eye over Archie's unmoving form and then met Steven's gaze once more. "Now, if you don't mind, I need to be with my son."

At Steven's silent nod, Cynthia spun and raced to Oscar's side. Scooping him up from the ground with a practiced swoop, she held him tight to her chest. With tears running down her cheeks, she looked around at all of them, a strange mix of apology and gratitude in her gaze. At first, she refused to meet Niklaus' gaze, having been the one responsible for his almost-death in D.C., but as both he and Victoria moved to join the mother and son in a long embrace, Steven recognized that at least in some ways, the healing had begun.

A quiet sob captured Steven's attention. Clarissa Lacan stood separate from the rest of the group, staring at the unmoving form in skintight black. Steven caught his Queen's gaze and inclined his head in the girl's direction. With a nod, Audrey slunk over and rested a reassuring hand on the terrified schoolgirl's shoulder.

"Now," Steven muttered, "what do we do about him?"

The Black Bishop's still form remained so but a second longer. A pained grunt escaping his lips, Archie began to writhe on the stone floor like a vampire dipped toes-first in holy water. With a scream ripped from the depths of his soul, he kicked and squirmed in an effort to push himself back onto the dark square beneath his shoulders, but his efforts proved futile as writhing arms of energy from each of the two squares, blindingly white and inscrutably black, encircled Archie's legs and arms respectively and soon worked to rip the man in two. If the previous screaming had proven unnerving, the gutted howl that erupted from Archibald Lacan's lips was infinitely worse and would haunt Steven's dreams for all his days.

Assuming, of course, that any of them made it out of there alive.

32

FOOL'S MATE

As all present looked on in wonder, waiting for what seemed an inevitable shower of gore, a miracle occurred. The form of Archibald Lacan indeed split in two, but the end result was anything but the dismembered body for which Steven had steeled his eyes, stomach, and soul.

One moment, a lone Bishop occupied the Board.

The next, there were two.

At least in a manner of speaking.

On the white marble square, returned to his natural age, stood the Archie that Steven had met in a hospital room in Roanoke, Virginia what seemed an eternity ago. Clothed again in the spotless ivory soutane, rochet, and miter of the White Bishop, Archie's aged yet strong hand gripped his poplar crosier, the silver cross and crescent moon at its head shining with a warm silver light. A peace that Steven had never seen in the elderly man's visage now permeated his every glance, movement, and gesture.

"PopPop!" Clarissa ran to Archie's side and hugged him around the waist. "You're all right!"

"I'm fine, child." He shot Steven a knowing look. "Better than I've been in some time, in fact."

"I don't understand, though." She raised a trembling finger toward the figure making his way to his feet in the next square. "You're old again and he's—"

"Those who take the power due them get to reap the benefits." Atop the opposite square of black granite, a man that both was and wasn't the much younger Archie they'd all come to know crouched like a cornered animal, his raiment anything but that befitting a holy man. A skintight body suit of black silk covered him from the tip of his curled-toed shoes to the four-point collar at his neck. A split cap the color of midnight with a silent bell at the point of each liliripe sat atop his head along with Black's crown resting unceremoniously crooked to one side. In his hand rested a two-foot scepter depicting a likeness of this version of Archie, right down to the jester's hat.

Both faces, wooden and flesh, bore the same look of utter depraved madness.

"Ah, my marotte," this Archie said, evincing an-over-the top French accent, "rhymes with garrote, as my predecessor found out oh so painfully."

Audrey approached Steven's side, not taking her eyes off the mysterious newcomer for an instant. "Who or what is that supposed to be?" she asked, taking her King's hand.

This Archie jerked his gaze in the White Queen's direction. "Typical American. You've been involved in a game of chess for the better part of a year. Did you not read? Did you not learn all you could about this Game that has come to define your very existence? In America, the King and Queen may be flanked by good little bishops, but in France..."

"Both king and queen have their fool." The older Archie looked up from his embrace with Clarissa. "God help us all."

"Precisely." The Archie in black leaned in conspiratorially. "It's actually quite a letdown, oh, Miss High and Mighty Queen," he sneered. "I mean, when you boil it down, this contest created by Grey and Zed is the only thing prolonging your disease-ridden life, my dear." A dismissive snort exited his nose. "Stupid cow."

The lone sphere of silver still orbiting the White Queen's shoulders flew at the sneering man in court jester attire, and only Steven's quick squeeze of her fingers kept Audrey from ending the Black Bishop then and there.

"Ah, ah, ah, dear Audrey. Temper, temper." he said, his grotesque grin growing more and more manic. "You may hold the upper hand for now, but our little Game is anything but done."

"The Game may not be complete," the White Bishop uttered, his tone unperturbed and even, "but your part in it, Fool, has come to an end."

"An end, you say?" This other Archie, unfettered from the man Steven and the others all thought they knew, spun in a circle within his square. "I just got here, Archibald." He spat the name. "And I'm not going anywhere." The mad jester wearing a twisted version of young Archie's face peered around at all of them. "In this Game, I may indeed be *Le Fou*, but it's all of *you* who are the fools."

"*Le Fou*." Steven recalled Archie's frantic warning from the King Tower in Atlanta when he'd first shifted into the accoutrement of the White Bishop. "You tried to warn me, Archie," he hung his head, "and I didn't listen."

"Ha." The dark jester's lips parted in a snarl. "I feared the old man's moment of clarity might doom my cause, but fortunately you were too dim-witted to—"

"Quiet, Fool." With a speed belying his years, Archie silenced his dark doppelganger's bile with a staff-strike to the throat before returning his attention to Steven. "Do not disparage yourself, my King." The White Bishop regarded him with kindness and compassion. "In all the many months we've known each other, it was only in that instant where I first donned the trappings of the White Bishop that I was free to speak the truth." His eyes shifted to the dark jester a square away. "This monster has held my strings for far too many years."

"I don't understand, Archie." Lena approached atop Rocinante, the stallion emitting an inquisitive whinny of his own. "Did we ever really know you?"

"Yes, child. In every way that mattered, you have known me as I have known you." He gestured to the Fool. "This monster may have been present within me since long before we met, pushing or pulling me in various directions to serve his own needs, but always, always you spoke with me." He lowered his head in shame. "As hard as it is for me to accept, in every way that matters, he *is* me."

"That can't be true." Audrey released Steven's hand and joined Archie in his square. "I know you, Archie. There is no part of you that even resembles this...thing."

"But that's just it, dear Audrey." His echoing of the dark jester's words raised the hairs on Steven's neck even as the White Bishop's calming words soothed his soul. "He is very much a part of me. A part without which I might not have survived some of the darkest times in my life."

"We all have a dark side, Richards." The Fool's voice cracked as he recovered from Archie's blow. "As you lay there on your death bed, your body eating itself from within, I suspect you would have done anything to save yourself from all the pain and misery. And was not your first act as Queen breaking the neck of the first Black Knight, a man who had spared your life? Would you care to know his name, girl? The name of his wife? His children?" His gaze flitted around the room, lighting first on William, still embodied within the gigantic oak, before settling on Niklaus, Victoria, Cynthia, and Oscar. "I'm sure you remember what your first Rook nearly did for lost love and what your second did for a cause he felt was just, not to mention what my own Rook was capable of, all to spare her only offspring." His eyes shifted to Lena. "You entered this room ready to kill the man who murdered your first and only love, did you not, Cervantes? Would you not have completed the dread task, given the opportunity?" His attention returned to Steven. "And you, Bauer. How many lies have you told to survive thus far, all in an effort to win a competition for a man who cared nothing about you, his literal Pawn?"

Steven pondered the Fool's words. "Every person walking this planet is comprised of many aspects, different facets and faces, some we show the world and some we hide. It may be that each of us contains a darkness like Archie's waiting to be loosed upon the world, but in your indictment of me and my friends, I believe you've missed your own point."

"Oh, really?" The dark jester seethed from his square of dark stone. "Do tell."

"Every charge you've leveled against us shares a common motivation." Steven's eyes softened. "All that each of us did, we did for love, something a creature like you would never understand."

The Fool rolled his eyes, but held his tongue.

"No matter what William did," Steven continued, "his love for his people and land guided his every move." He glanced at his Knight, so brave in her loss, and at his Rook, reunited for good or ill with a woman he once cared for more than any other. "As for Niklaus, Lena, and Cynthia, you said the word yourself." His eyes found Audrey's and in her hazel gaze and freckled smile, hope swelled anew in his chest. "And I'd be careful what you say about my Queen. Her love for her family, her friends, and, most important of all, herself has proven stronger than anything you or the universe could throw at her."

The Fool gazed around the room at each of them, a suspicious smile upon his face. "So that's it, then? The lot of you, clothed in your clear moral superiority, finally have me at your mercy. The bad man defeated, you plan to set aflame this winning lottery ticket you all share and relinquish your claim to this once in an era windfall, all at the word of a man who never even shared with you his real name?"

"The only name Grey needed was the one he chose," Steven crossed his arms, defiant of the Fool's attempted slight, "and in choosing such a name, he may not have given us the answer of how to win, but he certainly made it clear what to do with our victory."

"Pathetic." The Fool let out a derisive laugh. "Short-sighted drivel." After a thoughtful pause, he let out a disappointed sigh. "What then do you plan to do with me?"

A question Steven hadn't prepared for. "That's a problem for another day."

"Lock me up and throw away the key? Bury me under the jail? Perhaps a long walk off a short pier?" His ever-shifting features went deadly serious. "Then, the lot of you would be free to return to the tedium of your previous pedestrian lives." A mirthless laugh escaped his lips. "A grey outcome, indeed." He shot a withering gaze in the White Bishop's direction. "Never mind the fact that this man you all inherently love and trust held at his core a presence so vile that the merest touch on your loved ones' minds turned father against son, mother against daughter..." He turned his head toward a mound of shattered stone a few feet away, his wicked smile returning. "Wife against husband."

Steven followed the Fool's gaze to the pile of rubble and caught a flash of blond curls behind the jagged stone.

How could he have forgotten *her*?

"Ruth?"

"You bastard!" From behind the tiny hillock of marble rushed the final Black Pawn, bloodied and burned, her rapier brandished before her. "You killed Arthur!"

"No, Ruth Matheson Pedone," the Fool laughed. "That was you, *my dear*."

"He's dead because of you." Tears of fury streamed down her face. "And now, you're going to join him."

"Do it, though it changes nothing." The Fool's face twisted into his trademark sneer. "I pray to the darkest gods you see his face every time you close your eyes till the day you die."

"Pray for yourself, you son of a bitch," she whispered as she lunged at Archie.

"Ruth, please." Steven stepped between the two, hands raised before him, keeping the dark jester in his peripheral vision. "Don't do this."

"Out of the way, Steven." She ran a black sleeve across her eyes to clear her vision. "You can't let him get away with all of this."

"If you kill him, that's on your soul forever." Steven locked eyes with Ruth, his heart immediately transported to the back room of a New York diner in 1946. "Is that what you want?"

A frantic flutter from Amaryllis at his collarbone coupled with a quiet clink of metal on metal from behind jerked Steven back to the present. He'd taken his watchful gaze off the most dangerous man in the world, and this Fool who was anything but a fool had proven time and again that all he needed was half a second to cause chaos. Steven spun around in a desperate bid to defend himself, but before his sword was even halfway out of its sheath, Ruth shoved him aside and buried her own blade in the Fool's dark heart.

"Ruth," Steven whispered as she pulled the sword from their enemy's chest. "I'm sorry. You didn't have to—"

"But I did." Her eyes dropped to the jester's hand where his marotte now boasted a length of barbed chain between its dark wood and carved jester head no doubt meant for Steven's neck, proving the Fool's previous rhyme far more than a clever play on words. "He's already taken one man I love from me today." Her voice dropped to a whisper. "I'll be damned before I let him take another." She stepped past Steven and stood before the dying Fool. "You longed for your 'just desserts,'" Ruth whispered as the dark jester slumped to the ground. "Wait no longer."

The Black crown fell from the Fool's head and rolled to Steven's feet. As he knelt to retrieve the dark circle of metal, Archie rushed to his younger self's side, dropping to his knees to cradle the Fool's head. The selfless act stained his hands and spotless soutane with streaks of crimson.

"We could have had all the power we ever wanted, Archibald, all the power in Creation." The Fool let out a phlegmy cough, the spray of blood hitting the White Bishop center chest. "Power to remake the world the way we want it." His head lolled to one side so he could look upon Steven one last time. "But I suppose, in the end, you bested me. Too bad your time to enjoy your victory will be..." a peal of coughing left the last two words a quiet croak, "...so limited."

The dying Fool's body shuddered, and the enormous structure surrounding them answered in kind.

"Oh no," Steven's eyes shot to Cynthia. "What's happening?"

"It's not me," she answered, her fear-filled eyes dropping to Oscar.

The entire castle trembled again, worse than the first time.

Steven dropped to his knees by Archie and grabbed the Fool by his oversized collar. "What have you done?"

"What have I done, Bauer? Nothing." Another cough, this one weaker than before. "You've won, I'm dying, and the Game is over." His eyes rolled lazily up to the ceiling several stories above their head.

"With no Game to play, however, there's not much need for a granite and marble castle in the middle of Arizona, now is there?"

"Stop this." Steven's eyes shifted left and right frantically. "Archie can save you, if you'll let him."

"Nothing can save me now." He looked up at Ruth whose seething rage was quickly melting into wide-eyed terror. "This is it for me, not to mention each and every one of you as well." His lips parted in a pained smile. "At last, I succumb to *l'appel du vide.*"

Steven caught the White Bishop's eye. "And what the hell does that mean?"

"It's French." Archie locked gazes with the incarnate darkness of his own soul. "*The call of the void.*"

"Indeed." The Fool's eyes slid closed, the weak rise and fall of his chest producing a gurgling death rattle. "Oblivion calls," he whispered with one last blood-tinged cough, "and I must answer." He raised a trembling finger at the lone exit from the room. "But before I go…"

As the Fool breathed his last, a bolt of deepest violet flew from his hand, impacting the far wall above the room's only exit. The resulting blast further buried the massive double door and collapsed the adjoining wall, sealing shut the gouge in the stone left by Lena's mace.

"We're trapped," Lena shouted, as the tremors from before returned with a vengeance, sending a shower of dust and stone down upon their heads.

"That bastard." Ruth stared wide-eyed at the Fool's still form. "He wants to take us all with him."

"Not if I have anything to say about it." No sooner had Audrey sent a dozen tendrils of mist flying at the pile of rubble, than another section of the room caved in, crushing the Fool's throne.

"No time to clear the stone." Steven quickly surveyed the various wounded around the room as well as his own beleaguered forces, trying all the while to keep the chill of despair from stealing his focus.

"Cynthia," he shouted, "this place is all you. Can you buy us a minute?"

With a quick glance in her son's direction, the Rook's brown skin shifted into black granite. "With all I've got for as long as I'm able."

"I'll help." Niklaus dropped to one knee and placed his palms on the marble at his feet. For the first time since his sacrifice had bought them passage to Black's stronghold, his warm flesh shifted into cool marble. "If I can keep the Brooklyn Bridge from falling into the East River, surely I can keep this roof off our heads for a bit."

As Niklaus' hands fused with the castle itself, William stepped forward as well, the mighty oak boughs that formed his arms stretching wide. "My debt to you and the others, Steven Bauer, will never be repaid, but may this act help balance the scales." Green sprouted from every crack and crevice around the room, the roots and trunks and branches of countless trees and vines buttressing the castle's disintegrating walls, stabilizing the tons of stone above their heads, and blocking the falling debris that fell from above.

The three Rooks, from three very different worlds, had bought them time, though God only knew how much.

The rest, Steven knew all too well, was up to him.

"Audrey," he shouted, "grab everyone you can, White and Black, and bring them to the center of the room." His eyes shot to Lena. "You and Rocinante, grab Vago and his horse and fall in on Audrey."

"You've got to be kidding me," Lena grunted, the words barely audible over the rising cacophony. "You know what he—"

"Just do it." He turned his attention to Archie and Victoria. "You two, stay close and keep the kids safe."

The pair gave him a quick nod and huddled together with Clarissa and Oscar, the latter never taking his eyes off his mother who'd just turned to stone before his eyes.

"And what are you going to do, Steven?" Archie asked.

"I'm going to go save my dad."

He raced across the room to where the Black Rook's earlier blow had flung his father into the castle's unforgiving wall. As he knelt by Donald's sprawled form, he breathed a sigh of relief at seeing the rise and fall of his father's chest, though the odd angle of his upper right arm and the deep red wetness soaking through the white cloth of his sleeve gave him significant pause.

"Dad?" he shouted over the rumbling castle walls. "You still with us?"

"Get out of here, Steven," his father answered, barely able to lift his head, his words scarcely loud enough to be heard. "Leave me."

"Like hell I will." Steven grabbed Donald by the shoulders and helped him sit up. His stomach turned at the bruises along his father's face and the jagged bone protruding from the skin above his elbow. "I'm getting us both out of here."

"No, I'll only slow you down."

"I'm not leaving you," Steven grunted as he pulled Donald to his feet, "and that's final."

As he and his father forged their way for the center of the disintegrating Board, a quick scan of the room revealed his bare bones of an escape plan coming together.

Audrey's mists snaked around the room like the arms of some enormous sea creature, gathering together Arthur's pale form, Woody, and Ruth, as well as Magdalene and Wahnahtah. Her displeasure at being tasked with saving that last pair, both of whom had tried to kill her multiple times and more than once nearly succeeded, buffeted Steven through the ethereal connection they shared. Beneath the anger, however, lay a grudging acceptance that leaving anyone behind would be the very definition of wrong.

Audrey's indignation at rescuing Black's Queen and Pawn seemed infinitesimal next to Lena's palpable fury as she and Rocinante worked to free Sombra and the dark stallion's master from the mass of dark rubble at the room's edge. Dismounted, she dislodged stone after stone as Rocinante clamped down on Sombra's reins with his equine incisors and pulled with all his might to right both horse and rider.

As the White Knight and her steed finally accomplished their mission, Steven turned his attention upward. There, fingers of dark granite, bright marble, and branching wood ran up the walls and across the ceiling, all weaving together to form a canopy that held at bay the tons of rock above their heads. He'd no sooner mouthed a prayer that the three Rooks had the strength to keep them alive than the walls all around them fell inward, collapsing the roof. The already poor light grew dimmer by the second as he dragged his father toward the barely visible gathering of friend and enemy alike at the center of the Board. One fragmented square after another, they made their way across the sixty-four square battlefield with only the will of a Polish businessman, a proud Native American, and a tenacious young mother holding back the crushing death that hung over their heads like the Sword of Damocles. As Steven and his father joined the circle, however, he sensed that all three Rooks neared the end of their endurance. Without wasting a second, he ripped the pouch from his waist and held it before them.

"To the bridge," he whispered. "All of us."

In a flash, the dark room surrounding them was replaced by what should have been endless blue Arizona sky, the bright crimson that had ruled the upper stratosphere for weeks now the deep magenta of dried blood. Steven stood atop the checkered bridge with his father at his side. Audrey appeared next to him, her various saves still ensconced within her mists. Lena and Rocinante were next with an unconscious Vago still astride his dark charger, the man's leg mangled by the horse's fall. Archie and Victoria stepped from the silver shimmer next, with Clarissa and Oscar beneath their metaphorical wings. Last, a single tower of black stone, shining marble, and robust wood appeared at their center, dividing in an instant into the trio of Rooks who had saved them all.

Before their gathered eyes, the dark castle with its six towers of checkered stone collapsed inward on itself, leaving a mountain of rubble the US government would likely be trying to explain for the rest of history.

And that ignored the impossible bridge where stood gathered the Pieces of a Game that still had yet to end.

"Audrey?" The weak voice from behind them all grew stronger with repetition. "Audrey?"

Deborah Richards, still dressed in the ivory garb of a Pawn, weaved through the gathered Pieces and nearly tackled her daughter.

"Hi, Mom." Audrey laughed. "Did you think you'd never see me again?"

Her mother gave her a stern look that melted quickly into a smile. "You're okay. That's all that matters." She turned and looked Steven straight in the eye. "Everyone made it out, then?"

"Almost everyone." Steven helped his father to the ground and slipped quietly to the one scene on the entire planet he wished he'd never have to see again. Lena was already there, dismounted with Rocinante's reins in her grip, trembling by her aunt who had stood guard as instructed. Renata looked on in silence as a wailing White Knight knelt and pulled Emilio's pale form up into her lap. The visual evoked Michelangelo's *Pietà*, though the anguish in Lena's face was a far cry from the peace the sculptor carved into the Virgin Mary's features five centuries before.

"Lena?" Steven asked.

"I did everything you asked, Steven. *Everything*." She glared up at him through bloodshot eyes, her gaze flicking briefly in Audrey's direction. "Now, please, leave us alone."

"Very well." Steven backed away from the trio of huddled forms and returned to Audrey's side.

"Is Lena okay?" she asked.

"She will be." He glanced back at the mourning teen, but only for the briefest of seconds. He remembered experiencing voyeur's guilt at their first meeting as he intruded time and again on the young couple's private moments while seeking the first Piece for Grey's Game.

Apparently, he hadn't known the meaning of the word.

He gazed around at the remainder of the crowd.

Audrey and Deborah tended to Woody's injuries as well as his father's. Perhaps a portent of the future?

Niklaus and Victoria stared into each other's eyes, the pair closer than Steven would have imagined possible after all his friend had shared.

Archie knelt with Clarissa and wrapped her in a hug, while Cynthia held Oscar tight to her body, two families reunited after what must have seemed a shared eternity.

William stood guard over a sullen Wahnahtah, an emaciated and scarred Magdalene, and a still-unconscious Vago, any semblance of the trio's previous threat already a distant memory.

And lastly, his eyes fell on Ruth with her Arthur.

If Lena and Emilio's love was a book barely started when thrown on the fire, then Ruth and Arthur's was a novel whose last chapter had been ripped out and burned.

Steven glanced in Audrey's direction and caught her furtive smile, and the guilt that already ravaged his heart tore at him. He couldn't possibly have done more, and yet, he couldn't escape the feeling that even in their moment of victory he had failed.

Victory.

So preoccupied had he been with both winning the battle and getting everyone to safety that he'd forgotten one simple fact: in this Game in particular, to the victors went the spoils.

As if in answer, a rumble like thunder from another universe reverberated down from the heavens above, the ominous sound echoing in the canyon below. Above their heads, the crimson sky split asunder from horizon to horizon, the crack in reality running the gamut of every color Steven had ever seen and some he'd never even imagined. A storm of churning light and sound and power and magic gyrated above their heads, no doubt the vast energies of the current correction as filtered through the arrangement set in place by Grey and Zed's great Game.

This is it. Amaryllis' wings beat at Steven's armored chest, the sound like an angry rattlesnake. *The moment of truth.*

"Archie." He whispered as the old priest took in a phenomenon that likely both confirmed and challenged his deepest held beliefs. "I need one last favor before this is all over."

"As if anything I can offer will match the freedom your actions today have brought my soul." He left Clarissa with Cynthia and made his way to Steven's side. "What is it you need of me?"

"The power that awaits the Game's victor. As Grey explained it, I have to accept it into my being, at least temporarily, for all of this to truly end."

"That is how I understand it as well, though more than that even I do not know." Archie studied him. "What exactly is it you're asking?"

"What if temptation gets the better of me?" Steven shook from head to toe as if he'd touched a live wire. "What if I don't have the will to let go of such power?"

The priest shook his head and smiled. "Steven, it is as you said before. Grey may have selected you for this role in part for your excellent judgment of character, but Grey himself was no slouch in that department. There's no one he or I would trust more with that responsibility."

"Still, it took both of us to defeat our enemy." Steven lowered his head in deference. "We stand here neither as victor and vanquished nor in stalemate." He held out Black's crown to Archie. "I would share this moment with you, Archibald Lacan if you're willing."

"But..." Archie's eyes dropped. "You saw the thing that came out of me. How could you possibly trust me after that?"

"But that's just it." Steven waited till the priest looked him again in the eye. "The part of you that was the Fool is no more." His gaze crept to the unmoving form in black jester's garb all of them had avoided so much as looking at since their escape from Black's fortress. Shaking off the resultant chill, he rested a hand on Archie's shoulder. "Only my friend remains."

Archie considered for what seemed forever and then reached out and accepted the crown. "If this is truly what you think best, then I trust you my King, my friend, my brother."

The two turned shoulder to shoulder. Steven took Archie's hand, and together, each stretched their respective crown to the sky. Steven caught but a glimpse of Audrey's confused features before everything disappeared in a maelstrom of color and light and sound and majesty.

At once, Steven knew the answer to every question ever asked. All knowledge, every secret, anything he desired lay for the first time within his reach. Filled with all the power he would need to change the rules of the universe at a whim, his very consciousness threatened to rewrite reality.

His thoughts stole first to Audrey, with her auburn hair and hazel eyes that knew everything. He could save her, destroy the vile illness that devoured her from within, keep her with him for always. She was everything he'd ever wanted and more. He didn't have to lose her. Not after everything they'd been through. He had but to will it.

Next, his thoughts drifted to memories of Ruth from their months together in the past, with her infectious laugh and unstoppable zest for life. In his heart of hearts, he knew that she belonged with Arthur Pedone and Arthur with Ruth, and yet a part of Steven recognized that a simple nudge could shift reality and send her into his own waiting arms.

Inevitably, however, as it had every day since her death, a deep-seated grief drove away any other thought or desire and brought to center stage within his mind's eye one face and one face alone.

Katherine.

What harm would there be in bringing back one soul? A person whose life had been cut short so mercilessly early? An individual who had never done, as far as he knew, a bad thing in her life? Would such a reversal truly be considered a horrible outcome? Could returning her to life in any way be construed as wrong?

Hadn't he sacrificed enough to earn the ability to make that one tragic moment simply go the other way?

Let it go. Archie's calm words echoed across the ether and stole across Steven's thoughts. His five senses filled with the power of the Game, he could no longer see the priest with his eyes, but the strength in the aged man's hand remained firm in his trembling grasp. *End this, Steven. End it now.*

But...

Just let it go, Steven. Archie's quiet voice washed away the anxiety, leaving the victorious White King with a much-needed peace. *Let it all go.*

Steven held on for but a second longer and then, with an action as simple as releasing held breath, he allowed the power coursing through his body to return whence it came, back to an ever-churning, ever-changing, ever-capricious universe.

"That's it then." He released Archie's hand and fell to his knees, as weak as a newborn, the platinum crown of the White dropping to the black granite beneath him with a barely audible clang. "It's over."

Audrey rushed to his side. "Not yet, it isn't."

His eyes quickly adjusting again to the real world, Steven stared up at Archie, the aged priest now hovering several feet above the bridge surrounded in a nimbus of kaleidoscopic light.

"But," he could barely speak, "he told me to let it go. To end it."

Audrey pulled his head and shoulders up onto her lap. "Looks like he had other plans."

Terror gripped Steven's heart as he looked on helpless as Archie bathed in the power of a universal upheaval the likes of which hadn't occurred in centuries. The prismatic halo that surrounded him like a cocoon pulsed with the heartbeat of the cosmos and Steven feared what would emerge from this chrysalis of light, power, and majesty when all was said and done.

Had he come all this way, suffered so much, led the others through pain and loss and suffering and death only to hand the victory to a man who had already proven himself nefarious at his very core?

"No, Steven." The White Bishop's voice boomed from every direction at once, the mighty canyon below reverberating with the voice of Archibald Lacan. "Your judgment has not failed you this day. Understand that as you delivered me earlier, so have I delivered you from the siren song of limitless power."

"Follow your own advice, then, Archie." Renewed strength filled Steven's words. "Let it go."

"In a moment." A look of ecstasy filled the old priest's face. "For decades, I have served an almighty God though I have never truly seen his countenance." Suspended there, held aloft by unmitigated power sufficient to obliterate the entire world, Archie wept. "To bear witness to even this small aspect of his wonder and majesty is something I have coveted my entire life." His lips moved in a silent prayer and then, just as it had with Steven, the energies suspending his form in mid-air left him and Archie fell to the bridge by his King's side. The rift in the crimson sky that stretched from horizon to horizon sealed like an enormous eye closing for sleep. In less time than it took to say it, the heavens over Arizona resumed their normal azure hue.

"Thank you for that, Steven," Archie whispered feebly. "Though hopefully at no time in the near future, I can now die fulfilled, not only purged of the dark malignancy that has grown within my soul since I was a child, but having seen with my own eyes irrefutable evidence that my life of faith has ever been justified."

Steven stared at the man, incredulous. "You scared me for a minute there, old man."

348

"As you did me. Such power as we both just touched is not meant for any man. The allure of omnipotence, the utter temptation of unlimited influence, these are not paths once tread from which you return. Look what such unbridled desire for power did to Zed." His eyes slid shut. "Look what it did to me."

"You pulled me back from the edge."

"As you did me." Archie reached out with one trembling hand, the other somehow managing to hold onto Black's crown, and again grasped Steven's. "As we have since the beginning, we saw each other through a difficult time, did we not?"

"We did indeed." Steven squeezed the old man's fingers and then let go, turning his attention to the beautiful woman who held his head in her lap. "Hello there."

Her smile dazzled him as much as the cosmic lightshow from before. "Hi."

Archie looked away to give the pair at least the illusion of privacy.

"We won." Steven gazed into her upside-down eyes. "We're alive."

Audrey smiled her crooked smile. "Sure looks that way."

"So, where do we go from here?"

"That's up to you." She brushed his cheek with the back of her fingers. "Things are likely to go south like they have every time before." She looked away. "I'd understand if you...changed your mind."

Steven pulled in a deep breath and with all the strength he had, reached up for her chin and pulled her gaze back to his. "Wild horses couldn't pull me away." As if on cue, an excited whinny sounded from the other side of the bridge. "Not even that one."

"But you know what's coming for me. What's already come for me twice. I'm pretty sure my 'Get out of jail free' card has expired." She swallowed back the emotion. "Without the energies of the Game to keep the cancer at bay, it's simply a matter of time."

"Then we'll face it together." Steven pulled her face to his and placed a gentle kiss upon her soft lips. "No matter what."

"True love conquers all," Archie said with a knowing grin, "though in this case, I don't believe such self-sacrifice will be necessary."

Steven and Audrey turned their heads toward the priest and as one asked, "What's that supposed to mean?"

Before Archie could answer, an excited squeal followed by another whinny from Rocinante pulled all their attentions. Audrey pulled Steven around just in time to see Emilio sit up, hacking and coughing like a near-drowning victim, and fall into Lena's waiting arms as Renata and Rocinante both looked on in wonder. Before he could begin to process what he was seeing, another euphoric shout hit his ears from farther down the bridge.

"Arthur!" Her mystically-sustained youth fading by the moment, a middle-aged Ruth fell upon her quickly-aging-but-very-much-alive husband with tears of joy streaming down her face. "You're alive!"

"Of course I am," Arthur said weakly, his close-cropped hair greying by the second as he smiled at his wife of over six decades. "You think I'd leave you alone here in a place like this?"

Steven and Audrey shared an amazed gaze and then continued to take in all that was occurring.

Cynthia stood to one side, her son, Oscar on one hip and Clarissa Lacan on the other. Before Cynthia could stop her, Clarissa rushed to her great-grandfather and tackled him with all the exuberance of the young.

"PopPop!" she cried. "You're okay!"

"Indeed, child." He shot Steven a wink. "Now, don't smother me, sweetheart."

Where Deborah had sat desperately caring for both her wounded father as well as his own, now only excited laughter and exuberant hugs filled the air as two generations of family new and old celebrated a renewed lease on life.

"They're all right." Audrey looked on in wonder. "Both of them... just fine."

William continued to keep watch over their vanquished enemies, the trio of erstwhile Black Pieces as well as their dark stallion all returned to consciousness and in way better shape than Steven would have dreamed possible.

All of his wounds completely mended, Sombra stood silent with his head down, the time for fighting in his equine wisdom clearly long past.

Vago's various injuries appeared healed as well, though Miguel

Fausto Vasquez retained the look of a trapped animal ready to chew off its own leg to escape.

By his side, the man known as John Small sat slack-jawed, his leg restored, his body whole, and any vestige of Wahnahtah the Black Pawn erased from his placid features.

And none of that compared to the miraculous transformation of Magdalene Byrne.

Though returned to her natural age, her nonagenarian body showed not a bit of evidence of the scarring caused by the flames of yesteryear. Her skin, though loose and thin as would be expected per her years, remained unmarked, her hair hung from her head full and long and white, and her shrewd eyes, for once, exuded neither hate nor anger nor spite, but something not unlike gratitude.

Niklaus and Victoria, his arms wrapped around the lovely young woman's shoulders from behind, both gazed around the bridge, taking in the various wonders, their shared smile growing wider with each passing moment.

As his wandering gaze came full circle, Steven locked eyes with Archibald Lacan and the truth clicked.

"This is you. You did all this." He studied Archie's cautious half-grin. "That's why you held onto the power like you did."

Archie nodded, the gesture accompanied by a heartfelt sigh. "Though all of you together managed to exorcise the demon within me and free me from my darker side, I still have more sin to atone for than I have years left on this planet. The Game may have been set to occur regardless of my involvement, but all the death and destruction that led from my conspiracy with Zed now weighs upon my soul like an anchor of sin." He waved his arms wide, gesturing to all gathered. "I dared not attempt to correct all the death, destruction, and suffering across this continent stemming from our great contest, but among our cohort, both Black and White, it seemed only fair to rectify what I could."

"Wait, does that mean—" Audrey's voice choked with emotion.

Grasping her hand, Steven finished her question. "Did you heal Audrey as well, Archie? Is the cancer gone?"

"I wish I could say that such a miracle flowed from my thoughts and lips, as such would be a fitting gift of gratitude for what you two have done for me today, but alas, I could not heal her..."

"But—" Steven began.

"...*because*," Archie continued, "there was nothing to heal." He smiled kindly upon them both. "It would appear that Audrey's grand sacrifice in saving her King left her at death's door and possibly beyond." The priest rested his hand over Steven and Audrey's interlocked fingers. "When you crossed the final threshold and occupied Black's back rank to restore the White Queen to the Board, the Arbiters in their great wisdom apparently returned her whole and healed not only from her injuries, but the leukemia as well."

"Can it be true?" Audrey quivered with excitement. "Steven?"

"If there is one thing this Game has taught me," Steven allowed himself a quiet laugh, the floodgates of his heart opening wide with hope, "it's that a little faith can go a long way."

EPILOGUE

I - Full Circle

I just got a text from Lena." Audrey sauntered into Donald Bauer's living room from the kitchen with a tall glass of lemonade and sat on the couch next to Steven. "She and Emilio are getting off the highway and should be here in the next few minutes."

"So, looks like everyone is going to make it after all." Donald grabbed a handful of pretzels from the bowl on the coffee table next to their old chess set and commenced to munching. "After their flight got cancelled, I wasn't sure they'd make it."

"The days of having their bank pony turned white stallion double as a sentient street chopper may be over, but Emilio still has his little red road rocket." Steven chuckled under his breath. "Knowing those two, I wouldn't be surprised if he and Lena made better time than if they flew."

"Renata helped them find a nice farm north of Baltimore where our favorite horse can be taken care of while they're in school." Audrey squeezed Steven's knee as she addressed his father. "I wish Rocinante could have come, though. The lake out back is so peaceful."

"Any word from your Mom?" Donald asked.

"She and Grandpa finally heard from the insurance adjusters. It's going to be several months of living in hotels, but looks like we're going to be able to rebuild." Audrey shot Donald a wink. "Mom told me to tell you she's sorry she couldn't make it this time but asked for a raincheck."

Steven's father cleared his throat to respond, but before he could say a word, a knock signaled that the first guests had arrived. Donald insisted that Audrey stay seated and went to the door with a renewed spring in his step Steven hadn't seen in years.

"Welcome!" Donald boomed as he invited in the couple standing on his front porch. "First to arrive, the guests of honor."

Niklaus and Victoria, the latter sporting an understated yet sparkling diamond on her left ring finger, swept into the room and descended upon Steven and Audrey for a bout of excited hugs.

As Donald moved to close the door, a quiet clearing of the throat from beyond drew all their attentions.

"Good afternoon." William, his previous long black hair shorn in favor of a military high-and-tight, waited for an official invitation before entering. He cautiously stepped across the threshold, a small package in his hand, and deposited himself across the room in an old folding chair. "Didn't know what to bring, so..." He pulled a bottle of champagne from the brown paper bag and handed it to Niklaus. "For the happy couple to share at their wedding."

"Thank you, Mr. Two Trees." Victoria's hand went to her heart in gratitude. "You're invited, of course."

"I appreciate that," William said with a half-smile, "and it's William Lone Tree these days." His gaze flicked in the direction of the window. "New name. New start."

"I get it." Steven extended a hand to the man who'd served as his White Rook and sacrificed one of the two oaks that were his former namesake to keep the rest of them alive. "We're glad you came."

"Wouldn't have missed it." William tilted his head forward in a resigned nod. "Me and Nik, the way I see it, are brothers of a sort."

Niklaus laughed and shot William a beaming smile. "We are, at that."

Steven understood all too well what William was going through, having personally experienced the death of seven of his eight doppelgangers at the conclusion of their months long travail. His name and face being plastered all over cable news and the internet in association with the bombing in Alberta likely had a lot to do with the name change as well. Labeled both murderer and terrorist, a new start was exactly what the doctor ordered.

The crunch of gravel under tires signified another arrival. This time, Audrey went to the door.

"They made it." She shot Steven an amused wink. "Hey, sweetie, a couple of surprise guests for you."

He rose and joined Audrey at the door. Out on the gravel driveway of the house where he'd spent his formative years, an elderly couple exited a cab, an elderly couple he'd never dreamed would ever visit his family home.

"Arthur." Steven's jaw went slack, flabbergasted. "Ruth."

"She begged me not to tell you they were coming." Audrey rested her hand at the small of his back. "They both wanted to be a part of our little get-together and flew down last night."

Both returned to their proper chronological age, Arthur sported a new cane, not nearly as spry as he'd been the night he first welcomed Steven into his home, while Ruth strode toward the door with her trademark grace firmly intact. Steven's hand went to the chest pocket where he'd carried Amaryllis every waking hour since the final moments of the Game. Unwilling to part with the priceless adornment that had saved his life more times than he could count, he'd kept the bejeweled dragonfly near his heart ever since.

As Ruth stepped onto the porch, a single flutter over his chest let him know the old magic was still there.

"Hello, Ruth." Steven grinned. "Good to see you, Arthur." He motioned the pair inside. "Thanks for flying down." He raised a quizzical brow. "I had no idea you were coming."

"We wanted to surprise you, dear." Ruth hid her smile behind her hand. "It would appear we've succeeded."

"Ruthie insisted," Arthur added. "She said it only made sense to come see everyone since we were there pretty much every step of the way."

"In both the present..." Ruth's eyes dropped to the dragonfly-shaped bulge in Steven's chest pocket. "And the past."

Steven's heart raced at Ruth's mysterious comment as she and Arthur stepped inside, but before he could ask the obvious follow up, an arrest-me-red motorcycle carrying his two favorite teens pulled up at the curb. Audrey took off across the yard and met Lena halfway, the two women jumping up and down in an excited embrace reminiscent of long-lost sisters finally reunited after an eternity apart.

Emilio stepped around the pair with an amused eye roll and met Steven on the porch.

"Steven," he muttered.

"Emilio," he answered.

Emilio stretched out his hand, but as Steven reached out to accept the more formal greeting, the younger man pulled him into a brotherly hug. "Good to see you, *mi hermano*."

"Glad you two could make it."

The two men held their own embrace but a moment longer before joining Audrey and Lena by the old maple tree at the center of the front yard.

"How was your trip?" Audrey asked.

"Five hours counting pit stops and not a drop of rain." Lena slipped an arm around Emilio. "Not to mention some serious skills from my man here as we skirted a big traffic jam a couple hours in."

"I didn't want to be late." Emilio's gaze darted in the direction of the house. "Never know when all of us might be together again."

"Considering the rock on Victoria's left hand," Audrey offered, "I'm guessing sooner than later."

"They did it?" Lena squealed and ran inside.

Steven laughed. His eyes followed Lena until she was inside and then he locked gazes with Emilio. "You know, *hermanito*, when it's your turn..."

"He's going to make it unforgettable," Audrey finished the thought, "aren't you Emilio?"

A hint of pink hit the young man's cheeks. "Nothing I'd ever come up with would do justice to a girl like Lena, but you better believe when the time is right, I'm going to give it all I've got."

"I'd expect nothing less." Steven slapped Emilio's back and led him and Audrey inside where Donald had Ruth and Arthur in stitches showing them one embarrassing childhood picture of Steven after another.

"Careful," Steven shook his head, "or he'll drag out all the old albums, and you'll be checking out photos of me in all my 'naked toddler in a bathtub' glory."

Over on the couch, Lena admired the diamond on Victoria's hand breathlessly as if she were seeing her first sunrise. "Congratulations, you two!" She went in for the double hug, her well-established exuberance firing on all cylinders now that she and the rest of them no longer lived in the shadow of an impending battle to the death. "Have you set a date?"

"Not yet..." Niklaus started.

"But soon," Victoria finished, giving his knee a gentle squeeze.

"So," Steven sat across from the pair, "seems a lot can happen in a couple weeks."

Niklaus cleared his throat. "Vic and I had a lot to work out—"

"What Nik is trying to say," Victoria cut him off, "is that he had a lot of forgiving to do." She looked upon the man sitting next to her with eyes filled with such love that Steven finally understood what drove Niklaus to the top of the King Tower that night; to go from basking in the warmth of such adoration to losing your job and your love in the space of hours would be more than most could take. "Fortunately, I had opportunity to see him at his best, and he has accepted me after seeing me at my worst, so..."

They kissed, their walls down, both of them totally vulnerable and yet totally safe in each other's arms.

Emilio drew Lena close to his side, a pair so perfectly matched, the universe had chosen them to share a love, a steed, a destiny.

Who could have guessed the head of her mace hid one of Grey's final secrets, that sealed inside the mystic metal, the Knight icon had rested all along, waiting patiently for precisely the right time to reveal itself and bring a grieving young woman exactly what she needed to face her fears, balance the scales of justice, and win the day.

Arthur sneaked a look in Ruth's direction, the dazzled grin on his face unchanged from the one he'd first worn in a deli one fateful night in 1946.

Audrey studied Steven with a sidelong smile and curled into him as if she were an adjoining jigsaw piece.

"Well," Donald said after allowing the various couples their shared moment, "those burgers aren't going to cook themselves." He turned to Arthur. "I trust you've manned your share of grills, Mr. Pedone?"

"Ruth has done most of the cooking over the years, but she's always left the grilling to me." Arthur chuckled. "Just point me in the right direction."

As Arthur followed Donald out the back door, Ruth sat by Victoria on the couch and admired the younger woman's ring. "You know, Arthur and I got married in New York back in '47. It was a tiny service, but we did it up right. Still, it's just a day. The real beauty of it, though, is what you do every day after." She beamed a grandmotherly smile upon them both. "Don't ever forget that."

"Don't worry." Victoria blushed. "I won't be making the same mistake twice."

"Where are you going to get married?" Lena asked. "Georgia? Poland? Are you going to have a big wedding?" She paused. "Who are you going to ask to perform the service?"

"The only man who can, little *laska*." Niklaus whispered, his Polish accent brimming with a mix of mirth and somber reflection. "Having anyone but Archie preside after all we've been through would simply be wrong."

"In that case," came a deep Creole from the front door, "I accept."

All of them turned as one to find Archibald Lacan framed in the doorway. He wore the same penitent expression that had occupied his features since the day of the Game's final reckoning, the guilt of his darker nature's actions a constant weight regardless of everything the priest had done to set things right.

"Archie." Steven went to the door to welcome the aged priest. "You made it."

"My train got in around half past midnight." Archie pulled in a deep breath. "Made it to my hotel a little before two. One long brunch and a particularly chatty Uber driver later and here I am."

Archie joined the rest around the Bauer coffee table. Each of them stared at the old chess set that occupied one end of the scarred rectangle of wood. Resting in the spot where Steven and his father had matched wits over hundreds of tiny battles, the simple board of sixty-four squares in their midst captured them all one last time.

"So," Steven asked, shattering the silence, "we agreed not to discuss anything over telephone or the internet, but as all of us are gathered together in the safety of this house..." He paused. "Is it done?"

"Our part is finished," Niklaus said.

Emilio nodded. "Ours too."

"I have completed my task," William added.

"As have I," Archie whispered solemnly.

"Well," Audrey said, not looking anyone in the eye, "details?"

"John Small," William said, "the man you know as Wahnahtah, has returned to his reservation, grateful for the generous return of his leg. He has sworn never to seek out anyone from the Game, White or Black, for the rest of his life." His gaze dropped to his lap. "He asks for the same deference in return."

"And you believed him?" Lena asked.

William met her earnest gaze, his face a grim mask. "I did."

"We dropped off Vago with the Baltimore Police." Emilio shot Lena a sidelong glance. "I wanted to leave him with the Salvatruchas, but Lena insisted we do the 'right' thing."

"Justice, baby," Lena planted a peck on Emilio's cheek, "not vengeance."

"Right," Emilio replied, almost avoiding another eye roll, "of course."

"Magdalene is safe and sound back at her nursing home." Archie let out a mirthless laugh. "The entire staff was shocked to see her alive. They'd all figured she'd absconded and had met a not-quite-untimely end."

"But her scars," Steven pointed out, "they're gone. How'd they even recognize her?"

"In the months since she disappeared, there was apparently significant turnover at her nursing facility." Archie raised an eyebrow, his lips pulling into a smirk. "Those who did remember her spoke far more or her 'sparkling' personality than any outward scars." The priest crossed his arms. "Though she remains a boiling kettle filled to the brim with three quarters of a century of simmering hate, the staff there appeared quite kind and capable. I trust she will be well cared for over her remaining months on this side of eternity."

"Way more than she deserves." Steven let out a sigh and turned to Niklaus and Victoria. "And you two? Everything go okay?"

"As well as can be expected." Niklaus looked to his fiancée. "Vic and I accompanied Cynthia and her son back to their home in Biloxi. Unfortunately, after disappearing for months without an explanation, they'd been evicted. Their landlord tossed all their stuff a while ago."

"They're going to have to start over," Victoria said, "but my family has agreed to front a lot of their expenses to help them get back on their feet."

"They've got a long way to go," Niklaus added, "but they're going to make it."

"Her son, Oscar," Steven asked, "did he seem to be doing okay?" His eyes flicked in Archie's direction. "We've experienced what can happen when young eyes see too much of the Game, and Cynthia's boy saw way more than you ever did, Arch."

"He has indeed seen much for one so young," Archie sighed, "and though he seems quite resilient, I will reach out to the former Black Rook in the near future and check in on the young man." The priest smiled. "Shouldn't be much of an issue since Biloxi is just one state over."

"So, you *are* moving back to New Orleans?" Steven asked.

"Indeed." Archie gazed out the window into the front yard. "My family brought me here to Virginia when my visions of the Game became so intense that I could barely tell dream from reality, but now that I am free of the Fool's influence and my mind is my own, I wish to go home." His eyes slid shut. "But first, Steven…"

"Yes?"

"Your task, it seems," Archie muttered, "is the lone errand we've yet to discuss."

Steven cleared his throat. "My father and I took care of everything as per your wishes." He lowered his head as if in prayer. "It took some doing, but the remains of the Fool have been cremated and his ashes spread along the Appalachian Trail at a particularly beautiful vista, if I do say so myself."

"And the *Svartr Kyll*?" Archie asked. "The *Hvitr Kyll* of this century may remain missing, but its dark sister must be safeguarded until the next iteration lest everything we've suffered become irrelevant a century or two down the road."

"Taken care of." Steven mimed a locking safe. "Not only is Zed's pouch physically secured in a vault that Ocean's 11 would have trouble breaking into, but Dad and I are working with an estate attorney to ensure it remains in the family for generations." He motioned to all within the room. "And by family, I mean *us* and *our descendants*."

"Thank you, Steven." Archie shivered despite the late summer warmth. "Regardless of what we've all been through, I didn't relish the thought of attending to what in a way would have been my own final preparations, nor did the idea of being responsible for the nexus of darkness that a part of me coveted for the vast majority of my years sit well with my soul." His gaze found each of their eyes before settling back on his hands folded in his lap. "I still have a lot for which to atone, from whatever role I may have played in my sister's drowning all those years ago to my role in the Game and the untold suffering my actions brought upon each of you, not to mention the world, and the no doubt countless transgressions in-between. I just wanted to thank each of you for the opportunity to in some way make recompense for all the pain I have caused."

"All is forgiven, Archie." Audrey rose from her seat on the couch and embraced the elderly priest. "And that goes for all of us."

"Double for Vic and me." Niklaus chuckled as he pulled Victoria tight to his side. "We wouldn't have asked you to officiate at our wedding if there were any hard feelings, right?"

"The way I see it," William uttered, having remained a quiet observer for a bit, "a man in your line of work has forgiven a lot of people for a lot of stuff. Lord knows I could spend a couple hours in your confessional."

"Your point, young man?" Archie asked.

"My point is that you're going to have to learn to forgive yourself, you know?" William raised his hands in a subtle shrug. "Maybe grant yourself the absolution you've freely given so many over the years."

"Wise words," Archie whispered, "that I will reflect upon in the coming days."

Victoria's face brightened as the proverbial lightbulb went off in her mind. "Mr. Lone Tree, I know you brought this champagne for our wedding, but I think I would like to propose a toast."

Steven and Audrey gathered glasses as Niklaus and his fiancée popped the bubbly.

"To Archie," Victoria proclaimed, "and to overcoming what has come before so you can grab hold of what's meant for you now."

Niklaus raised his glass, his voice uncharacteristically somber. "As well as setting things in motion to reverse what would otherwise have been my untimely demise back in D.C."

Once the dust had settled after the Game's completion, Archie had finally been free to explain everything, primarily that the idea of Black Bishop as puppet master and White Bishop as marionette was far from the truth. While his darker side had indeed seized the lion's share of control early on, the two sides had played their own game of chess within Archie's mind, a game not visible to the outside world. For all the subtlety of his more devious aspect's various gambits, the good at Archie's core had chosen very specific instances to exert its own influence, not the least of which was the suggestion of leaving Niklaus' shattered form at the base of Mount Rushmore, formerly Six Grandfathers, one of the most powerful crossings of the entire North American continent. With an abundance of both mystical energies as well as fragmented stone with which to rebuild himself as he had in Atlanta that fateful first night, the rebirth of Niklaus as the White Rook had been left a simple matter of time. Once White's fortress of trees had grown, against all odds, from the rocky soil of the Grand

Canyon, the siren call of the Board did the rest, summoning Niklaus to his destiny.

As they all finished the first toast, Niklaus Zamek again raised his glass.

"Also, to William Lone Tree, for stepping up when I could not, for holding the line when it truly mattered, and to becoming more than he ever thought he could be."

William touched his glass to Niklaus', adding, "And to the brother I never had and his soon-to-be lovely bride, may their foundation be as strong as a stone tower and their family have as many branches as the mighty oak."

At Lena's latest barely restrained squeal, Ruth raised her own glass. "To the exuberance of youth."

Roses blossomed in Lena's cheeks. "To the wisdom and grace of years."

Emilio scrunched closer to his love. "Not to mention, to timeless beauty."

Ruth's hand went to her heart. "Thank you, Lena and Emilio."

Archie cleared his throat. "To our fair Queen, Audrey Richards, whose selflessness knows no bounds, and whose reward for a life well-lived and a Game well-played could not be more deserved."

Audrey grew silent, and Steven feared she might burst into tears. Instead, she reached for the priest's wrinkled hands and gave his fingers a gentle squeeze before raising her own glass.

"I'd like to propose a toast as well, if that's all right." She blinked away the tears welling at the corners of her eyes. "To the man who brought us all together, the man who somehow kept us all alive no matter what the enemy and the universe threw at us, the man who plucked us from the wreckage of each of our own lives and set us all on a new path, a path that has led to this..." She nearly choked on the word. "Family."

All but the man in question himself raised their glasses and as one said, "To Steven."

Silent in the emotion, Steven met each of their smiling gazes in turn, and then quietly added, "Last, but far from least, let us not forget the man whose Game we played, who saw in each of us the potential to be far more than we were, and without whom none of us would be sitting here today. A man Ruth and Arthur knew as Rex Caesius but the rest of us knew only as the color that guided his very philosophy, his every decision, and, as I can attest, basically every cryptic word that came out of his mouth. A name he chose as penance for a horrible act of necessity from his past, a travesty that at least in part has been made right."

The simple fact that very few of the gathered Pieces ever returned home after the Antarctic iteration almost five centuries ago remained unchanged; to the life, however, Steven had managed to spirit away all those still living that were thought lost beneath the avalanche Grey had summoned to prevent the far worse disaster of a second Black victory, a victory that would have left Zed nigh unstoppable. Steven had brought the remaining White Bishop as well as the surviving Pawns, Black and White alike, to the present in a last-ditch effort to free their loved ones from Zed's influence, only to return them all to their own century and homes when all was said and done, their brief service gladly given in exchange for their lives. Steven hoped that somehow, somewhere, Grey understood that the one act for which he could never forgive himself had been undone and that the unnecessary deaths of friend and enemy alike had been averted.

A quiet pulse at his hip brought Steven's brief reverie to an end. All eyes were on him, as he sat there mid-toast, his mind both centuries and half a world away.

"His identity went far beyond any name. He was a friend, mentor, guide, example." He shot Lena a raised eyebrow and smiled. "He had his favorites, of course, as do we all." He glanced in William's direction. "While some, he barely knew." He locked gazes with Emilio. "Some he quarreled with." He caught Niklaus' eye and chuckled. "And there were others with whom he shared laughter." He beamed at Audrey. "And even some for whom he became a surrogate father." He lowered his head. "Regardless, this man whose true name we will likely never know, means something to each of us, something more than the simple balance inherent in his chosen name." Steven raised his glass. "To Grey."

As one, they joined him in this final toast. "To Grey."

"Hear, hear!" Arthur popped in from outside with a plate full of sizzling burgers. "Looks like I'm missing some important stuff."

"Don't worry." Ruth shot her husband a soulful smile. "I'll catch you up over dinner." Biting her lip, she caught Steven's eye. "Can we talk?"

Steven joined her on the front porch, the sun a little further along its course in the beautiful blue Virginia sky.

"I'm curious as to what you're going to do about that." She gestured to the white leather pouch hanging at Steven's hip. "That particular item is of 1946 vintage, as I understand it. How are you planning on getting it back to its previous owner so that he can, in turn, give it to you when the time comes?"

"The most reliable doorway is likely the one at the Coral Castle down in Florida. It's out of the way, but I figure I can thumb my way back up to New York like Nik and I did the first time."

"And how will you get back to now?" Her eyes darted in the direction of the window that revealed the remainder of their gathering. Steven had little doubt for whose face she searched. "And more specifically, to *Audrey*?"

"All these doors seem to go both ways. Once I track down Grey, I'm sure he can take me to the nearest crossing and I'll be back like nothing happened."

"You won't have to hunt him down." She slipped a folded piece of paper from her pocket and pressed it into Steven's hand. "Do your best to aim for this date, time, and address." Her features twisted as if she might cry. "For God's sake, don't be late."

"I don't understand." Steven gently squeezed her aged fingers. "What's this all about?"

"You have to deliver the pouch to Grey, but that's not the only thing in your possession on loan."

Steven's face screwed up in a quizzical expression before melting into one of understanding. "I need to give him Amaryllis so he can give her to you for your wedding?"

"No." Her gaze dropped to the concrete beneath their feet. "That's not quite it."

"But you said Amaryllis was a wedding gift."

"Yes," Ruth's cheeks flared red, "from an *old friend*."

"You mean…"

"Yes." She again met his gaze, the kindness in her expression at war with the trembling of her lower lip. "You may have been able to avert the dark outcome of Grey's necessary cruelty in the past, but that doesn't change the fact that you still have your own left to commit."

"But, Ruth," Steven stammered. "I—"

"I'll get over it, Steven. My standing here in front of you right here, right now proves it. I'll be fine." She shook off the tremor of her lower lip and forced a smile. "Arthur and I have been very happy for our entire marriage. I haven't a doubt that he was, is, and always will be the man for me." For a moment, the years fell away and Steven saw the young girl he'd pulled out of a wrecked car in 1945. "Still, a girl's heart is a girl's heart."

"What am I supposed to say to you? How do I do this without being the bad guy? I don't want to break her—*your*—heart again."

"Steven, dear, I love Arthur Pedone, always have, always will, but there's a part of this heart of mine reserved for my very first love, and that part is yours to break."

"But—"

"Come back to me, Steven. One last time. You must." Ruth turned for the door. "I tell you this not only because that part of me still loves you after all these years, but because from my perspective," a tear meandered down her flushed cheek, "you already have."

As Ruth went back inside, Audrey stepped out onto the porch. The brief juxtaposition of the two women left Steven's head swimming.

"Everything okay?" The sun caught her auburn hair and glinted off those hazel eyes that had melted Steven's heart all those many months ago when they were basically all that remained of the radiant creature before him. "Looked pretty serious."

"Just catching up." He dodged the question. "In a roundabout way, I guess, we were talking about you."

"Me?" Audrey's head tilted to one side. "How so?"

"She was wondering a bit about our plans…." It was Steven's turn to bite his lip. "You know, for the future."

"The future, huh?" Her mouth curled into a playful smirk. "And what does that have to do with me?"

Steven stepped into Audrey's space and took her hand. "I'm staying with Dad for a few more days, and then…"

"Then it's back to Chicago, right?"

He shook his head. "Chicago was always just a placeholder for me, you know, a place I went to forget about everything from…before."

"You mean Katherine." Audrey sighed. "I know." She gave his fingers a squeeze. "What is it you're saying?"

Steven basked in the warmth of her touch and the kindness in her eyes. "That maybe it's time for another change in scenery."

"And where exactly were you thinking, Mr. Bauer?"

"I don't know." He gazed into those hazel eyes for the thousandth time, the racing of his heart no different than the first. "Maybe…Oregon?"

She raised a questioning brow. "And whatever would tempt you to move all the way to the West Coast?"

Steven's free hand went to the small of her back and gently pulled her body into his. "Only the most beautiful pair of eyes I've ever seen. The kindest soul. The purest heart."

"Who is this woman?" Audrey let fly a flutter of eyelashes. "She sounds pretty—"

Steven silenced her playful banter with a passionate kiss that left them both breathless. It was far from the first, but the moment clearly signified a new beginning.

The pinch below his collarbone reminded him, however, of the one task remaining before the two of them could embark on what he hoped would be their happily ever after.

"What is it?" Audrey asked. "Is it bad?"

"Just some unfinished business." Steven's fingers brushed the leather pouch at his waist that hadn't left his side in months. "For all of Archie's talk of moving forward and leaving what has gone before in the rearview mirror, it appears the past and I have one last stop to make before parting ways."

II - Something Borrowed

"YOU'RE...HERE." Ruth, her beautiful blond curls a good six inches longer than when he'd seen her last, stared at Steven with something akin to fear from behind those dark eyes that wouldn't diminish one iota over the six decades to follow. "On today, of all days."

"Yes." The distant sound of a pipe organ reverberated through the walls, the strains of Bach coupled with Ruth's pristine white dress and veil confirming that the *Hvitr Kyll* had deposited him at the exact moment in space and time he had intended. "My apologies, but I needed to see you."

"Does Arthur know you're here?"

"No," Steven said, "though you can tell him I came to take care of one last thing and then you two won't be seeing me again for a very long time."

"I don't understand."

"You will." He reached inside his coat and retrieved a small pendant in the shape of a dragonfly. "This is Amaryllis."

"You named a piece of jewelry."

"Amaryllis is more than just a 'piece of jewelry,' Ruth. She's something quite special."

Her lower lip trembled. "What do you want, Steven?"

"A very special woman gave this to me once in a time of great need. She said it was a wedding gift from an old friend. I'm just passing the gift along to another such woman in hopes that Amaryllis will bring you and Arthur as much good fortune as she's brought me." Steven's gaze dropped to Ruth's collarbone. "That necklace is lovely. A family heirloom?"

"It was my mother's." A tear formed at the corner of her eye. "God, I wish she were here today."

Steven fought the instinct to go to her. The time for such intimacy, if it ever existed, had long since passed.

"Not that you or your mother's necklace need any further adornment, but I'd love it if you'd accept my gift and wear it today on your most special of days."

Ruth considered, her expression inscrutable, and then unclasped the simple choker that encircled her neck and handed it to Steven. He, in turn, brought the necklace close to Amaryllis, the dragonfly's tiny legs grasping the silver chain as if the charm were alive.

She gasped. "Amaryllis, you say? Like the flower?"

"Yes." He stepped toward her. "May I?"

"Of course." Ruth raised her chin and allowed Steven to replace the choker. "I still can't believe you're here."

"I have but a few minutes more." He stepped back and admired the dragonfly pendant resting once more where it belonged, at the hollow of Ruth's neck. "Thank you once more, Ruth, for everything. Nik and I, we wouldn't have made it last year without you and your father."

"It was our pleasure." A sarcastic smile flashed across her features. "And it's not like you two didn't earn your keep."

Someone knocked at the door. "Ruth," came a woman's voice, "it's time."

Her eyes darted from Steven to the door and back. "This is so awkward. I have so much I want to say to you, but not today." Her gaze dropped to the floor. "Any day but today."

"Save it for next time." Steven summoned up the kindest smile in his arsenal. "Because I'll be seeing you again someday, Ruth Matheson Pedone."

She blanched for a second, the color quickly returning to her cheeks along with a knowing grin. "You knew all along that it would be me and Arthur. You knew."

"You'll understand someday. I promise you that." He stepped out of Ruth's path and offered a subtle bow, both of his hands directing her to the door. "Now, get out there and marry the man of your dreams."

Ruth stepped past him, rested her hand on the doorknob, and, before he could stop her, turned and planted a quick kiss on his cheek. "This pendant. It's my something borrowed, isn't it?"

"You could say that." Steven crossed his arms, forcing a certain distance between him and Ruth.

"That's quite fitting then, as that is what we were to each other." Her eyes slid closed. "Borrowed, I mean. Me from Arthur and you from this Audrey who holds your heart." Her lip trembled anew. "I'd love to meet such a woman that is worthy of someone like you."

"Perhaps you will someday." He stepped around her and opened the door. "Perhaps you will." The Bach shifted into Beethoven's "Ode to Joy," and Steven recognized their shared moment had come to an end. "Goodbye, Ruth. May you and Arthur have a long and happy life."

"Goodbye, Steven. Thank you for this." She took another step, looking back one last time. "Thank you...for everything."

As she passed through the doorway, her short train of lace held in her hand, Ruth set her eyes straight ahead and walked away without any further hesitation. Steven closed the door behind her and let out an exaggerated sigh.

"Now," he steepled his fingers at his chin, "just one last piece of business, and—"

"And what might that be, Steven?" Grey stepped out of a shimmer in the air. "Closing a few loops, it would seem?"

"How did you know I was here?" Steven's hands dropped to his side, his fingers brushing the pouch at his waist. "Oh, of course."

"Admittedly, I *was* already in the building." Grey's expression took on a wistful appearance. "I would not miss this particular wedding for the world, a sentiment you and I clearly share."

"I had something for Ruth," he unfastened the pouch from his belt, "just as I have something for you."

Grey furrowed his brow. "I take it then that the iteration from your native time has...reached its end?"

Images of Doctor Emmett Brown and Marty McFly from the *Back to the Future* movies swirled in Steven's head. "If I tell you, will I tear a hole in the time-space continuum?"

"I am not exactly certain what that means," Grey answered, "but if I surmise accurately what you are asking, then no."

"Understood." An image of Grey's pale form lying still and lifeless on parking lot asphalt, dead at the Fool's hand, flashed across his memory. "Though I think I'll watch what I say just the same."

"As you wish, Steven, though your mere presence here answers the question quite readily."

Steven held out the pouch to Grey. "I need to return this to you, so that someday you can give it to me, or at least the person I was before we met." He groaned in frustration. "God, this is confusing."

"You prefer not to leave things to chance, is that not correct, Steven Bauer?" Grey accepted the *Hvitr Kyll*. "Tie up all the loose knots, per se, dot the i's and cross the t's." He smiled. "I suspect that will be one of the things I grow to like about you someday."

"I suppose." Steven shrugged. "You told me you picked the best man for the job."

"If I know myself, I likely told you that you were the *only* man for the job." Grey studied him intently. "Despite the fact that your presence here confirms my future self was clearly correct in that assertion, your competence and tenacity have impressed me even here in your past since you first sought me out on the docks a year past."

"Something still puzzles me, though." Steven motioned to the pouch now resting again in its creator's grip. "I have, as you said, closed the loop on the pouch, returning it to you in my past so that you'll have it to give to me in your future."

"Indeed." Grey smiled, as if he already knew the question. "Go on."

"I would never have needed to borrow it in the first place if the Black Pawn hadn't sent it flying into the East River. In my time, the *Hvitr Kyll* is lost. What happens the next time the universe decides to have a seizure and the Game starts all over again?"

Grey laughed. "Fear not, Steven. This little sack of white leather and silver cord has survived centuries of war and abuse and the elements and is none the worse for wear. If it is lost, trust that it will not remain so forever, though you will most likely not see it again in your lifetime."

"So, after you send me back—which I'm hoping you can do—that's it?" Steven worked to keep the unexpected disappointment from his face. "No more magic? No more wonder?"

Grey's features took on their most fatherly aspect. "When last we spoke, you told me of a woman in your time, the White Queen of your iteration. Audrey was her name, I believe?"

"Yes." For all the frustrated chemistry that had filled the room when it was just him and Ruth, the mere mention of Audrey's name swept all else away. With so much at stake, she and Steven had each kept their distance as the Game played out to its inexorable end, both out of necessity and for fear of the heartbreak of loss. Now that the

Game was over, however, and their future again an empty page upon which to write, the pair had proven inseparable. Steven knew all too well that nothing lasts forever and that the other shoe can fall at any time, but with Audrey, for the first time in a long time, he was willing to put it all on the line.

"I know that look well," Grey answered, bringing him out of his reverie. "Believe me, Steven, for all the wonders you have seen along your path thus far, none match what await you in the days and years to come."

Steven locked eyes with the man who'd become so much more than mentor, sage, and advisor, but friend. "I'm going to miss you, you know."

"And I have many years to wait before I again have the pleasure of your company." Grey smirked. "Though I may check in on you from time to time, with your leave, of course."

"Of course." Steven pulled in a deep breath. "So, I had to go all the way back to Florida to get here. The Coral Castle was the only place I knew reliable enough to get me where and when I needed to go. Will we need to go back there to send me home?"

"Fortunately, no." Grey's eyes focused on something Steven couldn't see. "A tether exists between you and your own time, and I have at my command more than sufficient energy to empower the pouch to send you from here and back to where you belong." He held the pouch up between them. "Any last questions before we part ways for the better part of a century?"

Steven pondered. "Only one." His eyes went to the door where Ruth had disappeared before. "A loop I don't understand."

"The dragonfly."

"Yes." Steven's eyes narrowed in concentration. "Ruth gave Amaryllis to me in my own time when she was old. When she told me this magical artifact that saved my ass more times than I can count was a wedding gift from an old friend, I assumed she meant you." His gaze shifted to one side. "Turns out, the 'old friend' is me."

"Precisely."

"That still doesn't answer my question, though." He studied Grey's knowing smile. "If I gave Amaryllis to Ruth and her to me, then where did she come from in the first place?"

Grey crossed his arms. "A year ago, Steven, you told me of the love you had lost, a woman named Katherine as I recall, as well as the new love you had found within the Game. Trust that a blind man could also see the connection between you and Ruth. As I saw it at the time, one was your past, one your present, and one your future. In that moment, though, the bond between you and Miss Matheson was quite strong."

Steven flushed at the details of his heart laid plain by the man who would one day change his life forever. "All of that may be true, but I don't see what that has to do with my question? You once spoke of Amaryllis being one of only sixteen such works of combined art and magic ever created. If you know so much about the subject, why can't you tell me how she came to be in my possession? Or Ruth's for that matter?"

"But I have." Grey shook his head like a patient teacher explaining a simple idea to a student who simply isn't grasping the concept. "Did Ruth not give you Amaryllis, a gift that rested over her heart for better than six decades, out of a lifetime of unrequited love?"

Steven's cheeks went white hot. "I suppose."

"And did you not travel back through time simply to return a gift to a person who will always hold at least a small fraction of your heart? Unless you failed to tell me, it was not I who advised you to do so. You could have simply traveled back to this decade and left the pouch with me rather than interrupting her wedding day, an interruption that might have ended far less amicably. What compelled you to make such a decision, Steven Bauer?"

"Ruth told me to come back to her." Steven pondered the question. "But you're right. It was more than that. Somehow, I knew that I needed to see Ruth one last time."

"Then," Grey smiled, "if I may reiterate one last piece of wisdom before we return you to your own time, understand that not every question can be answered with a how or a why. As I told you during your last visit to this decade, sometimes things are simply meant to be."

J'ADOUBE

Quinn crept along the rocky coastline of New Brisbane, his eyes focused on the sun as it peeked above the Drowned City to the east. The solar turbines above his head captured both the sun's warm radiance and the rushing wind, generating the power that kept his family's home to the west both lit and cool on yet another day of the hottest summer on record. His body covered in reflective white, he rushed from tidal pool to tidal pool, searching the various outposts of marine life for the telltale delicacies his mother had requested he locate for their dinner, knowing all too well that as the sun came above the skyscrapers of centuries past, he would have to retire indoors whether he'd found the evening's sustenance or not.

Time and again, the pools proved empty, and yet Quinn refused to despair. At least another twenty minutes would pass before the sun was fully visible, and the constellation of pools a hundred feet up the rocky beach were often some of the best.

A short jog north along the tide's ebb and he hit the jackpot: a tiny water-filled indentation of stone full of sea urchins and his sister's favorite, a spanner crab. Donning his protective gloves, he dipped his fingers into the pool and snagged the crab first, smiling as he imagined her squeal of excitement at her preferred dinner treat. Shoving his most difficult quarry into the leather pouch at his waist, he returned his attention to the task at hand.

An octet of urchins waited, enough to supplement their dinner this evening with what had been a dwindling delicacy until the revocation of Oceania's treaty with the Asian Alliance sent the countless fishing boats that had littered their waters for years back north, leaving the waters surrounding the mainland of the Australian Protectorate fished by natives alone.

One by one, he gently plucked his spiny prey from their pool and deposited them in his pouch with the crab. The thick leather prevented the pinch of claws or the prick of an urchin's spine from ruining his daily hunt. He'd often marveled at the capacity of the simple sack and how there always seemed to be room for one more living morsel, even on a particularly fortuitous morning of searching.

What a find, indeed.

As he retrieved the last urchin from the tiny brine-filled crater, the sun crested the tallest skyscraper of the Drowned City and he knew it was time to go. The protective layers of poly-cotton would shield his skin from the blistering heat, but only for so long.

He ran due west for a solid ten minutes, his well-tuned body handling the long sprint as a matter of course, until he arrived back at his family's sliver of land.

Built in a crevice on the side of a small hill, Quinn's home was part tent, part cave, and a cobbled-together mishmash of left-over construction materials recovered by boat from the City in the Ocean. The awning that protected the area that served as their front stoop from the sun's scorching rays had been a personal find of Quinn himself, while many of the other materials they'd acquired through barter over the years. When he was younger, Quinn had mainly stayed around the house, and the neighboring men had performed much of the hunting and gathering, but now that he was days away from his seventeenth revolution, he was allowed to walk the tide shores by himself and provide for his mother and sister.

Stepping beneath the thick canvas, he flicked on one of the hanging lights and set the pouch down on the table where his mother and older sister prepared the food each day and the three of them ate every evening. They were both away, likely working in the communal garden and greenhouse getting the vegetables to go with the aquatic protein he'd been sent to collect.

Emptying the pouch as carefully as he'd filled it, he placed the urchins one by one in a straight line, almost as if he were setting up for one of the games he'd played with his mother and sister when he was still a child.

But the time for such games was over. He was the man of the house now, and with that came responsibility.

As he fished around in the pouch to retrieve the crab that would be his sister's evening delight, his gloved finger brushed against something hard. A rock perhaps? Or perhaps a discarded seashell from a long-dead mollusk. He pulled out the crab and placed it in his mother's largest pot and then returned his attention to the mysterious object.

The pouch felt strangely warm as his fingers crept back inside, warmer even than it had upon first returning home after baking beneath the Australian sun over his ten-minute scamper from the tide shore. As his fingertips explored the interior of the pouch, a low hum filled the air. Had he captured some sort of beetle that could be making such a sound?

Finally, carefully, his exploring fingertips encountered the object of their search. Strangely cool in contrast to the warm leather surrounding his hand and wrist, the smooth piece of stone felt carved rather than natural. Round at one end and flat on the other, Quinn had no recollection of placing such an object in his pouch.

Drawing the item from its leather prison, he set it on the table to study.

Between four and five centimeters in height, the carved marble appeared like a game piece from his sister's ragtag collection of boxed amusement cobbled together from another time. A sphere atop a tapered column resting on a wide round base, it shone dimly despite the shade from the canvas overhead.

As Quinn pondered what to do with such a find and whether the stone artifact, no doubt from another time, might in fact be worth something in trade along the tidal area, a murmur crept across his sensorium, a murmur he suspected only he could hear and that he half-wondered if he had merely imagined.

"*The first move, Quinn,*" came the cryptic whisper carried on the wind, "*is yours.*"

AUTHOR'S NOTE

At the end of the game,
the king and the pawn
go back in the same box.
Italian Proverb

Most well-played games of chess begin with a tightly choreographed opening, progress through an artful middle game, and inevitably culminate in an endgame where one move follows another until one side emerges victorious. While I plan to write many more books, the work you hold in your hands is the endgame of this particular story in which Steven Bauer and his friends somehow prevailed regardless of whatever I threw at them. While some folks survived that originally weren't destined to make it out the other side, at least one individual I'd not planned to permanently remove from the board met their inevitable demise. Regardless, in the end, everyone got the fate called for by this particular story, at least in my humble opinion. I sincerely hope all of you found this final installment as satisfying as I did.

The third book is a bit longer than the first two, as there were many loose ends requiring knots—or trimming—not to mention a several-chapter detour to go pick up a brand-new main character here in the third act, so thank you for hanging in there for the entire ride with all its many twists and turns. For a story that has been cooking in the back of my mind for well over three decades, it is such a relief to finally have it done and out of my head as well as such a joy to know that someone other than me finally knows what happens to everyone in the end. I already miss writing Steven, Audrey, Niklaus, Emilio, Lena, Archie, Grey, Zed, Wahnahtah, Vago, Cynthia, and especially Magdalene, but my surviving good guys have surely earned a long rest while my bad guys have all received their just desserts.

Life goes on, and I have new characters and worlds to explore. I've already finished the first book in a brand new series, an urban fantasy action adventure road trip (sound familiar?), and the second book is just shy of halfway complete. I currently plan for seven books in that particular series, and while the story is still revealing itself to me, I have to say that this one is pouring out of me relatively quickly and I think you are all going to love it.

But that is literally a story for another day.

The Pawn Stratagem is the reason I started writing in the first place. From the first seed of an idea from a sketch I drew back in junior high school, through its humble beginnings as a pastime during my 2003-2004 deployment to Iraq working on the company dentist's Panasonic Toughbook and saving the story each night on a Mosul-purchased thumb drive, to now being a series of books available to the world, I am quite frankly amazed that it's complete and so grateful for all the support from family, friends, coworkers, and my publisher as I finished this labor of love, not to mention my readers!

As always, I'd like to acknowledge some people who have made special contributions to my life and either directly or indirectly helped me get to this point.

To John Hartness and everyone at Falstaff Books, thank you for all your support and patience as I navigated all the obstacles, story-wise as well as real-world, that kept me so long from those ever out-of-reach words, THE END, and for working with me to get these roughly 126,000 words into shape for publication. It's done!

To Lucy Blue, thank you for taking on this third book in the trilogy and providing your expert editorial touch as well as to Tuppence Van de Vaarst and Erin Berner-Coe for excellent copy edits and proofreading respectively.

To Melissa MacArthur, thank you for your editing expertise on the first two volumes of this series and for the gorgeous covers that now grace all three.

To the outstanding employees at my four favorite Charlotte coffee shops for writing: Starbucks on East Boulevard, Caribou Coffee in Myers Park, Not Just Coffee in Dilworth, and Mugs down near SouthPark, thank you for the many cups of coffee and for just the right amount of background hubbub to focus my often-scattered thoughts.

To the various groups that kept me sane through pandemic times when we were all stuck at home on Zoom for social interaction—my ten-plus-year friends from Charlotte Writers, my Wednesday trips to the Secret Library (if I mention your names, then the secret is out!), the online Writing Tribe started by Venessa Giunta, and Friday night Zoom Calls with the awesome folks from Multiverse Convention—I can't thank you enough. We made it through!

To Dr. Anthony Martin, who recently celebrated his fortieth birthday and just welcomed his first child into the world, consider this book your birthday/Christmas/baby shower present for 2021! Also, to the remainder of my work family, thank you for helping make my day job as a family physician not just tolerable, but a place full of friendship, laughter, and heart.

No book of mine goes out without a thank you to not only my various teachers and professors over the years, but to all teachers everywhere. What you do is vital, and, as always, I salute you all.

To my Mom and Dad, thank you for unfaltering support for my first fifty years. No, I can't believe it either...

Lastly, to all the readers of this, the first series I ever conceived, I already said it above, but thank you so much for riding along with me, Steven, and the others as we travelled both North America and the world, crossed several centuries, and finally met our shared fate atop a darkened battlefield of sixty-four-squares.

Almost two decades in, it's time to put these particular pieces back in the box.

But never fear, for a new game is afoot...

ABOUT THE AUTHOR

Darin Kennedy, born and raised in Winston-Salem, North Carolina, is a graduate of Wake Forest University and Bowman Gray School of Medicine. After completing family medicine residency in the mountains of Virginia, he served eight years as a United States Army physician and wrote his first novel in the sands of northern Iraq, a novel that started this very trilogy.

His *Fugue and Fable* trilogy, also available from Falstaff Books, was born from a fusion of two of his lifelong loves: classical music and world mythology. *The Mussorgsky Riddle*, *The Stravinsky Intrigue*, and *The Tchaikovsky Finale*, are the beginning, middle, and end of the closest he will likely ever come to writing his own symphony. His lone YA novel, *Carol*, is a modern-day retelling of *A Christmas Carol* billed as *Scrooge* meets *Mean Girls*. His short stories can be found in numerous anthologies and magazines, and the best, particularly those about a certain *Necromancer for Hire*, are collected for your reading pleasure under Darin's imprint, 64Square Publishing.

Doctor by day and novelist by night, he writes and practices medicine in Charlotte, NC. When not engaged in either of the above activities, he has been known to strum the guitar, enjoy a bite of sushi, and, rumor has it, he even sleeps on occasion. Find him online at darinkennedy.com.

ALSO BY DARIN KENNEDY

FRIENDS OF FALSTAFF

The following people graciously support the work we do at Falstaff Books in bringing you the best of genre fiction's Misfit Toys.

Dino Hicks
Samuel Montgomery-Blinn
Scott Norris
Sheryl R. Hayes
Staci-Leigh Santore

You can join them by signing up as a patron at
www.patreon.com/falstaffbooks.